What's wrong? Hearing the hesitancy, I slowed automatically. Rourke glanced behind him and let out a small roar as he came to a full stop. He growled, his unease flowing through my veins. He was likely trying to talk to me and I wasn't answering.

This entire thing is much more dangerous than we'd originally thought, my father finally answered. *We figured that the fracture pack was buying the services of a voodoo priestess to achieve their agenda*—which was getting rid of me—*using her to create these abominations. But it seems the priestess has a mind of her own and she wants something so desperately she's willing to fight us to the death.*

What does she want?

Power of some kind.

A single voodoo priestess fighting a pack of werewolves was completely unheard of in our world. Priestesses were not stronger than witches, from what I understood.

And she thinks she can achieve that power through the Made wolves she's creating? I asked.

Yes. She's building an army.

By Amanda Carlson

Full Blooded
Hot Blooded
Cold Blooded
Red Blooded
Pure Blooded
Blooded: A Jessica McClain Novella (e-only)

PURE BLOODED

Jessica McClain:
Book Five

AMANDA CARLSON

www.orbitbooks.net

ORBIT

First published in Great Britain in 2015 by Orbit

1 3 5 7 9 10 8 6 4 2

A CIP catalogue record for this book
is available from the British Library.

ISBN 978-0-356-50406-3

Printed and bound by CPI Group (UK) Ltd, Croydon CR0 4YY

Papers used by Orbit are from well-managed forests
and other responsible sources.

MIX
Paper from
responsible sources
FSC® C104740

Orbit
An imprint of
Little, Brown Book Group
Carmelite House
50 Victoria Embankment
London EC4Y 0DZ

An Hachette UK Company
www.hachette.co.uk

www.orbitbooks.net

For Nat.
My favorite son.

1

"Juanita! Juanita!" I yelled into the cell phone. "What do you mean my life is in danger?" There was no answer. I pulled the phone out in front of me to take a look.

It was completely dead.

The screen was entirely white, which wasn't normal. I frowned as I tossed it back to Marcy, who snatched it in midair. She turned it over and raised a single eyebrow. "Please tell me that was not your Latina neighbor who just killed my cell phone? Because whatever supe she is, it's something ancient. The signature coming off this phone was off-the-charts crazy."

I gave her a single nod as foreboding washed over me. I leaned my head back against the airplane seat and closed my eyes for a brief few seconds.

I needed time to think.

Up until that very moment, Juanita had been my very *human* neighbor. I'd never guessed she'd been anything different, which is not exactly saying much, since I wouldn't have been able to detect her otherness when I'd been a human anyway. But once I'd made my first shift, I should've picked up on *something*. My wolf paced in my mind, not liking our circumstances either. *Did you ever feel a strange vibe from her?* I asked. She barked, ending on a snap of her muzzle. *I wonder how she hid her true nature from us.*

When I'd moved into my apartment, Juanita had already been living directly across from me. So her being there had been no coincidence. If she'd known I would move there, she had to be some kind of an oracle, knew an oracle…or was somehow tied up with Fate.

Fate would be my best guess.

I pressed my fingers into my temples and rubbed. I'd recently come back from the Underworld, where things had gone south in a big way. I'd killed Ardat Lili before her time, so Fate was angry with me—or at least the Hags were. They were the keepers of Fate, and I'd somehow managed to throw it off its true course. Assuming Juanita was connected to all of it was as good a hunch as any.

Ardat Lili, the powerful daughter of Lilith, had sat on the Coalition, and I'd ended her life before she'd had a chance to birth a child. The unborn child was the key. It would've led to the rebirth of one of the Hags, the one who had lost her life battling Lilith, Ardat Lili's mother.

It was a tangled web of power and greed.

But now, Fate was officially off its course because of me, and leaving the beautiful, peaceful Bahamian island where Rourke and I had just spent some much-needed quality time was beginning to feel like the biggest mistake I'd ever made. More foreboding crept over me and I rubbed my temples harder. Not that I could've avoided Fate's wrath on the island—but at least I'd have been on a sunny beach surrounded by luscious white sand, sipping fruity cocktails delivered in hollowed-out pineapples with umbrellas and pink straws.

To make matters more complicated, after killing Lili, I'd found out about my possible place on the Coalition. It had been big, earth-shattering news—the kind of news that makes your stomach roil uncontrollably. My place on the Coalition was the reason I'd been born a female. Only females were able to serve on it. My predecessor might have even been one of the very first.

Ardat Lili had been stronger than me, and I would've been killed had I not been given the power of five. The combined magic of five powerful supernaturals. Now it dwelled deep inside me, waiting for me to call on it. It'd been given to me freely by the Vampire Queen, the Prince of Hell, Rourke, Ray, and Selene.

Fae, demon, shifter, vampire, and witch.

My wolf had rejoiced and treated it like a second homecoming, but I wasn't sure about any of it yet. I hadn't had time to fully take it in. I was just thankful my wolf had stored it away and knew how to handle it, because I had no earthly idea. I'd only been a wolf for a few months.

This wasn't initiation to the supernatural world by fire—it was initiation by firing squad.

I finally opened my eyes and glanced over at Rourke, my mate and partner in all things. His expression was grim. We were seated next to each other on the private jet en route to Florida to aid my father and my Pack against a fracture pack of wolves who were wreaking havoc on a small town after soliciting the help of a powerful priestess who was turning humans into rabid wolves.

Rourke grabbed my hand, sensing my distress, and gave it a squeeze. "I heard every word she said, and Juanita wasn't talking about your life being in danger because of the fracture pack. She was talking about what happened with Lili in the Underworld."

I nodded in agreement. "I know. She was giving me a warning, and it makes me believe the Hags will strike sooner rather than later." Before we'd left the Underworld, Eudoxia, the Vampire

Queen, had speculated that the Hags might take years to follow up on their retribution. Her reasoning? We were supernatural and there was really no need to hurry. We'd all be around for a good long time. But I didn't buy it. Why wait when you could strike me down today? "My guess is Juanita is involved with Fate some-how. Either she's an oracle or she *is* a Hag herself." I shook my head. "I can't believe I didn't know she was a supe. It was a rookie mistake."

"Don't beat yourself up about it," Rourke said. "A supernatural that old, with that much magic, could've fooled anyone—even me. Powerful supes, especially the ancient ones, can keep their magic cloaked, no problem. If she didn't want you to know what she was, you didn't stand a chance of finding out."

Marcy sat up straighter in her seat across from me. "Did I just hear you say you think your neighbor might be a *Hag*? Like, as in a *Hag* Hag or a hag, as in she's ugly and awful and smelly?" I hadn't had any time to fill Marcy in on everything that had transpired in the Underworld. She'd arrived with Ray just before we all boarded the plane. Before I had a chance to answer, she continued, "Listen, Hags are pretty badass. They run the clock—so to speak. You don't want to mess with them unless you want to be royally screwed over. They will scramble your brains and smile like fiends while they do it."

I grinned at my friend. I'd truly missed her. It'd been three months since I'd seen her and I had so much to tell her. "Well, that's comforting news. And, yes, she might be a Hag—as in the all-powerful brain-scrambling kind. It makes sense, but I have no idea for sure. It's only a suspicion."

Marcy whistled low. "That's crazy. So what else do I need to know? Have you pissed off any gremlins? They do serious destruction on a very large scale. What about any serpentines? They're these creepy half snake, half man—"

I held up my hand. "Okay, I get it, I get it. I will share the details of my trip to the Underworld with you. Rourke and Ray were there for some of it, so they know a bit." Ray grunted from his seat across from Rourke. "But Naomi hasn't been debriefed yet either." Naomi had her arms braced over the top of my seat, likely eager to hear the details as well. I moved in closer to Marcy. "But before I start, you have to promise me you're not going to interrupt this recap or it will take more time than we've got on this plane. Understood?" Marcy nodded, running a finger and thumb over her lips to show me they were zipped, and then she mimed throwing away the key. "What are you, four?" I laughed.

"Hey"—she shrugged—"that's the timeless international signal for 'you have my undivided attention.'" She faked looking at her wrist with a wry expression on her face. "You just wasted seven seconds of story time asking if I was a four-year-old child. Now, get talking, you."

"All right. Here it goes..." Rourke kept a solid grip on my hand as I recounted what had happened to me in the Underworld, starting from the time I'd landed there to running through the tunnels, dodging the beasts and the demons who were dressed like janitors, meeting and then killing Lili, and reviving the Princess of Hell. His touch helped keep me calm. Reliving ordeals was never fun. Naomi listened quietly behind me, and surprisingly, so did Marcy. Every so often there was a garbled agreement from Ray, and I finished with "So all we can do now is wait. There aren't many options, since we don't know how the Hags operate. Juanita's call is the first thing that's happened since we rode the portal back. So by my reasoning, if she's involved with Fate, she either has to be a Hag or she's an oracle who works for them—I don't know for sure. It's only speculation at this point."

"Good grief." Marcy collapsed back into her seat like she'd just run a marathon, arms out to her sides. "That was a killer story—*literally.* So let me get this straight." She moved forward. "You killed this evil Lili character and now you think you've thrown Fate off its true course? And now Juanita is calling you to warn you—"

The plane took a sharp nosedive, tossing us around in our seats.

I grabbed on to the armrests, thankful I'd fastened my seat belt when the pilot warned us of turbulence. Rourke leapt up, roaring. Ray was just ahead of him, both of them racing toward the cockpit.

"The power's dead," Rourke called over his shoulder. I craned my neck and glimpsed the panicked pilot through the opening in the small doorway. He was frantically pushing levers and punching buttons.

Marcy met my gaze solidly across the seat, her face pale. "We're nearly over land," I told her calmly, "and we have two vamps who can fly. There's no need to panic. We're not going down without a fight."

"I know that." She shook herself, trying to relax, even though the plane was still in a nosedive. "I'm just a terrible flier. I always have been. Tally used to make fun of me whenever we flew together, the old biddy, and would purposefully make the plane bounce around in fake turbulence. But I'm a witch, for Pete's sake. I can fix this." Marcy had suffered from performance anxiety in the past, but she smiled at me as her eyes slid shut and she began chanting under her breath.

Her power swept over me in a hot breeze as the plane began to right itself slowly.

Go, Marcy.

"Rourke," I called, "have the pilots guide us down anywhere they can. We need to get off this plane."

"Damn straight we need to get off," Marcy muttered, her eyes still closed, a fierce look of concentration on her face. "I'm fixing the drop with a counterspell, but I can't undo whatever knocked the power out. Everything on the plane is dead, just like my phone. At least I think it's a spell...I can't even be sure. It all just feels *dead*." She continued to chant under her breath and the plane evened out completely.

"*Ma Reine*," Naomi whispered, crouching down in the aisle next to me. "I can leave the plane and help from below if need be."

I shook my head. "Not yet. Let's let Marcy handle it for now. She only has to keep the plane steady for a few more minutes until the pilots can guide it down. If we let you and Ray out, that means opening the doors and I don't want to freak out the pilots if we don't have to."

She nodded, alert as always. We'd been up in the air for a little more than an hour, and as I looked out the tiny window, I could see what was likely the Florida Keys passing below us.

We were closing on land quickly.

The pilot's voice came out of the cockpit in a rush. "We just passed Eagle Key. We're going to make it to the mainland, but just barely. We can't make it to any airstrip. We'll have to set it down in the marsh flats."

Rourke stood behind the two pilots, his arms crossed, his broad back taking up all the available doorway space. "I see plenty of open space to land down there. Just keep bringing us down and everything will be fine." His voice was calm.

"Fine?" Panic filled the plane, the pilot's voice wavering. "We're directly over the southern glades! All that's down there is sawgrass marsh with big channels of water and nothing else for miles and miles."

"Marsh means flat, right? You have to look at the positives," Ray kindly pointed out. He stood just behind Rourke, his back against the bathroom door. He leaned forward and glanced out the little window attached to the main door. "I don't see anything that will stand in our way. No pesky trees to worry about, no big structures. Just get us down. That's all we need you to do."

The copilot was a little more confident. "We can't radio in because the electrical is dead, but they should see us go down on the radar. We can do this, Larry. It's just like the simulator. We keep the wheels up and set her down belly-up. It'll be bumpy as hell, but this plane is solid. She should stay together."

Marcy still had her eyes firmly closed, and I leaned over to whisper, "Do you have a spell to wipe their memories once we land? Once we duck out, it's going to be a problem for them."

Marcy cracked one eye open. "I'm working here. And, yes, I can figure out what to do with them once we land. Not a problem."

I nodded and motioned Ray over.

He started for me right as the plane took another nosedive.

My head snapped back to Marcy. "What's going on?" I hadn't meant to yell so loud. "I thought you said you had this?"

"Something is fighting my spell!" she cried. "And whatever it is has some serious mojo."

"Can't you do something else?"

"I'm trying! But, balls to the walls, it's taking everything I've got." Marcy's knuckles were white as she gripped the armrests and fought for control. The plane bounced around like it was in the throes of wild turbulence as she tried another spell.

Rourke caught my eye from the cockpit doorway. He'd braced his body into the opening, his arms locked solidly in front of him. He nodded once and I turned to Naomi. "Okay, Naomi, it's time for plan B," I whispered. "Do you think you and Ray can position the plane up?"

"I do not know for sure, but we will certainly try, *Ma Reine*."

"Oh, we can do it," Ray piped up. "We will get this plane level even if I have to wrestle it to the ground. I'm not letting us burn up in a fiery crash. Not on my watch."

Land was coming up fast. Ray grabbed on to the handle of the door and pulled.

The pilot's voice was nothing less than a shriek as he heard the lever flip. "What are you doing? You can't open the door!"

Jessica, I have to knock them out, Rourke said in my mind. *They won't be able to process what's about to happen.*

Can you fly the plane? I asked.

If the vamps give me a good angle, I can get it down. I've flown before, but it's been a long time.

Let's have Marcy spell them. I don't want them hurt if we can help it.

Fine, but have her do it quick.

"Marcy." I reached out and tapped her leg. Her eyes flew open. "I need you to spell the pilots. Knock them out, quick like a bunny."

"I love bunnies." She muttered something and both pilots slumped forward in their seats. "How's that for quick?"

"Perfect."

Rourke wasted no time. He had them in the passenger seats beside us in about ten seconds. I rose to help, unbuckling my seat belt. "Secure that one." He nodded at the copilot.

I reached over and made sure they were both tightly belted. We were quickly running out of time.

Ray hollered, "We're going out." He tossed the door open and a rush of air filled the plane. In a blink he and Naomi were gone. The wind howled fiercely, sucking everything not tied down out the door.

I braced my legs and hands against the seats. We weren't at a high altitude, so breathing wasn't an issue. Rourke strapped himself into the cockpit and yelled, "Jessica! Buckle yourself in. We're going to crash in about thirty seconds!"

I glanced over at Marcy. Her face was white as a sheet, but she kept chanting the same spell over and over. "This damn interference is killing my craft," she moaned as I made a split decision and started for the front of the plane.

Almost immediately the plane began to nose up, slowing our rapid descent. The vamps were making it work. The landing wasn't going to be close to perfect, but at least we weren't going to crash headfirst. I took a seat next to Rourke and he arched an eyebrow at me.

"This seat is just as good as any," I answered as I grabbed the shoulder harness and clipped myself in. "What do we do now?"

"Put your hands on the yoke and pull back with me," he ordered. "We're going to help slow the plane down if we can."

I did as I was told, and with the aid of the vamps, the front of the plane continued to edge upward. But the ground was closing in exceedingly fast. We had only about ten seconds at most. "We're going to hit soon." I tried to keep the panic out of my voice. This was likely *not* going to kill us, unless of course the crash broke all our necks or the plane was engulfed in flames. But even if we weren't going to die, it was going to hurt like a bitch. Being broken and mangled from a plane crash was a serious injury for any supe.

"Hold on!" Rourke shouted as a sea of marshland, water, and scrubby brush sped in front us, filling the view out the windshield.

"I'm holding!" The yoke broke under my grip.

We hit once . . . and then bounced like a superball.

My eyebrows shot up as I glanced over at Rourke. "What's going on?" I asked. We went down again, almost in slow motion, and then bounced up like we were attached to a bungee cord.

"It's the best I can do!" Marcy yelled from her seat. "Whoever's messing with us managed to find a way to block the plane from my magic. But they can't block the entire earth, suckas!"

"Sweet," I called, continuing to grip the broken wheel in each of my fists. "But at this rate the plane is going to break apart."

"No it won't," Marcy said. "The plane is cushioned from below by a spell. I thought soft and bouncy, and my brain went straight to marshmallows. That's just how it works when I'm under pressure."

"So the plane is mimicking jumping from marshmallow to marshmallow?"

"That's right," she called, pride in her voice. "It was ingenious, if I do say so myself."

The plane began to slow to small bounces and I spotted Ray out the windshield. He was in the process of placing his body in front of the nose to try and slow us down to a complete stop. I assumed Naomi was helping him from below.

It was strange to see him out there, almost surreal.

We continued to spring over the small mounds of earth and water until the belly of the plane finally struck something hard.

The plane jerked to a stop, tossing us all forward. Then with almost no preamble, it cracked in half. I glanced back just in time to see Marcy tumble out of the belly of the plane, still strapped to her seat.

There was a splash below.

"I'm okay!" she called. "I broke my fall with a spell. Now I just have to figure out how to get marsh water out of my lady parts."

2

"Everyone okay?" Rourke called. A round of yeses chorused from outside the plane.

"I'm just fine, thanks to you." I leaned over and gave him a quick kiss on the lips. I pulled back, but before I could untangle myself from the seat, he ran a hand around my neck and pulled me into a deep, needy kiss. His relief that we were okay pounded through our shared connection, along with my own leftover adrenaline.

I slumped against him, bringing my hands up to stroke his face.

He let me go after a long moment. "I didn't do much other than try and keep the plane level," he sighed. "If you want to thank anyone, thank the vamps and Marcy for bouncing us like a ball instead of letting us crash."

He stood, reaching over to help me out of my seat. Once I was up, he positioned me in front of him and guided me forward. When we got to the rent in the plane, I jumped through to help

Marcy while Rourke went to check on the pilots who thankfully were still out cold and still in the plane.

I landed in thigh-high water.

Marcy was standing on top of her plane seat, dripping wet. "Good gravy, this stinks. It literally stinks—like week-old soggy laundry left in the washer." She shook her legs out, spraying marsh water all over.

"Don't you have a go-to drying spell? Or a change-of-clothes spell?" I asked wryly. "You're a talented witch who specializes in marshmallow landings. You must have something for cleaning up a spill in your repertoire."

"Hey, enough with the unfunny banter. Let's not forget I just saved our lives, shall we? I'm working on the drying part," she muttered. "Just trying not to freak out about all the creepy-crawlies that live here. You know, the venomous snakes, alligators, and seriously yucky things that call this place home. Healing from an alligator attack is not on my current to-do list. So, one thing at a time."

Naomi and Ray both stood off to the right on a dry area of land, looking incredibly happy we were all alive. "How does it look from over there, Ray?" I called. "Did you see anything interesting from above? Are we close to any civilization?"

"Nope, we're in the middle of one huge marshland. Nothing but swamp for miles and miles. We got lucky. But if the plane stayed on the radar, like the pilots thought, the air traffic controllers saw us go down. Activity will arrive shortly, so we gotta clear out fast."

I glanced at Marcy, who was already half dry, right as Rourke stuck his head out of the plane. "I buckled the two pilots back into the cockpit seats," he said, nodding to Marcy. "Now I need you to spell them into thinking they were alone and we were never here."

Marcy clucked her tongue. "I can do that, but they filled out a flight log in the Bahamas. There will be a record of us being on the flight. And before you ask"—she held a hand up—"I can't spell something when I don't know where it is."

Rourke arched an eye at her. "I don't care about the flight log. The investigators can interpret that information any way they want. If you wipe their memories and the plane clean, then there's no real evidence we were ever here. Can you take care of the black box too? There's a record of Ray opening the door of the plane midflight. Once that's taken care of, we should be all set."

Marcy muttered something under her breath about miracles and the abuses of witches. I smiled. "Fine," she answered. "But for spelling the pilots, I'm going to need something with their DNA attached. Get me a strand of hair or an eyelash or two. Whatever. I'll need to get back in the plane to deal with the black box." She crossed her arms and turned to me as Rourke went to fetch the DNA. "For performing my awesome spells on demand, I'll be requesting a cappuccino maker next to—*if not directly on*—my desk when we get home. As well as two additional weeks of paid vacation." She stared me down, daring me to object.

I had no intention of doing that. Instead, I said, "Done. In fact, I'm making you a partner, starting today." I grinned at her stunned expression. "Don't act like you don't deserve it. You kept the business alive while I was in the Underworld. You hired Naomi, which was genius. You're already head of operations. We'd be nothing without you. Nick will agree with the promotion wholeheartedly." I didn't have to address the fact that witches had to charge for their services. It was part of their creed. Marcy was on the Hannon & Michaels payroll, but spelling on demand required much, much more. So I was going to happily give it to her.

"Well, then, okay." She smoothed out her wrinkled but now perfectly dry pants. "I accept."

I chuckled. "Of course you do. That means from now on you get a third of the profits. And, out of curiosity, can you really spell it to seem like we were never here?" I asked. "That's fairly impressive and totally handy."

She placed her hands on her hips. "I can wipe this place clean faster than you can say 'your great aunt Fanny is a witch.'"

"Perfect."

"It's a good thing for you there's no supernatural union," she joked. "Or profit sharing might not be enough for my stellar spell-crafting."

"I have no doubt you'd start one if you could." I winked at her as I sloshed out of the muck toward Naomi and Ray, careful to make sure my shoes stayed attached. I was also on the lookout for snakes and gators. Marcy was right—this place was teeming with them. And even though I didn't see any, I could smell them, and that was just as bad.

Both vamps were on high alert, scanning the area as well as the sky.

"We have to get out of here, Hannon," Ray said as I came up to stand next to him. "Planes will be scouring the area soon. We're remote, but a helicopter or small jet can be here lickety-split."

"One of you is going to have to take Marcy," I said. "Rourke and I will shift and head out on foot. We'll meet you once we're clear of this area." I glanced over at Naomi. She had flown over this area last night on a scouting mission. "What direction do we head in?" I asked her.

"When I was high in the sky, I spotted our destination," she answered. "We will need to move north for some miles, before shifting to the west. We will plan to meet up with you in two hours. That should give you enough time to reach a paved road.

If you go northwest right away, there is very little land and much more water."

"Okay, so we'll head north for an hour, and then we'll edge northwest. We'll look for you two hours after we head out." I scanned the horizon. There was nothing but marshland for as far as the eye could see. Running and swimming through the Everglades was going to suck, there was no question about it. Naomi had told me before we boarded the plane that my father planned to exchange himself as a prisoner to free some of his wolves. I wanted to arrive before that happened. He'd already been cursed once, and the evil yellow masses that had coursed through his body had eaten him alive from the inside out. It had nearly taken his life and I wasn't willing to risk it again.

I turned a pointed look on Ray, my lips pursed.

"What?" he asked, shrugging. "What'd I do now?"

"Nothing," I said, hiding a smile. "But it seems at every turn we've taken, we're damn lucky to have you around. The cursed wolves are going to be extremely hard to deal with, and don't think I've forgotten that the only reason my father is alive right now is because of you—and your new skill set." Ray was a reaper *and* a vampire. His latent reaper genes had been activated by his transition into a vampire and a healthy dose of my blood. "Before this is over, I predict you're going to be one tired reaper."

Before Ray could respond, Rourke jumped out of the plane, handing Marcy what she needed from the pilots. He turned his attention on us, calling, "Naomi and Ray, you guys take to the sky immediately. We need you up there to get a read on our situation. If there are any planes in the air, we need to know which direction they're coming in from."

Ray nodded. "We're on it. But by the time we come back, you need to be ready to vacate."

"We'll be ready." Rourke waded over to me. "You and I will

shift, but if the planes are already on their way, they'll fly low, sweeping the area. Seeing a wolf and a big cat racing through the marsh is going to be an epic red flag. So Ray's right—we need to leave immediately, and once we do, we need to move fast."

"I have no doubt we can cover a lot of ground, but maybe Marcy can help us as well." I turned and called, "Hey, is it possible for you to conceal our animal forms from humans if they fly over?"

She looked up from the hank of hair she held in her hand—Rourke's contribution to the DNA. "Nope. Sorry to disappoint you. In order to do that, I'd need to be strapped to your back—which would be completely hilarious, and I'd be totally up for it, but something tells me that wouldn't be your thing. If I had an ingestible spell with me, it would be a different story. And can I just take a moment here to say that if I would've known ahead of time you were going to be pursued by the scariest, most ancient supes on the planet, I would have brewed up some potions." She leaned forward and cupped her empty hand around her mouth. "And, just between us, even though I'm not officially allowed to brew my own spells yet, they rock. It's against Coven rules for a non-member to brew, blah, blah, blah. But my spells are superior to anything those hacks can produce."

"I'm sure your spells are superior," I said, "but you're right, I'm not strapping you to my back, nor is Rourke. I'm sure we'll be fine, but to ensure that we need to leave soon. Ray is going to fly you out and the plan is to meet up in two hours."

She sighed. "I despise Vamp Air, but I guess it can't be helped. I can't even think about the amount of bugs that will be caught in my teeth over these swamplands."

"Well, maybe it would help if you just keep your mouth shut—"

Jessica! Can you hear me? Tyler's voice came rushing into my mind.

I grabbed Rourke's hand and gave it a squeeze to let him know what was happening. *Yes, I can hear you! Where are you?*

The better question is where are you? Both Danny and I got a huge pulse of distress from you a few minutes ago, and then it all went silent. What's going on?

"I do keep my mouth shut, so there," Marcy muttered. "Other than the screaming part. Now I need your man to lift me into the plane so I can spell the pilots."

Rourke nodded as he moved past me. "Stay here. I'll get the witch on the plane. Then we leave."

The plane we were in just went down. I'm sure that's what you felt.

Went down, as in crashed?

Kind of, yes, I answered. *It started with a strange call from Juanita warning me I was in danger, and then the electrical cut out. It would've been much worse if we didn't have the vamps or Marcy on board. But now we're stuck in the swamp. We have to get out of here before company comes. Where are you?*

Did you say Juanita? *Your Latina neighbor—that Juanita?* His voice was strained. I could sense he was running.

One and the same.

Jesus, Jess, it would be nice if you stayed out of life-and-death scenarios for five minutes.

You're telling me. I'd love nothing more than to go back to Rum Cay and leave all this crap behind, but unfortunately, that's not a current option. Helping Dad is. Where are you? I've got limited time before I have to shift and run.

We're just crossing the panhandle into Florida. It's slow going whenever we have to maneuver around a large city, but we're making good time. We'll probably be close to you in about four or five hours.

Sounds good. Once we're out of this area, I'll hit you with our location. Stay safe.

You too.

Right as I signed off with my brother, Ray landed next to me.

It took everything I had not to jump. "Jeez, Ray, a little warning would be helpful."

"You have supersonic hearing, Hannon," Ray groused. "I shouldn't have to announce my landing like a simpleton."

He was right, of course. But I wasn't going to give him the satisfaction of admitting I should've heard him. "I was having a conversation with Tyler in my head. Sometimes our senses are busy elsewhere." I hadn't realized it before, but when I talked internally, I did shut off almost everything else. In the future, it would be wise to keep things more open.

"Hannon, you have to stay vigilant, especially when the supernatural world is coming at you with a vengeance. What if I was some vamp coming to kill you? I would've had the jump on you just now."

"Spoken like a true cop, Ray. I guess some things never change." I chuckled. "But since it's daylight, and you and Naomi are some of the only vamps who can withstand the heat, thanks to my blood, I'm not super worried about a flying sneak attack."

"You never know, you just never know." Ray shook his head like he was sorry to have to breathe the same air as such a moron.

"Where's Naomi?" I asked. "Wasn't she with you?"

"She went a little farther to investigate. We spotted one plane coming out of the east. Not sure yet if it's headed this way."

"Once Marcy is finished with her spells, I want you guys to head out," I said.

"Directly north," Ray said, "about thirty miles you'll hit some dense sawgrass. The area is more exposed but looks easier to navigate and, from the sky, seems to have less water."

"That sounds good. We'll rendezvous with you guys soon."

Marcy stuck her head out of the plane. "All done," she chirped. "Now let's get out of here. This swamp is making my skin crawl.

Ray, can you come and get me? I don't want to have to use another drying spell. I'm taxed."

Ray grunted but moved forward to get her. "I'm sorry, but did you just use your brute strength to stop an airplane from crashing? If you did, I missed you out on the wing." Once he was positioned below her he said, "Jump and I'll catch you."

"Fine, but if you drop me, I *will* retaliate."

"I'm not going to drop you, witch. You weigh next to nothing. And as long as you keep your mouth shut on the flight and don't complain, the ride out of here will be stress free."

Marcy arched a look at the vamp. "You'd like me silent, wouldn't you—" The *you* ended on a long, extended high note as Ray snatched her up, tired of waiting for her to make up her mind and agree with him, and took to the air.

"They get along like Jekyll and Hyde," I said as Rourke walked up to me, taking my hand and leading me to a place where we could shift. "I hope Marcy spelled the area before Ray hijacked her. If not, we'll leave tracks."

"She said she did," Rourke said. "She also said we'd have exactly eight minutes after she left or it wouldn't cover us."

A whooshing sound came from above two seconds before Naomi landed ten feet in front of us.

"Did you see anything of note?" I asked, starting to disrobe in front of her.

"*Non*, there was nothing. And I don't believe there's any hurry. It's most peculiar, but it seems no one knows the plane went down. I found an airport in a city not too far from here. It would be a logical place to send out a search party, but there is no panic or activity whatsoever."

A plane doesn't usually pop off the radar without someone knowing. "That's great news for us, but bad for the pilots." I glanced over at the damaged plane.

Rourke nodded, and said, "Naomi, since there's no immediate pursuit, I want you to fly to the closest town you can find and call the crash in. Be obscure about how you discovered the information and make sure you use a phone that can't be traced back to us in any way. Snatch one from a human if you need to, and then meet up with Ray. We'll see you in two hours."

"*Oui*, no problem," Naomi said.

"Also," I added, handing her my shirt, "I want you to take our clothes after we shift. Tyler and Danny will need clothes too, once they arrive, which we hope will be in a few hours." I eyed my mate's white linen Bahamian outfit and tried to stifle a smile. They had been the only duds we could find on the island before we left. "Rourke will also need some...alternative clothing. Island linen isn't his first choice." He growled at my comment and I started peeling off my pants. I addressed my mate. "Tell her what size you need. She can stop somewhere after she calls in the crash."

"XXXL."

3

Naomi left after we undressed, taking both sets of our clothes and my backpack from the plane. I called to Rourke, who had stationed himself behind the plane to disrobe so he wouldn't embarrass Naomi. "Where do you want to shift?"

He walked around the plane looking strong, virile, and very, very naked.

I wished, with every fiber of my being, that we were back on Rum Cay at this very moment. But we weren't, so we had to make do. And we only had about four minutes left to get out of here before Marcy's spell ran out.

"There's no great place." He gestured in front of me as he came forward. "Pick anywhere. We're going to get wet, but it can't be helped. And, Jess, once we're in our animal forms, I need you to follow me no matter what."

"I have no issue with you taking point." I waded toward a very narrow patch of land surrounded by knee-deep water. "I haven't fully shifted in a long time, so my body feels itchy. I'm so ready for it." I lay down in the prickly brush trying not to be too disgruntled about where we had to make our transformations. However, my wolf howled in pleasure at the prospect of shifting. *Once we start running, I'm giving you control.* She barked her agreement. Having my wolf at the forefront in animal form was the best for both of us.

Rourke made his way to another small patch of marsh nearby and dropped to his knees. "I keep forgetting you haven't shifted very many times."

"It's easy to forget when I'm constantly in and out of my Lycan form." That form was almost second nature to me now. It wasn't the same as a full shift into a wolf, but it did give me a break from constantly craving a full change. "Do you think we'll be able to talk internally when we're in our animal forms?" We hadn't shifted together since we'd mated and made it official.

"I would assume so," he said, grinning over at me, "but we're about to find out."

Once I was down, almost instantaneously my back bowed and my arms and legs lengthened. It was a smooth, pain-free transition, and over before I knew it. Once we were done, we jumped to our feet. I'd forgotten how exaggerated everything was in this form. My hearing, sense of smell, and awareness were amplified. I turned my head toward Rourke. He was already up and it was all I could do not to cower. *How did we forget how awesome he is in this form?* My wolf howled and our muzzles lifted to the sky before I could rein her in.

The sound we made was beautiful as it echoed around the marshlands.

Rourke snuffed at us, turning his head north and nodding once. His fur was a beautiful dark gold with chocolate stripes flowing down his flank and over his legs. He was intimidating in this form, but now that we had coupled and had a bond, there was much less fear. His front incisors were curved and long, and as he lifted his head to roar, the ground shook.

He took off at a run and I followed without hesitation.

Rourke, can you hear me?

Yep, I can hear you loud and clear. Try to dodge the water and stay on higher ground. Do you scent the animals?

I raised my muzzle in the air. I did smell them. Over the smell of all the grasses, stagnant water, insects, and salt, there was an overlay of musky reptile. Several kinds from what I could detect.

When you smell one close, he said, *go around it. We're moving too fast for them to actually get a good bite, but if we surprise a large gator at the right moment, it's not going to be pretty.*

Got it. I don't smell many, thankfully.

Me neither. I think the water down here at the southern tip is not deep enough. The true Everglades will be to our left as we head north. We need to be tactical about how we're going to get there. Where did Naomi say the wolves were, exactly?

She didn't say. But before we took off on the plane, she said they were in something like an abandoned homestead. I'm thinking that kind of place has to be deep in the Everglades, very remote.

I agree. That means we have to find a reasonable way to get around the swamps once we get to the edge.

Like what?

We're going to need an airboat.

Okay. That sounds doable. We're in a swamp after all. I'd put Marcy on it once we met up.

The pace Rourke set was fast. My wolf worked overtime to keep up with him. We hit scattered patches of swamp, but we were moving so swiftly, flying over berms and channels, I hardly noticed. When we did hit a deeper patch, the water went no higher than my flank.

After a half hour of solid running, the topography changed to sawgrass growing on a firmer landscape with less water. It was much easier to maneuver over and we made great time. There were no sounds of any planes overhead, and that made us both breathe easier.

After another fifteen minutes, Rourke slowed. *I smell humans up ahead*, Rourke said. *We're too exposed to keep going straight toward them. We'll have to go around.*

I came shoulder to shoulder with him, both of us still loping. I was a fairly big wolf, but I was dwarfed by Rourke's massive frame. He was indeed a Big Cat. *Which way has less water? I vote for that.*

Let's veer west. We're supposed to do that in another fifteen minutes anyway. East will likely bring us closer to humans, so west it is.

We turned, heading left, and Rourke picked up the pace again. As we ran, I glimpsed the humans in a huge truck in the far distance. They were likely parked at the end of some lonely road that ran out here or had gone off-roading for fun. They couldn't see us unless they had binoculars, but I could see them.

As we ran, we dodged the growing smell of more alligators and deeper swamp water. I shrieked internally as my paw hit something scaly, but we passed over it too quickly for me to see what it was.

Jessica, is that you? Are you in trouble?

Dad? I nearly skidded to a halt hearing my dad's voice inside my head. It had been too long since we'd spoken internally. His voice was fuzzy, but I could make out most of the words. *I can hear you! Where are you? Please tell me you're okay.* There were a million things I wanted to tell him, but I had to settle for the immediate concerns first.

Rourke sensed the change in my emotions and turned his head back to huff at me as we ran. I bobbed my head up and down and kept running. I didn't want to switch off the channel with my father to tell him what was going on, so Rourke would have to wait until I was finished.

I'm fine. Good gods, Jessica, are you okay? I've been worried sick about you! Please tell me you're not still in the Underworld. Not knowing where you are and what is going on has been killing me.

I'm not in the Underworld. We're back, and actually heading toward you as we speak. There is so much to tell you, but in order to do that, I need to know how to find you.

It's not going to be easy to find us. We're in the middle of the god-forsaken cypress swamp, deep in the Glades. There's an entire area in here that's mystically spelled. It can't be seen by humans. It looks as though the priestess who's been causing all the trouble has called this place home for more than a hundred years. There's very little land and lots and lots of water.

Rourke says we need an airboat.

Yes, that's the only way in, unless you can fly. We've set up a wide perimeter around the main homestead we think she's using, but it's complicated. We're trying our damnedest to keep the rabid wolves contained, but it's taken all of our resources. The only thankful thing is that this place is in the middle of nowhere. Literally. We're living cobbled together on little spits of land—which consist mostly of old tree roots—and held together with nothing more than magic. But the Made wolves are creeping closer and closer to civilization each day. We've been able to find a way to kill them, once we catch them, but it's been dicey.

Naomi, the female vampire you met, flew over your area yesterday. I instructed her not to stop because none of your Pack know her, but she overheard a conversation that you were planning to swap yourself for some of your wolves. Please tell me that isn't in the works yet.

I've tried to broker a deal, but so far she hasn't taken the bait. The priestess is elusive at best. I have to find a way to stop it, including offering myself as ransom, because my wolves keep disappearing. Things have gone from bad to exceedingly worse in the last week. Five of my wolves have vanished into thin air, one a night for the last five nights. It's unacceptable.

Have you had a chance to talk to Tyler? He's on his way down from the panhandle.

Our communication has been spotty. I can't get any tangible information from him. It's been frustrating not being able to communicate with either of you.

I know, it's been hard for us too. I realized in that moment how much I missed my father. I looked forward to reuniting with him—I felt the need to be near my Alpha. There was so much for us to catch up on. He had no idea what had happened to me over the last week, which had actually been three months on this plane. *I'm not sure I'll be able to talk to you once I shift out of my wolf form, but I promise we'll find you. We'll figure out the airboats as soon as we arrive someplace more inhabited. I have Rourke, Marcy, Ray, and Naomi with me, and Tyler and Danny are on their way down.* I sprang over a small waterway, plunging after Rourke. He knew something was up and had slowed his pace a bit to allow me to better maneuver.

We will await your arrival. Send a vamp in to let us know when you get close. We'll likely have to come out to meet you, as this area is tricky. There was some hesitation lingering in his voice.

What's wrong? Hearing the hesitancy, I slowed automatically. Rourke glanced behind him and let out a small roar as he came to a full stop. He growled, his unease flowing through my veins. He was likely trying to talk to me and I wasn't answering.

This entire thing is much more dangerous than we'd originally thought, my father finally answered. *We figured that the fracture pack was buying the services of a voodoo priestess to achieve their agenda*—which was getting rid of me—*using her to create these abominations. But it seems the priestess has a mind of her own and she wants something so desperately she's willing to fight us to the death.*

What does she want?

Power of some kind.

A single voodoo priestess fighting a pack of werewolves was completely unheard of in our world. Priestesses were not stronger than witches, from what I understood.

And she thinks she can achieve that power through the Made wolves she's creating? I asked.

Yes. She's building an army.

Once I'd switched off with my father, I'd filled Rourke in.

We sped up, feeling the urgency of my father's words. Hearing from my dad had been wonderful and much needed. Relief and gladness swept through me, making me slightly euphoric. We made stellar time and were almost to the two-hour mark.

I scanned the horizon for the vamps, but I didn't spot any movement.

Jessica, let's stop up ahead. There are a few trees in the distance. I can smell the cypress to the west now.

Sounds good. Surprisingly my body wasn't tired, even after the long run. But I could use some food in a big way. My wolf clacked her muzzle at me and hinted we could hunt. *There's no way I'm eating a lizard*, I told her. I was always hungry, still in my new-born stage, but I managed to compartmentalize it. If I didn't, the constant hunger would make me crazy. In this form we burned even more calories, and my stomach felt hollow. It begged to be filled. My wolf growled. *I know you have no issue with it, but I can't eat a snake, or any reptile for that matter, so let it go.* She angled her nose up at my stupidity.

I think we're actually fairly close to a town, Rourke said, interrupting my wolf as he slowed to a stop. *I'm picking up on human smells. The vamps should be here soon. I'm going to shift back before they land.*

Because you don't want them to see you? Other than these two times I'd shifted with my mate, no one had seen his true form in centuries. Keeping his nature cloaked had aided him well as a mercenary.

No, because I want to talk to them. He chuckled, which sounded like a series of small sneezes tickling my senses.

I hope Naomi was successful in snagging you some new clothing or it's going to be a very one-sided conversation.

I'm sure she was. She's nothing if not reliable. I hope she spotted some water channels with parked airboats from the sky as well. We need to move quickly.

He had stopped at the base of a very small, scraggly tree. If you could even call it a tree. It had *a* branch. He lay down to begin to shift back, and I joined him. Hopefully we were close enough to our destination so we didn't have to change back and run.

By the time I finished, Rourke was already up scanning the area.

I stood and walked over, running my hands over his very naked back. He turned and growled low as he pulled me into his arms. "We don't have much time," he said, nuzzling my ear, "but what I wouldn't give to be able to whisk you away someplace private. It frustrates me I don't have the power to take you out of here."

"I know," I murmured, leaning into his lips. "We only have a few minutes at most to ourselves, but since we can't go back to Rum Cay, I'll take what I can get right here."

The kiss was blistering and urgent.

Our mouths fused together passionately with an intensity that weakened my knees. We both knew whatever lay ahead was going to be tough, and there never seemed to be enough time to bond with him the way I craved.

"You taste incredibly good," he said into my mouth as his tongue stroked my bottom lip. "But I hear something in the distance, so we have to make this shorter than I'd like. All the adrenaline from the change is making me crazy with need, and you standing naked so near is a dangerous combination. I need to back away from you now so I can calm myself down. I don't want to flash my bounding enthusiasm for my beautiful mate to the world."

"*Ha*," I said, glancing downward and licking my lips. "Would being naked and horny embarrass you?"

He leveled a hooded gaze on me. "Hell no, but I know it would embarrass *you*. You had me disrobe behind the plane so I wouldn't shock Naomi." He raised a single eyebrow in a very sexy way, laced with intent. "If you had less of a human nature, I'd already have you on the ground right now."

I shivered. "Well, as much as I would love that, we'd be caught in the act." On cue, a truck honked in the distance. Rourke maneuvered himself behind the small tree as best he could and I ducked down behind a single scrubby bush.

Before the truck arrived, which I saw was a souped-up pickup with huge tires that almost looked as though they could float, Naomi landed in front of me. Her cheeks were a little pink, indicating a blush, which made me think she'd been near enough to overhear our sexy banter.

"It is of no consequence, *Ma Reine*," Naomi stated, addressing my discomfort as she deftly tossed me my backpack. Then she turned and threw Rourke a bag of clothes. "Your mate is correct. Supernaturals don't have the same issues as humans when it comes to our bodies and…other personal things. But, you are my superior, and I would show you respect by not interrupting until I was sure you were not going to . . . interact. But in the future you don't need to be so shy."

"I think my shyness will be sticking around, Naomi," I muttered as I pulled my clothes out of the pack. "I'm new to all this, but I'm still a firm believer that some things are better left private. I don't see that changing any time soon."

The truck raced up as I yanked on my spandex.

"Come on, Hannon," Ray yelled out the window, laying on the horn. "Get your ass covered. We're wasting time here."

I pulled on my shirt and stood, making my way over to the vehicle—one that was only slightly less jacked-up than the Hummer we'd been forced to drive to Canada. The truck was bright orange with flames painted over the wheels. "Where in the world did you get this?" I asked.

"From the airboat guy." Ray chuckled from the open window. Then he thumbed his hand at Marcy, who was situated in the passenger seat. "She threatened him within an inch of his life. You should've seen it. And this was *after* she bought his goddamn airboat right out from under him."

4

Rourke came out from behind the tree fully clothed in brand-new jeans and a black T-shirt. Naomi did well. "How'd you know we'd need an airboat?" Rourke asked, nodding his head in appreciation for the commandeered vehicle.

Marcy stuck her head out of the passenger window. "The first thing I did when I de-boarded my awful flight on Vamp Air was purchase a new cell phone. James told me we'd need one and where the closest ones were. There's a bunch of places to rent them about thirty miles north of here, all clustered along the highway. We picked the most run-down operation we could see from the road, and knowing we couldn't bring along any company where we're going, I offered the owner more than he made in a year, and voilà, the boat was ours. Then I had to sign a bunch of safety waivers"—she dismissed their importance with a flick of her wrist—"but who cares. Get in."

Rourke and I made our way to the bed of the truck. There was no room for us inside. "You can't leave out the part about forcing him to lend us this truck to pick up our friends or you'd make sure his balls would ache for a week." Ray chuckled appreciatively. "That stuff never gets old."

"I didn't say balls, I said *groin*."

"Then she wound up for a fake punch and the guy nearly wet himself," Ray howled out the window. "Funniest thing I've witnessed in a long time."

I nodded as I sat down near the cab. The small partition in the back was open. "Did he hand this prize over immediately?" I leaned in to ask Marcy and smiled.

"Nah," Ray answered first, turning around. "I had to pull out my badge and tell him we were investigating drug smuggling in these parts and may have mentioned the moonshine operation they had in the back as extra incentive. The guy was caught off guard, and if he hadn't wet himself when Marcy feigned the punch, he did then. I couldn't tell him my supernatural sense of smell picked up on his illegal activities, but I was clear enough about the implications and he finally let us take the truck. But, honestly, I haven't had this much fun in a long time. Humans are so easy to manipulate." Ray gunned the engine for effect. "Like taking candy from a baby."

"How'd you get your badge?" I asked as Rourke and Naomi settled in beside me.

"I was buck-ass naked after that portal ripped every stitch of clothing off my body, so I went home to get new ones. My badge was sitting on the table where I left it, so I grabbed it. I thought it might come in handy, though not this soon, but turns out it did." Ray hit the gas and spun out, racing over the marshlands at high speed, bouncing us around like kids on a hayride, hooting like a kid with a new toy.

The huge tires, which appeared to be more like inflated donuts than actual tires, sprayed up an array of grasses and swamp water as we went. I scuttled to the middle of the truck bed to avoid being sprayed, but it was a losing battle.

"Too bad we don't have demon showers here," I muttered to my mate as he wrapped his arm around me. In the Underworld they had a formula that ate the dirt right off of you. "We're going to smell like dank swamp until we can wash off, and I can guarantee there won't be any decent showers where we're going."

We pounded along the bumpy terrain for a good twenty minutes.

My teeth rattled around until we finally evened out onto a small paved road. "Almost there," Ray yelled. "We got lucky with our directions. This direction is close to civilization. Any farther west and it would've been more complicated. Naomi tracked you before we went off-road, so we knew where you'd be."

Naomi nodded, her face amused by Ray's antics. Then she glanced over at Rourke appreciatively. "Your beast is fierce," she said to him. "I have not seen an equal to it in all my years. The rumors of your strength are renowned in the vampire world, and clearly they weren't exaggerated."

Rourke nodded once, accepting her praise, but didn't comment.

"I will not tell a soul," Naomi said. "My allegiance is to Jessica, and by proxy to you, and I won't risk putting us in jeopardy, nor will I ever talk of anything that would compromise us."

"There's no need to keep it quiet anymore, Naomi," Rourke said. "The game has changed for me forever and my old ways won't work any longer. If I don't adapt, I'll be the one who ultimately places us in jeopardy. And who knows? Maybe if supernaturals know what I am, and what I'm capable of, they'll think twice about pursuing us. Keeping Jessica safe is my number one priority, so it doesn't matter if anyone knows what I am."

Naomi sharpened her gaze, her eyes suddenly dancing. "If you'd like, I can spread rumors of your strength among the vampires. I still have a few contacts. Vampires love to gossip. They live for drama and it might help us."

Rourke chuckled. "I like your style, Naomi. Do whatever you see fit. I'm willing to do just about anything to keep the odds in our favor. Having the supernatural community renew their gossip about me might be a good thing."

Naomi nodded as she peered out at the scenery flying by. Ray must have been going at least eighty. I knew she would do whatever it took to keep all of us safe, just like Rourke, and she took her part seriously. I had no doubt she could come up with a tale that would paint Rourke as a fierce beast who could rip your throat out while you were still talking.

"When we get to the airboat place," I said, nudging Naomi out of her thoughts with the toe of my shoe, "I'm going to send you out ahead of us. I told my father you'd be arriving before us to get the coordinates. He said the place is warded from humans, but since you've already seen them, I'm sure you can find them again."

"*Oui*, I will do that," Naomi answered. "Are you going to wait for the wolf boys to join us before we depart? Or are we going to leave them to meet us later?"

"The 'wolf boys'?" I chortled, tossing back my head. "Now, that's something you don't hear every day."

"Well"—Naomi blushed, shrugging—"they are always together, those two. It will be easier to find a name that works for both of them. You refer to Ray and myself as 'the vamps,' and I agree, it's easier to group us together, so 'wolf boys' is the equivalent for me."

"I like it. And, Naomi, I think you're developing a sense of humor, and funny looks good on you. Let me check in with Tyler now so we can plan ahead. Gimme a second." I held up a finger.

Tyler, are you there? I called.

Yep, he said. *We're about an hour from a city called Homestead. We made good time. Where are you?*

Not sure yet. We're not near any town at the moment. But before we discuss that, I need to let you know I made contact with Dad. He's fine and the plan is to meet up soon. I hope you're close. If you are, we'll wait. Once we get to the airboat place, I'll let you know our exact location.

Glad you got in touch with Dad. I couldn't get through no matter how hard I tried. What's going on with them and the fracture pack? I hope they wiped those assholes off the face of the planet.

Dad said they've kept the Made wolves in check, but it sounds like there's trouble with the priestess. Apparently she's not in it for the money.

Tyler let out a low whistle in his mind. *If she's not doing it for payment, she's doing it for—*

Power.

Well, fuck.

The airboat place consisted of a few run-down shacks and a couple of cheesed-off backwater guides. They were both dressed in plaid shirts, dirty jeans, big-billed hats, and nasty scowls.

"See, we brought your baby back in perfect condition, no harm, no foul," Marcy chirped as she jumped out of the pickup. "Now, what I want is for you to show my friend here how to operate the boat we just purchased." She gestured to Rourke, and both men took a step back as he jumped down from the flatbed.

Rourke grinned and flashed his teeth, pushing his advantage. "I'm a quick learner, boys." Both guides didn't move an inch for a few beats.

I was still in the back, but Naomi had taken to the sky to wait for the wolf boys with extra clothes in hand. I walked to the edge of the truck and glanced down the long dock where the airboats were kept. The one we'd purchased was parked at the end, sitting on top of a big wooden platform that sloped downward on either side. The boat looked as though it'd served a long, battered life in the Glades. Two seats were set higher, right in front of the gigantic propeller fan. They were clearly the drivers' seats. Then there were two rows of passenger seats in front of them. Even from a distance I could see that the benches were covered with peeling red and white striped vinyl. The airboat looked like it could hold about ten people.

The taller of the guides followed my gaze out to the boat. "There ain't nothin' in these parts habitable, so I don't know what you're looking to find. Ain't no boats on the channels we don't know about, neither." He ambled forward, spitting on the ground. "But if you come to investigate the missin' folk, that's something altogether different. Some gone missin' in this neck of the swamp for a good few years now. Lowlife people, who most don't care nothin' about. Trappers mostly. No family to miss 'em. Regular folk blame the meth, but we know there's more to it than that. Guides who've been travelin' 'round here the longest know there's a place deep in 'em Glades where things just ain't right." He pinned his stare on me. "You coming to see about that?"

I appraised him before I answered. He wasn't well educated, but he'd been around about a thousand blocks and would likely pick up on a lie. "Yes," I said. "We're coming to take a look into that." I wasn't surprised humans would pick up on the negative energy after being exposed to it for so long. If the priestesses had been here for a hundred years, like my father had guessed, it was bound to have some residual consequences.

The shorter guide came within a few feet of Ray before he stopped. "He's right. Things just ain't right 'round here. So I guess they hired a fancy police officer from up in the north to come down here and do their dirty work, huh?" He pronounced *police* like "pole-eece." "So you just gonna set it all to rights, then?"

Ray stared at the guy so hard, he finally shied away, shuffling his feet as he went. But I had to give him credit, he lasted a lot longer than a regular human would. He must have been slightly off or he never would've approached Ray in the first place. "Something like that," Ray grumbled, crossing his arms. "But in order for me to 'set things to right,' I need you to tell me everything you know about these disappearances, got it? Leave nothing out. The more info we have, the better chance we have to catch these bastards. Let's go have a nice chat while the other boys figure out the boat." The short guide trailed after Ray, who was already peppering him with questions in a typical cop fashion.

The tall guide turned to Rourke. "I'll show you how to run the boat. It ain't too hard." They walked out to the end of the dock.

Marcy strode up to me, grinning.

"What?" I asked.

"This is going to be one heck of an adventure, isn't it?" Her eyes were gleaming. "The last one I had—being kidnapped by the sorcerers—was scary and hellish, but it did bring out one good thing."

"And what's that?"

"My thirst for adrenaline."

"You're an action junky now?" I eyed her, trying to keep a straight face.

"Not *exactly*, but I am trying to nurture the adventurer that has blossomed inside me like a tree taking roots. You know, encourage it to grow by watering it once in a while." She spread her arms wide. "Like right now. I'm fertilizing it as we speak. Then, I figure if I keep having adventures, they're bound to grow on me, like tiny shoots that will eventually turn into one big, kickass oak tree."

I snorted. "I'm not quite sure that's how it works."

"Oh, that's how, all right. Just you watch."

"Marcy, you're welcome to have all the adventures you want. I'm sure the Everglades will be exciting, but we have bigger things to worry about than a few alligators and a little black magic from this priestess. When the Hags choose to come after us, it will be adventure on steroids."

"Don't underestimate the power of black magic or this priestess," Marcy said gravely. "That's some serious juju. It's good you have me along with my twitchy fingers"—she wiggled them—"but even I can't undo black spells. That magic comes from a much different place than mine, like a good-versus-evil kind of thing. Those priestesses kill things and use the blood to do their bidding. It's heavy, and very, very dangerous." As she said it, her eyes were twinkling with excitement.

"And that excites you?" I chuckled. "You just told me that black magic is serious and we should be afraid. Death and destruction shouldn't be your go-to button for fun. You're acting like a little kid in a candy store."

"That's exactly it! I *am* in a candy store—for the very first time," she said. "My entire life I've been deemed not 'powerful enough' or 'not witchy enough,' and I've been relegated to the sidelines for everything. But now"—she hooted with joy, tossing a fist in the air—"I'm here to taste all the flavors life has to offer. This is the absolute best I've felt in years. I have James to thank for that too, because he's brought out all my positives and has punctuated them with delicious exclamation points, and even though I'm still mad at that rat-bellied toad for making me stay home and wait for you—"

"There's a baby alligator by your foot," I said.

She shrieked loudly and jumped into my arms. It happened so fast, I hoped the guides hadn't noticed her unnatural speed.

I chortled as I set her down. "I think adrenaline is your friend in more ways than one."

"That wasn't funny!" she accused, swatting me on the arm. "Having an alligator gnaw my foot off is not having an *adventure*. Do you know how long it would take me to regenerate a piece of my foot? And how badly that would hurt? I'm not an animal like you. Witches take a long time to heal."

Before I could comment on the unfairness of it all, and that most of the adventures I'd been involved with over the last month had had their share of hurts, my brother called my name outside my head. I turned to see him loping toward me, Danny close on his heels.

"Jessica!" I was happy to see he and Danny were both fully dressed, which meant Naomi had found them first.

"Where's Naomi?" I asked a second before I saw her emerge from behind the monster truck. "*Ohmygods*, are those hamburgers I smell?" My mouth instantly started to salivate and my wolf howled for joy.

Burgers beat raw reptile by several thousand country miles.

Naomi held up about ten greasy bags with a big grin on her face. "The wolf boys were hungry after their shift, so they sent me ahead to get food."

I turned to my brother. "That was the best decision you've ever made in your entire life."

5

After a quick but hearty meal of burgers and fries, we were finally ready to embark. Ray's face was grim after his chat with the guide, but he stayed quiet. We all boarded the airboat, Rourke and Tyler heading for the two driver's seats.

"Just like I said," the taller guide called. "It's as easy as one, two, three. This boat's name is *Betsy* and she's been suped up for speed. You can get 'er going to sixty. Find some nice flat vegetation to cross and you can go even faster. The green stuff gets the hull off the ground nice and quick like. You'll make good time that way getting to the deep cypress."

"Yeah, go and get dem assholes," the other piped in. "If you do, we got plenty of moonshine to celebrate with. It's not legal yet in Florida, but from where we come from it's like mother's milk, straight from the teat." He smiled wide, and I noticed he had more than a few teeth missing.

"Don't you worry," Danny called, holding up the old ceramic jug they'd given him and shaking it. "We will indeed find something to celebrate along the way." Danny popped the cork out and took a sniff. "Good gods, that's strong enough to take the hair off my mother's chest." Then he waggled his eyebrows. "But that's why I'm going to enjoy it to its fullest."

"Best stuff in the state of Florida," the tall guide called, "but be careful with it. That hooch'll leave you shitfaced and groggy for two solid weeks if you imbibe too much."

Rourke started the fan. It sounded like a jet engine readying for takeoff as the blades began to increase their speed. Very slowly he eased the throttle forward and began to glide us off the platform like he'd been operating this boat his entire life. "We go through the low grasses first to get to the main channel," Rourke said. "After that, the start of the cypress swamp begins. The particular patch of cypress the guides are concerned about ends in the mangroves, near the coast, which is likely how the priestess entered this area."

The fan found its rhythm, but it was irritatingly loud. None of us had to raise our voices to be heard if we didn't feel like it, however. The boat skimmed over small swamp grasses, and as Rourke opened up the throttle even more, it gained speed. The scenery over the open water was beautiful and majestic. The sun glinted off the water and plants, making everything sparkle.

"Naomi," I called. "Once we reach the cypress swamp, I want you to take off. I'm certain we'll all feel the magic when we get close enough, but you have to rendezvous with my father to get us the directions to their camp."

"*Oui.*" She nodded.

"Oh, and I never asked the first time, but when you were here last night did you notice any dark magic from the sky?"

"*Non,*" she answered. "I was too high up. I'm certain if I had come down farther, I would've detected something."

Marcy shook her head. "You might not have. Black magic is tangible only when you're right on top of it. It's like a creepy oil slick. Those human guides back there would've had to come right up next to it to feel anything, but once they did, I bet the hair on their arms jumped on end and it sent them scurrying as fast as their overalls would take them."

Rourke maneuvered the boat into a fairly wide channel littered with tall water lilies sprouting out of the water like they were trying to reach for the sky. Cypress trees were clustered in the distance, and we were closing in fast.

"Did the guide tell you which channel to take once we got there?" Tyler asked Rourke. "From here it looks like there might be a few options."

"Yep," Rourke answered. "We're taking the one on the far right."

We rode in silence, and once we reached the end of the channel, Rourke deftly turned the boat into the new lane, this one filled with trees. It was like entering a new world. Tall cypress trees jutted out into the water like gnarled fingers. The majority of their roots were exposed to the elements and their canopies were knit closely, blocking out most of the light as effectively as flipping a switch.

"Okay, Naomi." I motioned with my hand. "You can go. Once you touch base with my father, come find us."

"Okay, *Ma Reine*. I'll be back as soon as I can." She took to the sky immediately.

Ray turned to me. "Do you want me to go with her? I can scout around while she talks to your father. I'm curious about all this black magic hocus-pocus. I'm itching to get closer and see if I sense anything."

"If you want to scout it out, that's fine with me," I said, my eyes scanning the trees as we zoomed forward, searching for anything out of the ordinary. "But stay close. We have no idea what to expect."

Ray took off after Naomi.

I glanced at Rourke and my brother. Marcy sat beside me and Danny was in front of us. "Do you feel anything particular?" I asked my mate.

"Not yet," he said. "But according to the guide, we still have about ten miles to go. We're edging toward the coast. Keep your senses open. I don't have a good feeling about this." He shook his head gravely. "Whoever this priestess is, she knows we're coming."

We headed down the channel in silence for another few miles, all of us scouting and trying to sense any magic.

"Marcy, tell me what you know about voodoo," I murmured, not taking my eyes off the trees. "Before, you said it's magic based on sacrifice and blood. What else?"

"Voodoo is very old magic—possibly one of the oldest forms of all time. It's often referred to as *vodou* or *voudoun*. And from what I know—and my info is a little sketchy because it's been so long—the kind that's practiced in the U.S. was brought over from the West Indies a few hundred years ago. Voodoo worships the loa, which are literally spirits—like ghosts—but much more powerful. A priestess can summon the loa, and the spirit inhabits her body. It's called being 'ridden,' if you can believe it." She guffawed. "Not a ride I'd want to take."

"No, that sounds a little unpleasant," I mused.

"After they summon the loa, they're supposed to become stronger. There are a couple of groups of loas, if I remember correctly, but this is coming from my grade-school witch education, so take it with a pinch of salt. All spell casters are required to learn about the entire witchy community, so we know how to defeat them."

"Did you learn how to defeat them in grade school?" I asked, my voice hopeful.

"Heck no!" She laughed. "That's a specialized field of magic. They just teach us a broad overview and how to shield and bounce back certain spells. But now that I'm thinking about it, there might be a teensy thing that could make this entire thing worse." She turned toward me, her face appearing a little stricken.

"What is it? You just went pale."

"Talking about this made me remember. In voudoun, the priestesses are not the top of the food chain."

"They're not?"

"No. So pray to your great aunt Fanny that we're dealing with a priestess here, because if we're not, life is about to get much harder."

"Stop beating around the bush and just tell me what you're talking about! What's more powerful than a priestess?" I didn't really want to know, did I?

"A bokor."

The name rang a few tiny bells inside my head, but not enough to put it together on my own. "Explain."

"In a nutshell, they're the equivalent of a sorceress, and they deal primarily with the dead."

"Like a necromancer?" I asked, hoping she would tell me they were nothing like a necromancer.

"Kind of, I guess. I don't know much about it. We're talking fifth-grade learning here. But I do know they're supposed to be able to control their victims' brain activities, and I know this because we used to chase each other around on the playground pretending to 'voodoo' each other at recess. But who knows, really? Like anything in our world, it's all myth until you see it for yourself. If Tally were here, she'd set us straight." Marcy's eyes misted immediately and she glanced away. "Dang, I hope that old biddy is okay."

"Me too." I'd been worried about Tally too. Ever since we'd found out the witches had disappeared unexpectedly, my mind had been occupied with scenarios about what had happened to her, none of them good, and all of them involving me in some way. Tally had disappeared while she was helping me after

I'd killed Ardat Lili, who was the previous witch contingent on the Coalition. After we finished helping my father, aiding the witches would be my next order of business. I had no doubt Tally was in trouble because of me. "Do you have any hunches where she might be? Anything that can help us?"

"Not really. The only info I have was from that Romanian witch who said there was something brewing in Italy." Marcy had filled me in before we'd boarded the plane. To me, it was no coincidence that Julian de Rossi, the leader of the European Pack, was also in Italy. If there was a convergence of supernatural activity going on, they were all tied up in it together.

The air around us suddenly became heavier.

Both Marcy and I straightened in our seats. I darted a look back to Rourke. His face was set.

We'd all felt it. Black magic.

"I think it's best to pull the boat up and wait for your father," Rourke said. "We don't know what's real now, and what may be an illusion. From what I know about black magic, everything is tainted." He slowed the boat down by turning off the propeller and gliding us toward a thick bank of trees. These boats didn't have brakes. As Rourke nestled the boat in between cypress roots like a pro, the air around us pushed down on our chests, making it harder to breathe.

My wolf paced back and forth, lifting her muzzle to scent the area. The smell of rancid meat and rotting flesh started to creep into my senses. No wonder the guides didn't venture any farther. It was menacing here, and the trees were so thick that we could see only a few feet into the grove. Anything could be lurking there.

"Is that fog rolling in like on a movie set?" Marcy asked, her voice hitting a high note at the end. "This place is laced with negative energy."

There was indeed a fog creeping in. It was misting in front of us, straight up the waterway, blocking out any sun that had been trying to filter through.

"*Dammit*," Tyler swore. "This isn't good."

Rourke went to the side of the boat. "If I had to guess, I'd say we're about a mile farther in than the guides have ever been. I didn't feel any wards, but we definitely crossed a line of some kind back there." He glanced at the sky. "And the vamps should've been back by now. I say we turn around and head back to wait for them on the other side of the line. No reason to stay here like sitting ducks if we're in the priestess's domain." Rourke reached back to flip the fan back on.

Nothing happened.

Danny stepped over the bench in front of us, heading toward the guys. "Here, let me help. I have gifted fingers when it comes to starting things."

Rourke stepped aside. "By all means, wolf, give it your best shot." Danny flipped the switch and nothing happened. Tyler started to argue with him and Rourke drew closer to me. He leaned over and said, "If we're under some kind of attack, I want you to head straight back the way we came. Use the sun if you have to, but I want you to go."

I nodded absentmindedly, still scanning the trees in front of us. "The chances of us separating is slim, and you know it. I'm not leaving you here to fight the threat alone."

"If this priestess wants power," he said, crossing his arms, "she wants you. If she's a bokor like Marcy thinks, these Made wolves aren't cursed—they're *dead*. She's likely been in control of their minds the entire time, and if that's the case, she's had an agenda all along. We don't need much brainpower to reason that she's lured the Pack here on purpose, in hopes you would show up. And we played right into her hands."

I nodded. "That might be true, but we don't know anything for sure. It could be she was originally hired by the fracture pack and then decided to turn the tables when she realized how powerful her new wolves had become. Every supe we've encountered wants power any way they can get it. I might be the icing, now that I'm here, but there's a possibility I wasn't the main meal."

"I don't believe any of this was unintentional. She wants you," Rourke grumbled. "The air here is thick with hate. Nothing natural would live within these boundaries. Something that evil lies in wait for their prize, even if it means waiting a hundred years."

He was right. No self-respecting animal would live on cursed land if they could help it.

I looked over at my brother and Danny. "Hey," I called, "time to stop worrying about the motor. Let's get some long sticks and start moving this thing along like a gondola. We only went a mile or so before Rourke shut the boat down. Naomi and Ray should be back any moment. We'll meet them back the way we came."

Rourke leaned over the side and cracked a big branch off a cypress tree and placed it in the water.

Then he stilled mid-thrust.

"What?" I asked, reading his face. "What is it?"

He put his finger to his lips, his eyes pinned over my shoulder. *Don't move*, he told me internally.

Marcy stifled a shriek behind me and I closed my eyes.

My back was closest to the trees. Slowly, without moving my body, I tilted my eyes upward. Right into the face of a huge python. It slithered above me, slowly descending, not making a sound. It was ten feet from my head. We wouldn't be able to get the boat out fast enough by hand. We had to fight it.

Rourke changed his grip on the branch to hold it like a baseball bat. *Stay still. When I yell, you duck. It's only going to take one hit.*

Hurry up. That thing looks hungry and more than a little

possessed. There was no mistaking that the snake only had eyes for me. Its head never wavered.

As Rourke waited not so patiently for it to come, my brother crept to the side of the boat, yanking another huge branch off the nearby tree for himself and then one for Danny. "Stay calm, sis," he murmured. "I'm pretty sure that snake is dead, but it doesn't matter. All we need is to get it the fuck out of here, and then we haul ass out."

The serpent was as big around as a basketball and was so long I couldn't see where it ended. I also couldn't rip my eyes away from the spectacle of it, almost as if it had me mesmerized. I didn't feel any magic coming off it. *I'm throwing power at it,* I told Rourke, *but it's rebuffing me. Can it be an illusion? Tyler's right—it has no heartbeat or any signs it's actually alive.*

We're about to find out. "Now!" Rourke yelled.

I hit the floor of the boat as Rourke swung the tree branch a foot above the thing's head with supernatural force. The branch shattered instantly as it connected with the snake, but it was enough force to send the serpent flying. As the python went, it tore out the branch it had been coiled on, so it didn't go nearly far enough as we all would've liked.

It plunked in the water a measly five feet from us.

"That thing will be back as soon as it's able," Danny yelled, flipping the start button on and off frantically but still not getting the desired result. "Fighting a possessed python that could swallow us whole is not how I'd like to spend the rest of my day. Getting piss drunk on moonshine is a much better option."

"Danny's right, fighting that thing is not on the agenda," I said, scrambling back up. Because this thing was now supernatural and couldn't be killed easily, it was going to keep coming until it either killed us or took what it wanted. "Let's get out of here, and I don't care how we do it."

"Way ahead of you," Tyler grunted.

I glanced over and saw both Tyler and Rourke with branches the size of small trees in the water. They shoved them against the bank, their muscles bulging with effort, but we didn't move.

Not even an inch.

Marcy had turned white in panic, her hands fisted at her sides.

I leaned over and snapped my fingers in front of her face. "I need you to wake up, Marcy. This is exactly the kind of adventure you were looking for not twenty minutes ago. Your adrenaline should be up and running, and now that our happy fun time is beginning, I need you. You can help us get out of here, just like on the plane. Can you detect any spells? Something is holding us here and we need to break free."

She physically shook herself. "Okay, yes. Yes, okay, I'm on it!" She brought her fingertips to her temples and closed her eyes, but they snapped open after a mere second. "There's no spell! I can't pick up on anything. It all just feels…dead. Kind of like what happened on the airplane, but different. The plane was a void. This dead feels…*evil*."

I turned to Rourke. "Do you think there's any chance the Hags are using the priestess to get the job of killing me done?"

"I don't know," Rourke answered. "Could be. But we're not going to wait to find out. We have two choices. We fight that thing once it makes its way back here, or we bail out of the boat and try to make it back the way we came through the cypress trees." He motioned to the thick trees over his shoulder.

"Sorry, mate, there aren't two choices," Danny said, backing up until his shoulders hit the propeller screen. "The way I see it, there's only one."

I nodded numbly in agreement as I watched more snakes emerge out of the dense growth and slither toward us from all directions.

There was no fighting. We had no choice but to run.

6

Tyler jumped first because he was closest. He leapt to a clear spot on one of the bigger trees, one of only a few that wasn't covered in a snake. "Hurry," he urged. "From up here I can see more. There are literally hundreds. They've definitely been called into action, and we're the target."

"I'm right behind you," Marcy called as she launched herself over the side and landed next to Tyler.

Rourke placed his hands over my hips and said, "You're next. Once you get there, don't wait for Danny and me, start running. We'll keep back as many as we can, and then we'll join you."

"Goddamn bloody serpents," Danny yelled as he brought his stick down on the heads of some that had started to creep over the edges of the boat. If it wasn't so horrible, it might be comical. Attack of the Killer Swamp Snakes. "Get the holy feck out of here, you bloody bastards!" *Whap!* The blows only temporarily stunned them. Their tongues hissed as they came right back for more.

I jumped next, landing on the right side of Tyler. He grabbed my wrist and steadied me. We started to move immediately, which meant we bounded from one tree to the next, balancing on top of the roots. Marcy was right behind me, and when she started to fall behind, I tugged her along. I was directly behind Tyler, who was taking the clearest route around the snakes and doing a pretty decent job. But it wasn't going to last. The snakes would figure out where I was soon enough and start to converge, but I'd take it for the moment.

"I'm coming, I'm coming," Marcy muttered. "I don't need any more incentive to get away from this house of horrors."

"Keep trying to use your spells," I said. "Maybe if we get farther away, they'll work—"

Tyler blipped out of existence in front of us. One second he was there, the next gone.

Before I could yell for him, Marcy and I tumbled across some kind of warded boundary line. As we passed through, my body pulsed with strange magic. My wolf growled fiercely, snapping her jaws as the evil energy of the place raced along our skin. The ward tasted stale and very old.

The world in front of us slowly morphed into view.

Our environment before had been filled with healthy trees, interspersed with water. But now, like a watercolor being washed away, the space in front of us revealed another land entirely. What was left in its place was barren soil and dead trees. All the water was gone. We were standing along a ring of trees, a large circle of dead earth in the middle. The trunks were withered and gnarled, like old crones who had been forced to stand sentinel for their master. The sun had been cast into dark shadows, appearing like only a pale orange globe in the sky.

This was her land.

I could feel it as clearly as if she stood next to us. She was beckoning us, taunting us, daring us to move forward.

"Holy crap," Marcy said as my mate burst through the ward behind us.

"Thank gods," he roared as he made his way over. "When you disappeared, I thought it might have been through another goddamn portal." Danny was close on his heels. Rourke stalked through the tress, taking in his surroundings like the rest of us. He stopped next to me, reaching for my hand, his eyes alert.

"Well, this is a bit strange, isn't it?" Danny said, peering into the barren circle. "But the bloody snakes didn't follow us in, so maybe we've been given a short reprieve by finding this place?"

"I don't think a reprieve is what she has in mind," I murmured. "I'm pretty certain her snakes can enter, but I think she used them to chase us here. She gave us the only clear path to run, so we used it. She wanted us to find her."

"Well, she's not getting what she wants," Tyler said. He was twenty feet to the left of where I stood. "We're going back to the boat. The four of us will shift, and we can fight the snakes in our true forms. Our claws and fangs should be enough to hold them back until the vamps get back. Marcy, you send up flares. We should've done something like that from the beginning. Once the vamps arrive, they can take two of us out at a time."

"I can light up the sky like the Fourth of July," Marcy agreed, turning to follow Tyler without question. "I can also kindle a fire around us. That might keep them back. I know I have to start thinking better on my feet, but honestly, anyone in their right mind would freak out in the face of one of those monsters, much less hordes of them. I've never seen pythons that big in my entire life. And those red eyes. So hateful."

I didn't have a better plan, and fighting the priestess or whoever she was right now wouldn't be optimal. We all turned and started back the way we'd come.

After about ten feet, Rourke said, "We should've hit the boundary line by now. We all came through right around here." He turned in a circle. "But, honestly, I'm not sure if this place is an illusion or some kind of an alternate reality. If it's an illusion, we might be screwed."

I took in the scenery again. "The ground seems firm and real," I said, stomping on a tree root. "But I agree. This area gives off some weird, unnatural vibes. It's hard to know if what we're seeing is reality or not."

"It could be a place in between," Marcy said. "Not reality and not illusion."

"Like between dimensions?" Tyler asked. "I've heard those exist but never believed it."

"I would think the voudoun would seek out those kinds of places." Marcy nodded. "So I believe it. Maybe that's why she chose this location in the first place, because it was close to the in between."

"I visited a place kind of like this in the Underworld," I said. "The Scholls. Ardat Lili called it exactly that—a place in between. It was a spirit world for their half-dead, the demons who came back as wyvern. It was different than this but had the same thick air and menace." The air wasn't wavy like it had been in the Scholls, but it was similar enough. "I don't know anything about voudoun, but if the priestess who lives here communes with specific spirits, I think you might be right, Marcy. She could've come here to be closer to them." That seemed like the most logical. If a demon in the Underworld specialized in communing with the wyvern, they'd move to the Scholls.

"Where's the damn boundary?" Rourke growled as he continued to search in front of the group. "We should've hit it by now, but it's just more of the same."

"There's no channel either. The water has disappeared," Danny said. "No break in the trees like before."

We all turned in circles, spreading out to search for an exit. "Maybe it wasn't a boundary we crossed but a doorway we entered instead?" Tyler climbed up the roots of the nearest tree and placed his hands on the trunk. We all waited to see if he could push his way through. "If that's the case," he grunted, trying to force the tree open, "the priestess might be able to manipulate the door and place it wherever she wants. She directed us in here by chasing us with snakes. But in order to get out, we might have to open another doorway. Or force her to open one." Tyler gave up on that one and jumped to another.

I nodded. It made sense. "Maybe that's why Dad said it was so hard to communicate with her. He told me sometimes she's there and sometimes she's not. So she must be able to stay hidden within this boundary when she wants to."

"I'm just glad Ray and Naomi are on the outside," Rourke said. "Ray won't stop searching until he figures out where we've gone. He'll get your dad and they'll bring reinforcements. We either find a way out, or they'll find a way in."

"I agree—Ray won't stop. They'll get in if they can," I said. "But maybe we're going about this wrong. What if it's actually an advantage that we're stuck in here? I know battling this priestess without backup is not ideal, and having the entire Pack in attendance would give us better odds, but we came here to eliminate the threat. If the priestess, or the bokor, is our main opposition—and not the fracture pack—we're in the right place, right *now*."

"Jess," Tyler groaned. "We're not doing this. Dad is literally a few miles away with thirty-plus wolves. It would be a bad tactical error to attack now, especially if we can bolster our chances of defeating this thing with more force. There's no question."

"But Dad hasn't been able to figure out how to attack her here." I gestured at the dead land in front of us. "This priestess can keep them out if she wants to, or they would've been battling her here already. They've been here for weeks, and we've been here for five minutes and we're inside her lair. I say we use this to our advantage and end the threat ourselves, the sooner the better."

Marcy cleared her throat. "You're right about one thing, this priestess can keep them out whenever she wants. But I have to tell you, if my guy knew I was in here, and we had the chance to get back out to get reinforcements and didn't, he'd be furious with me." Then she grinned like a shrew. "But when Ray reports we've all disappeared, James will freak out and go all alpha on everyone to get me back. And that can only work in our favor, right? He's going to rip these trees apart trying to find me, so I'm voting with you. Let's push forward and assume the Pack is coming for us as soon as they can. If we get to her and start fighting, I bet we can weaken her hold on the wards."

My eyebrows shot up my forehead. "Two seconds ago you were heading back to the boat with Tyler," I said. "But you're right, James would never forgive us if something happened to you. Maybe going forward is not such a great idea."

She placed her hands on her waist, drumming her hips. "If you ruin this one chance we have to defeat the priestess because you're worried about me not being *man* enough, I'm going to be upset. I assure you, I can handle it. I know I lost it when I saw those things coming at us, but red eyes mean possession. Their sole purpose was to intimidate and threaten. But I swear to you right now, I'm ready. I can be an asset."

Marcy was a powerful witch, but she was extremely new to being a foot solider in this war. If she got hurt, I didn't need James's wrath—I'd never forgive myself anyway. But maybe there was a way around it. "Let's split the odds," I said. "Rourke, Tyler, and I will continue to investigate, but not engage, while you and Danny search for a doorway. Whoever finds what we're looking for first is the way we go."

"Okay, I can live with that." Then her voice fell a few octaves, to just above a whisper. "And, just so you know, if we run into serious trouble, I can make my magic dark if need be. I have ways to make it more potent, and if we're stuck between a possessed python and a hard place, that will give us a better edge. It would just take me a little time to get it ready, but once I was done, it would pack a punch."

"And how exactly would you make your magic dark?" I asked, my head inclined toward her. I didn't like where this conversation was headed.

She shrugged. "I'd use blood." She tried to make it sound blasé, like she used blood in all her spells, but it didn't work.

I threw my arms up. "Marcy, you can't be serious! I'm not letting you practice black magic under my watch. Not only will James rip me limb from limb, but your aunt will have my *head* if she finds out I sanctioned such a thing. No way in hell is that happening."

"Cool your jets, Glinda the Good Witch," Marcy countered. "I said it would take time to get it ready. I'm talking about brewing a dark spell, not sacrificing a chicken. Blood *brewed* in spells is different than ingesting it. Blood gives magic strength no matter what, but one way it's given freely and in another it's taken by force. If I drank your blood or ate your heart, and then gathered my magic from the blood sacrifice through my body, my magic would be jet black. But if I used a few drops of blood in a brewed spell, it gives it potency, but it doesn't make it black."

"But you just said your magic would be *dark*," I said. "Dark is bad."

"Yes, dark. But not *black*," she huffed, her long red hair

streaming down around her shoulders in a mass of beautiful curls. It was quite a stark contrast to our current environment. "I'm not insane. Once a witch nose-dives into black magic, there's very little that can bring her back. Blood magic is like smoking crack for witches. It makes them feel invincible—and many times they are, because their magic becomes super strong. But it also makes them crazed, which is why it's banned in every Coven in the entire world and has been for a thousand years. If all witches were walking around hopped up on blood magic, the world would've come to a grinding halt eons ago."

"So how exactly are you going to brew dark spells here?" I asked, gesturing around me. "We're in the middle of the Everglades in an alternate reality."

Marcy glanced around at the barren landscape. "Well, I never said it was... *ideal*. I just said I could do it if pressed. But, really, I only need a few things to make a simple protection spell. I always carry a vial of *fleur de sel* on me." She reached into her pants pocket and withdrew a small container of salt. "I can make fire, no problem, and I can spell the area to find other raw materials I need. I'd just need a pot of some kind to cook the spells in."

"Well," Tyler said, coming up to us, "that sounds easy enough to procure. I bet there's a Walmart on the other side of those dead trees." He gestured in the distance. "I'll be back in a few minutes with your cookware."

Danny elbowed him in the stomach. "Quit your grousing. You're not thinking craftily enough, mate. I think what she's talking about is a recon mission. If we can't find an exit, we go to plan C, which would be find the priestess's abode in this hellhole. She's bound to have a house—or at least someplace she can scuttle off to. And if she does, she has to eat. Eating means pots. We break in, steal one, and we're back before you know it."

"That's the dumbest thing you've ever—" Before Tyler could finish, there was a loud buzzing coming from Marcy.

All eyes went to her as she slowly reached around to her back pocket and pulled out her cell phone. We gathered around her as she placed it out in front so we could see:

GET OUT! GET OUT! GET OUT!

The message ran across the phone over and over again, ticking by so fast it was hard to read.

Rourke roared into the air, "And exactly where do we GET OUT?"

A heavy breeze laced with malice and intent rushed through the trees. Dead leaves rattled and shook, and low growls began to erupt from all around us.

"We're surrounded!" Tyler yelled. "She called in her wolves while we were debating cooking utensils."

Sure enough, red eyes began to light up the area as the possessed wolves crept closer through the trees on the other side of the circle.

"How many are there?" Rourke said.

"At least eight from my count," Tyler answered. "They're coming from all sides except behind us."

"Marcy, does the phone say anything else?" I said as I got down into a low crouch stance. "Keep looking."

"It says nothing!" she cried. "I'm shaking the dang thing and the message won't change." She held the phone up to her mouth and yelled into the speaker, "Listen, Jessica's neighbor, we know we have to get out, but you need to give us a little more help than this!"

There was a loud cracking sound, and the wolves howled their anger.

"Over there!" Tyler called. "Do you see it?" He pointed at a tree to our right. It had started to glow, pulsing through the yellow haze like a beacon.

"The phone is telling us to go to the tree," Marcy said.

We all took off, racing to reach it as the wolves closed in, yelping and snapping their jaws. Rourke arrived first, bracing his arms around the big trunk. One arm went through, which was a good sign. "It's a doorway, let's go!" He backed up and Danny lunged through, followed by Marcy. "Come on, Jessica, you're next!"

The rabid wolves were running hard across the clearing, trying to get to us. Tyler shoved me from behind, sending me shooting through right as a ghostly voice shivered along my spine, whispering, "We shall meet soon, *bèt nan bwa*."

7

"Where in the hell did you come from?" Ray yelled as we all landed at the edge of the channel, right in front of the boat.

"*Ma Reine*," Naomi said in a worried voice as she landed in front of me. "Are you all right?"

I picked myself up from the tangle of roots and followed Marcy, jumping into the boat. "I'm fine, I think. We were chased into some kind of alternate reality by possessed snakes, but found a way out thanks to Juanita. I'll explain later, but now we need to fire this boat up and get away from here." I turned to Danny, who was already by the fan. "Can you get it started?"

"Working on it," he said as Tyler landed in the boat behind me and hurried to join him.

"The snakes are gone," Marcy called from the front as she tentatively peered over the side. "But I'm putting a containment spell around the boat anyway."

"What snakes?" Ray asked in a bewildered tone. "When I got

here, this place was a ghost town. Not a sound for miles. It was like you, and everything else here, just up and disappeared."

"We did disappear. I told you, we were caught in some kind of alternate space," I replied. "The priestess surrounded the boat and forced us out because she wanted us in her realm." I turned to Marcy. "Can you hand me your phone, please?"

She set her phone in the palm of my outstretched hand. "Good luck." She grinned. "She killed it again."

I glanced down. Marcy was right. The screen was totally white. I punched the button on the front, but nothing happened.

"The snakes will be back as soon as she can summon them," Rourke said grimly as he landed in the boat, making it rock. He broke a branch off the nearest tree in the same motion. "Ray, kick the boat out with your feet as hard as you can. It's being held by something underneath. I don't think it's a spell. We're going to need a send-off."

The boys were still trying to get the fan to turn on, with no luck.

"I leave for ten minutes and all kinds of crazy shit happens," Ray grumbled as he took hold of a big tree branch above his head. Bending his knees, he shoved both feet into the side of the boat with enough force to knock us free. There was a huge crunching noise as something gave from below and we were finally launched into the middle of the channel.

As soon as we were free, the propeller roared to life.

Rourke ducked over the side to check out what had held us. "She must be able to control the trees somehow. The roots were suctioned to the bottom of the boat. There's a mass of them at the bottom now."

Ray swung himself from the branch and landed effortlessly in the boat. Rourke took the main chair and steered us around in the small space and zoomed out the way we'd come. Only once we'd reached the end of the cypress trees and were headed into the sawgrass and water lilies did Rourke lower the throttle.

"Okay, now that we're clear, can someone tell me, in detail, what the hell is going on?" Ray asked. "All traces of you had vanished. There are no smells, no footprints, nothing. That can't happen. We're in the middle of the goddamn *Everglades*. You couldn't have disappeared that soundly unless you went through a wormhole."

"That's a good name for it, because that's what it bloody felt like," Danny answered, picking up his jug of moonshine and petting it. "It was like we'd crossed over into a fifth dimension—one without life or love."

"We'll explain everything in a second, Ray," I said. "But first we need to get on the right channel to rendezvous with my dad. Where are they?"

Naomi answered. "Head south"—she gestured for Rourke to turn right—"and follow the tree line. The cypress swamp will stay to our right. There is another channel about two miles farther. They are on another boundary line of the priestess's territory. Your Pack has set up camp at the very edge."

"Does my father know we went missing?" I asked.

"*Non*," she said. "We had just arrived back at the boat when you emerged."

"Yeah," Ray added. "Before we were going to sound the alarm, we flew over the area thinking you went on a hike or found something to check out. But you were nowhere in sight."

"Did you feel anything strange when you flew over?" Marcy asked. "Any bad mojo?"

Naomi nodded. "*Oui*, something hit my senses once I flew closer. It was like a dark warning."

Ray snorted. "Yeah, the air right around where the boat was parked is absolutely full of shit. Like the devil blew his nose all over it."

"That's a pretty picture, Ray. What did it look like from above?" I asked curiously. "Did the swamp appear any different?"

They glanced at each other for a moment as look of confusion passed over both their faces.

Ray's eyes narrowed. "The funny thing is," he said, scratching his head, "now that you ask, I can't remember anything specific about it." He looked to Naomi. "Do you remember?"

She shook her head. "*Non*, I do not. The only memory I have begins when we arrived at the boat. My mind won't let me recall any other details. That's very peculiar."

"Do you think you could've landed there if you wanted to?" I asked. "Near the boat but on land?"

"I can answer that. I don't believe they could have," Marcy interjected. "The reason they don't remember is because black magic messes with your senses, as well as your mind. The space we were in was clouded with spells and strange, lethal energy. A place like that is meant to keep unwanted supernaturals away. But if they persist, then once they leave, I bet she has a spell trigger, meant to wipe their memories clear of the location. For humans, the spells alone are strong enough to deter them from getting close in the first place."

Danny uncorked the moonshine with a flourish. It made a big, thunking sound. "Well, if there was ever a time for a celebration, I believe it's right at this very moment. I think cheers are in order for escaping our mystic jailer, don't you?" He didn't wait for a go-ahead. He simply tipped the jug back and took two long swallows.

"Be careful, big guy," I called. "I can smell that stuff from here and I'm pretty sure it could take the finish off a floor."

He brought it down and grimaced, running his forearm across his mouth. "Woo-*eee*! Those humans weren't joking. It's been a long while since I've had the pleasure of tasting authentic moonshine. But a long while back, when I was pursuing a Shenandoah beauty who lived in a quaint hollow—the one I so fondly recalled when we were unceremoniously dumped into those same mountains exiting the horrid portal from the Underworld—her family invited me over several times to partake in their brew. And this, my friends"—he shook the jug and the contents splashed out—"rivals it in every way. Care for a taste?" He thrust the moonshine behind his head to Tyler, who took it from him and sniffed, then grimaced as he took a swallow.

Naomi leaned in close to me as the jug made it around and Rourke continued to take us closer to my father. "I must ask you who called you a *bèt nan bwa*?"

My eyebrows rose. "You heard that?" I was surprised. The voice had sounded like nothing more than a whisper in my ear, but it had happened right at the point of me leaving the realm and entering the regular world again.

"*Oui*," Naomi said. "But it was only a breath of a voice. I heard it right as you emerged."

"I don't know who said it, but do you know what it means, Naomi?" I asked. The voice held a small accent, and now that I thought about it, the words had sounded vaguely French.

She nodded. "It is a derivative of French, a dialect of Haitian Creole. *Bèt nan bwa* means 'wild animal.' But in your case, I'm certain it meant to call you a wolf, so the voice said, 'We shall meet soon, wild animal.'"

"Hmm," I said. "I'm assuming it was either the priestess or a loa. I have no idea. But something was definitely there with me in that moment. But it didn't feel like a threat...more like a promise or a warning."

Marcy turned to glance at me, her arm resting along the back of the seat in front of me as we sped forward. "It may have been a loa, or the priestess talking through one. But with the whole alternate reality, I'm really starting to believe she's a bokor. A sorceress makes much more sense, especially with the zombie aspect of those snakes and wolves. No normal priestess would be able to mind-control such a force and keep them contained as well as what we just witnessed. I bet those things are technically dead and she controls them through a potion or a curse. But however you care to slice it, she's got a crap-load of power."

"I think you might be right. But my father told me sometimes the wolves escape. They've been able to track them down before they hit a city," I said. "But that doesn't go along with her having supreme control over them."

Marcy shrugged. "Well, either she wants them loose or she has too many to control and some slip under the radar. Either way, it's very bad for us."

Rourke angled the boat down a new channel at Naomi's direction. "We're almost there," he called. "I can see boats up ahead."

A half mile down the new channel four airboats were roped to some trees on the side. Rourke cut the fan and maneuvered in behind them. On the bank there were several wolves in human form who I wasn't familiar with. One shouted and my father emerged on what looked to be a man-made wooden walkway.

I hopped out of the boat as soon as I could and ran toward him, which meant I had to scamper over the cypress roots, but it had been too long since I'd seen my father and I was excited.

"Jessica," he said as I jumped into his arms for a long hug, feeling like a little girl for one perfect, tiny moment. "I was so worried about you. It's such a relief to see you home safe. Going to the Underworld was no small thing, and when I found out you went unescorted, you gave me several gray hairs, which on a werewolf is a hard thing to do."

I laughed and hugged him a little harder. He engulfed me in his arms, not letting go. We'd always had a strong bond, but once I'd become a wolf, it had intensified. Swapping blood during an oath had made it even stronger. I was aware of him on a different level, and being this close made our internal connection burst. His love for me zipped along my veins, like a mini hurricane of emotion, making me feel content and happy. A wolf needed to be close to their Alpha at regular intervals.

I finally pulled back, feeling a little sheepish I'd held on for so long. My brother cleared his throat behind me while I kissed my father on the cheek.

"Some of us are waiting here," Tyler said.

"Sorry about the gray hair," I told my father, "but I survived Hell, so there's that. We have a lot to discuss."

"Yes, we do. We'll talk immediately after everyone gets situated." He turned to embrace my brother in a wolfish hug, which meant a quick pull followed by a few back slaps on the back. No deep emotional words were spoken, but I felt their affection for each other and it made me happy once again.

Rourke came up behind me and placed one hand on my waist and reached around with the other to shake my father's hand. My dad took it and gave him a warm smile. "You went after her to the Underworld and kept her safe. I owe you my life." My father inclined his head down.

"You owe me nothing. She was the one who kept *us* safe. Your daughter is a natural leader, and a very powerful one at that. She did your Pack proud in the Underworld."

My father's head angled toward me, and I could tell he was trying to process my new signature. "Lots of changes, I see," he said, a single eyebrow raised. "Let's head over to our less-than-adequate headquarters and discuss it then, shall we?"

We followed him on the skinny wooden planks that ran through the trees. "How did you do this?" I asked, noticing the pathways branching off in a few directions.

He shook his head. "It's been as tough as hell to live here, let me tell you. We had to take multiple trips to get the supplies we needed, and once they were here, we had to build a sustainable place to live, which as you can see, isn't easy in a swamp. When we were done building, we had to employ two witches to spell the area from humans. This is a national park, so we're breaking many human laws, but it was necessary. We have three small areas like this staked out around the priestess's perimeter. The Made wolves are a danger to every human they meet, and they also pose a threat to exposing our secret. Supernaturals are cloaked from humans for a reason, and allowing this priestess to break that law is unacceptable. So we've done what we saw fit to contain this dreadful situation."

"What about the fracture pack?" Tyler said, glancing around us. "I can't believe those deserters live like this in the swamp." Tyler was referring to the wolves who joined together to move against me. I took out their leader, but they were still operational, which is why my father had come here in the first place.

"No, they set up shop in a nearby populated town. We took out almost all of those wolves when we arrived three weeks ago. They'd already been largely leaderless, so it wasn't hard to do. Once they were gone, we figured we'd erased the threat. But then we found two Made wolves lurking on the periphery and chased them, and they ultimately led us here." He spread his arms. "We tracked them all the way in, through this godforsaken swamp, but they disappeared before we could get to them. But we waited them out, and it became clear that was their home base. Since we've set up shop, surrounding her, she has struck against us four times, kidnapping our wolves in the middle of the night. I have a total of eight men gone. We have no idea how she's taking them, but in the process of going up against her, we've figured out how to efficiently kill the Made wolves without getting cursed."

We stopped at a ten-by-ten-foot wooden platform set up with a crude table and chairs and a rain tarp strung up between the trees. "How are you killing them without getting cursed?" I asked, thinking back to the big battle we'd fought with the vamps and witches against the demons, when we first discovered my dad had been cursed. Tally had managed to explode one and Ray had sucked the life out of the others.

"Basically we have to give them a lobotomy. Once their brain function is dead, they crumple like marionettes," he answered as he pulled out a chair and sat down. He gestured for us to sit. Rourke, Tyler, Danny, and I complied, while Naomi and Ray stood behind. For the first time, I noticed Marcy wasn't with us. I glanced around the small space. She must have made a beeline to find her man. I smiled, thinking of how sweet their reunion would be.

"How is that done, then?" Danny asked. "Do you have to tear their heads off?"

My father shook his head. "No, we've all been carrying these around." He unsheathed a sharp blade, about three inches long, from its holder on his waist. "We stick it right behind their eye socket. It happened by chance the first time. We'd been breaking their necks, their bones, everything, and those suckers wouldn't die. We started taking up arms, guns, knives, anything to combat them. Then one attacked and Nicolas managed to get a knife securely into the brain and the thing dropped like a bag of garbage."

"Oh my goodness, Nick! Where is he?" I asked, restraining myself from jumping out of the chair to go search for him. "I can't wait to see him."

"He's at the far camp, two over from here," my father answered. "I put him in charge and he's doing a fine job. He's grown into a great leader with a keen mind." There was pride in his voice, and it was nice to hear it. Life growing up on the Compound had never been easy for Nick. And if a fox was in charge of wolves, then his standing in the Pack had definitely gone up since I'd left. "Don't worry. You'll see him soon. He'll be over here tomorrow morning for a prearranged check-in."

I nodded. "I always knew Nick would be a great leader. He managed to keep me safe for all my formative years, and that took some gumption. How many status fights has he had?"

"Three," my father said. "After that, I placed him in charge of the younger wolves, and there have been no further issues. He's like a son to me, and my wolves know that, wolf or not. But I will not tolerate any underhanded dealings. If one of my wolves wants to challenge him, as they will, we'll set it up appropriately. For now, next to James, he is the best person I have to keep these camps running so we can efficiently take out the threat."

"One more question before we discuss what happened to me while I was away, which I know you want to hear sooner than later," I said. "You keep referring to this threat as a 'priestess.' Do you know for sure that's what she is?"

My father shook his head. "I'm not sure of anything, but I refer to her as that because that's what Redman called her. When I came down here the first time and tried to talk some sense into the Southern Pack, he insisted that she had been in 'his' territory for years and that they previously had an understanding. She kept to herself and they left her alone. That's how the fracture wolves knew how to find her. She's a legend in these parts."

"And he said 'priestess' for sure?" I asked.

"He said something like that, but mainly he called her a nuisance. Why do you ask?"

"Because Marcy seems to think she's not a priestess, but something more powerful."

"And what would that be?"

"A sorceress."

8

"A sorceress?" My father scratched his head. "I guess that makes some sense given she can make rabid wolves. My understanding of priestesses is that they feed the ghosts they worship or some such nonsense. I've never paid much attention."

"I don't know the role a priestess plays, but in voudoun Marcy said the sorceresses are called bokors." I wished Marcy was here to explain, but I would do my best to relay her thoughts.

"That sounds about right. I've heard of them before, but only vaguely." My father shifted in his tiny seat.

Rourke cleared his throat. "I'm not up on the practices of Haitian voodoo in the last few hundred years, but I agree with Marcy's assessment. I'm somewhat familiar with voudoun. I know it started in the Congo at least a thousand years ago, and from what I've heard on my travels, a bokor does indeed specialize in mind control. I'm not sure if the creatures they puppet are dead or cursed, but it seems to fit the bill here. They also use fetishes. It's their specialty. I know this because some supernaturals are willing to pay large sums of money to procure them."

"I'm assuming you're talking about an object—that kind of fetish?" Danny asked. "Or are they just really into certain things, like feet or belly buttons? I can totally understand the belly button part, because who doesn't love a good navel? But feet? No, sir, I've never been a fan."

Rourke arched an eye at Danny. "They trap magic into objects to enhance their power when they need it later. No navels."

I drummed my fingers on the table. "So this is another supernatural who can harness power and magic?"

My mate turned to me, his face grim. "There are no accidents or coincidences where you're concerned, Jess. I believe that. Like Eudoxia said in the Underworld, the fact that we're where we are right now is not a mistake. This bokor is aware of you. My guess is she knew you'd show up eventually if she kept sending rabid wolves out. The minute we entered her territory, she let you in, and when you left, she gave you an ominous message. None of that was a mistake."

"What did this sorceress say?" my dad asked, leaning forward.

"She said that we would meet again soon," I answered. "And she called me a wild animal in some kind of Creole. Naomi heard it."

My father raked a hand through his hair and leaned back in his chair. "If she's a bokor, and those Made wolves are dead, this just became more complicated. Dammit." He blew out a frustrated breath. "I wanted to eradicate this threat and be home before you arrived back from the Underworld, but that clearly didn't happen. So here we sit, playing chess with a sorceress who wants to harm my daughter by draining her power."

"A sorceress who's likely been playing games with us since before Stuart brought his ragtag pack of wolves to her doorstep," I said. "She must have taken one look at him and saw her opportunity. She set this up so we'd be forced to come here, and if she can pull power or magic out of me, there's no doubt she'll try."

"The question is, how do we fight her?" Tyler asked. "Do we know enough about her magic to gain an advantage?"

My father shook his head. "No, we don't know anything about her, but that doesn't mean we can't find a way to best her. I'll put a call in to Devon as soon as I can. He's been busy gathering information from a home base in Florida. But before we try to figure out a game plan, I need both of you to fill me in on what happened while you were in the Underworld. I can sense your signature change, Jessica"—he leaned over, his eyes grave as they met mine—"and your power feels layered. I need to know what's going on."

"Of course," I said. I had so much to share. "Is this the only place we can talk?" I glanced around at the small space. "Where do you eat and sleep?"

"We have another area where we keep our food and supplies. We can move over there, though it's not much more comfortable than this," my father answered. "We had to take some trees down to gain the space. But you're right, let's head over there first and get situated. I want James to hear this too. There are twelve of us in this camp, and fifteen in both the others. James usually stays at one of the others, but we knew you were coming, so he's here now."

I chuckled as I stood, following my father's lead. "He might be a bit busy at the moment. Marcy came with us. But she needs to be in on whatever we're doing. She's the only one of us who knows anything about the kind of magic we're dealing with."

Relaying the entire story of our Underworld escapades took two full hours. I told my father every detail, ending with the power of five, killing Lili, the fact that I'd made a mistake by ending her life one hundred years too soon, my possible place on the Coalition, the Hags' anger, Juanita, and finally the plane crash. Then I filled him in on what the airboat guides had told us of this place and how we'd just escaped the priestess's alternate reality. My brother told his part, including the length of time that had passed for him in the Underworld, his torture at the hands of the demons, and added details I didn't have about the rescue of the Prince of Hell.

My father sat back, his face set as he absorbed it all. Finally he said, "That was quite a story. I'm not sure where to begin." James sat next to him at another makeshift table, this one a little bigger. We were surrounded by crates of supplies and hammocks strung through cypress trees. "How about we talk about Jessica's new power acquisition first. What can you do now that you have the power of five? I've never heard of a supernatural absorbing magic before you. It's truly amazing. I'm at a loss for words."

I stared at him and blinked. "That's a good question." I nibbled my lower lip. "I'm not sure. I barely figured out how to harness the demon magic while I was in the Underworld, as I told you. My wolf sort of stored it away as fast as we gathered it." My wolf growled, showing us glowing with multicolored magic. "My wolf is indicating that we can pull it apart as needed, but I don't know how to do that...yet."

"Well, it makes sense it would take some time to figure it out, but it means you're extremely powerful," my father said with finality. "It took me fifty years to figure out all my strengths and weaknesses. I don't want you to feel any pressure. I just wanted to try and get a gauge on what we're dealing with here."

"Jessica," James interjected. "Your new power gives you one thing for sure. It ensures that you can defend yourself, and that will be your biggest asset."

My father nodded. "James is right. That's the most important piece in all of this, and it's what will keep you alive."

"There's one more thing," I said. "It concerns Tally and the witches. I told you the witches disappeared, that the circle was dead in the Underworld. But I'm going to let Marcy share what she found out from a witch in Europe. Things might be brewing in Italy."

My father turned to Marcy. She was perched on the edge of James's leg. She straightened under his intense gaze. "Jessica's right. According to the witch I spoke with, there's been a convergence of supernatural activity in Italy. Florence, to be precise. She told me supes were flocking there by the hundreds. I feel, because of that, it's a good indication of where my aunt may have gone—either by choice or against her will—but her leaving without sending word, whatever the circumstances, is highly unusual. We are the only true family we have. My feeling is she was taken, kidnapped or worse, and her witches went after her."

I nodded along. "Tally wouldn't have broken her word and left us stranded in the Underworld unless something extreme had happened. She's proven herself loyal." I glanced around the table. "And I also believe the event of her leaving or being taken coincided with me killing Ardat Lili."

"You can't know that for sure," my father said. "It could be an internal power struggle, witches fighting witches. But, I agree, there is some merit to it. From my understanding, if there's an open seat on the Coalition to be filled by a particular Sect, the power shift is felt by all in that Sect. I haven't felt anything yet, but that doesn't mean we won't. I suspect, across the board, there will be skirmishes to gain power before the final five supernaturals take their permanent positions. It could be all-out civil war inside each Sect until that final day comes."

"What do you mean? I thought we were fated to our seat on

the Coalition?" I asked, my wolf echoing my sentiments in my mind.

"Fate has something to do with it, and in your case particularly—as there are no other female wolves to fight you. But that doesn't mean there won't be powerful female supes vying for a place on the Coalition. No supernatural will step aside willingly if they think it's their right. Fate can shift, as you've now seen firsthand." He raised his eyebrows. "It's not infallible. Choices are made, paths shift, and supernaturals will die. Sitting on the Coalition is the ultimate station in our world. Now we know all five will share power, making the entity of the Coalition the strongest supernatural group on earth. We believed they were in stasis all this time—at least I did—but they were clever. A rebirth means all five seats will be filled at once."

Marcy gasped, slapping her hands on the table. "That's true! That might be *it*—the reason my old biddy of an aunt has disappeared."

"What?" Tyler asked.

"Your father hit on something. My aunt is indisputably the most powerful witch in the world. The power of our Sect lies insider her, so logically, if the seat was open, it would go to her. But there's bad blood between her and a witch who ascended to godhood. When the previous Mistress of the Covens, our leader, died around four hundred years ago, this witch figured the mantle of our Sect would shift to her, because she was both a witch *and* a goddess. When it didn't—and it went to my aunt instead—she lashed out. Tally defeated her, three times to be exact, but she's always carried a grudge. I can assure you she thinks that seat belongs to her."

"Who is it?" Danny asked. "Which goddess?"

"Ceres," Marcy answered.

"Angie the Awful's *sister*? The Goddess of Fertility?" I gasped.

Angie was the irritating witch who gave us a scooter to escape the sorcerers, knowing it would leave us open and exposed. "I don't really get it, though. Doesn't being a goddess trump being a regular witch? Why didn't the power of the Sect transfer to Ceres?"

"The short answer is the witches never do anything the easy way," Marcy said. "The long is godhood doesn't equal total power when it comes to ruling a Sect. Godhood is about immortality, and think about it, once you attain it, you don't really need a Sect any longer. Sects by definition are formed to make a species strong. Strength in numbers and all that."

I shook my head. The entire godhood thing was confusing at best. "How does anyone actually become a god or goddess?" I asked. "Do you know?"

"I must confess," Danny interjected, "I've never understood that part either. It seems very random and contrived, if you ask me. Why couldn't I just declare myself the God of Thunder? Oh, wait, that title is already taken," Danny snickered. "No matter, I'll just become the God of *Tundra* instead. It makes no sense, and who needs immortality anyway? The wolves have never needed it. We regenerate just fine. If you manage not to die, it's not an issue."

Marcy shook her head at Danny, smiling. "Very funny, God of Tundra. It's humans. Humans are the ones who decide godhood."

"Humans?" I said. That's the last thing I thought would come out of her mouth.

Marcy arched a look at me. "Yes, humans. That's why there hasn't been a new god or goddess—at least that I know about—in centuries. Humans don't pray to new gods anymore. I think it might be time for a supernatural intervention with you. We can call it Marcy's Magical History Hour."

"Hilarious," I said. "I've been a wolf for a total of five minutes in the scope of things. Wolves, from what I know"—I glanced at my father—"have kept themselves in the dark about supernatural things on purpose. Our motto has been 'If it doesn't concern us, we don't bother.'"

"That's true," my father said. "It's never been our practice to concern ourselves with the outside world—but, in our defense, we've never had a need. We keep our heads down and fight our own battles. I believe it's always been our way. But I can see those ways won't work for us now. It's time for a rebirth for us too." He grinned. "The wolves, under my command, will become educated in all things supernatural. They will be aware of every possible threat so we can take care of them efficiently."

Marcy shook head and muttered, "Men. So typical."

James growled, his arms wrapping around his mate's middle. "Men you must now have pity on. Enlighten us. Let's have it, lass. Tell us about how gods are made."

She leaned over and planted a chaste kiss on James's cheek. "You people are incorrigible. There's not enough time to give you the full monty, so I'll give you the abridged version. Gods and goddesses are worshipped, right?" We all nodded. "Well, they gain their power from the act of humans gathering to give them fealty, repeatedly. The power inside a supernatural is sizable, and we use it to wield our magic. Humans have power, too, but it's nominal. But you get enough of them together and it acts like a power transfer straight to the god or goddess they pray to." She leaned over and set her hand on my forearm. "Just like this." She pushed a tiny bit of her power into me and it tingled up my arm. "Small zaps just like this, from millions of humans, equal one powerful supe. Over time, the gods or goddesses build up enough power that they'll never die. They can mend even the gravest injury, thus securing their immortality and living forever."

How she explained it made sense. "So Ceres and Selene were worshipped by humans and gained massive power over time? But how did they become goddesses in the first place? Did they nominate themselves?" I pictured Selene campaigning for the job and stifled a laugh.

Marcy shrugged. "That predates any knowledge I have. I'm not sure anyone knows for sure. But I do know you have to have a sponsor, another god or goddess in your corner, which I'm assuming is so humans can find out who you are. How else would millions be keyed in otherwise? But once the humans begin to pray, all bets are off."

"So what you're really saying is, becoming a god or goddess is nearly impossible these days?" Tyler asked. "Humans would have to believe in a new god in large numbers, and that doesn't happen anymore."

"I wouldn't rule it out, but yes, I think it would be harder," Marcy said. "Humans are eternal searchers of hope, however. In the old days, the gods and goddesses would actually perform 'miracles.' It kept them gorged on power. So, could it happen today? Maybe. Under the right circumstances."

"Tyler's right," I said. "Humans don't pray to gods and goddesses much anymore. Maybe that's what's motivating Ceres to take a place on the Coalition? Her power can't be what it used to be."

Marcy nodded. "That would be just like her. Needy and delusional."

My father interrupted. "Marcy, do you know where Ceres is located?"

"Yes," she said. "She's in Italy."

9

The sun had set by the time we'd finished up our discussions, and we were all exhausted. We'd tossed around rough plans about how to deal with the bokor. Defeating her was a must, but the question was how? My father was going to wait for more information before we moved forward with anything concrete tomorrow.

"I'm not sleeping in one of these without you." Rourke gestured to the hammock. "It would never hold the two of us together anyway."

I nodded. That thing wouldn't even hold Rourke alone. "Maybe we can have Marcy spell it?" I said as I strapped the skinny knife my father had given me to use against the Made wolves in a holster on my upper arm.

"Marcy and James already left for the other camp. Let's go back to the first platform and sleep there," he said. "Your father said wolves disappear during the night. I find it nearly impossible for werewolves to vanish without a trace, so there's something big going on. I plan to stay awake, but I want you close."

"I don't care where we lie down. I just need to get horizontal before I collapse. I'll ask my dad if they have some extra blankets."

We were settled a short time later on the first platform we arrived at.

Even though we'd slept on the island, not having had any rest in the Underworld still wore on me. Going head-to-head with the bokor was going to take strength, and I needed sleep. Rourke threw an arm around my waist and tugged me to him tightly. "Get some rest," he whispered in my ear. "I can't help thinking we should've headed back to real land tonight. This swamp is making my beast edgy."

The air did hold a heavy vibe. "I think it's impossible to run from her at this point, unless we got completely out of Florida." I turned in his arms and placed my hands on his face. "But I promise you, we're going to defeat her. And once it's done, I will never come back here. That's going to be our new motto: *Defeat the threat and move the hell on.*"

"I'm with you. It would take a supernatural crowbar and about twenty trolls to drag me back here. But if this bokor is kidnapping wolves right out from under the Alpha's nose, it's serious business."

I snuggled into his side and sighed. "I wonder how she's getting them out."

"I don't want to know," he grumbled. "She just better not try to mess with me or mine."

"You're really not going to sleep a wink, are you?" I leaned up and kissed his cheek.

"Hell no," he retorted with a half laugh. "But I want you to sleep. You're going to need your rest."

"Let's face it—I'm probably not going to sleep either," I said. "And kissing you sounds like a much better way to pass the time."

His lips were on mine before the last words were out of my

mouth. I ran my hands around his shoulders and wrapped them up in the back of his hair. "*Mmm*, you taste good," I murmured into his mouth.

He rolled me on top of him and grinned as he nipped my chin. "I like you like this. The way it should be. Safe in my arms."

I woke with a start.

My heart was beating like a hummingbird's. I felt it inside my rib cage, fluttering quickly against my breastbone. I hadn't realized I'd fallen asleep. The last thing I remembered was kissing my mate thoroughly, and then nothing.

It was deathly quiet all around me. A thick blanket of fog had rolled in and I couldn't see the tops of the trees in front of me.

My best guess was it was an hour before dawn.

Something brushed by my face.

I reached out to swat it away and a voice whispered next to my ear. *She's gone.* It slid in and out of earshot, making it sound eerie. *You must find… her. Her* was drawn out, ending on a shallow breath.

I sat up, glancing over at my mate, who was out cold. "Rourke." I shook his shoulder. "Wake up. Something's here."

He didn't respond.

"Oh my gods." I jumped up, fully shaking off my sleepy haze, comprehension finally penetrating my brain.

Something had knocked us all out cold.

And in order to do that, it had to be heavy magic—black magic. But I couldn't sense a spell. "Who's gone?" I called desperately into the air. "Tell me!"

No answer.

"Dammit!" I shouted. "You're the one who woke *me* up! You want me to know. Now tell me *who's* gone."

Vampire. The breath was only inches from my ear and it was followed by crackling laughter. *You must find her before it's too late...* The voice popped out of existence and the fog evaporated from the air into nothingness in front of me.

Danny shouted and I started to run.

No, not Naomi! I shouted in my mind. *She's already been through too much. Please, not her.*

"Jessica!" Rourke roared as he awoke behind me.

The bokor took Naomi, I told him in my mind. *We have to get her back.*

I nearly collided with Danny, who was sprinting toward me on the skinny planking. "She's bloody gone!" he shouted, his face as angry as I've ever seen it. "I don't know how it happened, but she was there one minute, then gone the next. The priestess snatched her right out of thin air. How can that even *happen*?"

I grabbed his arm. It was vibrating, echoing the adrenaline racing through my own veins. "How do you know she's been taken? Maybe she just went on a scouting mission?" I knew it wasn't true, but I still felt hopeful that maybe the bokor was lying just to mess with our minds. "She could be doing a perimeter sweep for us. Vampires don't sleep like we do."

"I know she's gone because I found this in her hammock," he said, thrusting a small ebony figurine into my hand.

I grasped hold and the power inside of it almost brought me to my knees.

It was churning with black magic.

I uncurled my fingers and let it drop to the ground. It bounced a few times before coming to a stop right on the edge of the walkway.

I bent over to catch my breath as Rourke rushed up behind me. "Oh my gods," I breathed. "That thing looks like Naomi."

I gestured to the tiny carved face. Rourke reached down and I yelled, "Don't touch it! It's a black magic fetish and it packs a punch." I eased up to a standing position.

"I have to go after her." Danny brushed past me and I immediately turned and started to jog after him. Rourke was right behind us. I snagged Danny's arm before he could leap into one of the airboats.

"Wait a minute," I said, turning him around. "You can't go like this. We all want to find her. It's our top priority." He tried to shake me off, but I braced my hand against his forearm. "Danny, listen to me. We'll come up with a plan as soon as we can, and once we do, we'll go together." A moment later, my father, Tyler, and Ray showed up. Without taking my eyes off Danny, I said to Ray, "I want you to fly over the area. Naomi's missing. See if you can detect anything, but don't land anywhere. And if you start to feel anything strange, come back immediately."

Ray nodded once and shot into the air.

I glanced over Danny's shoulder at my father and brother, who both stood with pursed lips. "Can you give us a minute?" I asked. I was still Danny's Alpha, and his emotions and confusion were racing through my veins at top speed. I needed to calm him down.

My father nodded once. "When you're finished, meet me at the main table."

"We're going to need Marcy back here," I called to his retreating back. "She told us she can brew spells that can aid us against the bokor. Send word to James."

"Will do."

Rourke sensed the need to give us space, even without me asking. He followed my father but stopped about twenty feet away, resting his back against a tree. That's all I was going to get.

Once they were gone, I peered into Danny's face. It was full of anguish. I ran my hand along his arm. "We're going to get her back. I need you to believe that. The odds will be better if we gather all the wolves and come up with a good tactic. We can't go barreling back in there unarmed with no plan. It won't help anyone."

Danny tipped his head down and whispered, "She's my mate."

The news wasn't as shocking as it could've been, because I'd suspected as much. Their chemistry was palpable, and had been from the start. The fact that the two of them had managed to avoid the inevitable pull up until now had been nothing short of incredible. I'd only denied Rourke for a single day, and it had cost me. "When did you find out?"

"The very first time I set eyes on her." There was a deep sadness in his voice. "But I've been in rabid denial—that, and she won't willingly talk to me in private so we've never been able to sort it out. I've refused to believe what was in front of me. I'd like to think it was out of fear, but I believe it was my own cowardice. Now I've gone and messed it up before it could even start."

"It's not all your fault. Naomi is a very private person," I reassured him. "She is likely grappling with the same feelings you are. You're both very similar and very different at the same time. You complement each other well, but a vampire and a wolf together? I've never heard of a match like that before in our world."

"You're telling me." Danny ran a hand along the back of his neck. "Up until right this minute I've been cursing Fate for playing such a cruel joke on us. But now that Naomi's been taken from me, my wolf has gone crazy with need. Jessica, you have to understand, I can't stay here. I must go after her. I *have* to make this right." His voice held panic. "There is no other choice for me—for us."

I nodded. Nothing kept Rourke from following me to the Underworld, and I would've done the same if he had been taken.

"Danny, you have to listen. Naomi is going to make you a perfect partner, when we get her back. Our best chance of freeing her is to do it together."

Danny stepped toward the boats and I let go of his arm. "I can't wait. I can't think straight knowing she's in harm's way. Jessica, please. By the time you're ready, and agree on a plan, it may be too late. My wolf won't rest until I make her completely mine. And I'm not bringing her back here, into danger, until we've forged our bond together, whatever it takes. Please don't make me ask you for permission." His face was masked in the kind of sorrow that burrows deep and holds on.

I was his Alpha and he was asking for my acceptance, even if he wasn't asking for my permission.

"Danny, my Alpha instinct is to keep you here and protect you until we come up with a plan, but my heart understands. Nothing would keep me from going after Rourke. I'm not sure you're going to find her, but you have my blessing to try. We'll be right behind you as fast as we possibly can."

He drew me into a quick embrace. "You being my Alpha feels right," he whispered in my ear, "and as we move forward, you have my fealty, as well as Naomi's. I won't make another troth to your father now, so you're stuck with me, for better or worse."

I pulled back. "I appreciate that, Danny. Our bond is strong and I'm thankful to have you behind me. I'll let my father know. I don't think there will be an issue."

"I'm taking a boat." He moved to the closest one. "I'll head back to where we went into the priestess's lands the first time. I hope like hell she will let me in. If anything, I will try to delay whatever she has planned by wreaking havoc where I can."

"Promise me you'll keep your wits about you, even if you see Naomi in pain. That's the most important part." I remembered clearly how I felt when I found Rourke in Selene's cave. "I know you're wily, but you need to keep your emotions in check for this. If you lose control, you'll be vulnerable."

"I will try my best."

"Like I said, we'll be right behind you. Play the sorceress's game as long as you can."

He gave me a two-finger salute as he pushed off from the trees. Without glancing back, he turned on the motor, maneuvered the boat around, and took off.

Once he was out of sight, I made my way to Rourke, who pulled me into his arms immediately and murmured, "You did the right thing. Nothing could've kept him here."

"Then why does it feel like I just sacrificed him to the bokor?"

"He may prove just what we need to upset the apple cart over there. Your dad is getting making plans to move as we speak. We'll be right behind him."

We found the wolves deep in conversation. Someone had managed to pick up the fetish from the walkway, and it sat in the middle of the table. It was ugly and crudely made. I shuddered.

My father said, "So it turns out the goddamn sorceress can render us all unconscious. I hadn't guessed that she was capable of that much power. That was my mistake. None of us have any recollection of the nights when she took the wolves, not even a trace."

"I was knocked out too, but she woke me up," I said as I pulled out a chair and sat. "She wanted me to know—she wants me in her lands. I just wish I knew why she chose Naomi and not another wolf. It doesn't make sense. She wants wolves to control and humans to change into Made wolves, but why would she want a vampire? I don't think she can turn Naomi into a wolf."

"If this fetish is any indication"—Rourke gestured to Naomi's likeness—"I think she's telling us she plans to take Naomi's power and transfer it into one of those for herself." Rourke stood behind me, hands resting on my shoulders. "Naomi is now an incredibly powerful vampire, thanks to your blood. The priestess or the bokor wants that power."

It made me sick to think about it. I addressed my father. "I let Danny go after her."

My father crossed his arms. "That's a tactical disadvantage and Daniel Walker knows better than to do something like that."

"I did it because she's his mate."

I glanced over at Tyler as I said it. He ran a hand through his hair, so like our father, but he didn't look at all surprised. "I knew she was his mate, but Danny wouldn't talk about it. For a while I was pissed off for him. A vamp for a mate is a shitty draw if you ask me. But once I got to know Naomi, I realized they are actually great together. And damn if she isn't as fierce and loyal as a wolf. It makes sense in a strange way. His guts must be in his throat. Even if you had made him stay, he would've found a way to slip out. That's Danny."

"Daniel will have a hard road ahead of him with a vampire for a mate," my father said. "I don't know her well, but they have my blessing." That was all he had to say on the matter. Then he turned to me. "James and Marcy are on their way."

"I want to leave shortly after they arrive," I said. "Backing Danny up is our number one priority."

"We go as soon as they get here, but if Marcy can brew the spells you were talking about, it would be in our benefit to let her do that." My father leaned forward. "Now that we know the bokor is strong, there's a good chance she can separate us if we poise an attack, and I don't know how to prevent that from happening. If Marcy has a good idea, we'll have to listen to her."

Rourke addressed my father. "I have no idea how to kill a bokor, do you?"

"I might know a thing or two." Nick's voice carried ahead of him. I'd heard two boats come up to the landing, but I'd assumed it was some of my dad's wolves escorting James and Marcy.

"Nick!" I yelled, jumping up to give him a hug. "I'm so glad to see you!"

"Jess," he said, gripping me tightly, before letting go. His brown curls were tousled around his head and his amber eyes bright. It appeared like my father had raised the alarms and called in his wolves. "I think it's safe to say I'm the one who's happy to see *you*. When I heard you were here, I was ecstatic. A round-trip ticket to the Underworld is quite impressive."

I laughed. "Not as impressive as you might think. I'll fill you in later. But first, what do you know about bokors and priestesses?"

"I've been doing some digging. We have a crappy satellite feed, which gives me spotty Internet, but it's been enough to gather some information that may help. It seems they are fallible, which is good news."

"I have some good news too," Marcy chirped as she strode up behind Nick, James right behind her, his hand at her waist. "Lookit what I managed to brew up last night." She shook a bag. "Goodies for defeating a bokor."

"Are they dark spells?" I asked, peering into the bag.

"No," she replied with a wink, "but they will be soon."

10

"Stop wiggling," Marcy commanded. "All I need is a few more drops. Quit being such a baby."

I was perched at an awkward angle over a small fire she had kindled, my hand wrapped around her body so I didn't have to witness the cutting. "I'm hardly being a baby. This is the fifth time you've sliced me open with a hunting knife, the kind used for skinning large prey. It's not exactly like a needle prick," I grumbled.

"If you'd stop healing the moment I poked you, we'd be golden. We need your blood. It's the only thing that will cement these spells and make them strong enough to go up against the bokor's magic." She readjusted her grip on my wrist, tugging it over the pot. "And I just need a few more drops. Hold still."

I gritted my teeth. "Hurry up." My wrist throbbed. Marcy had brewed the initial spells at her camp but had to get them bubbling again to add my blood.

We were losing time.

She poked me again and I flinched. "No go. Nada. Healed up already. What are you anyway? Hercules? Who heals so fast a single drop of blood can't drip out? I'll have to make the gash longer and pray for just one little red bead."

I closed my eyes as she slashed again. Even though I healed the wound almost instantaneously, it still burned like crazy. "Healing this fast is new for me," I commented through a clenched jaw as she sawed on me one more time. "I had no idea, because I haven't had the pleasure of encountering a hunting knife since I've been back from the Underworld."

Rourke watched with his arms crossed. "I'm losing my patience, witch. One more time and you're done."

"It can't hurt that bad. I'm not severing your arm," Marcy said as she sliced and squeezed. "There, I got one. Just need one more. Calm your cat down. Lie and tell him it doesn't hurt."

The pain wasn't actually that bad. "I think my human side is making it worse, if that makes any sense. I'm anticipating how badly it *should* hurt. There's a burn, but then it eases up fairly quick—*ow*!" Marcy slashed deep and a single drop of blood plunked down into the pot, and the entire brew sizzled like water sprinkled on hot oil.

"Done." Marcy chanted something under her breath. "Your blood is behaving like nothing I've ever seen before. My pot is popping with action. I'm considering that a win. There's an old witch's proverb: The stronger the blood, the more potent the spell." The pot continued to sizzle as Marcy leaned over it. "I've just never seen blood this concentrated." She released my arm and I brought it back to my side.

"That doesn't sound like a proverb."

"Fine, you got me. I just made it up. But look at it go."

I peered over the bubbling pot. She was right. It looked like it was full of Pop Rocks.

"What spell are you brewing now?" my brother asked from his spot on the other side of the fire, leaning over to investigate. "It smells like moth balls crossed with grapefruit. Stale citrus."

"It's a protection spell," Marcy answered proudly. "If Jessica explodes this, a five-foot wall of protection will erupt around her like a shield."

"How long will it last once I use it?" That sounded like something I needed.

"You'll be lucky if it lasts three minutes." She chuckled. "If this bokor is extremely powerful, she may be able to bash through it in less than three, but for an average opponent, this spell, mixed dark with your blood, would give you upward of ten minutes. Too bad you're not fighting a regular sorceress. But it's better than nothing."

"What other spells do you have?" Nick asked curiously. He stood near Tyler. Marcy had quite an audience. "And how did you make them with such limited resources?"

I had to admit, I was impressed too.

"All of these spells"—she gestured at the array of pots around her—"are made with simple organic material. Witches' magic is made of the earth, and these are what we call *base spells*. You can substitute things on hand for these kinds of spells. It's only when you start getting technical do you need 'a single Balm of Gilead bud picked under the new moon' or the like. Those kinds of spells are hardwired to do something exact. These"—she waved her arm in an arc—"are broad. Last night I had the wolves at our camp hunt for a few things, and then James took me out on the boat. The Everglades is certainly not like shopping at the local alchemy store, but I made it happen."

"According to that sizzle, you certainly did," I commented. "Are you almost done? We need to get a move on."

"Yep," she said. "These last two are almost done. With any

luck, they'll all work and you can give her some whoop-ass in a bag. Sorry, I didn't bring any fancy vials, so plastic baggies will have to do. Once these cool, I'll dump them in and we can go."

Ray arrived five feet from us in a rush of air, his feet landing cleanly and without impact on the walkway. "I located Danny's boat. It's parked in the same spot you guys were in yesterday, but he's nowhere to be found. We need to leave right now." Ray's voice was hard. Even though he likely wouldn't admit it, he loved Danny and Naomi as much as the rest of us.

"The bokor let him in just like that?" I asked.

"That's my guess. I didn't see any of those snakes you talked about before, and this time the black magic around the area didn't fuck with me as much. Maybe because I was just there. But I flew over the top to check it out and remember more details. The trees all look dead from above, gnarled and black. The memory is fading quickly, but that place is rotten from the inside out."

"We're almost done here," I said. "Marcy just has to put the spells in bags."

My father stood from his place at the table where he'd watched Marcy work. "When we go, we take all the airboats. The channel where you crossed over into her land has two entrances. There's another channel farther west. We'll split up and meet where Daniel parked his boat."

It was the only viable option we had. The bokor would be expecting us, and she wasn't about to let an angry army of were-wolves invade her land. We all knew it but had no choice but to move forward and hope we could breach her wards.

I stood and Rourke laid a hand on my back and leaned around to my ear, rubbing his stubble along my neck. "She's not going to play nice. If we get separated, remember the power inside you. Call on it individually if you need to. Each supernatural has a different strength."

Marcy poured the spells into the bags, tying the ends with a makeshift closure made of wire, so they looked like little water balloons. "He's right," she said. "If you can find a way to concentrate anything Selene gave you and push it into the words attached to these spells"—she shook the bags—"like uttering a power word, the spell will become even stronger. Each of these spells has a keyword attached. I'll give them to you on the boat."

I nodded. I'd managed to separate the demon essence inside me in the Underworld and use it to my advantage. Since receiving the power of five, it'd been stored away in my body and I hadn't focused on it. I'd left it to my wolf. *Can we easily pull magic individually when needed?* I asked my wolf. She snapped her jaw, showing us taking what we wanted. *How do I pull just one kind?* Magic erupted inside my mind, a kaleidoscope of colors—my wolf's way of showing me that each magic had a different signature. Mine was gold. Eudoxia's was white—and now pale orange, which must be her fae magic. Demon essence was black. Selene's was pink. Rourke's was slate green. It was the first time I realized I had my mate's magic signature inside me.

"I have a piece of your magic," I said to Rourke, a little surprised to find it there, even though I *knew* it was there.

He chuckled as he began to lead me toward the waiting boats. "That you do."

"Do you think I can turn into a cat now?" I joked. "Because that would be awesome."

"No." He grinned. "That's hardwired into my DNA. But I *do* think you'll be able to run faster now, especially in your animal form. Did you feel different when we ran after the crash?"

"I wasn't paying attention," I admitted. "I was too worried about dodging hungry alligators and getting out of there with both my legs intact. But I kept up with you, no problem, so I'd say that's a yes."

Four airboats pulled alongside Danny's boat, two from one end and two from another. There were nineteen of us total. The short trip over had been uneventful, even though once we crossed into her territory, the air was denser than it had been before, heavy with intent.

She knew we were coming and she was preparing herself.

Ray dropped out of the sky onto the cypress roots next to our boat. "Storm clouds are gathering directly above us. I can't believe this bokor can mess with the weather, but something is definitely brewing up there." He pointed to the sky and my eyes tracked upward. Sure enough, big, dark clouds were pulling together, forming a huge front right above our heads.

"She's going to do everything she can to protect her realm from attack," I said. "I'm not surprised. She only has two choices. She either has to bide her time or launch a preemptive attack. We have to prepare ourselves for her to pick the latter."

My father sat in the boat directly across from me. "We all go in at once and scour the area. Naomi's and Daniel's scent are all over this area. I know we can find them, but we'll have to be tenacious about it."

Behind me, in our boat, James was quietly arguing with Marcy to stay put, but she was loudly having none of it. "You can't be serious," she addressed her mate. "There's no part of me that's going to sit on the sidelines and watch the people I love get hurt while I can help." She stood, and James raised his head up to the sky in defeat, reluctantly standing to help her out of the boat. Once she was out, I followed. She handed me the baggies and a pouch with a long strip of fabric to tie around my waist. "Here you go," she said. "They're all ready to use. They're as airtight as I could make them. The important thing to remember is to split the bag open while uttering the words. You can either toss it to the ground or explode it in your fist." The words she'd given me were in Latin and corresponded to the colors of the spells. "I made a little pouch for them out of an old shirt, and once you wrap the ties around you, I spelled them to stay put. Again, not ideal, but it should work."

I did as she asked, taking the strip of fabric and tying it around my hips. Once I cinched it tight, I felt the spell activate. I tried to move the pouch, but it wouldn't budge. "How do I pick the right one, at the right time?"

"There's no need to pick," Marcy said. "They are all defensive. Just make sure you pair the color with the right word."

All the wolves disembarked from the airboats around me and someone shouted, "Alligators!"

I craned my neck around and saw an army of alligators heading toward us from both directions. "Into the trees," my father ordered. "They can't climb trees."

We all began to jump onto the root banks, and then from tree to tree. Some of the younger wolves scampered higher into the branches, trying to scout our situation better. Rourke took the lead and I followed. Within a minute or two we arrived at roughly the same place we'd crossed over into the priestess's boundary before.

This time nothing happened.

"Spread out," my father called from his position down from us. "And stay vigilant."

I could scent both Danny and Naomi, just as my father had said. Their smells were all over this place and it was incredibly frustrating. James and Marcy were behind us, with Tyler bringing up the rear. Ray had taken to the sky again, but he was hovering close. We were all on the lookout for a potential threat.

Behind us, the alligators were thrashing in the water.

"There must be a hundred of them down there," Ray called from the air. "It's totally nuts. All their eyes are beady red."

I took another careful step over some roots and felt something whisper past my neck. *We've been waiting*, the breathy voice said, almost too soft to detect. I stopped in my tracks. "Did anyone hear that?" I called.

Rourke froze ahead of me, sensing my unease, and glanced back. "I didn't hear anything. Was it the same voice you heard before?"

I nodded. Marcy was right behind me. I turned back to her. "Did you hear it?"

"No, but I believe you," she answered gravely. "The hairs on my arm are yelling at me." She lifted her arm, and sure enough, goose bumps had erupted. "We're definitely inside her zone. I've sent out magical feelers and tried to push a few spells through her ward, but nothing is working."

Something brushed by my ear again.

I'd had some interactions with ghosts once before in New Orleans, but this was decidedly different. The ghosts there had felt like gusts of cool air brushing against my skin. This was a hot wind, dragging long tendrils in its wake, slashing at me as it passed by.

It was full of evil.

The temperature around us suddenly dropped exponentially.

Rourke's nose immediately rose in the air. I heard my father yell a command, but I couldn't understand what he was saying.

Suddenly I was falling, the ground beneath me giving way like it wasn't even there. I glanced up, my face a mask of surprise. Rourke was shouting, furious, but it sounded like he was talking in slow motion. I couldn't make out any words. My arms cartwheeled as he reached out for me.

Something clamped onto me from behind and I fell backward like a lead weight.

Right into her world.

11

I landed hard. Onto something soft that uttered a small gasp.

"Jeez, you weigh a lot," a familiar voice sputtered. "What, are your bones made of steel?" Marcy shoved me. "Get off me, Hercules. I can't suck in a single breath."

I rolled once and sprang up. "Marcy?" I choked. "What are you doing here?"

Marcy arched a single eyebrow at me from her position on the ground as she brushed dirt off of her. "Shouldn't you be asking what *we're* doing here?"

"Well . . . technically, yes." I peered around at our familiar surroundings. We were right inside the same ring of dead trees where we stood yesterday, just ten yards to the right. "But I thought the bokor targeted me on purpose. I'm pretty sure she didn't mean to bring you along too."

"Of course she didn't," Marcy quipped as she stood. "That's why I held on so tight, like a baby cheetah clinging to her mother's back."

"Um"—I stifled a laugh—"I'm pretty sure baby cheetahs don't ride on their moms' backs, those would be monkeys, and why did you hold on?" I asked suspiciously. "Did you know I was coming here?"

She placed her hands on her hips, her red curls swaying. "No. Well, I had no idea. When you started flailing like a fish on a line, I sleuthed it out fairly quickly. Then there was the dramatic temperature drop, always a good cue for danger." She shrugged. "So I latched on. So what?"

I narrowed my eyes. "You're a terrible liar, you know that? What gives? Spit it out. How did you know to jump on my back?"

"Fine," she sighed in exasperation. "You want to know how? I've been in contact with Juanita, that's how. And she told me exactly what I had to do, down to the baby cheetah claw-you-in-the-back technique. She said I *had* to come here with you, and that I had to hold on tight, so here we are." She held a hand up. "And before you start blaming me, she said if I didn't accompany you here, then you would *die*. How's that for a good reason?" She crossed her arms and gave me a look.

My mouth opened and I snapped it shut. It was hard to argue with her when she mentioned death. Finally I decided on "Why didn't you just tell me? How could you keep that from all of us? That's something the entire Pack should've known and decided on. And exactly how has she been in contact with you anyway?"

"First, I couldn't tell you because it was, *duh*, a secret." She shook her head at me like I was a clueless baby cheetah. "And second, she only popped back up on my phone last night. She was actually responsible for me finding some of the supplies I needed to brew the spells last night." Marcy had the decency to look a little sheepish. "And then she gave me some advice on how to make them more potent by using your blood."

I glanced around the alternate reality. "You sneaky little witch."

"I had no choice," Marcy hedged. "She told me if I uttered a word to anyone, I wouldn't be here and you would die. I needed to come with you *and* we needed the spells. I had to trust her—she's likely a Hag, for cripessake!"

I put my hand to my forehead. "James…James is going to kill me."

"No, he's not"—she bit her lip—"well, he better not. This was my decision. He's not my mother." She took a step forward and wagged her finger at me. "And you better listen to me when I say this, and listen closely. This is not a game. If we have any chance at all to defeat this bokor and save Naomi and free Danny, we have to work as a team. We're all we've got. You can't treat me like I'm breakable or hang back to protect me. This is you and me on a mission—*Thelma and Louise* style. Do you hear me?"

"I hear you," I said, "but how do you honestly expect me not to try and protect you? You're my best friend! And you've never been in a real battle before. If something happened to you, James won't be the only one who would be devastated—it would kill me."

"My case in point. I did not come to this place to die." She jabbed her finger at the ground, surprising me with her vigor. "So let's clear that up right now. I came to fight against this evil and win. If James has taught me anything, and believe me he's taught me a lot"—her eyes sparkled—"it's that you fight for the people you love. Period. I believe in Juanita. And according to her, this is your only shot. Something has gone wrong with your Fated path. But we are *fixing* it right here or we're both going to die trying. Together. Do you feel me?"

"I feel you." I smiled at my courageous friend. I knew deep down she had to be terrified she was here.

"Good." Then she surprised me by pulling me into a bear hug. "Because as scared as I am, I know we can do this. But you have to promise me you won't waste your time trying to protect me or you'll be distracted. I can take care of myself."

"Baby cheetah style?"

"BCS. It's all the rage."

I pulled back, admiring my friend, feeling lucky and loved all at once. "Did Juanita tell you what to expect? Did she give you any useful details?"

Marcy shook her head. "Nope, just that you needed me and where to find the ingredients to the spells. Oh, and she also made me practice some verbal ones. She's handy, that one." She patted the side of her hip. "I also brought along the dagger James gave me for the rabid zombie wolves."

"Okay." I blew out a breath, deciding to accept the road we were on. "I guess we're in agreement to go in and fight. Together." Rourke, my father, and my brother would all be equally furious with me for not trying to break out and seek backup. But Juanita had given us the way out before, and I had to assume she would try to help us again if things became dire. In a desperate moment, I called out to each of them in my mind, hoping the alternate reality wouldn't keep out our communication, and at the very least to tell them we were okay.

No response.

Marcy held out her hand to me, grinning. "I want you to shake on it, before you get second thoughts and try and toss me out the nearest tree. Juanita said this was the only way we would ever have a chance to defeat the bokor. In fact, she drilled it across my phone with words like 'ONLY WAY' and 'THIS IS IT.' So swear you're not going to get rid of me."

I shook her hand. "I swear I'll keep you around. Do you still have your phone on you?"

"Of course." She drew it out of her back pocket and handed it to me. Its face was dead white again. "That's not much help." As soon as the words left my mouth, the phone started to vibrate in my hand. Then blinking words scrolled across the screen:

YOU ARE IN DANGER. YOU ARE IN DANGER. YOU ARE IN DANGER.

"No shit!" I yelled into the air, spinning my head around to find the danger. "We know that. But how do we fight against it?"

WOLVES. WOLVES. WOLVES.

As soon as I read the screen, I heard the growls.

"Marcy, stay still." I handed the phone back to her and crouched into my fighting stance, scanning the circle. "The wolves want me, not you. Remember that."

"I don't think those mutants are picky. Fresh meat is fresh meat."

"The bokor pulled me in, but she wasn't looking for a twofer. If there are too many, I want you to climb the nearest tree and wait them out."

"See, you're already doing it. Stop," Marcy muttered. "You promised you weren't going to protect me. We can handle this. How many do you see?"

"Four." I scanned the area to make sure. The wolves were lurking in the shadows directly across from us, only their red eyes visible. "We're going to need to take care of them systematically. If you're going to fight, pull out your dagger."

"It's already out." I glanced over to see that she had a firm grip on the handle. The blade was longer than mine, but she needed the extra length because she wasn't as strong as I was. Score one for James.

"Once they charge, I'll hold them down," I said, "and you stick the knife right behind their eyes. Got it? We work as a team."

"How are you going to—"

One of the wolves broke from the tree line and loped head-long toward us. I leapt into the clearing, morphing instantly into my Lycan form. Right as it closed in. I grabbed on to its neck, careful to stay away from its teeth, and hit the ground, one arm clamped around its middle. It lashed out in a fury, snapping and growling, trying to free itself. It smelled like decay and its organs were mushy and soft under my grasp. Gross.

Marcy rushed toward us, her knife shaking slightly. "Marcy, do it fast." I gritted my teeth as the wolf struggled in my arms.

She lunged forward, plunging the blade into the wolf's head, quick as lightning. The wolf instantly went limp in my arms and I glanced up, smiling. Marcy appeared a little wild-eyed, but she took hold of the wolf by the scruff and tossed the mangy thing to the side as I stood.

"That was impressive—" I turned. "Look out!"

Two wolves barreled toward us at the same time, sprinting into the clearing. I rushed forward to intercept them, springing out to kick one in the flank, sending it flying as I took the other one behind the ears, tearing it off the ground and tossing it out of the circle. The wolf sailed far into the trees, crashing through them as it landed. Neither would die, but I hoped this would buy us time, and only one would recover at a time.

"Jeez, I'm amending the name Hercules, and from now on I'm going to refer to you as Wonder Wolf." Marcy whistled. "You moved so fast I could barely make out your form. That wolf flew clear across the clearing into the trees over there." She gestured right as the thing sprang back into view. "Dang, they don't stay down long, do they?"

"Marcy, I may be strong, but I can't be in two places at once." I turned as the other one rose. At least now they were coming at us from different directions. I moved toward the wolf closest to us, the one I'd kicked, as both he and his buddy closed in. They bared their yellow, decaying teeth and snarled.

"Don't worry." Marcy placed a hand out in front of her and started chanting right as the wolf began to run. "I've got this one."

"Okay." I turned as the wolf in front of me sprang. In one motion, I unsheathed the knife strapped to my arm and angled my body to the side, striking the wolf through the brain as it leapt past me in midair. It collapsed to the ground and I moved back to help Marcy, only to see that the other wolf was already down in front of her and she was pulling the knife out of its head with a satisfied grunt.

It was hard not to be impressed.

There was one wolf left.

This one had watched all the action from the sidelines, just behind the tree line. It had huge patches of fur missing and seemed older. Its eyes were cloudy and somewhat vacant, but its pupils were alert, which made sense if the bokor was controlling them like zombie wolves. "I see you," I called to the wolf. "You're not fooling us, sorceress. I know this wolf is your puppet." I waved my hand in the air. "And I know you can see me. I want you to know, we're coming for you. You're not going to succeed in hurting my friends. And once I find you, it's not going to be pretty."

In response, the wolf turned its muzzle up at me in a gruesome smile. If that dirty thing could talk, it would tell me good luck and have fun trying. Either that or it would tell me to fuck off.

The mangy beast glanced behind him, back over the trees. "What? Aren't you going to attack us now?" I asked. "Afraid we can kill you just like the others?"

It snapped its maw at us, yellow slime running between its jaws, and then it abruptly turned tail and ran, disappearing into the cypress trees.

"Well, that worked well," Marcy commented. "Now what? Do we follow it?"

"Yes." I sighed. "We follow it. I don't have a better plan, but we'll have to be watchful. She's expecting us."

As we began to track the wolf, Marcy's back pocket vibrated. She drew her phone out and held it in front of her.

The screen held two words.

MOVE CAREFULLY.

12

"It would be nice if Juanita would explain what's going on in more than two or three words. An actual phone call would be nice," I grumbled as we climbed across dead, broken tree roots, trying not to stumble. "Have you ever tried to call her?"

"And how exactly would I call her?" Marcy asked, tripping behind me but catching herself before she tumbled through the roots. "I don't exactly have a coverage plan that includes friend-to-friend calling with ancient supernaturals. Plus, I'd need her number and she killed my phone. The only thing this phone is good for anymore is her ticker tape messages. She doesn't leave any traces behind. Nada."

I stopped for a moment to assess the area. "I feel like we're going around in circles. It all looks the same. How do the zombie wolves run through this stuff?" The cypress trees were tangly and hard to maneuver around. "It wouldn't be easy on four legs."

"Maybe we missed a path?" Marcy said. "I'm thinking there must be a trail of some kind and she's not letting us see it."

We'd followed the wolf out of the clearing and into the trees. I knew the actual acreage the bokor inhabited couldn't possibly be that big. I couldn't track any scent, because everything smelled like decay, death, and rot. "My guess is she's either blocking the way to her lair or this realm extends wider than we think."

"Wait a second." Marcy held up her hand. "My backside is ringing again." She reached around and plucked out her phone.

I leaned over to read it with her.

SOUTH.

I sighed. "Seriously? That's it?" I called into the trees. "I have no idea where south is. We can't even see the sun from here." I glanced at the sky to get a sense of our location, but only a sliver of light filtered through the thick overcast.

"Hey, look." Marcy pointed. "She's giving us helpful hints." A tree began to glow off to our left. It was a soft yellow light, radiating outward like someone had turned a nightlight on inside the trunk. "She's a tricky one, you gotta hand it to her."

"Tricky, and much too secretive for her own good." I moved toward the glowing tree, and right as we reached it, another tree in the distance blinked on.

As we picked our way through, Marcy shook her head. "I wish I knew more about this kind of magic. Being able to create an alternate reality is heavy-duty. It's extremely old magic. This bokor must worship lots of loa to gather that much strength."

Right as Marcy uttered the word *loa*, something swished by my face. I batted the air. "We've got company."

There was a short pause, and then a soft voice purred next to my ear. *We've been waiting a long time for you... female wolf...*

I glanced back at Marcy, my eyebrow arched. "You heard that, right?" I asked.

"Heard what?"

"The hot gusty cloud of air that just said, 'We've been waiting a long time for you, female wolf'?"

"Nope," she said. "But all my hairs are on end again. See?" She held up her arm. "I can sense a presence, but that's it. I guess those words are only for your ears."

"But Naomi heard them before. I don't get it." I pondered that as another gust blew by me. If I had to guess, it felt like this thing was trying to push me back the way we'd come. "I think the spirit, or whatever, is pissed Juanita is leading us in the right direction. I think it wants me to go back. Something tells me we're jumping the bokor's timetable. Maybe she's not ready for us?" I angled my head up at the treetops. "Is this an inopportune time for you, sorceress?" I called. Hot wind assaulted my body and I stumbled backward, tripping on low-lying branches. "I guess I'm right."

Marcy was propped against a tree. "If this bokor is indeed trying to steal Naomi's power and stuff it into a fetish, she'd need to perform some kind of ceremony to do it. That's a huge magic transfer. It can't be rushed. If changing Danny into one of her zombie wolves is on the agenda as well, who knows how long that will take? But my guess is she has to prepare some kind of mumbo-jumbo potion first. So maybe you're right. We are interrupting her and she's not happy."

I shuddered, and my arms prickled as thoughts of harm coming to Danny or Naomi washed over me. "I guess that means we double our pace and hurry. Juanita wants us to get there or she wouldn't be leading the way. Let's go."

We maneuvered through the trees as fast as we could manage. We made it about fifty yards when something slammed into me from the side. I was caught completely off guard, and grabbed on to a root to steady myself.

At least I thought it was a root.

When it moved with me, and I fell to the ground, I knew something was wrong.

Marcy shrieked, "It's unraveling quickly! Let go before it wraps its slithery, awful body around you!"

The thing hissed, its forked tongue inches from my face. I was on my back, but thankfully I had a tight grip on it behind the neck. Its red eyes pulsed, but there was also something else there. "Marcy, I bet we can kill these zombie snakes just like the wolves. Get your knife out!"

She was beside me in an instant, her hand steadily gripping her new best friend. "That thing reeks of magic. It might not work."

The bottom of the python's massive body slithered around my legs. It was getting ready to strangle the life out of me. "Marcy, use one of your spells at the same time you stab it. It can't hurt." The muscles in the snake's body were heavy and rigid, like they'd been reinforced with steel. And Marcy was right—there was powerful magic attached to it.

"Okay, but if a verbal spell isn't strong enough, we'll have to use one of the dark ones." Marcy began chanting, and the air around us tingled with power. The snake's gaze slid toward her as it began to vibrate under my grasp. "Marcy, it's working! Now stab it and see what happens."

Marcy was clearly in a zone, but she moved forward, her eyes glazed in concentration as she expertly struck the snake right behind the eyes. She used so much strength, the knife lodged into its brain and she couldn't pull it out. The red eyes above me began to blink like Christmas lights on the fritz.

Marcy kept yanking at the knife, trying to get it out. "Leave it in!" I shouted. "I can feel the thing weakening. Just keep doing whatever you're doing with the spell."

She immediately let go and stepped back, closing her eyes,

bringing her hands up in front of her. To my surprise, her hair began to lift at the ends as the air shifted around us.

The snake began to shake like a tuning fork, vibrating so fast I had no choice but to let go of it.

A few seconds later the thing exploded.

Right on my chest.

I managed to look away in time, shielding my mouth and eyes with my hands a few seconds before it erupted. Snake guts had exploded everywhere. They were sticky and putrid. This thing had been good and dead before it had been reanimated by the bokor.

I ran a hand over my neck and chest as I glanced up at Marcy, coughing. "I think we can safely say that you just bested the bokor and her stupid snake. What kind of spell was that anyway? Good lords, woman. That was nothing short of amazing."

Marcy's eyes were bright as she extended her hand to help me up. "It was a tricky one. It was part null, to combat the bokor's magic, and part boil." Once I was up, she actually clapped her hands together excitedly. "I wasn't sure I could do it, because it's actually a dual spell, but I've been practicing them lately. You take a piece of one spell and combine it with another. It's extremely hard to master and usually takes a young witch years to hone. But I only started doing them a month ago. Yay!"

I whapped the biggest, stinkiest bits of carcass off my body, trying to clean it the best I could with my hands. The smell was putrid. "Yay is right. You rocked it out. But now I hope you have a hose-me-off spell. In the Underworld they had these amazing showers that washed you and your clothes on the spot. I would kill for one of those now."

It was really the only good thing about the Underworld.

"I have a cleaning spell, but it's more of an 'incinerate the crap off you' spell. I don't think a bathing spell even exists. That would be handy, but too risky. The spell would have to attack your actual skin. Lots of ways to backfire." She smiled as she aimed her fingers at me. She said a few words and the bloody snake guts sizzled and burned up like ash and fell to the ground.

I glanced down the front of my shirt. "You took some material with it." I put a finger through a hole on the hem and wiggled it.

"Good grief!" Marcy said with exasperation. "You can't expect perfection a hundred percent of the time, O Grand Taskmaster." She steepled her hands and faked a bow. "I just defeated a possessed python the size of five kindergarteners end to end. My brain is completely fried. You're lucky your shirt is still attached to your body."

I laughed. "Well, the guts are gone, so that's all that matters."

"Of course that's all that matters. Now, let's get out of here. That carcass is making me gag and we need to get to Naomi and Danny. Plus, I want out before any more possessed reptiles slither out of the woodwork."

I started after her. "After your impressive display of magic, and how handily we took care of the wolves, I don't think the bokor will risk any more of her precious pets. We're systematically reducing her flock of terror one creature at a time. I'm betting she won't pull any punches till we show up at her front door."

As we made it to one glowing tree, another would light up.

We quickened our pace, meaning we continued to stumble over roots and knotted growth as fast as we possibly could, mostly jumping from tree to tree. The only positive thing was there wasn't any water. In the regular world this place would have water everywhere, seeping in between the trees. "I wonder how she filters the water out," I pondered as we went. "Seems like too much hassle and energy to keep it dry here."

Marcy grunted. "She must live in a house or something, so she needs land to operate. My guess is it's just easier to spell the entire area the same way, rather than pick places to drain it. That's what I'd do."

"I wonder why the loa has left us alone. It must be able to do more than catch me off guard so I'm forced to grab on to a snake."

"I have no idea, but I do know a loa is strongest right after it has a ride in its host. It siphons energy while it's inside. So maybe this one wasn't primed on enough bokor juice?" I made a face. "That was the best explanation I had."

"Well, I hope that's the case, because I'd prefer to fight a tired bokor—"

A scream rent the air, followed by a strangled howl.

It sounded like a cross between a wounded cub and an anguished siren. "Oh my gods, that's Naomi!" But before I could move more than five paces forward, something crashed into me from the front, bowling me over.

You won't get to her in time, the voice said in my ear as I hit the ground. *Your blood will taste deeeelicious. We will devour it gladly. But you must wait your turn.*

I punched the air in front of me but came in contact with nothing. And just as quickly it was gone. "You're not getting her!" I shouted to the sky. "You'll have to kill me first!"

"Jess." Marcy stood over me, her voice quaking slightly. "The air smells like black pepper and lavender."

"So?" I stood up and brushed myself off. "Did you finally hear what it said? It's going to drink Naomi's blood. We have to stop it. It doesn't want us to get to her and it's trying to slow us down."

"No, you don't understand." She grabbed my arm, pulling me up short. "That is a very *particular* scent, and once I smelled it, it triggered something that was taught to me a long time ago, like clicking the last cog into place."

"What does it mean?" I asked. When she didn't talk immediately I urged, "Marcy, spit it out!"

"If what I was taught is correct, the loa harassing us is the spirit of Marinette."

"Who's that?" I asked as I dragged Marcy along with me. "Come on, talk to me while we move."

She followed, frowning. "How can you *not* know who that is? She's renowned in the lore as one of the most powerful and vicious spirits around. The rumor, at least for the witches, is she started out as an extremely powerful goddess, who was killed or punished for her wrongdoings—which is almost unheard of. Then she came back as a spirit to seek revenge and wreak havoc on the supernatural world." We scrambled over trees, trying to make up for lost time. "Honestly, when you learn things as a child, it's in one ear and out the other—until you see, or in this case smell, some kind of real proof. Well, that scent is enough proof for me. It's a huge part of the story. No one else smells like black pepper, much less coupled with lavender. But there's one more key piece—" Marcy stumbled over some roots and I grabbed her arm to steady her.

"What is it?" I stopped, turning to face her. "I know I'm not going to like it, so just get it over with."

"Marinette is the patron of werewolves."

I processed that bit of information. Werewolves?

Marcy was impatient. "Do you understanding what I'm saying? She's a former goddess—the goddess of werewolves. As in, she was the first one to create them."

I was too stunned to respond.

Marcy nodded sympathetically. "I know this is crazy, and must be a lot to process, but who do the wolves consider as their creation myth?"

Marcy was right to call it a "myth." Supernaturals had inhabited the earth long before there had been any written documentation. For a millennium, only oral legends had been handed down through each Sect, which were highly susceptible to being embellished or exaggerated, as anything is if it's handed down through that many years of history. Our Pack Bible had many facts, but our creation, the birth of the first wolf, was considered legend—loosely interpreted—but believed nonetheless.

"Our creation myth states that the first human was turned into a werewolf," I recited from memory, "by an ancient Scottish goddess who'd been rebuffed by him. He'd been a great warrior—the greatest the world had seen—and was cursed to live out a life of immortality without his lover."

"A Scottish goddess, huh?" Marcy's voice held some irony. "Voudoun is an ancient magic that has been around for eons. Your goddess creation story could easily be entwined with some myths and legends of the voudoun, which would be how she ended up a loa. Honestly, Celtic and African myths are not such strange bedfellows when you go back millennia." She shrugged as we began to walk again. "I'm telling you though, that scent is unmistakable. It sent all the hairs on my arms jumping at once."

"So what you're saying is, if this *is* Marinette, there's a chance I might be heading to do battle against my creator?" I was dumbfounded even thinking that something like that could be true.

Marcy tucked an errant curl behind her ear. "I have no idea. I'm just telling you what I learned as a young, impressionable witch. Witches like to hammer scary folklore crap into our brains to prepare us for the unexpected, and this"—she waved her arm around—"is about as unexpected as I've ever seen. The goddess of your creation myth *could* be her, but who knows? There's no way for us to know for sure until we know for sure."

"Eloquent," I said wryly. Another scream rent the air and I took off, yelling, "We're coming, Naomi! Hold on!"

13

As I raced forward, my mind replayed everything Marcy had just told me. I leapt and bounded over roots and trees, mindless of anything else. My wolf snapped her jaws, urging us on. *We're close*, I told her. *I can sense it.*

We'd shot ahead of Marcy, but she wasn't very far behind.

My wolf held her nose in the air. And as we ran, the scent of black pepper and lavender grew stronger. *I think I see something up ahead*, I told my wolf. *There's a break in the trees.*

I soared through the opening and somersaulted onto an expanse of cracked, dry earth—if you could call it earth. It was more like a bunch of accumulated dust. I was up on the balls of my feet in a low crouch before I came to a full stop. In front of me stood an old, dilapidated wooden shack that looked to have been constructed sometime during Prohibition.

The old building was in bad need of repair. There were boards missing, window glass was gone, the porch was decayed and slanting at an angle, and the entire thing was covered in hanging fetishes, old animal parts, dried herbs, and other things I couldn't—and didn't care to—identify. They hung from every available space on the house, from the dormer all the way up the roofline, and they chimed together eerily in the soft breeze.

The house is empty, I told my wolf. I didn't sense any movement. She put her muzzle in the air and scented. Then I heard it.

Chanting.

I spotted a path across the expanse to my right, but before I could take off, Marcy burst out of the trees behind me, panting.

"It's about time," I told her.

"Shut it." She bent over, gasping in a few harried breaths. "Last time I checked, I had no animal in me, but making sure I wasn't python bait was a big motivator to move quicker than I ever have."

"Something's going on over there. I hear chanting." I gestured to the path across the way and turned to start moving forward when Marcy grabbed my arm once again.

"Hold it, Wonder Wolf," she ordered as she manhandled me back, tugging at the bag around my waist. "I need you focused. You can't just barrel in there without protection at the ready. You're going to need your dark-magic baggies." She opened the pouch. "We need to throw a wedge into her evil plans, and this is the only way to do it." She dug her hand in and pulled out two spells. "Perfect." She set them in my hands, one in each palm. "One stun spell"—she curled my left hand into a fist around it—"and one protection." She did the same thing with my right. "Once we get in there, I want you to throw these in front of you at the same time and speak both words. I'll be there to back you up."

I noted the colors. "Say both words in one breath?" I asked as she made sure the pouch was accessible to my hand.

"Yes." She set her hands on my shoulders. "And, Jess, it's not going to be pretty in there. Whatever she's doing is evil. Don't let your emotions get in the way. If you have any Achilles' heel, it's that you have too much human empathy, something supes who are born supernatural never have. The prime objective is to kill her and eliminate the evil—even if it's at a cost."

I nodded. Marcy knew me well. If the cost was Naomi's and Danny's lives, it was too steep a price to pay, but I wasn't going to argue with Marcy. I would make the tough decisions as I went. "The only one who is losing her life is the bokor."

The chanting picked up, coming faster and in more hurried tones. "It sounds like she's performing some kind of ritual," Marcy whispered. "That's probably why the loa didn't come back. She's probably inside the bokor. The best way to stop what's about to happen is to disrupt the ceremony before they get a chance to finish it. Mess it up completely, which I know firsthand you're good at."

"Like physically destroy it?"

"Yes, exactly. There should be an altar, and nearby potions or bowls of blood. Destroy anything and everything you can get your sharp claws on."

"You got it." I headed down the path, a spell clutched in each hand, Marcy close behind me.

"Oh, and expect there to have been a blood sacrifice, so don't let it catch you off guard."

I started to trot. "What kind of blood sacrifice?" I glanced over my shoulder and grimaced.

"My guess would be human."

I stifled a gag. "Why not a wild boar or chicken?"

"Because death is the best kind of energy for the darkest magic, and the bigger, and more intelligent, the better. Remember, this bokor is a supernatural without conscience. I just told you we don't have much empathy as an entire race, but most of us do have a conscience. The evil ones don't. They kill without thought, vying only for power."

"If she wanted the strongest magic, why wouldn't she just sacrifice a supe?" My mind instantly shot to Danny. That's why she let him in! Before Marcy answered, I shouted, "She *would* sacrifice a supe."

We both ran down the winding path. At the end, we came to a wall of trees and nothing else.

"This can't be a dead end!" I exclaimed. "I can scent her, and I can hear the chanting." I placed my hands on the bark nearest me and it hummed with magic.

"This is just a strongly warded illusion," Marcy said, closing her eyes as she began to murmur. "Push some of some of your magic into that tree and see if you can break the ward while I try a spell."

I closed my eyes. *We need Selene's or Eudoxia's magic for this,* I told my wolf. For the first time, she uncurled the power of five. She grabbed Selene's red signature and mixed it with Eudoxia's white. As the magic moved forward, it churned through my body, a ribbon of pink. It was strong. *We toss it at the tree all at once.* "Marcy, get ready," I said. "I'm going to blast it on three."

"I was born ready."

"One, two . . . *three*!" I forced the magic from my body, shocking the ward at the same time Marcy shouted her incantation.

There was one pulse and all of a sudden it burst open. The impact threw us backward. What stood before us was terrible.

"No," I breathed.

Naomi was laid out on top of an earthen altar, her body still, covered by a gray blanket that could've been white at some point.

"You are too late, lone wolf." The voice coming out of the bokor's mouth held an accent, possibly Haitian.

"She's stalling," Marcy whispered from right beside me as we both stood and stared. "The ceremony isn't finished. I can feel the magic vibrating for release. You have to go now." She elbowed me. "Destroy it before she can say anything else."

Needing no more prodding, I bounded into the area.

It was a perfect circle, lined with tree trunks carved into gruesome totem poles with expressions of death and destruction detailed onto each tier. Tied to every pole was a rabid wolf, each baring its teeth and snarling. In the trees behind the totem poles, snakes of various sizes slithered here and there between the branches and skated across tops of the structures in eerie silence.

It was a grisly scene.

But the capper to the entire show was the female, who stood tall at the head of the altar. She was thin, her skin a deep milk chocolate, her hair pure white and sheared close to her scalp. She wore a multicolored robe, the sleeves draped to her elbows, her hands raised high in the air. Her nails were long and yellow, curved around her fingertips like claws. And blood dripped from her palms.

As I entered the circle, her head rose slowly to meet my gaze.

Her irises were the color of ice.

The effect was immediate. It was like she could see through me, straight into my soul.

Naomi lay in front of her. The altar was crude, made of mud and twigs, and as I rushed closer, I noticed that under the gray blanket, Naomi was dressed in a simple sheer gown, her hands restrained by thin iron rings.

She didn't move, which was distressing.

I was going to destroy everything I could find.

"Halt!" This time the voice that came out of the bokor's mouth was different. It sounded ancient. The loa's voice was authoritative, the Haitian accent gone. I stopped in my tracks. "You came too late to save this one. The blood that rides within this host has already been consumed." The bokor grinned, an expression that looked unnatural since the command had been issued from the loa. I noticed now she had a red smear mark on both her cheeks, and as she smiled, her teeth were broken and blackened.

I narrowed my gaze on Naomi and edged to the side to get a

better look at her. One of her arms had been recently cut and a bone knife covered in blood lay next to her head. Her blood had been contained in a small bowl, made of what looked like ivory, which sat next to the knife.

"I don't care if you've consumed her blood." I took a bold step forward. There wasn't much here to destroy except for the altar. "You're not going to live long enough to do anything with it, so it doesn't matter."

The bokor tossed her head back as the loa laughed. The sound was manic.

"You fear me." Her gaze landed on mine, and her irises were like tides washing over a clear sea. "That makes me satisfied. I have been planning this for longer than humans have inhabited these lands. Look around you." The bokor's body awkwardly swept a bony arm outward, her robe riding up to expose no more than a skeleton covered in skin. The loa's voice sounded hollow in her host's throat the more she spoke. "This is my world. It's a place where the Earth collides with the spirit realm at a perfect apex. In the beginning, I filled it with water and beasts to keep the humans out, but they have wound their way back in. So now I must cloak myself within these trees so none discover me. But I have been patient all these years, biding my time, knowing that soon I will be free again. Free to roam the Earth as I did once long ago."

I pretended to be devastated by the news that she wanted to rise again, which likely had something to do with me. My eyes were downcast as I drew slowly closer to Naomi, the spells still in each of my hands. This loa was clearly out of touch with reality. She must've lived in this swamp for hundreds of years, not doing much of anything. In order to keep her thinking I was interested while I figured out how to take apart the altar, I asked, "If you've been waiting all these years for me to set you free, you're going to be sorely disappointed. I'm not here to grant your wish. In fact, just the opposite." At the same time, I lobbed the spells down in front of me, shouting the Latin words in unison.

They exploded in a cloud of black and green smoke as I dove for Naomi.

I skidded across the altar, scooping her body along with me as I went. The iron shackles snapped on impact, and they came sailing along with us as I landed on the ground, cradling an unconscious Naomi in my arms.

That's when I saw him.

I knew it wasn't Danny, but my heart rose in my throat anyway. The body was prone in the soil in front of the altar, right where the bokor had stood. His hair was the same dark shade as Danny's and he had a similar build. I knew he was one of my father's wolves, and when his scent hit me full force I swallowed, biting back my human emotions.

I had to stay focused. There was nothing I could do for him now.

The rabid wolves strained at their leashes, snapping and gnashing their teeth. They must be tethered there because the bokor couldn't control them when she was ridden. But it was only a guess.

I tucked Naomi against the side of the altar, as far away as I could get from any of the wolves, and stuck my head up. Marcy had cast a spell right after I'd thrown mine. She said we'd get three minutes if we were lucky. I now had a protection spell five feet around me and if both spells had worked, the bokor was stunned. It didn't bode well that she wasn't standing where she'd been, but I had to trust she was down for at least a moment. The air was dense with smoke and I had to act now.

Marcy wanted carnage, and I was going to give it to her.

I leapt over the altar in my Lycan form, destroying and upturning everything I could get my hands on. My claws raked away huge hunks of mud and twigs, while my legs exploded the bowl and sent the knife and anything that touched me sailing. I swiped at candles lining the circle, slicing them in half, destroying more bowls that had been placed on a small table with my fists. As the smoke from the spell began to clear, a laugh swept by my ear. *You think I'm a child who can be felled so easily by a simple spell? Think again.* The loa crashed into my stomach, sending me hurtling backward in the air.

I gasped as I hit the ground. "You were forced out of your host. I take that as a win." I'd landed within a hairsbreadth of a wolf, and without hesitation I drew my knife and plunged it into its brain.

A scream pierced the air.

My head shot up and I spotted Marcy standing over the bokor on the other side of the circle. I leapt up and ran toward them. "What happened?" I asked. "Why is she down?"

"She's weak. The loa took all her strength. But she's trying to access her wolves. She must have connected to one of them right as you killed it."

I raised my eyebrows. "Then we need to keep our advantage going. Your spells worked like champs. They forced the loa out and weakened the bokor. That's more than I'd hoped for." I turned, glancing at the remaining wolves. There were some who were still rabid and uncontrolled, straining their leashes like they were trying to get out of their skin to get to us. But others had calmed and seemed to be assessing me with intent.

The bokor was grappling for control but was too weak to take over all their minds. I bolted toward the wolves I knew she was puppeteering, striking them down quickly.

She shouted and writhed on the ground in obvious pain.

Marcy called, "I'll take the wolves on this side—"

"No!" I yelled as Marcy flew backward, arms flailing. Her eyes were wide as her mouth gasped for air.

Something had her by the throat.

It had to be the loa. I dug my hand into the pouch as I ran, withdrawing another spell. I couldn't remember what color did what, but I knew the word to use. This one was orange and I shouted, "*Irrata!*" as I threw it down on the ground.

It exploded in a burst around us.

The power of the spell shot me backward and I crashed into a totem pole, luckily not one with a wolf attached. I was back at Marcy's side in an instant, thick orange smoke lingering in the air. She was rubbing her neck and coughing, still trying to catch her breath.

"Did it work?" I asked. "What spell was that?" I reached down and held my arm out to her.

She took it and I pulled her up. "It was a null," she said. "And I think it worked better than expected." She swished the fading orange cloud away with her hand. "I think I underestimated your blood, Wonder Wolf. Those spells are packing some serious power." She blew her hair out of her eyes. "Honestly, they shouldn't be working as well as they are against this kind of strength. That loa is fierce. Her magic is so strong, it crackles with energy."

"Maybe we should've brewed more?"

She chuckled. "I did what I could. But we're lucky—without these, we'd be fresh meat. Where's Naomi?"

"I tucked her behind the altar. Better question is where is the bokor?"

Marcy glanced around. "I don't know. She was right here on the ground a second ago."

I spun in a circle. The wolves had gone eerily quiet too.

"Oh no," Marcy whispered, tapping my shoulder.

I slowly turned to where she was pointing. The bokor stood twenty feet from us, her remaining wolves surrounding her, calm and at the ready, with the strongest one at the forefront.

Danny.

14

"Nooo!" I wailed, anguish tearing at my throat. "Please, no!" I tried to get to him, but Marcy held my waist firmly, keeping me rooted.

"This may be an illusion," she murmured close to my ear. "She's playing with us. He can't be dead from her usual methods. He's supernatural, and he wasn't in the circle before. She just called him in, likely because he's not completely under her control yet."

Danny's wolf was fierce.

He stood shoulders above the other rabid wolves, but his brown coat was already coming off in patches, his muzzle dripping with yellowed saliva.

"He is one of mine now," the bokor said, her Haitian accent back. The cadence was oddly hypnotic. "And he will do my bidding as I ask it."

I straightened, my wolf howling. I called out to Danny in my mind, and to my happiness, my Alpha connection was present. It wasn't as strong as it had been before, but it was still there. "I bet he won't."

"We shall see." She grinned. "Go, my beast!" She set him loose and he launched himself at me without hesitation.

I let him come.

His front paws slammed into my shoulders and we both flew. My back crashed into the ground, and as we slid, I took my hands and wrapped them around his neck, fisting the fur tightly in my grasp. Once we stopped, he went for my throat, snarling and snapping. It took all my combined strength and magic to hold him just inches away from my face. But I was in my Lycan form, and I could hold him for as long as it took now that I had him. "Daniel Walker!" I shouted, infusing as much power as I could into my words. "Stop!"

He faltered for a moment, his overly bright eyes dimming. But a moment later something ignited in them once again and he began to snarl. He smelled sickly, like my father had when he'd been cursed, but he wasn't dead, so that was something.

"Marcy!" I yelled. "Take the bokor down! She's in his head."

Marcy charged the priestess, her fingers out front wiggling.

"Danny." I gritted my teeth as I turned us over, bracing my stomach and legs against his squirming torso, effectively pinning him. "You have to *quit this*! It's me, Jessica! Your Alpha." I threw power into his body, my breath hitching when I sensed the same mustard-yellow masses coating his insides that had infiltrated my father. The curse would kill him if we didn't get it out, and once he was fully dead he would be in her control forever.

I wasn't about to let that happen.

Marcy shouted, "Listen, you ancient witch for hire! I can play games too. How about this?"

I couldn't see what was happening, but the bokor shouted in pain in response to Marcy's spell, and Danny's eyes flickered. "Do more of that, Marcy," I urged. "It's working."

I told my wolf, *When she hits the bokor again, we send our power into Danny's body and try to force the rest of her control out. Her presence shouldn't be too hard to detect.* I hoped.

Marcy incanted another spell as I pushed power into Danny, trying to shove out the spell or however she was controlling him.

As I did it, Danny lost some of his will to fight me and relaxed. I tried to reason with him again. "It's me, Danny," I murmured in calm, soothing tones, praying I was getting through to him as I continued to force her out. The yellow masses pulsed but didn't disappear. I tried to insert my power between them and his body, just like I had done with my father. "Listen, you have to help me out here. We need to cut this sorceress off. I know you're still in there, and I'm not letting you go without a fight, but having you cooperate would be extremely helpful right now."

He cocked his head at me and I read his confusion, and then his eyes lit with the unnatural brightness once more and he began to snarl at me, lunging and snapping at my face.

"Dammit," I grumbled, holding him down with a forearm locked over his neck. "If you're not going to do it for me, then you need to do it for Naomi." He struggled beneath me, not heeding my words, growling and biting. "Danny! Do you hear me?" I got as close as I dared to his face. "Your mate needs you!" I sent more power into his body.

This isn't working. We'll have to use magic to force her out, I told my wolf. *I don't know what it will do to him. I don't want to blow him up, so we need to tread lightly.*

Transferring power was different than blasting something with magic. One acted like jumper cables on a battery and the other would tear through him like a hurricane. What I needed to do was find the sorceress's signature—whatever she was using to control him. It was in there somewhere.

I concentrated on the task as Marcy and the bokor went back and forth, spell for spell. My friend was holding her own and I was extremely proud of her. I slowly threaded magic into Danny's body until I found something. *There, I see it,* I told my wolf. *Those thin, almost transparent yellow lines connecting the masses together? We concentrate our magic on those places and destroy the connection.* I prayed it would be enough as I sent a multicolored burst of magic into his body and aimed it directly at the yellow lines.

Danny jumped like he'd been defibrillated, and the bokor let out a bloodcurdling scream. "You don't like that, huh?" I called as I sent one more blast of concentrated magic into his system and all the lines snapped at once.

Danny shook his huge wolfy head as his haze finally lifted. He glanced up at me and seemed to be surprised to find me over him. Then, without hesitation, he ran his huge tongue completely over my face. I chuckled. "I knew I hadn't lost you yet." I gave him a quick hug and eased off him, wiping the saliva away with the back of my arm.

Danny rose on unsteady paws, staggering as one of his knees gave out. My magic hadn't gotten rid of the masses. I had only broken her mind control over him. We had to get him out of this realm and to Ray as soon as possible. That was the only thing that could help him now. Danny made a move to lie down and shift back into human form.

I shook my head. "Not yet," I said. "Naomi needs your protection, and shifting right now is too risky in your condition. I didn't just free you from her hold to have her snare you again."

At the mention of his mate's name, he growled, pinning his ears back. He angled his muzzle in the air, and once he found her scent, he took off. I let him go.

I stood, turning to where Marcy and the bokor were still circling each other. With surprise, I saw that the rest of the rabid wolves were lying on their sides. "How'd you do that?" I called as I moved toward them.

"I figured out the spell she was using," Marcy said triumphantly. "So I countered it with one of my own. It was a deceptively easy one. I almost missed it. It's the kind of spell you learn in grade school."

"You know nothing," the sorceress intoned in a flat voice. "My wolves are part of me. They have only gone to sleep but I will raise them shortly."

"They went to sleep because I kicked your spell to the curb." Marcy had her fingers up, ready for the next round.

I came up behind Marcy and addressed the bokor. "Are you the one who's making these people into wolves? Or is it the loa?"

The sorceress threw her head back and cackled, her multicolored robes flashing, her grimy, broken teeth exposed to full effect. "My magic is beyond your understanding, female wolf. But mine coupled with my darling Marinette's—we are a force like nothing you've ever witnessed."

"So it's true," I said, trying not to be too stunned. "The loa is Marinette." I glanced at Marcy. "You were right."

"Imagine that. I mean, by strict percentages, I'm bound to be correct at least half the time," Marcy answered. "But I can tell you, I wish I had been wrong about this one."

Something whispered by my ear. *Your time has come*, it said. *I have dreamed of this day.*

I swatted the air in front of my face. "Marinette," I called. "I see you've finally recovered from the last black spell we gave you. Your henchman here is claiming you are both extremely powerful, but we drove you away fairly easily. You're not looking too incredibly fierce to me now."

The bokor started to laugh and it sent the hairs on the back of my neck straight upward. I glanced at Marcy. Dammit, we were missing something big here. She shrugged and said, "I have no idea what's going on, but I don't like it either. Something's off."

"You wanted me here, Marinette, so I'm here. Let's finish this," I called. "Or are you too weak?"

Hot air wafted by my face, prickling my skin. *I created you... now I will take back what's mine.*

It took me a moment to process what was about to happen, but when I did, I shouted to Marcy, "She's going to try and get—" All at once, dank air infiltrated every part of me, pouring through my nose, my ears, my eyes, pushing into me with relentless strength and energy.

She was inside me, devouring me in an instant. And I fell to my knees.

I heard Marcy yell, "Grab a spell! Grab a spell!"

Mindlessly I jammed my hand into the pouch and grabbed the last three spells. I drew them out, but instead of throwing them to the ground, I took one deep breath and smashed the bags against my body, saying all the words. The spells were crafted for me, with my blood, so I assumed they wouldn't render me unconscious or do anything overly nefarious.

There was a crushing noise as they all exploded, making my eardrums ring, but I managed to keep myself steady. Then suddenly the smoky, spell-filled air around me went totally still.

I coughed and wiggled my fingers, swishing away the cloud of mingled aftereffects. I couldn't feel the loa in my body. The air in front of me was muddy brown. "Marcy, what happened?" I called.

She came up behind me. "Well, you successfully froze, stunned, and protected yourself against the loa. Can you feel her in the air? Was she doing what I thought she was doing?"

"She was inside me. I don't sense her right now, but that doesn't mean anything."

"Wait," Marcy said. "If you froze her with that spell, then we should try and do something more, and we only have a few minutes at best."

"What do you have in mind?" I glanced through the haze and spotted the bokor on the ground. "She looks asleep." I raised my eyebrows at Marcy. "Or is she dead? That would be the better scenario."

"She's asleep or stunned, or both. But that was all me. I hit her with another combo. I have no idea which one worked, or if they both did. But it doesn't matter, we need to hurry and deal with the loa first. She's the bigger fish we need to fry in this dead swamp." Marcy waved her fingers in front of me and magic brushed by my face. It made a crinkling sound, like a potato chip bag being rustled, and the air around me started to pop and crackle.

I stood, brushing myself off. "What are you doing?"

"No, stay still. I'm exploding all the air particles around you. If the loa was in your body, and you successfully shot her out and froze the air around you, then maybe we can get rid of her by exploding the particles around you."

"Good thinking," I said. "Hit close to the ground too. Maybe some of her ghostly particles landed in the dirt."

Marcy aimed downward. As she did, I backed away slowly. "I'm going to check on Naomi and Danny." Marcy nodded as she kept her focus aimed at the place where I'd just been standing. I rounded the altar and gasped. I kneeled immediately, plunging my hands into Danny's fur, trying to ignore when it came away in tufts in my hands. "It's going to be okay," I murmured in his ear. "I promise you."

He whined at me from his position lying over Naomi's back. He had nudged her away from the altar and had draped his body over hers, protecting her. She still hadn't woken. But he was clearly in distress, the curse eating away at his insides.

"Danny. I need you to roll off of her." He growled at my instruction. "I know you don't want to leave her, but I have to examine her for injury. She should've woken up by now." He grudgingly let me maneuver him away, but I settled him as close to her as I could. "It's going to be okay." I stroked his fur while searching

Naomi's body. "We're going to eliminate the threat, and once we do, we'll get you both out of here."

He lifted his snout and snapped his jaws. Then he shook his head. "I don't care if you don't believe me." I turned to address him. "That's the way it's going to be. Everyone is getting out of here in one piece. All of us. Now, let me see what's wrong with your mate." I got down on my knees and hovered over her. There was nothing outwardly wrong with her that I could detect. "Naomi." I shook her lightly. "I need you to wake up."

No response.

I placed my hands on her abdomen and sent a trickle of power in, searching for what was wrong. I was so focused on my task, I didn't hear Marcy approach.

"What's that mark on her shoulder?" she asked as she leaned down and peeled a piece of Naomi's dress back to expose a sickle-shaped mark that appeared to be inflamed and pulsing.

"I'm not entirely sure, but I think that's the mark she got when she fought Selene," I said. "Once she woke from her torture in the cave, it was there. I remember seeing it. But now it looks angry. Do you know what it is?"

Marcy knelt down beside me and said, "It's called a flora."

"What does it mean?"

"It means Selene marked her. She placed some concentrated magic into her body to use at will. They are rare, and hard to craft properly. They're meant to do one thing very well, and they are very hard to break. This one looks like it was used to knock her out—like a sleeping spell? But that's just a guess. Was she unconscious when you found her in Selene's lair?"

"Yes, she was out cold," I answered, panic edging my voice. "Please tell me we can break this magical flora on our own."

Marcy bit her lip. "I'm not sure. How did she wake up before? Did Selene do it? Or did she wake up another way?"

"No, Selene was occupied." I thought back for a moment. "I'm not entirely positive, but I think the first time she woke was when my brother gave her his blood."

Marcy's eyes widened. "Huh. I didn't think wolves ever fed vampires willingly, but go, Tyler. Then blood must be the ticket here."

"I'm not sure if it was only that, and how would blood break the spell of the flora? That seems too easy."

"The only way it would work, in my mind, is if his blood was stronger than Selene's spell. I don't know that much about floras, since they're incredibly hard to perfect, and they backfire like no ones business, so most witches don't bother. But whatever Naomi needed, it came from his blood."

"It makes some sense, since he'd taken some of my blood just before we got there. If his blood worked with only a trace of mine, full potency should do the trick." I rolled up my sleeve and brought my wrist up to my mouth, slashing it open with my dull teeth, trying not to wince. It sealed immediately. "Dammit, I'm healing too fast." As I made the second slash with my teeth, Danny growled, staggering to stand. Once he was up on shaky legs, he pushed his snout against my arm to move me away. "Danny, you need to settle down. I've already fed her twice. A third time won't make any difference. And you're in no way capable of feeding her yourself." He snapped his jaws. "Do you want to risk giving her your curse? Either I feed her or she stays asleep, and that worries me. We all want to know if she's okay. Let me do this without arguing with me." He sat down with a thump and then laid his head on his paws, inches from her body, and whined. "I know. I hate this too. But I promise you she's going to be okay. You're going to have to trust me."

I ripped my wrist open once again, this time making a huge rent, and brought it down to Naomi's mouth.

Right as something rammed into me from the back.

15

I somersaulted headfirst over Naomi, rolling once, and then I was up. There was nothing in front of me. "Marcy," I called, "can you see her?" When there was no answer, I turned my head around to look for my friend.

Marcy was lying facedown in front of the altar next to the sacrifice, not far from Naomi.

You think you can best me? I think not. Blistering wind whipped by my face at top speed. At the same time, the air temperature around me dropped significantly.

Danny whined and tried to stand.

"No," I commanded him. "Stay and guard these two and don't let the bokor get near them if you can help it." He growled and shook his head, trying to refuse my order and come to my aid. "I'm still your Alpha, Daniel Walker. Do as I say. I need you to protect them." He whined, but sat.

You are strong, yet weak. You interest me. The breeze ruffled my hair and I swatted at the space in front of me as I backed up. *I had*

132

not thought you to be so young...and inexperienced. And you have no more spells to use.

"Yeah, my age isn't ideal, but I had no control over the timing of my birth." She was right. I was out of spells. "What do you want?" I turned in a slow circle, edging away from Danny to give them ample space.

What does everyone want from you? I shivered as my breath came out in a soft plume of white. The air temp had dropped to bone-chilling. *I want life. I want power. I want strength. My life was taken from me. I was immortal!* Currents of cold and hot air zipped around me. *But I will rewrite my fate and make up for the injustice that was done to me.*

"How do you know so much about me?" I asked, stalling.

The breeze was reaching a cyclone level. My hair began to sway and I was forced to close my eyes against the current. The loa was everywhere and she was pissed.

I know about you because I am you. Laughter echoed on the wind.

"You're going to have to be a little more clear." I took a few steps backward. "How can you be me? You can't be my reincarnate, because I already have one of those." My wolf barked her agreement.

There was a whisper of mirth next to my ear, and just as quickly it was gone. *I am not she, but I am your creator, and a piece of my soul resides inside you.*

My wolf growled and snarled.

I maneuvered around the altar, making sure I stayed on the opposite side of my friends. Behind me and to the left there was a noise as the bokor stood. I turned to her. "This loa claims to be my creator," I said to the sorceress, still biding my time, quietly willing Marcy to wake up. "Is that true?"

The priestess turned her icy stare on me and grinned. She

looked no worse for wear from Marcy's spells. "Marinette is infinite. She is all. She graces us with her own free will."

"That's not helpful," I grumbled as I moved forward. "Nor was it an answer to the question I asked. I want to know if she was the one who was responsible for creating the first werewolf."

Yesssss drifted by my ear.

The bokor was clearly old, but not nearly as old as the spirit who was harassing me at the moment. The bokor finally said, "She is the creator of all."

"All *what*? All shifters? All wolves?"

"Yes."

"Hmm, still not helpful." I edged closer to the sorceress. I couldn't fight the loa without any more spells, but I could take down the bokor with physical strength.

I am Marinette, goddess of wolves.

"So only werewolves, then?" I asked. I had to grab my hair and pull it out of my face because the wind wouldn't stop. Marinette was clearly gearing up for something.

The bokor opened her arms and spread them wide, her robe gaping, arms opening like cloth wings. She pinned me with her gaze as she intoned, "We have been awaiting your arrival. And now we will do what is necessary."

"And what exactly is necessary?"

"Marinette will rise again." The bokor's voice was firm and unyielding. She believed exactly what she was telling me.

"So she's going to ride me, then what? And that's really not going to work for me in the long-term, because I'm kind of attached to my body." I bent down to a fighting stance. This sorceress was nothing more than skin and bones. One snap of the neck and I had one adversary down.

"No, she won't ride you. She will *become* you," the bokor cackled.

A noise pinged in the air.

My head snapped to Marcy. *That was her phone!* I told my wolf. Juanita wanted to chat. Not an opportune time, but since I had no idea how to win against Marinette, I knew I had to get to that phone. I spun, lunging over the altar. But before I could fully clear it, something struck my side.

I rolled and came to a stop—right into the jaws of a rabid wolf.

I tried to wrench my body away, but it was too late. The grimy wolf embedded its broken teeth into my left thigh before I could scramble out of the way. The pain was immediate, searing, and intense.

White-hot lightning shot up my leg.

I brought my fist around and crashed it into the beast's head, hard enough to knock its jaws loose. I unsheathed my knife, and with another stroke and the wolf went down. I had to yank hard to get my knife out of its skull.

The priestess screamed behind me as I killed her wolf, but I ignored her.

Marcy's phone was still beeping and I had to get to it even if my leg was engulfed with the curse. It seared through my bloodstream as I crawled toward Marcy. My wolf urged us to shift, her instinct to protect us rearing its head. But shifting was the wrong choice. That's what the bokor wanted. She wanted us in wolf form. *We aren't going to shift*, I told my wolf. *We need to get to Marcy's phone. If we pass out, the loa and the bokor have us where they want us. Juanita is the only shot we've got.* I maneuvered onto my stomach and started crawling.

The bokor had crumpled to the ground when I killed her wolf. She must have to regenerate something when one of them was killed. I'd have to remember that. As I moved, I told my wolf, *Focus on cutting off the flow of poison.* Immediately she threw magic over the creeping yellow masses growing in our system, but it didn't do anything. *Keep trying.*

The temp around us was still ice cold, and it was only exacerbated when another hot wind blew by my face. *Do you like the feel of my blood settling into your bones?* the loa said on a long breath. *My blood will change you, and once you succumb, you will be free for the taking.*

"I'm not down yet." I gritted my teeth as I moved stubbornly forward. My leg was now immobile and the pain was shocking. My wolf was having some luck getting the creeping yellow to stop by erecting up a magic barrier around my upper thigh.

The loa nudged by me again. *You cannot ever recover from my blood, you know. You are doomed.*

"We'll see about that." I was almost to my friend when the bokor stepped in front of me, a rabid wolf on either side of her. Marcy's phone was still beeping. Juanita wasn't giving up, and neither was I.

"You are ours now," the sorceress said. "Marinette is right. You cannot recover from her curse. It flows through you now, and once you are under its spell, I will add my control and it will be finished."

I glanced up, giving the bokor a cynical look. "Nothing is ever really finished, is it? Don't you wonder how my father escaped this same curse? According to your logic, he should be dead right now." I was still doggedly moving forward, but at a snail's pace, which was maddening. "I know you've seen him here. He's alive and well, despite your best efforts to control him. And, I shouldn't have to point out, he didn't die."

The bokor looked mildly surprised, but just as quickly her face clouded. "Your father is the Alpha of his kind. He is very strong. But make no mistake, if he hadn't escaped, the result would have been much different."

"Ah, but he was able to escape," I said. "He bested your spell even if he couldn't cure the yellow masses himself. But he had help with that. And I do too."

"By the time your aid arrives, it will be too late," she said, dismissing me. "You are already going through the first transformation. Feel how it takes from you, eating you from the inside out. It's meant to be painful, so you realize every second that your life is ending."

I was almost to Marcy. The phone was still going off, its beeping rhythmic and constant. I wondered for a moment if only I could hear it.

She cannot help you, a breath whispered by my ear. *This is inevitable.*

That answered that question. "What are you waiting for, then?" I yelled, still grappling forward. I was to Marcy's shoe. "Why not strike me down now?"

There was soft laughter. *Why take you now when I can wait until my blood incapacitates you and does my work for me?*

Danny whined, nosing toward me. "Stay back, Danny."

Instead of listening, he got up on shaky paws and stumbled toward Marcy, knowing my intent was to reach the phone. I hadn't seen what took Marcy down, but I assumed it was a spell from the bokor or something Marinette did. *She couldn't have been bitten, right?* I asked my wolf, my voice filled with anxiety. I hadn't thought of that. If Marcy had been bitten, it would be dire. I was to her leg when I heard a soft moan. "Thank goodness," I muttered. Once I got to her, she lifted her head up. "I thought you might've been cursed."

"What happened?" Marcy said slowly, still fully waking. "I had the advantage. I was sure of it—"

The bokor hit her with another spell and Marcy's body lifted with the impact and collapsed back down, out cold.

I was furious, but there was nothing I could do to retaliate. "Was that really necessary in the scope of things? She was barely conscious."

"Keeping her incapacitated is easy," the bokor crooned. "I will not allow her to aid you again."

The phone was still beeping, bless its heart. But now it was facing the ground, since Marcy had flipped over. I had to roll her. Danny tried to help, whining as he pushed his muzzle into Marcy. I slid my hand under her to reach it when something grabbed my ankles, yanking me sharply back.

I kicked my legs as I turned.

A rabid wolf snarled over me. I saw the sorceress's careful attention in its eyes. I peered over at her and she was smiling a gruesome, broken-toothed smile.

"I will not allow her to help you."

Danny snarled and started toward the wolf. He was going to protect me or die trying. His growl was ferocious, and he was huge. Much bigger than the wolf hovering over me. Another wolf sidled over to stand next to it, but the one who had been over my body stepped back. The bokor wasn't going to take any chances. She had only these two left, as far as I could tell. We'd killed all her others.

"Daniel Walker, stand down," I ordered. "This is not worth getting your neck torn out over. Plus, I'm getting out of this myself." With a little help from Juanita.

He ignored me in favor of half stumbling, half walking to stand guard over my shoulder. Instead of moving him out of the way, which I could have done, I brought a hand up to his fur, letting him know my intent. I pressed him lightly, indicating where I wanted him to go with my fingers. He obliged and moved, and I casually rolled with him, reaching under Marcy to get the phone that was still beeping with Danny as my shield. My fingertips plucked the side of it right as the loa entered the bokor in front of me.

The change in the sorceress was immediate.

Her eyes flickered as the loa began to speak through her. The earth around us began to vibrate and the temperature dropped yet again, which seemed impossible since it was already so cold. "You cannot escape your fate. I will inhabit you and finally seek my resurrection."

The ground began to shake in earnest, and I watched in horror as the bokor's body began to convulse. Her eyes rolled back into her head, leaving only the whites, and she collapsed to her knees, her arms held wide.

There was another gurgling sound, and the two rabid wolves fell at my feet.

"Danny!" I yelled. "Get over to Naomi! I think this is Marinette's last hurrah. She's gathering power—"

A horrid scream pierced the air as the bokor keened, her body withering before my eyes as Marinette sucked every last drop from her.

Danny dove for Naomi, sensing the danger. The temperature was so cold my fingers were numb. I pulled myself up on my knees, ignoring the searing pain in my thigh, and I picked Marcy up under the arms, dragging her backward away from the spectacle.

The priestess's cheeks hollowed out, her fingers began to shrivel, and then one by one her teeth fell out. Marinette was greedy in her taking, and once she was finished, she would be even more powerful.

And I was her next target.

I had to get my friends out of the way. "Danny, follow me. Pull Naomi out of the circle, but be careful not to prick her with your teeth. When Marinette is done, she's coming after me." If I was overtaken, she wouldn't spare them. "Once they are out of the circle, I need you to go try to find help!" Danny began to tug Naomi along, whining as he went, fearful he would hurt her.

My wolf was still focused on making sure the yellow masses couldn't enter the rest of my body. So far it had been working, but I was going to need my magic to battle Marinette. It couldn't be tied up fixing my leg. *There's no doubt she's coming after us,* I told my wolf. *This is it. We're going to need our magic to battle her. Do you think we can we do both? Fight and keep the yellow from spreading?* My wolf growled. I took that as a no. *Well, we have no other choice.*

The bokor gave one last moan and collapsed on the ground, face-first.

She was nothing more than a skeleton. Marcy was outside the circle, tucked behind a totem pole. She was beginning to groan and that was a good sign. With the sorceress dead, she should be able to break the spell. Danny was right behind me with Naomi. "Stay back here with them until you see the loa enter me," I told him. "Do not go out there, whatever happens. Once Marinette is occupied with me, go for help. Try and find your way out of this realm. The Pack is right outside searching for us."

Danny snapped his muzzle and gave me a low, disapproving bark.

"It doesn't matter what you think," I countered. "I won't be able to keep Marinette out of me. I don't have any more spells, and nothing you can do will stop her. She'll just kill you once and for all. Now, focus on finding the Pack and leading them here. Ray is the only one who can save you. Don't you dare give up. Do you hear me, Daniel Walker?"

Danny leaned over and rubbed his flank against me. He was hanging on because he was a strong wolf. I pointedly ignored his yellowing eyes and the missing fur. He had to be okay, and in order for me to make sure he was, I had to fight this loa and win. I just wish I knew how.

There was a snapping noise. It was the sound of bones breaking.

I peered into the circle. *Ew.* She was taking the bokor's bone marrow.

Suddenly the phone beeped.

I'd never gotten to it and hadn't realized it had stopped ringing while I'd been occupied getting Marcy out of the circle. I bent over and plucked it out of Marcy's pocket. It vibrated in my hand.

I turned it over right as air brushed by my face. There were only three words scrolling across the screen.

SHE IS YOU!

"What?" I shouted into the air. What did that mean? "That doesn't help. I need—" I glanced up right as Danny lunged for me, barking wildly. Wind twisted my hair, and with the force of a tornado, the loa struck, knocking me back into the circle.

She was inside me before I could take my next breath.

16

Coldness filled me, consuming me with its intensity. My limbs were not my own and my veins were filled with ice water. My wolf howled, furious.

The possession was immediate.

By the time I hit the ground, she was in control. She had more power than I'd ever thought possible. The bokor had amped her up by giving her everything, even if it had been unwilling. The combined magic tore through me, unwelcome and reckless, overpowering anything I had inside me.

Try, I told my wolf as my head spun, *to grab on to her magic...*

I am here now. The voice in my head was crystal clear, like we were having a real conversation. *It's only a matter of time before you succumb. I will infiltrate every piece of you until you are no longer here and only I am left. Once I do, I will become you.*

Juanita had just told me the same thing.

SHE IS YOU.

What the hell did that mean? *I'm not giving up without a fight*, I told her.

Fighting me will not work. I've been preparing for this for centuries and I am too powerful for you. She snickered, enjoying herself.

I was immobile physically—Marinette had control of my limbs—and I could no longer sense anything around me. Her magic was an unruly mass, and as I lay there, it began to attach itself to my magic one strand at a time. *NO!* I shouted. *You can't take it away from me.* To my wolf, I said, *If she absorbs it, it will be hers to wield!*

Exactly, she cackled.

My wolf struggled to keep our magic away from her, trying to yank it back, but it had become slippery and cold, like everything else in my body, and there was no place to take it. My stomach heaved. Suddenly I was on my side retching, expelling everything from my body.

That's right, Marinette said. *All of your body functions will be laid to waste one by one. I will have no need of them.*

I shivered, my teeth clattering. The yellow masses in my thigh began to change. I could see the poison pooling in my mind. It had become fluid, like thick amber flowing through me. This was her magic—her signature. As it moved, it attached itself to everything. I could no longer see my own magic. *Can you intercept it?* I asked my wolf. She howled her anger and frustration.

You cannot. You are not stronger than your creator, my child. Marinette's voice was harsh. *My magic defines you, defines all wolves. Your magic comes to me naturally. It yearns for its master. It matters not that it is muddled with others' signatures. That will be a bonus to me once I inhabit your body, but it is of no consequence.*

I gulped for air. My lungs were shutting down. I couldn't fight this. It was different from anything else I'd come in contact with in my life. I wasn't going to be able to blow this up or knock her out. My brain was starting to get hazy. Marinette was succeeding and I was slowly losing control of all my faculties. My wolf yelped, urging me to do something—try anything. She was battling to keep Marinette back, but we had very little power left.

Then I felt it. My hand was vibrating.

I could barely detect it, but something was needling my senses, making me aware. I hadn't let the cell phone drop from my hands. Juanita was trying to get my attention.

The Hag cannot help you now, Marinette said. *She is too late and this is proof that the Fates can be changed. I will be living proof.*

My mind was growing more and more muddled as Marinette's anger whipped through me. The beeping continued, but I couldn't find the strength to lift my lids.

My arm began to shake.

I was still on my side from when I had emptied my stomach, and with insurmountable effort I forced my eyes open. I couldn't see anything at first. I concentrated on clearing my vision, but I realized there was a thick coating of film covering them. Everything looked milky.

You can try all you like, Marinette said. *Whatever she is trying to tell you is inconsequential.*

I ignored the loa. I couldn't access my magic, but I still had some scant power left. I pushed it into my eyes, forcing myself to focus. I squinted at the phone but could only make out a blur. "Make it bigger!" I yelled into the air, my vocal cords failing at the end like ice had frozen them solid. My teeth chattered hard.

I finally caught sight of one word.

TAKE

"Take what?" I whispered, barely getting the words out.

What is she talking about? I asked my wolf. *What does she mean by* take?

She is grasping at straws, Marinette answered before my wolf could. *It will be over soon, don't you worry.*

I had to do something. I couldn't just die here without a fight.

My body wouldn't move any longer at my command, so I did the only thing I could think of—I tried to distract her and buy us some time to figure out what Juanita wanted us to do. If she was still reaching out to me, that meant there was a way out. *Why are you doing this?* I asked Marinette.

Instead of words, I began to perceive a clear image of Marinette in my mind. *That's right. I was glorious and will be again very soon.*

She was in fact glorious. Long blonde hair billowed out behind her as she stood atop a rocky crag, dressed in a gown of what appeared to be spun gold. Her features were feminine and linear, her eyes the purest blue. She was beautiful.

Why were you killed? I asked groggily. *I thought immortals couldn't die.*

That's not important.

I beg to differ, I said. *It's the reason I'm lying here right now. You were an immortal goddess and you died. Because of that, you are seeking revenge. I feel your bitterness and your rage like it was my own. This involves me. You're taking what's mine and I have the right to know.*

I felt her impersonal shrug, like it wasn't my business, but who cared if I knew. *Fate deemed I was no longer fit to be a goddess, so the Hags stripped me of my form, but try as they might, they could not take my soul.*

Why weren't you fit to be a goddess? Because you created were-wolves without their permission?

No. She sniffed. *Creating a race of powerful supernaturals was what I was born to do. The Earth was evolving and supernaturals who had formed in the beginning were becoming uncontrolled. Unchecked, the supernatural races would've taken over, each Sect trying to kill off the other in a perpetual war. Eventually all humans would have died and there would have been none left to breed or to pray to the gods and goddesses. Everything would've been lost. So immortals, like myself, were each tasked with creating a new, powerful race—races that would control the balance. More intelligent beings. I chose mine wisely.*

Then why were you punished? I was fading fast and Marinette knew it. Her voice was filled with glee. She would answer any questions now, but only because she no longer had anything to fear. She had what she wanted. I struggled to stay coherent, to hear her answers because they were important. And as I did, something about Juanita's word pushed at my consciousness, forcing me to listen to her carefully. TAKE.

They deemed me unfit because I veered from Fate's path.

On purpose? I asked.

Oh yes, she positively cackled. *My race was growing strong, fighting and amassing great power, taking down the weak, protecting the humans. The humans were aware that the tides had shifted and they paid me with their homage and prayers, and my power grew by unfathomable degrees. It was a wondrous time.*

It couldn't have been that wondrous if you died, I pointed out.

I did what I had to do. I have no regrets. Her voice was harsh.

You've got a captive audience here, and I'm dying to know what you did to piss off Fate.

Her magic was now intertwined inside every piece of me. We were one and I was hanging on by a thread. My wolf was the only reason we hadn't succumbed just yet. She was still fighting, trying to push Marinette back with everything she had. *I created you.*

I gasped. *Me? I was the reason you were killed?*

SHE IS YOU. The knowledge of Juanita's words dangled in front of me, needling me, begging me to understand.

Your predecessor, to be exact, Marinette spat. *The very same wolf who resides inside you now, who fights me even though you have already given up.* I didn't feel like I'd given up, but I was awful sleepy. I couldn't see my wolf in my mind any longer. Marinette had masked her from me. *Do you not wonder why you—and you alone—have two souls?*

I have two souls? I sputtered. I was equal parts thunderstruck and baffled by her admission. It was true, I could hold a conversation with my wolf, see her clearly in my mind as an individual. She was pushy and independent, but I'd never considered her as *separate*. I only had myself to go on, and I figured every wolf could communicate with their inner wolf like I could. But, come to think of it, I'd really never asked anyone.

Marinette laughed at my confusion. *Yes, your wolf is separate, of her own mind, unlike your Pack mates. She was actually created with a piece of my very own soul, bred to be the most powerful wolf on the planet. Your predecessor was my greatest achievement, as well as my undoing. Once they found out what I had done, the Hags were only able to kill my living body because my soul was halved. It is also the reason why your body cannot fight me now. Inside you resides my existence, and I've finally come back to retrieve what's mine, like a mother to her child.*

Realization dawned on me with crushing clarity.

My wolf had been created so this greedy goddess, my creator, could rule the supernatural world through her. Marinette's hasty actions had probably led to the necessity of a supernatural Coalition—which had been made up of powerful *females*— females who had likely come into existence to keep what Marinette had created in check.

Yes. Marinette fed on my mind. She knew my thoughts without me having to project them. *Up until then every supernatural had been male. We were only allowed to create males to ensure that humans would remain essential.* Her voice held disdain for what she likely considered the lesser race. *The male races had been cre-ated by magic, fed by Fate, and manifested by the gods and goddesses. But as my valiant Sect, powerful and hungry, fought for their right-ful place at the top, they began to falter. The vampires and the fae were gaining leverage and I was forced to do something critical, so I created something that would be a game changer for the supernatural world and everything in it.*

And one female wolf did all that? It was clear to me my creator suffered from delusions of grandeur, but I knew she wasn't alone in this mind-set. If she hadn't done it, another god or goddess would've done something similar, all to gain the perceived upper hand.

I pictured a lone female wolf forced to battle all the races herself and shuddered.

No, not just a female, Marinette corrected me. *A female cre-ated from my flesh and bones. Created by my blood—my very soul! She would be mine in every way, connected to me for all time, and with that strength used together we would become the ruler of all the races—the single strongest supernatural anyone had ever seen.* Her words echoed what Lili had said in the Underworld. The quest for supreme power.

I struggled to respond to Marinette, to keep her talking. *I shouldn't have to point out to you that the supernatural races wouldn't survive by a rule of one. It would've brought more chaos and more fighting. By creating me, you single-handedly brought about the demise of humans and supernaturals alike. Fate knew that.*

They were blind! she shrieked in my mind. *They could not see the vision that was right within their grasp.*

Oh, I think they saw it just fine, I responded. *That's why they killed you and created more females—entire female races like the witches, to turn Fate back on to its original path.*

TAKE.

Juanita's word filtered through my mind again and again.

TAKE.

Take what? I still don't understand. I called to Juanita in my mind.

Marinette thought my words were for her and replied, *Of course you don't understand. I take what I want.* Her voice shook with rage. *And I will not be denied this time.*

This time? A spasm of understanding overtook me.

TAKE. DON'T FIGHT.

Oh my gods. I finally understood. *Your powerful female wolf creation disobeyed you, didn't she! She had your soul inside her, but she wasn't you. You didn't have the control you dreamed you'd have, because she had a mind of her own. That's why you died. She ultimately sided with Fate!*

Fury boiled in my bloodstream, heating my freezing veins for a precious second. *You know nothing! Fate corrupted her so they could kill me. Now I will exact my revenge. I created the most powerful being the world had ever seen. Now I will* become *the most powerful being.* She blew through my body, her magic so cold it made me ache once more.

But she couldn't take hold.

My wolf was still fighting her.

TAKE. DON'T FIGHT.

Your signature is almost the same color as my own, I said. *It's yellow, though it's a darker shade than mine.*

That matters not. Soon all the magic in your body will be mine.

Her signature was yellow, same as mine.

TAKE.

Dawning washed over me. I sent out a silent prayer to Juanita that this was what I had to do. *WE HAVE TO STOP FIGHT-ING HER!* I yelled to my wolf. *WE HAVE TO ABSORB HER MAGIC.* I tore through my mind, trying to find my wolf. A new batch of adrenaline raced through me, bolstering me. I heard her bark. *Do it now! Stop fighting and grab on to her magic.*

You cannot wrestle my magic from me. It's impossible—

My blood warmed by a few degrees as another bark sounded in my mind. My wolf had heard me and was doing what I asked. *Yes!* I urged her. *Let it become a part of us. LET GO!* My wolf howled in response and my temperature began to rise in earnest. Marinette's amber signature began to undulate. My wolf threw the magic she had kept close at the stream, and I watched it collide, coming together with Marinette's, the two yellows melding, becoming brighter.

This can't happen! Marinette raged. *You are not strong enough to do such a thing!*

It has nothing to do with strength or power, I said. *My wolf is simply taking her just deserts.*

What are you talking about? I owe her nothing!

Oh, on the contrary. You created her with half, but she deserves the whole.

Impossible!

No, Marinette. You made a mistake by infiltrating us. This is what Juanita was leading us toward the entire time! You hand delivered exactly what we needed—what Fate wanted—to finally set things to right after all these years. Your soul. The half we need to make my wolf complete, what she should've received from you from the beginning. You made an error thinking you would be the victor, that your half was stronger—but clearly it's not. You were never going to win. We just had to stop fighting you. I was waking internally now and could see my wolf. She had her muzzle up, howling her joy. My body opened up in a rush as my magic absorbed Marinette's amber signature as quickly as it could, melding with it like Marinette had stated—like mother to child. It was a homecoming.

I cannot die this way, Marinette screamed, her voice fading fast. *I am immortal!*

I had no idea if she was actually dying in the classic sense. My guess was that she would snap out of existence once my wolf took her soul. That had been the only thing tethering her as a spirit all these years—she'd told us that already. If she lingered after, that would be a very bad thing. My wolf snarled her agreement, both of us on the same wavelength. As my magic swallowed up Marinette, I felt euphoric.

You may be able to take my magic, but you cannot have my soul, Marinette whispered in my mind, trying to tear free of our grasp. My body temperature began to cool slightly as she fought against us.

We might have to rip it from her once and for all, I told my wolf. *Can you connect it to yours and take it completely?* I couldn't see Marinette's soul in a physical sense, but I knew my wolf could. She began to snarl and keen, a high-pitched sound that brought tears to my eyes. Her voice was strong and determined. She was calling to her other half, that piece of her she'd been yearning for all this time. It was a beautiful cry, and our magic jumped in response.

I knew then why I was different.

Not only why I was a female, but also why I could partially change. This was the reason my wolf acted like an Alpha. I was a part of two halves. My wolf had brought her own legacy to me, and together we'd made one completely unique supernatural. Marinette had created her all those years ago, but I'd brought her new life. And in this one, she would be whole.

Marinette's soul answered my wolf's call, and with a huge rush of power, it coalesced inside of us with a big snap. For a single moment, my body felt like it was engulfed in flames. My chest rose and I cried out.

Then power exploded all around us in one huge surge.

17

I opened my eyes. Marcy stood over me, hands on her hips. "Way to go, champ. You just blew this place to smithereens."

I lifted my head slightly and ran my hands through my hair, sliding them to my temples, and rubbed. I couldn't feel a trace of Marinette inside me anywhere. *Do you sense her, or is she gone?* I asked my wolf. She barked happily. I took that as a sign that the goddess was gone for good.

Then I heard a roar.

"Rourke?" I croaked as I sat up. "Are they here?" I asked Marcy, my throat still sore.

Marcy ignored my question, her face a mask of both fear and frustration. "You looked dead, you know"—she tapped her foot—"and you weren't breathing. And your body was totally blue. Your eyes were open and they were vacant and spooky and covered in a white film. Then all of a sudden there was a gigantic popping noise and all the wards exploded. You scared the tar out of me! Then I thought the loa would be ejected or there would be some sort of shift in magic, and once it was over she would be you and dominate us all"—Marcy peered down at me—"but she didn't come out, did she?"

I grinned up at my concerned friend and simply said, "I love you too."

"You scared me senseless. That wasn't funny."

"I know, and I'm sorry. That wasn't my intention. And, Marcy, I promise to tell you everything you want to know, but we have to get out of here first." The ground beneath us began to shake. Now that the wards were gone, the makeshift island that had housed the bokor for so long was crumbling apart.

"You're right, we do have to get out of here." She glanced around her, making a face. "Water is already seeping in."

"Where are Danny and Naomi?" I asked, rubbing the back of my neck.

"I am here, *Ma Reine*," Naomi said, almost too quietly for me to hear.

My body responded to the sound of sorrow in her voice and I jumped to my feet and began to run. Naomi was awake, sitting behind one of the totem poles, the flora on her shoulder bright red.

She cradled Danny in her arms. He was still in his wolf form.

Marcy came up behind me. "I sort of gave her my blood, because I didn't know what else to do. You were playing dead and none of my spells worked. And wouldn't you know it, she woke right up."

The anguish in Naomi's eyes brought me to my knees in front of her. Danny's listless body was draped in her arms, dwarfing her slim figure. Blood tears ran in rivulets down her face. She bowed her head and said, "He is gone."

Her words shot to my core.

She spoke the truth, but I didn't want to believe it—couldn't believe it. Instead, I plowed my hands into his fur and frantically sent power rushing into his body, searching for any signs of life, and for his connection to me as Alpha so I could help him. But I couldn't find the bond anywhere.

There was a void where he should have been.

He was dead.

I angled my head up to the sky and raged, screaming, my hands fisted at my sides.

"Jessica!" Rourke shouted in response. "We're almost there. Hold on!" The realm was evaporating quickly. The natural environment was taking over, setting things to rights.

Marcy touched my shoulder. "I'm so sorry," she whispered. "But, Jess, we have to get out of here. We need to get to the airboats before this area is submerged. All the black magic buildup over all these years will have lingering effects, none of which we want to encounter. It's silly to stay."

My body shook where I sat. "We're not leaving him." My voice broke. "I refuse to leave him here."

"*Non*, we will not leave him." Naomi's voice was filled with sadness. "I will take him."

I fought to control my emotions. My battle with Marinette had taken too long. I had no idea how long I'd been out, but it was too late. I'd lost him. Danny had tried his best to protect me and he'd run out of time. I let it happen. "Naomi, his wolf form is too big for you to handle on your own. I'll carry him out."

Rourke broke through the deteriorating circle right as Ray landed in front of us. Rourke crossed the expanse in no time. Then his hands were on me, helping me to my feet. "What's going on?" he asked. I couldn't speak. "Jessica, what's happened here?" He glanced down at Naomi and Danny.

"Um"—Marcy cleared her voice behind me—"we lost Danny. He was poisoned with the bokor's curse and he...just ran out of time."

Ray walked over to Naomi and bent down to look at Danny. Naomi immediately tensed, tightening her hold on her mate.

"It's okay," Ray told Naomi, his voice quiet and soothing. "I'm not going to hurt him. I just want to take a look."

I turned to Rourke, resting my forehead against his chest. "His bond to me has vanished," I murmured. "I can't feel him any longer. He's dead."

"It's true," Ray added. "He's gone. He's not breathing and his heart isn't beating. All his functions have shut down."

I lifted my head off of Rourke as Naomi eased Danny onto the ground in front of her. Right then my father and his wolves entered the circle.

My father's voice boomed over the quietness. "What's going on here?"

"Danny is gone," I answered.

My father came forward and bent on one knee, his hand going into Danny's fur to check. "Well, he certainly isn't breathing, but he's still in his wolf form"—my father glanced up, meeting my gaze—"but wolves always shift back to human when they die."

Naomi nodded. "He just passed. I am certain he will shift soon."

Her quiet fortitude rocked me and I had to tamp down my anguish once again. If she could handle herself with such grace, I had to do the same. I moved to her side and took her hand while we all waited for Danny to change back.

Ray shook his head, regret in his voice. "What a loss. And there was nothing I could do. It's clear he was cursed, but I didn't see anything to get rid of inside him. It's not like it was with Jessica's father. There's nothing to take out, but his soul is hanging on by a thread, so go figure."

"What do you mean there's no curse? There has to be," I sputtered. "That's what killed him!"

"Nope, his body is clean," Ray said. "No curse."

I cried as I broke away from Naomi's grasp and plunged my hands into Danny's fur once again, pouring my power into him, searching for Marinette's magic.

Ray was right.

The curse was nowhere in sight. But that couldn't be right. How could it have disappeared?

Rourke stood behind me, and my father moved in next to me, putting his hands on Danny's head. "Jessica," my father addressed me. "I know this is hard for you. Losing a wolf always is. Daniel Walker was bonded to you. Because of that, I cannot help him. But he's still in his wolf form. I'm not saying it will work, but there might be a chance. Try to save him if you can."

"I'm trying"—tears rushed down my face—"but his bond to me is broken. I can't feel anything. I'm transferring my power to him and he's not waking up. His heart is not beating."

"Jessica." Rourke knelt down next to me. "We all know you're doing your best. Keep trying, we have time—not a lot, but we can spare a few more moments. There might be something we're missing."

"I'm trying to find it," I said miserably, "but there's nothing here." *Do you sense anything? What killed him?* I asked my wolf.

Tyler burst into the clearing. "Hey," he yelled, "water is filling this place up like a bathtub and there are more than a few gators out there that seem interested. We have to get going. I sent some wolves back out to gather the boats and come around to this side—" He stopped dead in his tracks. I knew the instant he figured out what had happened. "No. He can't be dead. It's not possible." He dropped to his knees beside me, as Rourke moved to make room, his eyes furious. "Why aren't you helping him?" he accused. "He's not dead! He can't be dead. You have to fix this! You're his Alpha, for chrissake."

Grief wound its way through my heart. Tyler was right. I'd let Danny down. I was his Alpha and I'd sent him here on his own to fight a battle he couldn't win.

My father responded for me. "We are doing all we can. Jessica is pouring power into him right now. He's unresponsive, and has been for some time."

"I'm so sorry, Tyler." I bowed my head. "I don't know how else to help him. He was like this when I woke up."

"Woke up from what?" Tyler asked. "What the hell happened in here?"

Marcy stepped in when I didn't answer. "In a very basic nutshell," she said, "we were pulled into this realm on purpose. Once we found the bokor, she was trying to drain Naomi's magic, and she'd already cursed Danny. We both battled her and the loa with spells, which worked in the short term." Marcy's voice held her distress. "But then Jessica got bit by a rabid wolf, and from what I could surmise—once I woke up from my spell—the loa, who was actually Marinette, the powerful goddess of werewolves, had drained the bokor of all her power, killing her, and then entered Jessica's body. I woke up and thought Jessica was dead—I mean she looked totally dead—but then she blew this place apart and woke up. The loa hasn't been back since."

I glanced up at Marcy. "Wait a minute. I *looked* dead. But I obviously wasn't. Was I breathing?"

"Um, I don't think so. That's part of the reason I thought you were dead, duh," Marcy said.

"Then that's the same as Danny. You said my eyes were filmy, right?" Every one of our gazes shot down to Danny as my hands flew to one of his eyes. The lids were closed, but I gently pried one of them open.

There was a thick, filmy coating covering it. "I don't know what this means," I cried, feeling hope for the first time, "but while the loa was inside me, she told me that the curse was actually her blood, which I took to mean her magic signature. I don't feel her magic in Danny right now, but her magic had to go somewhere when I killed her, right?" I looked up, my eyes wide. "Right?"

"Jess, we have no idea what the hell you're talking about—but whatever it is, just do it!" Tyler yelled. "Even if he's dead," my brother choked, "we have to get rid of whatever is left in him so he can shift back and we can bury him properly."

I felt numb as I ran my hands over Danny's coat, pushing more power into him, searching to see what was wrong, praying like crazy I could fix this.

"You can do it, Hannon," Ray coached from the sidelines. "His soul is still there. It hasn't left yet."

It wasn't until I felt Rourke's hands on my shoulders that I finally took a much-needed breath. He infused calm into me as he said, *It's okay, Jess. Danny's death is not your fault. We all know the risks we take in battle, and we take them willingly. If Danny had been given a choice, and he knew what the outcome would be, he would do it again without pause.*

I know, but that doesn't make this any easier to take. I took in another labored breath and focused my power on Danny, seeking to find what was wrong. If there was a way to save him, I had to find it.

After several minutes of trying with no results, Naomi broke the silence. "I believe this is Fate's plan, *Ma Reine*." Her voice was solemn. "Even if it is hard for us to accept, we must. We will grieve, but in the end, he would not want us to—"

"Wait!" Something caught my attention. *Do you see that?* I asked my wolf. *Our magic signature is back to our sunlight color. When did that happen?* I hadn't noticed the change. When we battled Marinette, it had been a muddy amber.

She barked and shook her head.

As she did, I immediately noticed she was clearer in my mind, sharper than ever before. She had beautiful thick, inky fur and she radiated power. I was in awe of her for a moment. She had become her own entity.

"Jessica?" Tyler asked. "What's going on?"

I shook my head. "I'm sorry. I can't sense anything in Danny with my power alone. I'm going to have to send my magic in." I glanced up at the group. "But I'm worried my magic will be toxic to him"—there was no way for me to explain quickly how my signature had changed once again—"and instead of the possibility of finding something lingering from the curse, it might be enough to give him a true death."

"Hannon," Ray said in a gentle tone, "he's essentially dead already. Whatever you do is not going to be *more* harmful to him. Go ahead and use your magic. This is the only way to settle this, one way or another. It must to be done."

I nodded. Ray was right. We had no other options.

Naomi's hand settled over mine. "I believe in you, *Ma Reine*. He cannot remain like this. He must die a true death or wake from whatever it is that's holding him, but in my heart I don't believe you will kill him with your magic, as he has a piece of you inside himself already."

She was referring to the blood we'd swapped, but that made me realize something incredibly important. "Naomi, I don't think my blood has anything to do with this, but he did have something in him already—Marinette's magic!" I exclaimed excitedly. "I might know how this happened, but I'm not sure I can fix it. The only thing I can do is try." A flicker of hope ignited inside me as I spread my hands across Danny's flank.

"What are you talking about, Jess?" my brother asked. "What does the magic have to do with anything?"

"I think he's in the same state I was in a few minutes ago—but only because we both had Marinette's signature inside us when I defeated her. The whole theory of magic being, it has to go somewhere."

Naomi shook her head. "I don't understand."

"It's just a hunch, but if Danny was *alive* when I took Marinette's soul it means I caused his current state by killing her"—I gestured down at his limp body—"but if he was already dead, I don't think I can save him," I answered truthfully.

"So you think you blew up Marinette's magic inside his body?" Ray asked.

I nodded. "Something like that. The curse was eating him alive when I defeated her, and when it exploded, this might have happened. Maybe he's in a form of stasis from the shock?" My voice rose in excitement. "Marcy said I blew up the wards, which were hers. Well, the magic in his body must have done something equally as big. Now I just have to figure out what—and try to undo it."

"*Oui*," Naomi replied, a hesitant smile on her face. "If there is life inside him, I know you can find it."

I buried my hands firmly in Danny's fur and murmured, "Come on, Daniel Walker. Let's do this." I grabbed on to my magic and began to push it inside him, careful to go slow. My magic felt strong and heady, and once it hit Danny's system, it took off on its own, rushing through his body too quickly for me to control. *We have to pull it back!* I shouted at my wolf. *It's too much—*

It hit something.

I watched in awe as my golden signature broke apart, each color bursting alive at the junction of his brain and spine. *What is it doing?* I asked. Each piece of magic seemed to have a different task to do. The base of the neck was a key connection point for all wolves. One that decided life and death. A broken neck meant there was no communication from the brain to the body. *Is that Marinette's signature lingering there?* It was hard to tell because it was so faint. It was possible when the curse exploded inside him that it had done major damage to his spine—damage Danny couldn't repair because the connection points had been too badly injured. But if the tiniest bit of her residual magic had hung on, he had a chance. It had kept him from dying completely.

As my magic separated, it began to try to heal the damage. All at once there was a popping sound and Danny's body thrummed below mine. I fed him continuous magic until I swayed.

"Jessica," Rourke said. "It's time to pull back."

"Yeah," Ray added. "Easy does it, tiger."

When I let go of him, I felt drained, my magic snapping back into my body in a rush. I fell to the side, exhausted by the effort. "Danny, I hope that was enough."

Then I closed my eyes.

18

A moment later, a wet tongue lashed up my face. My eyes sprung open. I was so relieved to see Danny awake I threw my arms around his neck. He began to shift back into human form immediately and Rourke helped me up. We all took a few steps back to give Danny some space.

Except Naomi.

She remained locked into place beside him. She wasn't going to leave him easily.

"Let's give them some room," Ray said, ushering us backward. "They're going to need some privacy so they can...you know... bond or something."

"They're not going to bond right here," Marcy tsked. "But I agree. Let's give them some space. Hey, speaking of mates, has anyone seen mine?"

"I'm sorry, Marcy. I forgot to let you know. I left him in charge of keeping things clear on the outside. We didn't know what we would find in here or if this bokor had called in backup," my father answered. "I just summoned him. He should be here shortly, and he'll be very happy to see you unharmed."

"That's good to know. And you don't fool me one bit, Callum. He would've been of no use to you in here if I were in trouble. It's smart to keep us apart if you want your second in command to act like a second. I wholeheartedly agree with your choices and hope you keep it that way. But now I need a little mate fix." Marcy dusted off her hands. "It's been a hell of a day."

Instead of being offended, my father tossed his head back and laughed. "You've got a good head on you, witch. James is a lucky man."

I turned to walk away and give Naomi and Danny some space, but she rose and moved forward, grabbing my hand. Her eyes were filled with emotion. I swallowed as she said, "I had no doubt that you could help him if it was within your power. I thank you from the bottom of my soul. I am grateful I am going to get a chance to get to know my... mate, and it happened because of you."

"There's absolutely no need to thank me, Naomi," I replied. "If any one of us could've saved him, we would have. We love Danny and we're all happy to see the two of you together." Naomi had a yearning in her eyes I'd never seen. Danny was almost done shifting, most likely needing more time since he'd just been on the brink of death. "Go be with him, Naomi." I nudged her forward. "You two deserve it. But you'll only have moments before we have to leave."

I turned to join Rourke and Tyler and we started to walk to where the boats were waiting. "What's up?" I asked Tyler, whose face was lined with worry, as I linked one arm through his elbow and one through Rourke's. It felt so good to have my family back, and for the next five seconds not feel like the world was going to crumble.

"I've been close to Danny since the day I turned into a wolf," Tyler answered. "He's been my friend and mentor all this time. But it never crossed my mind he could die—or that any of us could die, for that matter. We're *supernatural*. This is not supposed to happen." He turned to meet my gaze. "Honestly, Jess, I miss the lake. I miss my home. I miss running through the woods not thinking about anything other than the freedom to run as long as I want." He ran his free hand around the back of his neck. "This battle is going to be tough and sometimes it feels like no matter how long we keep fighting, we're never going to get back to normal."

"I hear you, Tyler," I said, understanding his position completely. What he didn't realize was that while he might be able to go back to normal—and I was desperately hoping that was going to happen for him—my old normal was no longer an option for me. "I think all the wolves will get back to normal eventually, but for me, I'd settle for a new normal that didn't include being under constant attack or running from the next threat."

Rourke slid his hand around my waist. "I'd settle for getting the hell out of the Everglades. My beast is restless. We circled this island no less than twenty times and couldn't find a way in. I want us as far away from here as possible."

"We're almost to the boats," Tyler said. "I hear the motors."

We picked our way through the trees. Marcy was in front of us, my father and a few of his wolves in front of her. My father stopped short and turned. "We'll head back to our camp first before we depart this place," he called. "I want to go over what happened in detail. It looks as though you killed the remaining rabid wolves. I'm leaving a few of my wolves behind to make sure their bodies are destroyed. Once my wolves arrive back at camp, we leave."

I said, "Did you see the wolf the bokor sacrificed for the ceremony? We stopped her before she could steal Naomi's magic and place it in a fetish, but we were too late to save him."

"We have him," my father said gruffly. "Two of my wolves have already taken him away. I'll send another airboat once we get back. That particular wolf was from the Southern Territories. I didn't know him that well, but he was loyal to me in the short time he was part of my Pack. When I killed Redman Martin, a few of his wolves joined us—very few, since most of them were traitorous, just like their Alpha. But this wolf was decent. I'll make sure he's given a proper burial."

If I never saw another cypress, I'd be a happy girl. "I'm glad Redman is gone. I'm assuming the wolves of his who chose not to assimilate with your Pack went to the fracture pack and were dealt with."

My father stopped ahead of us, reaching the channel. "Yes. The fracture pack is no more. There wasn't a strong wolf among them."

The airboats were a welcome sight.

"We're getting out of here as soon as possible," Rourke said in my ear. "I think the safest plan we have is to head home and search for Juanita. If she's there, she'll have answers."

"I have a lot to tell you, but Marinette, the powerful spirit I battled, called Juanita a Hag. We'd only guessed before, but now we have confirmation."

My father turned to me. "Are you positive?"

I nodded once. "Yes."

Tyler was the first one to hop into an airboat and gestured us down. "I never would've guessed it, Jess," he mused. "Juanita was so...normal. And she had no signature whatsoever, at least that I ever detected, and that's saying something because I can pick up on almost anything with this." Tyler touched his nose. He did have a killer sense of smell.

"Hags are among the most powerful of any supernatural," Rourke said as he helped me into one of the boats. "She would be able to cloak herself well. I've never met her, so I don't know if I would've picked up on it or not, but I'd like to think I would have." He grinned. "But it's unlikely."

"You're going to love her," I said. "She's a piece of work in the best way possible."

"James!" Marcy shrieked.

James emerged from the trees and made his way along the edge of the channel at top speed. Marcy's face was bright with happiness, and I knew the feeling. She rushed toward him and he growled his greeting. It must have killed him to stay out here, but my father had been smart.

I sat down in the front seat of the boat, Rourke next to me. My father was in the row behind with two of his wolves.

"We're not waiting for the lovebirds," Tyler said as he took the driver's seat. "They can wait for Naomi and Danny." Tyler shouted a command to another wolf to wait for the two couples and we took off.

As we sped away, I glanced back. The dead trees, which were revealed once the wards came down, stood in stark contrast to the green ones around us. "Did anyone see what happened to the old cabin?"

My father grunted. "The swamp has already taken it. I'm not worried that humans will venture in here to investigate any time soon. The pall of evil and malice will linger for a while. It will only clear up once new growth and animals start to inhabit the space again."

"Speaking of evil and animals," I said. "What about her snakes and gators? I hope they all disappeared."

"They're all gone," Tyler called over the fan. "When you blew the place up, I watched one wither away instantly. It was cool as hell, like a slo-mo video, nothing but old, rotted bones left over. There are, however, lots of gators lingering on the outside of her boundary, attracted by the noise and action. But they were real, not possessed."

It was funny to me that we'd be happy to see live gators after all this. But it was the truth.

I woke, gasping.

The dream had been so real. Marinette stood on another rocky crag, her face full of anger and rage, and as I watched, she turned to face me, morphing slowly into Lili, her hair changing, growing longer, her gold dress becoming the one Lili had worn in the Underworld. The one with demon glyphs that shimmered when she moved. On top of her head a crown, covered in serpents, appeared. Lili's eyes were alight with pain. She said four words to me: "It will be you."

"What is it?" Rourke was up next to me instantly, his arms pulling me tightly against his chest. His heart was beating fast, no doubt wondering if I was going to disappear on him again.

We'd all been up late, talking into the night. We'd gone over the implications of everything that had happened to me—both in the Underworld and with Marinette. I told them the loa had been our maker, the patron goddess of werewolves, who had been killed, but her spirit had endured, holding on with half a soul. It'd been a shock for everyone to hear, but once I explained what she'd told me about her connection to my wolf, and how she'd made her, it had been easier for everyone to digest.

What was done was done. There was no going back now.

We were leaving this place at first light and I couldn't wait.

"I'm okay." I rubbed my fingers over his beautiful tattoos.

"I just had a very realistic dream about the evil ladies in my life. I guess when you become a killer, you have to deal with the fall-out. No getting around it." I snuggled deeper into his body for warmth. "Having blood on my hands is not easy for me. It still feels very strange. I know ending Lili's life was necessary, and my job moving forward with the Coalition will require me to do things like that, but it's going to take me some time to adjust. Marinette didn't even have a body, but knowing I ended her existence makes it tough."

He kissed my temple. "It gets easier," he murmured, sliding his lips down my neck. "You have to look at it as a necessary evil or it plays with your mind. What you did when you killed Lili saved thousands of lives, possibly hundreds of thousands. Lili was a threat to the human race, as well as the supernatural. It had to be done. But you spared Selene, so I believe you're already finding a balance. I think with you, there will always be balance and we're luckier for it."

"I can only hope," I said. "As the Enforcer, my job criteria will only get more intense, but I'm glad I have you by my side. There is no one better to help me through it than you."

He turned me in his arms so I faced him. "Jessica"—he leaned in for a lingering kiss—"I will happily take whatever burdens I can from you. That's my primary focus from now on—that and protecting you, which has been hard to do when you keep disappearing," he growled. "But you don't have to do all the enforcing on your own. You have a team behind you, one that will stay by your side every step of this journey. No one is going anywhere."

I knew my team would go with me, but I didn't want to gyp them out of a normal life. "Do you think we have to live somewhere special once I take a seat on the Coalition?" I asked. "Like a remote castle built on an impenetrable fjord?"

Rourke tilted his head back and laughed. "No, I think with modern technology the remote castle on the fjord is no longer a requirement. Though the members do need solid protection. But I think this rebirth will be different. There's no way to keep the identity of the new members a secret. Times have changed too much for that, and I think it's for the best. That will allow us to rally around you openly and use your Pack for position and power. Every Sect will know where you belong, and if they mess with you, they mess with all of us. That will erase many threats before they even develop."

"You make it sound easy, like taking a corporate job at a firm. It's not going to be that smooth and you know it." I leaned up to nip his chin. "You're just trying to make sure I don't implode or have some serious PTSD once things get rolling."

"There might be some of that," he admitted, "but I don't think it's going to be harder than what we've gone through thus far. Think of it like this. You've been in a Coalition boot camp, so to speak, and once you take your official seat, you'll be ready. We'll look at this like a new job. We'll be together, you'll have your friends and family around you, and each step will bring us closer to our main goal—"

"Which is peace, I hope?" I asked. "That's what I want. I want the supernatural race to take a few minutes and breathe." I knew there would be trouble at the start with supernatural challenges to the new reign of power, but after a few years I was hoping that the Coalition would use their power to quell the unrest and create some kind of peaceful state—at least for a while.

"I think that's an achievable goal," he said. "Once the dust settles, I'm hoping, like you, that there will be a period of calm for us."

"I'll do whatever it takes to keep that peace once we have it," I said. "I can almost taste the victory, and it's delicious." I snuggled into his chest.

"You have to remember, it's in the nature of supernaturals to fight." His chest rumbled in his low bass. "I'm certain it won't be calm forever, but my guess is this new Coalition will be the most powerful one to date. That will give us a decided advantage and likely buy us big chunks of peace."

"Why do you think it will be the most powerful?" I asked, bringing my hand up to stroke his face, loving the feel of stubble under my fingertips.

"Because you're on it," he said simply. "I can feel the swell of magic inside you. You have tremendous power. Not to mention Eudoxia, who is not only a powerful vampire, but also fae. I see the Coalition members coming in with their root abilities and having a mix of power—almost like hybrids. And once you all share your magic, you will be unstoppable."

"Do you think I have more power than you now?" I teased.

"Much more. And it's raw. Jessica, you vibrate with strength. It's amazing. It's unbelievable to me that you have no idea how strong you are." He grinned as he slanted his lips over mine.

I took his kiss greedily.

I broke from him, panting lightly. He tasted wonderful. "I know I have power, I can feel the concentrated magic in my body, but my wolf is in control of it. Now that I know she's her own being, I trust her to deal with it, and because of that—and that alone—it allows me to feel more normal. Even after all of this. Without her, I don't think I could do this. I really don't."

Rourke lay back and brought me with him, rolling me on top of him, his arms crushing me in their grasp. "You are perfect, you know that? You are handling this," he murmured, "with your wolf. You're a team, like we're a team. I've never heard of a shifter and their beast being separate, sharing one body. Mine is very much a part of me—an extension of myself. I have feelings and lots of animal instincts that rear up inside me without warning, but it's still just me. It makes us decidedly different, but I like that. I think having your wolf separate will keep you levelheaded and able to make good, solid decisions in a stressful time. That's an asset."

"It's strange, because I don't feel separate from her. I still consider her 'my wolf.' But having the knowledge that we're different, each with our own soul, makes it easier moving forward. I felt that immediately. It lessens any competition for control on my end when it comes to supernatural issues. I can trust her to think for herself, and she knows a lot more than I do, and there's no way to put a price on that. But we still don't agree when it comes to my human issues. Her tendencies are decidedly supernatural, mine are not, and I'm not willing to give up my control on that. I will keep my humanness, whatever happens."

"It makes sense you'd push back on that and hold your ground, and, Jess, your humanness is what makes you who you are. Your wolf will come to see that. And even though she might be irritated with you, she will respect you for it in the end."

"She might, grudgingly." I laughed. "I already feel like we understand each other better and it's only been a handful of hours since it happened—"

"*Ma Reine*." Naomi's voice was quiet in the darkness but I jumped nonetheless. "We are sorry to bother you, but we must have a word."

19

"Well, we're not exactly *sorry* to interrupt you, per se," Danny added as I scrambled to stand, Rourke right behind me, a very low chuckle rumbling under his breath, "but I am, however, apologetic it's the middle of the night. See, we heard you chatting, even though you were doing your best to be quiet, and my girl and I"—his face broke into a huge grin as he beamed at Naomi—"would like your permission to get the hell out of here."

"But only if that's okay," Naomi added hastily. "We know you will need us, but in light of what happened, we were hoping—"

"—with me almost losing my life and such," Danny interjected smoothly, "we decided we have some catching up to do. And here"—he glanced around the planking and the trees—"is not the bloody place to do it." He cleared his throat. "The kind of catching up we need to do is of a delicate nature." Then he winked.

Rourke started to laugh openly and Naomi stiffened.

She blushed so hard, it resonated in the moonlight. I slapped Rourke on the chest with the back of my hand and inclined my head. "I hope Naomi is well aware that she's going to have her hands full with you, Daniel Walker. And of course you can leave. You have my permission to get out of here ASAP. We're going to be heading back at first light, and we'll meet you at home."

Danny replied, "Oh, Naomi knows what she's in for, and she's told me herself she's in."

"He speaks frankly," Naomi said. "I am definitely...invested. But our duty to you comes first. We would not leave you knowingly in danger, but if you feel you are safe for a time, we would appreciate a few days away."

"Well, let's not be hasty. It could take weeks to complete the—" Danny said.

Naomi elbowed him in the ribs and he smiled like he'd just won the lottery.

"Of course, take your time. You two deserve it," I said. "We'll rendezvous at home. If anything happens, I'll get word to you. Check the Pack phones daily."

"We will, *Ma Reine*." Naomi's face broke into a wide grin. "I swear to it."

Danny moved forward and took my hand, surprising me. "There's just one more thing I must do before I leave." He knelt down on one knee in front of me. "You are blood-bonded to my mate already, and we were bonded as well, until my untimely semi-death wiped the troth away. I would swear another one to you right now before we leave. Before all gathered here, I choose you, Jessica McClain, to be my Alpha. I was meant to serve you, and you alone, and I will continue to do so until I take my last dying breath." He put his other hand over his heart.

"Well done, Daniel." My father strode toward us from the other sleeping area. I knew the entire camp had heard our conversation. He turned to me. "Daniel Walker is unfaltering in his loyalty to you, and that's the best kind of ally you can have. As we move forward, my dream is to have an army of wolves who are loyal to you, and who will swear an oath to protect you at all costs."

Tyler walked up, his hair tousled from sleep. "I'm keeping my allegiance to you, too, Jess, and any wolf who doesn't like it can answer to me."

My father nodded his agreement. I glanced between my brother and my father and smiled, feeling proud to call them family. Danny still had my hand. He gave it a small tug. "Shall we get on with it, then?" he asked. The look on his face was so serene and content, it made me smile. It was hard to believe we'd almost lost him.

I nodded and Rourke handed me a knife, which I gave to Danny. "You'll have to go first. I heal too quickly, so this might be a challenge," I said.

"Happily," he answered as Naomi moved to stand behind him. She looked as joyful as I'd ever seen her. Her loyalty to me was absolute and I knew she and Danny were going to make perfect partners.

I remembered the words for the troth and had no need for a prompt this time. I projected my voice as I started, "Of my mind and body, I ask thee, Daniel Walker. Do you pledge of me freely?"

Danny slashed his palm, handing me the knife, and answered, "I pledge to you freely with body and soul."

I sliced my own hand in a long, deep gash, bringing it to his as fast as I could. "With the blood that mixes, it binds us together. You are my Pack and I am your Alpha." I barely had the words out when Danny was tossed backward violently, narrowly missing taking his mate with him. He smashed into a cypress tree, tangling in its roots. "Are you okay?" I gasped as I rushed over.

"Good gods, woman." Danny lay faceup, unmoving. "That was a killer dose. Your blood is much more potent than before." He lifted a fist and pumped it in the air. "I feel like I could rule a small country or quite possibly bench press a metric ton at the moment."

"Don't get ahead of yourself," Rourke muttered. "Let's start with obeying your Alpha first." I moved toward my mate and wrapped an arm around his waist, tugging him close. Our mate bond trumped all others, but me being tied to other wolves wasn't the best scenario for him. I reached up and gave him a kiss on the cheek and he growled his reply, a small grin on his lips. He knew he had me, heart and soul, but it was nice to show it to the world occasionally.

Tyler helped Danny off the ground by grabbing his wrist and hoisting him up. "That was pretty sweet," Tyler said, thumping him on the back once he was up. "No wolf is going to challenge you now."

"Why would they?" Danny answered gleefully as he moved over to Naomi and slung his arm around her shoulders. They already looked comfortable, like they'd always been a couple. "I've just become Jessica's second. That would be silly."

My eyebrows shot up my forehead. He was right. "You *are* my second," I said. "I can feel it. This time our connection is more powerful." James was my father's second in command—his most trusted wolf and the second most powerful in the Pack. James and Marcy were at the other camp for the night, or they'd be standing here with us. "How did that happen?"

"The oath this time was given freely by Daniel," my father answered. "And you weren't in extenuating circumstances like before. You are not his temporary Alpha—you are his permanent one. The bond is strong. I can sense it. The link of second comes automatically to the strongest wolf in the Pack. If you were to rebond with Tyler, I'm not sure—"

"No need for us to explore that option," Danny asserted, waving a hand in dismissal. "I like where I am just fine."

Tyler chuckled. "No need to worry, Danny. Jessica and I are bound in a totally different way. By blood and genetics first, Pack status second. If you remember, when we were in those mountains, I never gave Jessica an oath. We did exchange blood—and something definitely changed between us—but even if we swapped blood again and I actually swore my fealty to her, I don't think I'd be her second. I would be something completely separate. If that's something you want to explore"—he nodded his head at me—"we should think long and hard about the impact before we do it. But having Danny as your second is perfect. I couldn't choose a better wolf for the task." Tyler grinned.

"I now have a first and a second." I rested my head against Rourke's shoulder. No one could take the top spot away from Rourke. He was my protector in all things.

Naomi moved forward. "We will head out now, if it's still all right. But we will be in contact and will rendezvous with you when you arrive home."

"Yep," Danny added, taking her hand. "My bachelor pad could use a little pick-me-up. It'll be nice to be home."

"Safe travels to you both," I said. "After we try and connect with Juanita, the next order of business is finding Tally. It's a growing possibility that Ceres has her in Europe, and if that's the case, we're headed there immediately." The moonlight filtered into our small area, giving it a surreal effect, like we were all standing in the middle of a painting frozen in time. It was the early hours of the morning and my family surrounded me in the dark. I'd never felt safer.

"I will have a long talk with Julian when we get home," my father said. "He should know what's going on in his backyard, and once we're apprised and have support from him, we take action. Although I haven't always been in favor of an alliance with the witches, I cannot deny the role they play in your safety, Jessica.

We will ally with them, and if that means finding Tallulah and making sure things are set to right, so be it."

I nodded, agreeing with him. "We owe Tally," I said. "Without her, Tyler wouldn't be here." I didn't have to mention that James was now mated to Tally's niece, which made them blood kin.

"That's the best plan we've got, but let's not forget, our first priority is to get off this makeshift island," Tyler said. He turned to address Danny. "Are you going to just fly on out of here? Or take a boat?"

"Fly," Danny answered. "I enjoy flying, really. The wind in my hair, a beautiful woman with her arms wrapped tightly around me, gripping me in all the right places. It's quickly become my favorite method of transportation."

"You've only done it once that I know of," I said, chuckling. Naomi had flown him one time at the vamp headquarters. "And this is going to be a much longer journey. You might not love it as much as you think you do at the end."

"Oh, we're not flying straight through." He waggled his eyebrows at me. "I'm certain there will be plenty of pitstops, and I plan to thoroughly enjoy our flight time together as well." He turned toward Naomi. "Can you snog while you're flying, love?"

She elbowed him in the stomach, and then wrapped her arms around his middle, a slight grin playing on her lips. I'd bet money that she was going to be doing her fair share of snogging during the flight to make up for lost time. She turned to me. "Thank you, *Ma Reine*. We will see you soon." As they shot upward, Danny's shouts echoed on the air.

I snickered. "She's going to teach the boy a lesson or two he won't forget, guaranteed. I think they are a perfect pairing."

"I agree," Tyler said. "Never in a million years did I think I would, but seeing them together makes sense."

Amanda Carlson

My father grunted as he turned to go. "We leave at first light, which is only in a few hours from now. I'm going to get the wolves started on packing the boats now." I could tell he respected Naomi and loved Danny like a son, but that's all we were going to get from him. A wolf-vampire pairing was unprecedented.

Like everything else in my life. That's why it made perfect sense.

Tyler trailed after him, adding, "Get some sleep, why don't you? And no more talking. You can hear a pin drop in this godforsaken place."

"All I hear are the frogs. So many frogs," I joked as Rourke folded me into his arms. I turned into his chest and murmured, "Home will feel nice for us too. I can't wait." My apartment was still pretty bare, but I did have a bed.

"Waiting is not my strong suit," Rourke whispered, "but it looks like we have no other choice."

"Well, there might be a few other choices," I said as I leaned up and kissed him.

20

"You brang it back?" The shorter guide scratched his head like the concept was too much to process. "And you don't want no money for it?"

The airboat we'd purchased was already parked on top of the dock, and Rourke, Ray, Tyler, Nick, Marcy, James, and I stood there waiting for the guides to get over their shock. My father and the rest of his wolves had gone back to the place they'd purchased theirs from and were heading back home by plane. No one thought getting on an airplane with me was a wise plan, so we were going to rent a vehicle and drive home. We figured it would be safer that way.

"That's what I just finished telling you," Marcy answered. "The boat is yours, but on one condition."

"And what's that?" the taller guide asked, his voice indicating that he knew there was going to be a hitch.

"We need a vehicle. One that will carry all of us. And once we're gone, you saw nothing, you remember nothing." A little magic shot out of Marcy's fingertips as she said the last part and I knew she was insuring us with a spell.

Once we left, we'd fade from their memories altogether.

The taller guide sized her up for a second before he answered, glancing around our group, trying to read our inscrutable faces. He was clearly the more intelligent of the two. He saw his opportunity to gain back what he lost, and then some. "Deal." He drew a cell phone out of his overalls pocket. "My nephew Teddy might have what you need. He's got a few of them big old vans he takes gator tours in. I'll dial him up."

The shorter guide assessed us. "Well, the least we can do is get you some more of that moonshine fer your troubles. I don't see the jug in the boat, nor the guy who had it, so I'm 'ssuming that he enjoyed his drink."

I couldn't tell him we'd lost his precious hooch in a scuffle with a bunch of possessed snakes. "That'd be...nice of you," I said. Nothing like a jug or two of moonshine for the road. "And one more thing—if you hear any gossip in this area, or if any of the other guides start talking, we'd like you to assure them that everything is back to normal. No one is going to bother anyone here anymore. No more mysterious disappearances."

"Good to know," the taller guide said as he clicked off his phone. "The lot of you are welcome in these parts anytime. Free airboat rides for the family for life. Anythin' we can do, consider it done."

"Thanks, but we're not planning on coming back," my brother said. Then he whispered too low for him to hear, "At least not in your lifetime."

"Well, then, moonshine whenever you need it." He fished something out of his front pocket. "Just gimme a call. We ship anywhere in the world." Tyler took the card and grinned as he passed it to me.

It read:

JIMMY'S MOONSHINE
Better than yo' mama's moonshine.
We ship anywhere in the world.
www.jimmyshooch.com

"Thanks," I said, tucking the card away. "If we find a need for it, we'll be sure to get in touch with you."

We began to walk up the banks to a dirt road. Right as we got there a brightly colored van turned into the drive. The vehicle was orange with lime-green accents—which appeared to be hand-painted drawings of tall swamp grass with a few alligator heads poking out. The side was crudely printed with EVERGLADES TOURS. SEE DEM GATORS UP CLOSE.

"Good criminy," Ray muttered. "These people are beyond backwoods. They're so far back, they're only a step or two up from cavemen."

"They are quite...uncivilized, aren't they," Nick added. He had joined us this morning, and insisted on accompanying us home. He'd been relegated to watching over the camps during the takedown of Marinette and the priestess, which I knew had been my father's way of making sure he stayed safe. Nick was a fox, and if he'd been taken by the bokor, it would've ended very badly. My father loved him like a son, and even though I knew Nick was unhappy with my father's decision to keep him back, he didn't complain. That wasn't his style. "But they do have a certain charm."

"This must be what happens when you're born and raised in a swamp," I said. "But they deliver. We asked for a vehicle, and we got one within three minutes. Beggars can't be choosers."

"That thing looks like it's made of Legos, constructed in some kid's garage," Ray grumbled. "These guys don't have two brain cells to rub together."

"They're harmless," Rourke said. "And now they owe us. We brought their boat back, and that buys us considerable loyalty."

Ray shrugged. "It might, but what are they really going to do for us?"

I gestured toward the van. "That."

The driver got out of the car and Marcy reached in the window and honked the horn. "We're ready to go," she called. She'd been negotiating with Teddy since he'd arrived. He was supposed to be the tall guide's nephew, but he appeared to be older—considerably older. We walked toward the van. Marcy came around the front. "James is driving and I'm riding shotgun. Anyone complains, I don't give two hoots. I have to make a quick phone call before we head out so I can wire Teddy here some money for his beautiful van." She nodded toward Teddy, who with his long, grizzly beard had a ZZ Top vibe going.

Tyler made a show of inspecting the vehicle as Marcy borrowed a cell phone from the shorter guide to make the call. "Will it make it eighteen hundred miles?" he asked Teddy, skepticism in his voice.

"Sure 'nough," Teddy said as he spit on the ground in front of us. "This here van is sound. My twin brother, Glenn, is a mechanic." He patted the hood. "She's been rebuilt more than ten times. Won't be no issue for you."

Ten times? I hoped Marcy wasn't paying him much.

"Last rebuilt when?" my brother asked.

"Oh, about seven years ago," Teddy answered. "But that ain't no problem. He tinkers with it a lot."

Before my brother could tell him off, I held up my hand. "Thank you for bringing it over so quickly. I'm sure it'll get us home just fine. If it doesn't, we'll cope." I turned to Tyler. "And here I didn't think anything could trump the bright yellow Hummer *you* bought for us. Looks like you and Teddy have similar taste in vehicles, and I'm sure Glenn did a great job on the most recent rebuild."

"That Hummer was built to withstand a war. This thing smells like it burns oil and gas every time the tires spin," Tyler countered, irritated with me. "And that many rebuilds means its engine has parts from fifty different vehicles. It'll be a miracle if we can limp back home in this piece of sh—"

"Done." Marcy clapped her hands as she gave the cell phone back to Shorty and turned to the vehicle owner. "Teddy, the money is in your account. You can go check if you don't trust me. We'll take it from here."

"Oh, I know you're good for it, Red," he said, tossing the keys to James, who was heading for the driver's side. "Just like my uncle's boat, feel free to bring it back anytime." He winked and grinned at his own joke. I think we'd underestimated ol' Teddy. Wrapping my head around how he was the taller guide's nephew was too much trouble, so I turned and piled into the back with everyone else.

"How much did you pay for this thing?" Tyler grumbled as he climbed in behind me.

"Don't ask," Marcy said from the front. "It's better for everyone that way."

James revved it up, and it did the opposite of purr. It sounded more like a junkyard dog scrabbling for his next meal in a bunch of tin cans. Rourke and I were in the last row and I immediately lay down, sprawling out on his lap. It was a twenty-seven-hour drive in human time. But James would break the speed limit by a good fifty miles an hour and Marcy would make sure no cop stopped us.

I flew off Rourke's lap, my body hitting the seat in front of me, before the van skidded to a stop. James's outraged bellow followed one second later, and we were all instantly wide awake.

I scrambled back onto my seat, Rourke leaning down to assist me. "What is it, Irish?" Rourke called. He made sure I was fine and then maneuvered himself toward the van's side door. "Did you hit something? Or is something out there?"

"I didn't hit anything," James said. "The van just died. On its own. It was all I could do to get us to the side of the road. A small tree took pity on us and stopped us."

"Did the van die because it's a complete piece of shit or was it something supernatural?" Tyler asked, getting out of his seat to look out the window.

"I have no idea," James said, peering over the steering wheel into the darkness. "It just died."

"I don't feel any spells," Marcy said. "But that doesn't mean much. I didn't on the plane either."

"Where are we?" I asked. I'd been asleep the entire time up until this point.

Marcy turned around. "We crossed into Georgia about an hour ago. We're on some small country road. Too many cops for me to keep spelling the highways. Since James insists on going over a hundred miles an hour, it's made it difficult. It's a miracle this rattletrap can even maintain that speed. It's possible we just blew out the engine."

We'd all discovered quickly that this van shook at high speeds. "Wouldn't there be smoke or noise if the engine blew?" I said. "I didn't hear anything, but I was asleep."

"Jess is right," Nick said. "I was awake and I didn't hear anything. The van just stopped working."

That meant trouble.

Ray had opted to fly an hour in, muttering about smells and gator vans, so he was somewhere out there.

The boys piled out of the van.

"Marcy, do you have your cell phone on you still?" I asked as I went to sit closer to her.

"Yep. I've been checking it religiously, but all's been quiet in Juanita-Land. I've been secretly hoping she would send me little flashes to help us, but there's no dire message blinking on the screen." She pulled it out to double-check. "Nope, nothing there."

"Are you sure you don't sense a spell?"

"I don't," Marcy said. "But that's not saying much. If it's anything like what killed the plane, I likely won't detect it."

"If the van really stopped because of a mechanical failure, do you think you could fix it?"

"I can try," she said. "I have no idea how to spell a motor, but it can't be that hard. But, honestly, who are we kidding? I highly doubt it's mechanical. It happened too abruptly."

"Yeah, that would be too easy—"

There was a loud crash in the trees just outside the van. Marcy and I both sprang out of our seats, and right as we opened the doors, both our mates yelled in unison, "Stay in the car!"

"Yeah, right," Marcy called, answering for us, "like that's happening!"

We jumped out and headed over to where the guys stood just outside the tree line. "What do think that was?" I asked Rourke. "And why in the world would you tell me to stay in the car? I shouldn't have to remind you that Marcy and I just took out the big bad ourselves."

He growled. "It was just a gut reaction. I'm sick of seeing you in danger. The van is the only cover we've got at the moment."

"That gator van is hardly going to protect us against anything—"

Twenty feet in front of us there was another loud explosion and we were all knocked backward from the force.

Each of us was up in a moment, glancing around but finding nothing.

Tyler called, "I don't sense any magic, but there's no question something's coming."

"We need to move out of here now!" Rourke tugged me back. "Everyone back in the vehicle." He glanced at Marcy and nodded to James. "Open the hood and see if she can fix it with a spell."

"Agreed." James moved forward with Marcy tucked to his side.

I reached the side of the van first and wrenched the door open. I took one step inside and the door snapped shut behind me on its own, locking everyone else out. I turned, rattling the door handle, but it wouldn't budge.

"Jessica!" Rourke shouted on the other side. "What's going on?" He pounded his fists against the window, but it held when it should've shattered.

"I have no idea," I called through the glass. "The door won't open—"

The van's motor turned over.

It revved once and snapped into gear. Before I could do anything else, I was tossed in between the seats as it sped off down the road, faster than it should've been able to go. "What do you want?" I shouted into the air as I maneuvered myself up from between the seats and made my way to the driver's side. I climbed in and sat down, grabbing the wheel, but it wouldn't budge. I jammed my foot onto the brake, taking it down to the floor, over and over again, but it was useless.

I glanced into the rearview mirror, and to my surprise my mate, along with the others who had run after the van, pulled up short, stopping, looking around confused as I sped away.

"You're cloaking the van?" I shouted. "Is that really necessary? Come on!" The vehicle veered wildly as we barreled along the country roads, but it seemed to have a destination in mind.

I knew Rourke would follow no matter what, and once Ray landed and was told what happened, he would scout the air. It would help if I could break a window. Then they could catch my scent. I began to pound on the driver's side glass as my wolf flooded me with adrenaline. I morphed into my Lycan form, but no matter how hard I pounded on it, it wouldn't break. Jeez. This was heavy-duty magic. And even though all this was happening, I still didn't detect any magic.

I was about to turn and use my feet on the windshield when the van careened over an embankment and shot straight into the woods. There was barely enough room between the trees for it to maneuver, but it zigged and zagged fairly effortlessly. I righted myself in my seat, grabbing the wheel to steady myself. The van appeared to be heading down a small logging road, but it was hard to know for sure in the dark. The moon was occluded by clouds at that moment and the van's headlights were dim.

A few more yards and the vehicle sputtered and died.

But the momentum caused it to bounce over a few more dips in the ground, and then with a final snap it jolted to a stop, just short of crashing into a large tree.

I sat for a few minutes catching my breath and peeling my fingers off the steering wheel. It was a miracle I hadn't pulled the damn thing off. I was in my human form already and I tried the door, but it was still locked. "What do you want?" I yelled, rattling the door handle in anger. "You have me. I'm here! Now show yourself or let me out!"

There was no response for a few beats, and then the doors all popped as they unlocked. I tentatively pushed the driver's door all the way open.

As I set my foot on the grass, I asked my wolf, *Can you sense anything?* She had forced all our magic outward as a shield once we'd been kidnapped, now she growled and huffed. She couldn't detect anything either. It was unsettling for both of us. *I don't know if this is the other Hag or not,* I said. *But whoever it is, they didn't take us very far. Our backup will be here soon. Keep our magic ready to go. Whatever we're dealing with here is incredibly strong.*

I moved around the front of the van cautiously, my senses alert, my power jumping out in front of me. I was relieved the headlights were still on. It was the only illumination for miles.

The thought hadn't even had time to take seed when the lights snapped off.

The darkness was complete. "Dammit. Figures." It took my eyes less than four seconds to adjust. Everything snapped into focus and I heard a rustling coming from a group of trees to my right. I stilled.

Then a single male voice called into the air, "I am the ambassador. Come closer. I will not harm you if you do as I say."

21

"Ambassador of what?" I cautiously moved toward the voice. The supe was cloaked in the trees beyond the van, so I couldn't see him. "Why should I blindly trust that you won't hurt me? You just kidnapped me—which was totally unnecessary, by the way. All you had to do was ask for a meet. If you're really not going to hurt me, my answer would've been yes." I wasn't sensing a heavy threat from him, but I knew he was powerful if he had just been behind the carjacking, so I had to be cautious.

"My way was necessary," he said. "You are never alone." That sounded like a tsk-tsk. "I had to ensure our privacy for this meeting, so I did what I had to do. Getting you here, in this way, was highly inconvenient for me, if you must know. I haven't traveled this far away from home in centuries. I'd almost forgotten how to get around. Too many human changes in this era for my liking."

This era?

As I moved closer, I felt more confident that he wasn't out to kill me. His responses were normal enough and seemed to be non-threatening, but my magic was coiled tightly around me just in case. "Why do you need me alone? I trust my team with my life."

"The business I must discuss with you is of a delicate nature, of course." He sniffed. "Secrecy has always been our way." He said it like I should've known.

There was more rustling and he finally stepped from behind a tree in front of me.

My mouth opened, and then closed. I had no earthly idea what kind of a supe he was. He was short—under five feet—and his dark brown hair was spiked up around his head like a porcupine. He was dressed casually in khaki pants and a white long-sleeved button-up, paired with a navy blazer. The nicely pressed outfit conflicted with his full beard, bushy eyebrows, spiked hair, and overall unkempt look. "What are you?" I asked before I could help it.

He appeared to be offended at my question, dusting off his shirtsleeves before answering. "My name is Jebediah Amel and I'm a warlock." He ended with another sniff. "Most of the time when I encounter another supernatural, they introduce themselves first and then ask my name, not what I am, which is quite personal to most supes."

"I'm sorry," I replied, feeling a little flustered. He was so proper, and he obviously thought I should know the supernatural etiquette of things, which I didn't. "You took me by surprise. I've never seen a warlock before and, as excuses go, I'm a young supe, which you probably already know. But you did take me hostage," I pointed out, "so niceties at this point are not exactly high on my list. I'm not in the habit of asking someone's name after they *kidnap* me."

"You are very young," he agreed, nodding quickly, the spikes on his head not swaying an inch. "I will give you that. The youngest

I've ever had the pleasure of dealing with." He'd uttered the word "pleasure" like it was a dirty word. "But some advice for the future? In order for you to succeed in this business, you must be professional at all times. You must address powerful supernaturals in a way that they justly deserve. Anything else is an insult."

"Business?" I was too stymied by the first part to worry about the second. "Succeed in what business?" I asked.

"The Coalition, of course," Jeb said as he folded his hands in front of him.

"You consider the Coalition a *business*?" The thought was preposterous.

He nodded like I was daft. "Of course it's a business. Keeping the peace and dealing with the supernatural race is nothing *but* a business. Think of it like a kingdom—or a queendom, as it stands—and the supernaturals who inhabit the world are your serfs. Running it smoothly takes hard work, but in the end it boils down to efficiency and paperwork."

"*Paperwork?*" I gaped. This night couldn't get any stranger. There was no way I was having a conversation in the middle of the woods with a warlock who looked like Zach Galifianakis. *What do you think? Is this guy a raving lunatic?* I asked my wolf. *Did we just get kidnapped by some sort of supernatural deviant?* She growled, flashing me a picture of Jeb long ago. *Wow, he really hasn't changed that much.* Still had the beard and the hair. My wolf seemed to be familiar with him, even though she didn't give me any more information.

"Well, paperwork completed by myself and my underling. For you, since your work will mostly be out in the field, there will be less paperwork and more combat. But once you are done with a specific assignment, there will, of course, be papers and such to fill out." He waved his hand in dismissal like the busywork I'd have to complete would be a minor inconvenience.

"So you're telling me *you* give me assignments, and my job as Enforcer is considered 'fieldwork'?" I'd never imagined the Coalition would run like my PI firm. Marcy took the calls, scheduled the appointments, and Nick and I went out on the jobs.

Jeb made this giant life change sound simple.

"Yes, of course that's how it works." His expression was comical, his eyes scrunching up and his thick eyebrows going in low to form a V over his nose. "How did you *think* you were going to be alerted when things needed to be set right in the supernatural world? Did you assume there would be some kind of supernatural gong that would go off every time there was an emergency? Or a light shone into the sky like humans like to portray in the movies?" he asked.

"Are you talking about the *bat signal*?" I asked.

He waved me off. "It is of no consequence. The assignments come from me"—he gave his chest a clap and then had to stifle a cough—"as my special talent is scrying for such things, which is why I attained this position in the first place, like my father before me."

"I see." I didn't see at all.

"Then once your assignments are completed, you must fill out the appropriate forms in triplicate." From my confused expression, he ended with "Well, how did you think we keep records of all the things? We must have reports, and they must be filed in several places. Things are known to get lost over time."

I moved forward, my wolf warning me to be wary. His signature was very faint and weird. "To tell you the truth, Jeb, I haven't had time to give any real thought to the Coalition and how it might work. If pressed hard enough, I would've answered that all the job assignments and record keeping happens 'by magic.'"

"Yes"—he nodded quickly—"by scrying magic, and that belongs

to me." He shuffled his feet and kicked away some leaves. He was agitated. I was certain I wasn't measuring up to his vision of hierarchy in the supernatural world. I was young and clueless. It must suck to have to deal with such incompetence. "The Coalition is naturally made up of powerful supernaturals, but nothing would be complete without firsthand reports. They are essential."

I crossed my arms. "Okay, Jeb. You're going to have to come clean and tell me why you brought me here. I just found out a very, very short time ago that I have a position on the Coalition, and frankly, my main goal these days is staying alive, not worrying about the future job of the Enforcer. It's been kind of a rocky road since I left the Underworld, to tell you the truth, and what would be helpful now are answers. You're wasting my time by giving me anything less, so feel free to lay them on me."

He nodded along, his hair still ramrod straight, no bounce at all. "This is very true!"

"What's true?" I asked, settling my hands on my hips. "You're wasting my time?"

"No, that you're in a very precarious place. You've volleyed between life and death a number of times in the last month, like a Wimbledon master, and it's been quite amazing to witness, if I must say so myself. Precarious, indeed!"

I dropped my arms and took a step forward. "Jeb, how do you know that?" I sized him up. He didn't look like he should be an all-powerful supernatural who knew everything. He looked like he should be working a stage in Vegas.

He barely kept the indignant gasp out of his voice. "Because I am the High Ambassador, that's why! It's my job to know. Who did you think you are dealing with? I'm not some young supernatural trying to prove myself. I'm Jebediah Amel, first warlock of the great Amelentia Line. I take my position very seriously and I've come to talk to you about *business*."

"Hmm," I said. "I hear what you're telling me, Jeb, and it sounds very impressive, but your signature is strange. You're cloaking yourself, aren't you?" I ran my power over him, pressing it firmly against his body, trying to figure out the warlock puzzle that was Jebediah Amel.

"Stop doing that," he ordered, his hands fisting at his sides. He was just short of stamping his foot like a child. "Yes, of course I am cloaking myself! Do you honestly think a warlock of my stature can just walk freely around this realm? I'm a target—just as you are—and once the supernatural world figures out I am away from the protection of my home, it could be chaos!"

"I'm sorry to inform you, but none of that means anything to me," I said, hands back on my hips. "It can't be chaos if the most powerful supes on the planet don't know who you are." If Jeb was really a bigwig supe, there would be some record of him. My father would've mentioned him. I would bet my eyeteeth Rourke had never heard of him—and he was the oldest supe I knew.

He seemed a bit stunned by my words. "You . . . you really don't know who I *am*?"

"I have no earthly idea who you are. I've never even heard a whisper of your name. But you will be happy to know that my wolf remembers you, which is why I'm not currently trying to put you in a headlock, even though your hairstyle would make it tough to do." My humor was lost on him.

He looked dejected. "I see."

"But I do know you're strong . . . strangely so." I took a few steps closer. "And I'm not sure even Tally could do what you did with the van. Your spell casting is amazing, and your ability to cloak yourself is impressive. Did you take the plane down too?"

"I had no part in the plane crash," he huffed. "That is not how I do business."

"No, carjacking is a much better way to achieve your goal."

"I was left with no choice. You are always accompanied by many and I had to make contact with you before you arrived home, and that was the only way I could see to get you here safely."

" 'Safely' is going a bit too far. That was a crazy. If I'd gotten on a plane with my father, would you have been left with no choice but to take that particular plane down?" I asked curiously. Then I pointed out, "You just said you had to get to me before I got home."

"No," he said, more to the ground than to me, "I would've found a way to get to you before you boarded."

"I already said you could've asked to meet me alone. I'm usually fairly accommodating when someone isn't trying to kill me." I rubbed my neck. I knew Rourke was still searching for me, so I had to wrap this up. "But, Jeb, we're done debating this. I need you to explain to me the real reason why you brought me here. And if you want my trust and cooperation, I suggest you stop cloaking your true nature. I don't suffer fools or pretenders, and I'm warning you, I don't trust easily." I crossed my arms and waited for him to make up his mind.

"Fine," he said. "I will do as you ask." He flung his arms wide, in what was becoming a decidedly Jeb-like flare, and chanted something into the air. Powerful magic gathered around him, swirling, causing the air to change until there was one final surge. His clothes transformed with a loud whoosh, leaving him in flowing white robes.

I hadn't been expecting that.

The robes were a touch comical because he was so short. The effect wasn't as dramatic as I think he'd intended. His arms were now extra hairy and thick with muscle, and his hair was even longer on top but still stuck straight out. No amount of gel in the world could have given it that effect, so it had to be either natural, or magically secured into place.

He held something in his arms. It was a leather-bound book of some kind, and it was gold and glossy and took up his arm space. His power prickled me and I took a reluctant step back. "Holy cow," I said. "Your magic is potent. It's making my hair stand on end."

"I am the Gatekeeper of Fate, the High Ambassador of the Coalition." He sniffed, for what must have been the fifth time tonight. "As I told you, I am the keeper of *all* things supernatural. Every supernatural on earth, and throughout the realms, must pass through me to get to you. And once you assume your place at the head of the Coalition—"

"Wait." I held a hand out to stop him. "What did you just say?"

"I said once you take your seat at the head, I will be at your service—"

"The 'head' part I don't understand. I'm just the Enforcer. I can't be the head of anything. The Coalition is a team, made up of five equal members." At least that's how I envisioned it all working.

"You are the chosen leader of the Coalition. The female wolf, who acts as the Enforcer, is the head of the council. It's always been that way. And I am your secretary, if you will. Your chief operating officer, as a better term." He inclined his head in a slight bow.

"Just because it's always been that way doesn't meant it has to stay that way, does it?" I could hear Eudoxia, the Vamp Queen, right now in my ear, moaning and constantly complaining about my lack of everything necessary to lead the council. I didn't want to suffer through that daily if I didn't have to, and she was right, for the most part. I was very green. Not an ideal candidate to rule.

Jeb raised a furry eyebrow at me. "I suppose it could be another, but that would be unprecedented."

"Somehow I think that will become the unofficial tagline for the new Coalition: The Unprecedented Bunch. I can already promise you, we aren't going to act like the old guard. This is a new era, Jeb. You said so yourself. The other women on the Coalition will be much better qualified to run things than me. It's likely that we will vote on most things. There'll be five of us, so that makes it easier. We'll always have a tiebreak."

"So be it," he nodded, "but no matter who will sit at the head of the table, you will always be the leader, and I will answer to you, for it is you who I give the assignments directly to."

"Jeb, you're not hearing me. The ladies will vote me out. I can promise you, I will not be the leader."

"You will." His face was set. He wasn't going to listen to any more rational explanations, and honestly, it really didn't matter now anyway. This entire thing was a ways off, and who knew what would happen between now and then? And almost like he was reading my mind, he added, "But all of this is conjecture if you don't heed my warning right now. You have angered the Hags." He shifted his weight and opened the big book with a flourish. The pages moved on their own, stopping toward the end. His big finger went over the lines as he paraphrased. "The Hags are only one station above me, but they like to think they are the supreme rulers of the entire universe. But from what I can see here, you have no choices left to you. You must appease them if you want to live." His lips moved as he read the words silently to himself. "To do that, you must find a way to settle your debt to Fate and put yourself back on your true path."

"Okay, I'm in. How do I do such a thing?" For the first time I had a glimmer of hope that maybe this strange warlock had an answer to all my problems inside his big gold book.

"It will take some time, but first we must figure out how you're going to survive the night. Then we can talk of future dealings."

"*I'm not going to survive the night?*" I said. That wasn't what I wanted to come out of that book.

"Not as I have it here." He ran his finger over more words I couldn't see. "That's why it was imperative for me to find you now. You have angered someone very powerful, and as of right now, she cannot be convinced it can be fixed without your death. And she has a point. With your death, there is a resolution. Even though her sister disagrees and has been championing you for quite some time—it was she who took the plane down, and lucky for you she did because if she hadn't, your path would've ended in disaster in that swamp. You must find a way to mend the rent in Fate that doesn't include your dying, and according to what I see in here, there are very, very few options left to you—"

"Juanita took the plane down?" I interjected. It was the only thing I could focus on at the moment. "She could've killed us."

"She had no other choice," he said dismissively. "If not, the plane would have been redirected by her sister Enid, and you would not have survived. That would've been a more dire outcome. Juanita did what was necessary, as have I. But on your current path, as I've just stated, you will not live through the next two hours. Your outlook is dreary. If you *do* survive, however, the next task will be to figure out how to redirect your Fated path. This will not be simple either, but it will be a tad easier than being dead."

I pressed my fingers to my temple. "Okay, we have to break this up. What are my choices for the next two hours? That seems like the most pressing, wouldn't you agree?"

"Yes. For one, you need to stay out of all transportation devices. They are far too easy to manipulate. Enid cannot blow your body up, per se, but she is well versed in bringing down powerful supernaturals by other means, and you are not a goddess, so there's no chance of regeneration."

"How do I get home without transportation?" I asked stupidly.

My brain was still processing the fact that I was supposed to die soon—*really* die. My wolf howled in anger.

"You must run, of course." He cocked his head at me oddly. "You do have that capability, do you not?"

"I do," I said sheepishly. "But that would take longer than I'd...intended." That was about as lame as I could get. I had nothing specific to do once I got home, except find Juanita and then help Tally.

But I couldn't do any of that if I was dead. So, duh, I could run.

"It's the only option to you, long or not," he replied with a curt nod. "You will take your...partner along and no one else. If you do not listen to this advice, you will put your entire party at risk. And I am beginning to understand, by your actions, that you don't take harm to your family and friends lightly. That is a commendable trait, but not always advisable. Sometimes, for the greater good, sacrifices must be made."

"I will never sacrifice my family." Rage bubbled up inside me before I could tamp it down. I could almost handle the thought of dying, but thinking about being responsible for someone I loved dying was unacceptable. "So don't ask me to, now or in the future, for any reason."

"Well," Jeb scoffed. "In our world, it's impossible to assign the same value to all lives. The sooner you understand this, the better. Our world is much different than the human world."

"I don't agree," I argued. "How can anyone choose which lives will bring more value, human or supe? It's not possible."

"I can and I do. For example, if you were to die, it would lead to catastrophic consequences for us *all*. Countless lives would be lost, both human and supernatural. How's that for hierarchy of value? For many, if they died, it would trigger no change in Fate's fabric. And I can't speak for every living soul, but a great many, I believe, would willingly sacrifice themselves for the greater good.

Keeping you alive is one of those greater goods, in my book." He shook his golden book for emphasis.

My mouth closed with a rebuttal on my tongue.

It was hard to argue against knowledge like that, but I loathed being the one who would have to choose whether someone lived or died. Instead, I asked, "I understand I made a mistake when I killed Ardat Lili and now I have to right my wrongs, but why does the rest of it—like if I die, the supernatural race is in peril—seem to sit on my shoulders alone? Since the first day I shifted, I've felt the pressure of the supernatural race on top of me, slowly choking me with its need—quite possibly I've felt it since the day I was born. But I'm not the only person who is going to sit on the Coalition. It's supposed to be made up of five powerful supernaturals. Shouldn't we all share the burden of the end of the supernatural race?"

He gave me a once-over, his expression shifting slightly as he glanced over the top of his book. "You are different than all the rest, of course. I thought you were aware of that. You're not only the Enforcer, but you are also the *catalyst*. The change maker, if you will. Your birth was a significant event in our world. It set into motion much that had been patiently waiting, and that's just the way it is." He shrugged. "It can't be changed. You are who you are and you have a specific role to play. There is only one catalyst born every thousand years or so. But everything about you has been late in coming—you are actually four hundred and forty years late to this gathering."

Huh? "*Late?*" I had no idea how to respond to that. "How can my birth be late when I wasn't supposed to kill Lili for another hundred years?" I turned in a slow circle, searching for something tangible, something to let me know I wasn't really having this conversation. I was sick of things not making sense. My fingers wandered back to my temples. I was starting to hope this was a dream and I'd wake up any minute in Rourke's warm lap. I stopped and faced Jeb again. "If my birth was late, wouldn't that be what threw off Fate and angered Enid, and not the other stuff? I would think all this is interrelated—kind of like the snowball effect of bad karma."

"I can't answer that. I guess it could be." He shrugged, appearing to be unsure of himself for the first time tonight. "I'm not a seer—I'm an intuit. Things come to me, and I write them down. I don't ever see the entire picture. That would be too telling. Instead I receive knowledge about the supernatural world through my magic, like reading a report, and from there I figure out what things need to be dealt with, in what order. The Hags are seers, and they like to think they know everything, but I know for a fact they do not. Fate has always been tricky that way. It is ever changing. Which is why it is imperative that you figure out a way to bring your path back around, from whatever got it off track— your late birth or your actions, it makes no difference. If you do not, all is lost." He snapped his book shut to accentuate his point. He didn't need to, because I understood now how dire this was.

"Any more advice for me? How am I supposed to bring it back around?"

"That I do not know. But if you can remain alive tonight, there is hope. I see that in the writings, but nothing specific has been stated...yet. I believe it is up to you to figure it out, and once you do, it will show up in the book." He smiled, happy with his sleuthful deductions.

"That's reassuring."

He shrugged. "As I said, it's not written yet. If something changes, I will let you know immediately, as keeping you alive, and back on your Fated path, means life and happiness for us all."

"No pressure there. And next time you want to get in touch, can you use a phone? No more hijackings."

"Yes, that can be arranged."

I glanced around, surprised for the first time my family hadn't found me yet. "Jeb, you didn't take me that far into the woods," I said. "Why can't my team find me?"

"I have the entire area cloaked, of course," he said.

"Then I need you to drop it," I said. I hadn't considered he would keep everyone out. "If my life is in danger, I need them here, plus they need to know what's going on. They will help protect me."

"No," he said firmly. "I will keep us concealed until I take my leave. It is for your own protection. Enid cannot see you through my barrier, but once it's gone, she will know where you are."

"I don't care about Enid. She's going to do what she's going to do regardless of being cloaked for five more minutes. I have to leave this place sooner or later, so what's the difference? Drop it now so they can find us."

"I will not."

I bared my teeth and stalked forward. I wasn't going to be flexible on this. "You're not starting us out on the right foot, Jeb. You just told me you work for me, correct? You're my secretary. If that's the truth, then I want you to drop whatever wards you have up so my team can find me. Now."

He shuffled backward a few paces, clutching his precious book to his chest, robes tangling at his feet. "Technically, you haven't spoken the sacred vows yet, so I'm not bound to you yet." I continued forward. "I came here of my own free will to help you!" he spouted as I growled some more. "Lest you not forget, I came here to save your life. If I drop my cloaking wards, we will become instant targets. I will not have it!"

I crossed my arms, stopping right inside his personal space.

He cringed. "Jeb, you are planning on letting me leave here alone, correct?" I asked with all the patience I could muster. "Or are you planning to accompany me and change into a wolf so we can run up north together?"

Jeb cleared his throat, tripping once more on his robe as he took a big step back. "You will be allowed to leave alone, but I will remain cloaked. Even now, my power is leaking around the edges because you forced me to drop my glamour. We are at risk." He stuck out his chin, trying to regain his footing. "Enid will be able to spot us soon enough, but I refuse to make it easier on her."

"How about this—if I promise to you that once you drop your wards, my team will be here within minutes, and once they arrive, we won't linger for more than a moment, will that be enough? You will be rid of us and free to cloak yourself again. I'm certain Enid can't act that fast—you'll be safe." He wasn't convinced, his body language hostile, so I continued with "Listen, times have changed, Jeb. And if you and I are going to get along, you need to evolve your way of thinking and be open to new ways of doing things. If you're going to be my right hand, you need to follow my directions immediately. That's how you begin to earn my trust. I'm the one who has to do the heavy lifting around here. You have to trust that I can formulate a good plan. With Enid breathing down my neck, and only a two-hour window to figure out how to survive, I *need* my team. The sooner the better. Wherever I go, my family goes. Once I take a seat on the Coalition, it will be the same. There's no getting around it."

Jeb sighed, a look of defeat causing his bushy eyebrows to buckle above his eyes like a pair of sad, hairy caterpillars. I had a feeling I'd never get sick of looking at them. "I knew you were going to be stubborn, but I had hoped it was an error in the paperwork. So be it. I will drop my wards, but only for three minutes. If they do not find us in that time, I will put them back into place and we will agree to finish our discussions and you will go."

"Agreed. Three minutes will be more than enough time," I said.

He whipped out an arm in a long flourish, his hairy wrist coming into view as his robe flopped back, and instantly there was a loud booming noise, like thunder, and then the reverberations hit my chest. Jeb didn't mess around. He had some serious magic.

I closed my eyes and counted down in my mind... *three, two, one*.

A loud, terrifying roar filled the air and there was rustling in the forest, not fifty feet from us.

Jeb paled and I opened my eyes, grinning like a shrew.

It had taken Rourke three seconds to find us.

22

My mate was spectacular as he bounded into the area. He was in his beast form, fangs curved, a snarl on his lips. His muscular shoulders spanned at least three feet. I'd just seen him in this form, but he still took my breath away.

He rushed over and rubbed his flank against me, marking me with his scent and reassuring himself I was okay. Then he turned his ferocious glare on the warlock.

Jeb took a few shaky steps backward, waving a hand in front of him. "I meant her no harm, cat. This was a necessary meet—"

Rourke silenced him with a terrifying roar that shook the trees.

I grinned at the flustered warlock. "See, I told you he'd find me in less than three minutes. And if you don't want to deal with an angry cat, like I said, next time call me."

"Well, yes, I see that three minutes was adequate—"

A whooshing noise tore through the area and Ray landed next to me, hands already on his hips. "What the fuck's going on?

Who's this guy?" He thumbed his fist at Jeb. "Do we need to take him out for you?"

Tyler barreled into the area before I could answer, emerging from the woods right where Rourke had come in, Nick behind him. Tyler had recently shifted out of his wolf form, still donning the clothes Nick held out to him as they walked. Marcy came next, holding Rourke's clothing in her arms like a small bundle of laundry. I could hear James shifting back in the brush.

My entire team in under a minute. I smiled wide.

"Who's this guy?" Marcy asked dryly as she passed by him. "The power in this area is ridiculous, but something isn't right. And why is he wearing a bathrobe?" She came to stand by my side and leaned over. "And what's with the crazy hairdo? Porcupines look better put together."

I swallowed back a laugh as Jeb sniffed at the insults. There was going to be a lot of sniffing around this group. "I'm a warlock, if you must know," Jeb answered even though the questions hadn't been directed at him. "Now that we have all gathered, I will re-ward the area, to make sure"—he swallowed as Rourke pinned his gaze on him—"we stay safe."

Absentmindedly, I ran a hand through Rourke's fur, grabbing on and luxuriating in the feel of him. His body was warm next to mine and I knew he wasn't going to change back just yet. Jeb's signature was too strong. In order to fight a powerful old supe like that, Rourke would be better off in his beast form. I inclined my head toward Jeb. "This is Jebediah Amel," I said as a way of introduction. "He's the High Ambassador to the Coalition and kidnapped me so he could tell me my life was in danger."

"If that was all it was, you could've just told us," Ray said, irritation at the forefront. "Why send us on a big cloak-and-dagger goose chase in the middle of the woods? What a waste of time."

Jeb cleared his throat. "My allegiance is to Jessica, and Jessica alone. Anything I discuss with her is private. The Coalition has never shared its business with any outsiders in over a thousand years. This is"—he cleared his throat again—"a first. Not completely unwelcome, mind you." He waved his hand out in front of him, his eyebrows bunching again. "But highly unusual. It will take some getting used to."

"We don't care if you ever get used to it," Tyler commented as he zipped up his pants. "We're here to protect my sister at all costs. We've pledged our lives to her. If you're on our side and have an allegiance to Jessica, then there should be no issues."

"I can see that more clearly now," Jeb said. "In fact, you all... smell like her." He made a show of sniffing the air in front of him. "As if you have all taken a piece of her inside you somehow. It's most particular." He continued to scent the air. I was going to have to nickname him Sniffy. "This indicates that you have all shared blood bonds with her." His voice held some surprise, but also irritation.

I nodded. "That's true. I've shared blood or power with most of them." I glanced around the group. I'd given Marcy my essence to heal her when the Prince of Hell had blasted her. I felt our connection, though it was faint. Tyler, Ray, Naomi, and Danny had all taken in my blood. My gaze landed on Nick and he grinned. I arched an eye at him.

"Don't you remember? You shared your blood with me," Nick said. "But it was back when we were both kids. You hadn't shifted for the first time yet. We were in the woods behind the lodge and we swore an oath to each other and cut open our palms, reciting some nonsensical thing. But I swore to protect you that day, and nothing has changed. Once you shifted for the first time, I felt our bond grow, but I didn't understand why. Now it makes more sense."

My face brightened at the memory. I hadn't thought about it

in years. We'd been no more than ten years old at the most. We'd both pledged our loyalty to each other. My wound had taken weeks to heal. "I remember." I grinned. "You were my knight in shining armor in those days. One of my only allies." I was stunned that my blood, given that long ago, could still bind us together. I didn't feel the same connection to him as those who had taken my blood recently, but there was a tingling there when I brushed my power over him.

"When you decided to leave the Compound for good," Nick said, "I went with you willingly, but I also had a burning urge to stay close and keep protecting you."

"Little did we know that when we exchanged that blood and a nonsensical childhood oath, all these years later we'd find that you actually became my real, bonded brother that day."

"It was the best-case scenario. And, as your father indicated to me when I saw him last, I will freely give you my troth as soon as you have time to take it." His chest expanded. "And this time it will be formal, not as two kids in the woods."

"That would make me happy," I said to him as Jeb cleared his throat. This time with more oomph.

"We must get down to the business at hand," the warlock said. "You are running out of time." Jeb appeared a little flustered as he continued. "I'm happy this homecoming has been so beneficial to you, but having those kinds of bonds to others is highly unusual. Only the Five share their essences with each other, and by doing so it makes them very strong. You have"—he coughed into his fist—"shared the wealth, so to speak. I'm not sure what to make of it, but I'm certain I will have information forthcoming, as it pertains to your future."

"Do you think that might be my 'special gift'? My ability to bond by blood with other supes?"

"I can't answer that," Jeb said. "It is not written anywhere yet, but if you want my best educated guess, I would say you've developed a much-needed coping strategy." His head shook with his intensity as he spoke, but his spikes stayed still.

"Coping strategy?" I asked. I'd never thought of it like that.

He gestured around the group. "Without your team, as you put it, you would likely have perished already, so something or someone had the foresight to guard you against that. Even as a child you were driven to seek protection. It makes sense."

"By who?" I asked.

"Maybe yourself or your wolf?" Jeb answered. "Despite my ability to know all important events, there are things at work we can never fully understand—nor are we meant to."

"Before, you said you brought my sister here because her life was in danger. If she dies, what happens?" Tyler asked.

"The supernatural race would be launched into chaos until the time of another rebirth, one thousand years from now," Jeb informed the group. "I can't impress the importance of this, but Jessica must survive at all costs. Before you all...descended, I was informing her of the odds of achieving that very thing. They are quite low, which is unacceptable. That is why I went to great lengths to get her here. In fact"—he glanced directly at me, his eyebrows shooting up—"if you don't leave within a minute or so, the exact way I tell you, the odds will be even less in your favor. I have cloaked the area once again, but Enid is now on the hunt. I can feel her magic pressing in on me. We cannot linger."

Rourke huffed and rubbed his flank into me before walking up to Marcy.

"Boy, you're one big kitty, aren't you?" she said as she put his clothes into his mouth.

He tossed his head and trotted into the woods to shift, right as James came out.

"Okay, Jeb," I said. "We're all ears. Tell us how to do this."

"I don't like it," Ray grumbled. "I don't care if that little spiky-haired bastard is right or not. You two going alone feels wrong to me."

Tyler paced nearby. Rourke was silent, lost in thought for the moment. He'd been quiet after Jeb had told us what to do, not even commenting when Jeb vanished into thin air.

One minute the warlock was there, and the next he wasn't.

It had been the weirdest thing I'd ever seen. Now the air was deadly quiet, all the magic gone. But Enid was on the move. We had to act quickly, and fighting about it wasn't helping.

James had already maneuvered the van around so it was pointing back toward the road. It was idling and Marcy and Nick were already inside waiting for the signal to go.

"We have no choice but to trust him, Ray," I said. "You heard everything he said. He's been working for the good of the Coalition for thousands of years, and more importantly? He wants me to survive. We go with his plan."

"I thought he was sincere enough," Tyler agreed. "I kept trying to catch a scent of a lie and none ever came, but that's not saying much. If that warlock can cloak his power signature, he can likely do anything."

Rourke finally turned to me, his eyes intensely focused. "We have to do as he says, and go now. I have a faint recollection of this warlock in my mind, though it's very fuzzy. I believe he is required to help—as his station in the Coalition dictates. Jessica and I go alone." He turned to a still disgruntled Ray. "You and

Tyler have to stay back, like the warlock said, at least two hundred miles. No closer. My suggestion is to go somewhere and get some rest. Start out again in the morning. If we run into trouble, Jessica can reach her brother in her mind."

"I don't *sleep*," Ray said. "I'll do what you ask and stay back exactly two hundred miles. If there is a disturbance, I should be able to feel it. I can cover that stretch fairly quickly."

"That sounds reasonable," I told Ray, cutting Rourke off. "Jeb was specific about distance, so make it two hundred and fifty to be certain. You'll still be within contact at that distance, so no griping."

Tyler added, "I'll run under Ray as he flies. He can make sure we stay the right amount of miles back. I can run faster than any other shifter, so I can be there for backup in enough time to help as well."

Jeb had warned the entire team to stay back in the beginning, but once Enid engaged us, we could call them in. But by that time all might be lost. It was a chance we had no choice but to take. The real hope was to evade whatever her nefarious plans were—plans that Jeb said he had no clue how to interpret. He said the words had been cloaked, but the intent was "tainted."

Whatever that meant, but the word "tainted" couldn't be good.

Rourke took my hand and tugged me into the woods to shift. Tyler would gather our clothes and give them to Marcy after we changed.

We stopped a few yards in and found some brush. Rourke was still very quiet. "Are you okay?" I asked as I took off my shirt. "You're a little too introspective for me right now."

He came over and encircled my waist, leaning down to take my lips in his. It was a light kiss that spoke volumes. He broke the kiss with effort, his eyes shining with emotion. "When the warlock finally dropped his ward and I found you, the scent of his magic hit me hard. It's old. Very old. I've never met the warlock formally, but I knew then, beyond a shadow of a doubt, that it was ancient magic. It made my beast wary and me very aware of the difficulty I have in protecting you. Against that kind of magic, it would be nearly impossible. My insides are knotted. Knowing the Hag will strike tonight is unacceptable. I'm just trying to ready my beast for whatever it takes."

My hands threaded into his hair. "You heard Jeb as well as I did. Without my 'team,' I would've died already. You are necessary to my survival, but what's more important is the way we work together. This is going to be hard, but we have to stay in sync. I need you in touch with me so we can work flawlessly as a *team*. If we do that, we have a chance." I leaned up and gave him a tender kiss.

We stood like that for a few moments. I knew we had to get going, but this was necessary too. We needed to connect before we headed into known danger.

"I agree, we go in as a team," he said as he pulled back. I let him go. "When the warlock said you should've already died, it was devastating. I can't lie." He brought his head down. "For my entire life I've always been one of the most powerful supernaturals around. Other supes cower in front of me. My battle skills, back when people used to fight with their fists and swords, were unparalleled. As my Pride began to die off, and there was nothing I could do to stop it, it changed something in me. After that I swore"—he arched back to look at the sky—"I *swore* I would never allow myself to care like that about another again." He brought his forehead down slowly, placing it against mine. His eyes focused on me, drawing in my gaze like they held their own gravity. "But things didn't go according to my plan. Now I care more than I ever have about one single person, and I find myself once again powerless to do much of anything to stop the same fate from befalling you that befell my family."

I stroked his face with both my hands. "I'm so sorry," I whispered. It was all I could say. "I know you loved your family. It had to be crushing to see them go."

"Jessica," he said. "I love you. With everything I have, and everything I am. And I'm willing to risk my life a dozen times over to save you. But even if I forfeit my life, I fear it won't be enough to save you."

"No one is going to need saving. We are both going to survive, and there will be no *forfeiting* anything," I said firmly. "Not my life, not your life. We're a team. We help each other and will keep each other alive. That's the way this is going to work." I refused to believe anything different.

Rourke didn't look convinced.

I added, "I once explained to my brother and Danny that an army of anything could defeat even the most powerful supernatural. We're that army now. Nobody is going to mess with our strength. We have too much firepower. I believe with all my heart we will survive—*together.*"

"I'm not sure of anything anymore," he growled, separating from me to shift. "Enid is powerful and dangerous. The warlock said it was going to be a treacherous road."

"Yeah," I countered as I lay down next to him on the cool ground, "but we have Juanita."

23

We'd been running for over three hours and still nothing. No signs of any trouble. We'd been staying to rural, densely forested areas as much as we could. We rounded a thick copse of trees and Rourke slowed in front of me for the first time. I followed suit. His nose was up in the air, so I raised my muzzle and sniffed.

There was a strange, pungent tang in the air. *What do you think it is?* I asked him.

I don't know, but it's not good, he replied. *It smells decayed.*

Jeb said Enid would have no trouble tracking us, and once we suspected trouble we should try and do the opposite of what we thought was right. His take—it was the only way to throw her off track. She was an oracle, so she knew what was *supposed* to happen, but things changed—especially if you made decisions counter to your beliefs.

I've smelled something like this before, I said. I ran my memory over the scent, hoping it would spur some recognition. All of a sudden, a picture leapt into my brain.

Oh no.

I froze. Not willing to take another step forward.

I figured it out, Rourke growled, so low it sounded like nothing more than a rumble.

I did too. It's a ghoul, isn't it? I asked. *That's what I'm coming up with. Tyler and I ran into one in the Underworld. It was foul, but didn't harm us.*

Yes, it's a ghoul, he said. *It's either being operated by a necromancer or it's a dead necromancer. Either way, it spells trouble.*

The one in the Underworld didn't seem too threatening, I said. *I think we can take it out without much resistance.*

Rourke shook his tawny head and huffed out loud. *A ghoul is deadly only if it's being controlled. If the one you saw had no one manning its brain, it would just sort of wander around. But if a necromancer is directing the ghoul, it will have deadly precision, and if it bites you, it's all over.*

What do you mean all over? That sounded ominous.

If a ghoul bites you, you become worse than a ghoul. A ghoul is a dead body, reanimated. Healthy people who are bitten become wendigos. Alive, yet dead. Supernaturals who get bitten by a ghoul are like wendigos on steroids. We turn into powerful flesh-eating beings that can take out a small town and raise an army of killers in no time flat. I don't know any supernatural who is immune to the bite of a ghoul, which Enid is well aware of. Not to mention, raising a ghoul to bite someone is against every supernatural High Law we've ever had. The penalty for doing such is death.

I guess Enid doesn't care if she dies. How do you kill a ghoul? I asked.

You have to disassemble the brain without being bit. If there's more than a couple, then we're in serious trouble. We'll have to go slow for the next few miles and hope we stay out of their way. Tell your brother and Ray to back off immediately. We can't have them follow us into this.

Rourke's tone was as serious as I'd ever heard it. *On it,* I told him. Then I switched gears in my mind. *Tyler,* I called. *Are you there?*

Yep, he answered. I heard his labored breaths as he ran. *We're staying back two hundred and fifty miles so don't you worry.*

Change of plans. You can't follow us any longer. We need to slow way down and find a new route. We're scenting ghouls here. Right as I said it, I detected more than a few. The air was getting thick with putrescence. I switched a channel in my brain and said, *Rourke, there's more than one.*

I'm picking up on that. Their scent is getting stronger too, he replied. He glanced back at me, his eyes radiating emerald. *I don't want to alarm you, but I think we're at the edge of a large cemetery.*

I swallowed. Cemetery meant lots of dead bodies to reanimate. *Can we turn back?* I asked.

I don't think so. Enid has been tracking us for hours. She knew which way we were headed before we did. The necromancer likely has dead scattered all over this place, at every possible point on our path, even coming in behind us now. There's no backtracking. We move forward and use our noses and try to circumvent them.

Jess, what's going on? Tyler asked

Tyler, you and Ray have to find a different route. I mean it. Once we're clear of here, I'll get back to you. For now, go thirty miles west immediately.

Jess, I'm not leaving you in danger. We'll go fifty more miles and stop. That way we can be behind you if need be. His voice filled with concern. *I'll change back, and Ray and I will come up with a plan. If you get around the danger, fine, we'll take a detour, but if you don't, we'll be there to back you up.*

I hated this part. Bringing my family into a fight with the ghouls was dangerous, but it was necessary. *Fine. That sounds reasonable, but be careful of the distance. If you cross within two*

hundred miles of us, you could put us all in jeopardy. Jeb said it was
a must to stay back.

We will, he replied. *Yell if you need me. Ray can be there in a*
snap and I'll be right behind him. Ray has something set up with
Marcy too. She gave him a trigger spell or some such thing. We will
alert them when the time comes.

Got it, I conceded. *I'll let you know if things get out of hand. You*
have my word. Then I switched him off and turned my attention
on Rourke, who had begun to snarl, his body focused on a thick
copse of trees. It was near dawn, but it was still dark.

Enid had chosen her trap well.

How many? I asked.

At least four in front of us, he said. *I don't think we should try and*
disable them. I think we dodge them and try to clear the area. But it's
imperative we stay together. No separating. That's what she wants. It
makes us easy to pick off.

I'll stick as close as I can. Do ghouls have any other special abili-
ties? Something to watch out for? I asked.

They're not that fast—not like wendigos. Their main objective
is to bite us anywhere they can. Ghouls are usually recently dead,
but don't mistake them for zombies. Necromancers pick bodies that
haven't fully decomposed yet, because they need specific brain elements
in place. Embalming practices on humans in the recent century make
that much easier. The necromancer operates them like robots, seeing
through their eyes. But, Jessica, like I said before, if you're bitten, and
their essence enters your bloodstream, you don't become a ghoul—you
become a wendigo. Death to the living.

His intensity stilled me. He was more worried than I'd ever
heard him, even when we were in the Underworld. *I understand.*
We can't get bit.

He snarled his agreement, pacing forward slowly, edging to the
left of the trees.

I followed cautiously. *Do you think Enid is a powerful enough Hag to be a necromancer? Or did she hire this out?* I asked.

My guess is she found someone in this area to do her bidding. My understanding is a necromancer has to be close to her creations. Distance plays a factor.

We reached another grove of trees, this one spread out in front of us. There was no choice but to go through. Rourke began to pace into them quietly, not making a sound. I followed closely—as close as I could get without jumping on his back. My wolf scented the area as we went. She'd already pushed much of our magic out as a shield to help protect us. I had no idea if it would keep the ghouls off us or not, but it did make me feel better. Rourke led us through the trees. They became denser as we went.

I heard rustling to our right.

Rourke began to trot. We veered away from the noise as quickly as we could, but I wasn't fooling myself. We weren't going to make it through this without incident. After a few moments, the forest fell away in front of us. We stood at the edge of a massive cemetery. The grounds were hilly, like soft rolling waves, full of shiny marble grave markers reflecting in the dusky twilight as far as we could see.

See all the mounds of freshly dug-up dirt? Rourke indicated with his tawny head.

I saw them. They didn't look like someone had uncovered them nicely with a shovel. Instead it looked like a scene out of *Night of the Living Dead*. These ghouls had clawed their way out of the earth with their own bony fingers. *I see quite a few*, I said. *That seems like a lot of recently dead bodies for one cemetery.*

For a cemetery this size, it's about right. We must be on the outskirts of a big city.

So, do we go around the edges or are we heading through? I glanced out into the expanse, trying to sense any movement. Nothing caught my eye, but the scent of decay was everywhere.

Let's stick to the perimeter for now. That way we can either duck into the trees for cover or take off through the cemetery if the threat comes from the woods.

Sounds good to me.

He took off, moving at a brisk pace. Within a few moments, there was rustling in the trees to our left. Rourke roared his anger as he spotted them, but the two ghouls kept on coming, heedless of the scary big cat. One appeared to be an older man, his gray hair hanging limply in a few places. The other was a young girl, maybe ten years old, her long brown hair still mostly intact.

They came at us with surprising speed, but we were faster.

Go! Rourke yelled.

We took off at a run. It was more dangerous to run, because the smells were everywhere and we couldn't tell precisely where they were coming from, not to mention it was harder to locate all the sounds.

Look out! I shouted. Three more ghouls emerged from the trees fifty yards in front of us.

I see them, he said. *Time to veer back into the woods.*

Do you think that's safer than running through the open cemetery? At least we can see what's coming at us from a distance if we go in the open.

Rourke growled, clearly not liking either scenario. In the forest we might have a chance to hide from them, but out here we were exposed. I followed his lead as we raced back into the woods. Rourke went wide, arcing away from the cemetery grounds, plunging deeper into the dense tree growth.

There was rustling up ahead.

Then, all of a sudden, it sounded like it was coming from

everywhere. *We're surrounded,* Rourke roared in my mind. *Turn back the way we came!*

We both slid to a precarious stop. As I backed up a few steps, wondering what to do, something reached out toward me and grabbed hold. *Something has me!* I yelled.

Don't let its mouth get near you. Rourke turned like lightning toward me.

I snarled and snapped my jaws, dancing to the side. The ghoul wouldn't let go. Its bony, awful fingers were intertwined in my fur. It was going to bite as soon as it could.

Rourke charged it from the side and sent it flying. It took tufts of my fur with it.

By the time we were done with that one, five more had closed in on us.

Good gods, I cried. *Enid knew we would be right here in this spot! We can't win against someone who knows our every move before we do. I didn't even hear that ghoul behind the tree until it was on me.*

She's not going to win, Rourke snarled, his anger tearing through the woods. *We're just going to have to keep changing up what we do. I see an opening, straight and to the right. We're taking it. Now!*

He herded me forward, nudging my flank, trying to make me run faster. We broke through the small opening between two ghouls, dodging them, and ran.

Turn west, Rourke said. *Even though that's technically heading back the way we just came. We're out of options.* We weaved our way west for only a few yards before there were more sounds everywhere.

I'm voting for sprinting full-out, I said. *Maybe we can move too fast for them to bite us.*

It only takes one small nip, Rourke said. *And just like you said, if Enid knows where we're already headed, going blindly makes it riskier. If we go at a speed we can scent and track them, it gives us better odds.*

I couldn't really argue because it was two sides of the same coin. Quick or not, we were still in a shitstorm of trouble. I had to remind myself these weren't mindless zombies. These were calculating horrors operated by a powerful supernatural. Whoever was pulling the strings was a master.

Rourke, I said. *I think we need to really change our tactics, like out-of-the-box change.*

How?

If we don't do the opposite of our gut response, like Jeb said, we will never survive this. We need to stop making rational choices. I think it will only take one big change to throw us off the path we're on that Enid can see. If that crumbles, she will lose her advantage.

That's easier said than done, he said. *In fact, I don't think my mind works that way. My beast won't allow me to lower my guard like that.*

I'll take the lead, then, I said. *We have to be unpredictable, and my wolf is on board. I'll let her take the reins first.* How we were going to achieve this was anyone's guess, but it was worth a shot. He growled, but moved to the side so I could take the lead. *Clear our brain the best you can,* I told my wolf. This was going to be easier for her to do than it ever would be for me. *Think of nothing until the moment we do it.* She barked, assuring me she had it. *If we can do this successfully, we have a chance.*

There was movement all around us. I took off at a trot, thinking about the last good book I read to take my mind off what we were doing to help my wolf. It seemed like eons ago when I actually had time to do something other than fight the next supe in line or battle through a ghoul-infested forest.

Rourke snuffed at me from behind, voicing his trepidation, but went along with the plan, staying close to me.

What was the last good book you read? I asked him as my wolf began to zigzag, based only on smell.

What? His response couldn't have been more incredulous.

Just play along. Instead, what's your all-time favorite book? You know, when you used to have spare time? My wolf was doing a good job of dodging the threats, but there were so many. I didn't know how long it would take to throw Enid off—if it was even possible. *You had to have read a book sometime in your life before you met me and our lives were turned upside down.*

Jessica, I haven't read a book in too long to remember. Watch out for those two! he yelled. Two ghouls, one a female about seventy and one thirtysomething male, came at us from behind a huge pine tree. The male was moving faster. Maybe age had something to do with it?

I see them. My wolf smoothly dodged them but picked up the pace immediately. *And I'm not letting you off the hook about your lack of reading. We're going to fix that in the future. But since we're talking about it, my favorite of all time is* Lord of the Rings. *After the movies came out, I read them all one after another. So good.*

He huffed at me. *This is not the time for this discussion.*

It's the perfect time for this discussion—because we shouldn't be having it! My wolf wove us in and out of trees, while I kept my mind on good books. Each time I heard a rustling, we shifted our movements and then shifted again. She had great reflexes.

Rourke followed me with no issue, but he was on high alert and couldn't shut it off. I just hoped Enid had been tracking *my* movements and not ours together. *Jessica, you're moving toward the cemetery,* Rourke said. *I don't think that's a good idea.*

My wolf is in control, I said. *The sounds are coming more infrequently now. I think it might be working. If Enid doesn't know we're heading there, the cemetery can be safe, because all the ghouls are in the woods.*

Nothing is safe, Rourke grumbled, veering with me out into the open.

I switched my mind to my favorite TV shows as we sped past several tombstones. I was feeling quite confident that maybe we'd thrown Enid off.

Not a second later, low moans came from a hill to our right. My head snapped to it in alarm.

Run! Rourke shouted, shoving into me from the behind. *As fast as you can. Now!*

The horror scorched into my mind like a blistering brand as I watched them come at us like loping zombies over the grassy knolls.

Wendigos.

24

Keep to the open spaces! Rourke yelled as we dodged and leapt over gravestones. The wendigos were running hard. They were very different from the ghouls. These guys were alive. *We can't fight off both ghouls and wendigos. We're going to have to do something drastic.*

Like what? I asked, glancing behind me. We'd gotten in front of them. I spotted only two, but that didn't mean there weren't more.

I don't know yet. When I think of it, I'll tell you.

We continued to run. And the wendigos continued to gain. They were clearly supernatural now, with the essence of the necromancer inside them. I took a peek over my shoulder. They looked disheveled, their faces smudged with dirt and their clothes ratty. *I think they were cemetery workers. One guy looks like he could be a grave digger. Do they even have those anymore?*

They've been turned recently, Rourke agreed.

Rourke turned and followed a path over another hill. At the

top we caught sight of the other edge of the cemetery. It was at least a hundred yards away. *Rourke, we have to make a decision. They're gaining on us. I'm not sure we'll make the other side, and when we do, there's a wall of ghouls to contend with.* A line of ghouls was emerging from out of the woods on the far end. They weren't moving very fast and were likely just going to sit and wait for us to be dumb enough to try and get through them.

We have to fight the wendigos. They're the biggest threat, Rourke said. *We keep running until they're almost on us, then we turn and attack. Use your claws and slash right through their necks. It's risky, but we have no other choice. But whatever happens, don't let them bite you!*

That was easier said than done, especially if that's what Enid thought we'd do. *I promised Tyler I'd get in touch with him if things went south,* I panted as we continued running. *This is pretty far south. Ray can be here in a matter of minutes and Tyler will follow quickly. If Ray shows up, we can use him as a distraction, and because he can fly, maybe he'll be safer?*

Go ahead and sound the alarm, and then I want you to get ready to fight.

Tyler! I called. *We're in trouble! Not only ghouls, but we're also being chased by wendigos. Get here as soon as you can.*

We're on it, my brother answered immediately. *We guessed it would get bad. We have your scent. Ray will be there soon.*

Tyler, you have to be very cautious. You can't risk getting bit. Contact me before you hit the area and I'll give you the plan.

Got it.

I tuned him out and focused on our situation. Then I had a thought. *Rourke, my gut is we have to make change happen in a big way right now. If we don't, we're going to become wendigos.*

We just tried that and it didn't work! he answered.

No, we were still moving forward in the same way, just putting our minds on something else. I'm talking about doing something completely unexpected.

Like what? I could tell by his tone he was leery of my plan already.

I don't know, but it has to be out of character—something shocking. I leapt over a tall grave marker and spotted something in the distance. It gave me an idea. *This way.* I careened to the right, not giving him a choice. Rourke followed, staying close to my flank.

Where are we going? He nudged closer.

I saw some mausoleums. Two, side by side. We're going to jump on top of them and hide.

Jessica, they will see us do that. Even if we aren't doing something predictable, like hiding, they can follow us by sight.

Not if we can reach the buildings before the wendigos see us, and the key word was "hide."

I still don't get it.

Follow me and find out, I said as I made a sharp turn. I raced downhill over the terrain, thanking my lucky stars these mausoleums were over the next hill. I'd just gotten a glimpse of their roofs at the right time. If we ran fast enough, we could get there before the wendigos rounded the incline behind us, giving us a few precious seconds where the hill would obstruct their line of sight.

This is crazy. These guys are gaining on us and they can jump just as high as we can.

I huffed. *I'm trying to do something unexpected, and having you not on board is actually perfect. Just follow me and try to stop overthinking it. I just need to make sure they can't see us for a few seconds. Look behind us and watch. Let me know when we duck out of their line of vision.* I raced toward our goal. Once we rounded the top of the next hill, I could see the mausoleums clearly. They each had flat roofs and large columns and a small peak in front, which would give us something we could crouch behind.

Okay, we have about four seconds before they come over the top of the last hill, Rourke called.

Perfect. I sprinted the last few yards and leapt, stretching my body as far as I could, landing on the roof of the closest building. The mausoleums were at least fifteen feet high. Rourke made a move to follow me but I yelled, *Jump on top of the other one!*

Rourke swerved at the last minute and did as I asked but was snorting his dislike as he went.

Now duck down, I said. *Flatten yourself out so you're smaller.*

He did it as best he could and then turned his big tawny head toward me. *Jessica, this is the craziest thing you've ever had us do so far.*

No, it's the most brilliant, and you want to know why?

If cats could look sarcastic, he was achieving it. *I can't wait to find out. Why?*

Because it feels wrong.

He stayed down, but his ears were pinned back and he snarled, *What do you mean it feels* wrong? *That's not what I want to hear right now.*

No, wrong in a good way. We're hiding from the threat. It wouldn't normally be something we would do. A few minutes ago you wanted us to fight them, and I agreed with you. I poked my head up and looked, careful not to make a sound. The wendigos were barreling over the hill in front of us but were not aiming for the mausoleums.

Even if the wendigos pass us by, they'll figure it out soon enough and turn around, Rourke said. *They won't give up the hunt.*

Probably, but I don't think it will matter. By jumping up here to hide, the die has been cast, I said. *All we needed to do was to change the game enough—to make the future a little more unpredictable. If we achieved that, we survive. If not, we become horrible flesh-eating supernaturals.*

I'm not sure it's going to work like you hope—

There was a whooshing noise and Ray landed on the mausoleum next to me. "What the hell are you two knuckleheads doing up here?" he bellowed. "Don't you know you're under attack by a horde of shitty, awful-looking zombies?"

I huffed at him, my ears down, showing him my displeasure. I couldn't talk to Ray internally, so there was no real way to tell him to leave besides swiping at him with my paw and trying to knock him off the roof. I raised my front leg to give it a try.

"Hold on," he said. "Don't get your undies in a bunch. We can fight these things. They don't look that tough."

I glanced over at Rourke. *Do you see the wendigos? They must have heard Ray's yelling.* Tyler must not have stressed to Ray how dangerous this was. Ray was too new and cocky to know better.

I snarled.

"You don't have to thank me yet, Hannon," Ray said. "We're not outta the woods by a long shot. Those two ran past, down the—"

The wendigos howled as they changed their direction. I poked my head up. They were running at top speed toward us. The reason Rourke hadn't answered me was because he'd readied himself for a fight, crouching low. The wendigos made good time, and when the first one sprang toward me, I was ready. But before I could do anything, Ray intercepted it in midair and tossed it effortlessly to the ground.

It bounced and rolled a few feet and then was up again, snarling, pus and drool running down its chin. I howled as the next one flew at Rourke. With his huge paw, Rourke batted it away, tearing open its middle. The wendigo tumbled through the air and landed with a loud thunk on the ground.

They were both back in business within a minute.

The action had alerted the ghouls, and now they streamed in from all directions, surrounding us. They were reanimated corpses, so they couldn't jump very well or get on the roof, but they weren't going anywhere either.

The wendigos circled the buildings, calculating their next attack.

If we can find the necromancer and disarm her, do you think they would all stop fighting us? I asked Rourke.

The ghouls should drop like rocks and go back to being corpses, but the wendigos would still be a threat. They are infected, and while the necromancer might have some *control, these guys are largely on their own. They crave flesh any way they can find it. If they stop being interested in us, they will hunt down the next available option.*

Good gods, I said as visions of a town being turned into an army of hungry wendigos assaulted me. *Okay, then, we have to kill them and find the necromancer. I'm going to put Tyler on finding the necromancer if he can,* I told Rourke.

Rourke didn't answer, as he was occupied when one of the wendigos launched himself onto the roof again. He efficiently sliced the wendigo up the side. Rourke was being as careful as he could so the thing couldn't bite him, but it was still unsettling to watch. The wendigo fell back to the ground, but it still wasn't down for the count.

I angled my head at Ray and nodded my muzzle toward Rourke, indicating he should go help.

"I'm going, I'm going, but I don't think your boy really needs my help. Did you see that? He just clawed his arm off with one swipe." Ray's voice held some awe. This was the first time he'd seen Rourke in action in his true form. I nudged my head against Ray's leg to get him to move. "All right, I'll go, but if one comes here, I'll be back."

Rourke was indeed incredible to watch, but I wasn't going to breathe easy until the wendigo went flying off the roof without its head. Rourke roared, and the sound shook the buildings. It was so close to dawn the sky was beginning to turn from black to blue. Humans would be up and around soon. We were running out of time. We had to finish this.

Tyler, can you hear me? I asked.

Yep, I'm almost to you, he said. *And I smell a whole hell of a lot of interesting things coming my way. None of them make me happy.*

Great. Don't head to where we are. I want you to find the necromancer. Use your nose. Rourke says they have to be stationed close by to operate these things, and there's a whole bunch of them. I'm thinking the necromancer has to be on the cemetery grounds somewhere. If we can take him or her down, we have a chance to stop these ghouls. No operator means no more attack.

I'm on it, he said. *Marcy and James are close too. Ray sounded the alarm. I'll keep an ear out for the van. She can help by throwing some spells out if I can't pick up the scent.*

I knew he would do his best to find the necromancer, and for a moment I hoped Juanita had been in contact with Marcy. We needed an edge. I brought my attention back to the scene in front of me. The wendigos had decided to work in tandem and Rourke had his hands full, even with Ray's help.

I leapt cleanly to Rourke's rooftop, where Ray had already landed, and glanced over the side. There were at least sixty ghouls surrounding us and one headless wendigo on the ground. Rourke had finally hit his mark. But, ridiculously, its one arm was trying to locate its head, doing the pat-pat-pat around its body. Not sure what would happen if it managed to grab it, but I couldn't imagine the wendigo could function very well again without its head secured on.

The remaining wendigo crouched a few feet away, separated a bit from the ghouls, ready to spring again, its vacant eyes never leaving the roof for a second.

"That bastard's not dead," Ray complained, gesturing to the headless wendigo. "You took one arm and its head off and the sucker is still trying to function. I can't kill these guys like I usually do, because their souls have already left the building. We'll have to bash their brains in or something."

I stood, nodding my head toward the other wendigo, who was edging himself closer.

"I see him, I see him," Ray muttered. "But he'd be a fool to come up here. He's outnumbered. These others"—he gestured at the crowd of ghouls that were now clawing at the walls of the mausoleum—"are no threat. We just have to stay away from their teeth."

Keep your eye on that one, I told Rourke. *Tyler is going to try and find the necromancer.*

I'm watching him, Rourke answered. *I thought they'd be quicker, but their reflexes are slower than a shifter's. The ghouls also seem to be slowing down. The necromancer must be overloaded trying to control all these things at once.*

Ray made a move to fly off the mausoleum and I snapped my jaws on the end of his shirt to keep him rooted in place.

"Jesus, Hannon. I'm not going near them. I'm not that stupid. I was just going to take a look overhead," he said. "This necromancer has to be close by, right? That's a horde down there. That would make anyone tired." Ray's brain was in the right place, but I had no way to tell him that I'd just sent Tyler on that same mission.

But it wouldn't hurt for him to do some surveillance. I let go of his shirt.

"I'll be right back," he said.

Ray took off and I edged closer to Rourke, whose gaze was still locked on the wendigo.

How do you want to do this? I asked.

We wait him out, he answered. *I've been watching him closely for a while now and he seems unsure. I think Ray's right. This necromancer is overwhelmed. Even though whoever is running things might not be keyed in fully to the wendigos, all the undead are slowing.*

Seeming to finally make up its mind, the wendigo began to run at us. Rourke and I stood, lowering our bodies, reading for an attack.

I said, *You go for the legs, I'll take the neck.*

I'm not sure this wendigo is going to make the jump.

As it ran forward, it stumbled, and just as it was about to spring, a high-pitched scream came from the woods.

The wendigo took a halfhearted leap, and Rourke reached out, his claws making a clean cut, severing the head. The wendigo went down, and then all around us the ghouls fell one by one.

Tyler's voice hit my mind a second later and it was frantic. *I found her. She was nearby.* He gave a guttural internal cry and then yelled, *No!*

I was instantly on my feet. *Tyler, what's wrong? What's going on?* I made a move to jump down, but Rourke held me back with his big tawny head, snarling furiously.

I howled my frustration into the air. *Tyler, answer me!*

His voice wasn't more than a whisper. *Please, she can't be dead.*

25

Jessica, I have to eliminate the threat completely while they're down, Rourke said, brushing against my flank to get my attention. *The wendigos aren't fully dead yet. Stay up here until I know for sure it's safe. The ghouls don't look like they're going to rise, but stranger things have happened.*

Fine, I agreed. *But do it quickly. Tyler found the necromancer and something's wrong.* Ray hadn't returned either. My guess was he had found Tyler. My brother's voice had been full of anguish and I didn't know what to make of it.

Ray landed beside me. "Brace yourself, Hannon," he said. "I saw Tyler running into an old building on the grounds, busting right through the door. Marcy, James, and Nick were close behind, but by the time we all got there, he wouldn't let anyone in. I have no idea what's going on, but it smells like a pile of shit to me."

I paced the length of the roof, not knowing what to do as I watched my mate finish killing the wendigos. Fully dismantling their brains with his claws wasn't a pretty sight.

Before I could talk to Rourke and figure out what we should do, I spotted Tyler in the hazy dawn, just over the hill in front of us. He was half walking, half staggering, holding something tightly in his arms.

He was naked. He hadn't had time to dress yet.

I sprung off the roof without a word and soared through the air toward him. I landed at a run and could feel both Ray and Rourke close behind me.

I slowed about twenty yards from Tyler, sensing his distress.

The form in his arms appeared tiny in his grasp. Her long dark hair hung almost to the ground. Her skin was pale yet bronze in color. Her delicate neck was tossed backward, and I could see she was breathing, but it was shallow at best.

She wore nothing more than a dirty nightgown with small flowers dotted on it, and her feet were bare. On further inspection, I noted that her wrists were damaged—ugly red welts ran in a circle around them both and a bit of loose rope hung between her and Tyler.

Tyler stopped in his tracks, his face a mask of pain.

I had to tread with caution. I'd never seen my brother in this state. *What happened?* I asked. *Who is she?*

Tyler seemed stunned at my question. He glanced down at her and said out loud, "I...I don't know. I just saw her...and my wolf went wild...and then she collapsed...I think she's dead..."

You have to set her down so we can help her, I told him calmly in my mind. Her shallow breaths were uneven and coming too far apart. I had no idea what the life span of a necromancer was or how easily they could die.

"We can't help her....She's dangerous...," Tyler stammered. "She's...she's going to have to...be stopped...We can't risk it..." His voice trailed off as he glanced down at her again, his face unreadable.

Rourke snarled next to me, catching my eye, and then bobbed his head. *I know*, I said. *I'm trying.* Ray mumbled something and Marcy and James came into view behind Tyler.

Marcy had a questioning look on her face. I addressed my brother again. *You need to set her down.* Tyler didn't move. *We're not going to hurt her. She did this against her will. Look at her wrists.* As he did, his eyebrows drew together, but he held her close to his chest, unmoving. *We can't help her if you don't let her go. Lay her down on the grass. Time is running out and we need to hurry.*

Marcy held our clothes in her arms, so we were ready when we shifted back to human. Nick came up from the side, circling around so he stood behind Rourke and me, likely trying to put himself between us and the pile of ghouls and dead wendigos up the hill. So very Nick.

Come on, Tyler, lay her down, I coaxed.

Tyler hesitated before he set her gently down in front of him, making sure she was covered by her scrap of a soiled nightgown.

I moved toward them slowly and huffed at Rourke to stay behind me. *Let me handle this. Tyler is an extremely protective wolf, and for some reason he feels he needs to protect this necromancer. He's going to react strongly to anything until we can get him to calm down.*

I'll be right by your side, Rourke replied. *I can understand his concern. That necromancer looks very young. She almost worked herself to death. Enid must have held something significant over her to get her to do it, and by the looks of it, she was snatched right out of her own bed.*

She had to have been taken from her home. No one would come to work in a nightgown. Once I arrived at Tyler's side, I gently placed my muzzle near the girl's body and scented. Her signature was powerful and strange. I'd never met a necromancer before, other than the dead one in Hell, but this one kept her power coiled tightly inside her.

Marcy walked up, James right behind her. "I have your clothes here. How about you guys shift back so we can all help this girl? She's obviously in some distress. Sound okay?" Her movements were measured and easy. James had her back, and all eyes were on Tyler.

Tyler, I said carefully. *Take the clothes from Marcy and put them on. Rourke and I will go change and we'll come back. I can't help her in my wolf form.*

Tyler nodded, absentmindedly grabbing the clothing Marcy held out. He started to dress, his gaze never leaving the necromancer's body. Marcy beckoned me and I moved toward her. She held out both mine and Rourke's clothes, and when I took mine in between my jaws, she whispered, "Make it snappy. The sun is up and this place will be hopping soon. James has the van ready to go so we can move quickly."

I nodded and padded into the woods, Rourke right behind me.

We shifted back and dressed in under two minutes, and as we walked back side by side, Rourke said, "You help the girl while Nick and I gather the bodies. I'll send Ray off to search for something to set them on fire. We're going to need a big blaze. Ray can light it after we take off."

"We'll have to take the necromancer with us," I said definitively. "Alive or dead."

"Agreed. From what I can sense, she's alive, but barely," he answered. "If anyone can help her, you can. She probably needs a power jump so she can refuel her own magic herself, but be careful. Once she has that, she might wake up, and who knows what she'll do when she finds herself caught."

"I'll be careful. If she snaps out of it, she's going to be in for one hell of a surprise. She doesn't look more than twenty-two at most."

Marcy was on the ground next to the girl when we arrived, and

James stood between Tyler and his mate, arms crossed. The van was idling at the edge of the cemetery. James had parked it on the grass just in front of the trees.

Rourke's voice was full of authority. "Irish," he said, addressing James, "come with me." He nodded toward Nick. "You too. We need to pile the dead up and burn them. Ray, you go find something flammable. We need a strong, hot fire. Humans are going to be talking about this for centuries, but it can't be helped." Rourke turned and began to walk back toward the mausoleums. Nick followed immediately, and after a moment, so did James.

I nodded to James, letting him know I had this as I knelt next to Marcy. "Did you find anything?" I asked her. "What do you think happened to her?"

"Necromancy is powerful magic. It takes a lot of juice." Marcy shot me a wry glance. "She's just a little slip of a thing, isn't she? I'm not sure how she did it—controlling that many." Marcy ran her hands lightly over the girl's body. "I can't find any serious injuries. I think she just burned herself out, which can be dangerous. A supe can short-circuit themselves with magic if they push too hard."

Marcy moved back so I could scoot in. I laid my hands on the girl's stomach and addressed my wolf. *Can you spot anything?* We began to ease our power in, trying to jump-start her magic. *Wow, do you see that?* Her signature was a vibrant orange and alive, buzzing and bouncing throughout her system. It was like nothing I'd ever seen before. I turned to Marcy. "I'm going to transfer some of my power to her. Be ready to restrain her. She's not going to be happy to see us when she comes to."

"My fingers are at the ready," Marcy answered, wiggling them. "I've never met a necromancer before, which is kind of weird since I'm a witch and they're kind of witchy. I have no idea what to expect. When she wakes up, there's a possibility she'll order forty ghouls to jump out of the woods and attack us. She might have a backup plan in place for this very thing."

I shook my head. "I don't think so, but just in case, I'll knock her out the good old-fashioned way if it looks like trouble." Tyler began to pace in front of us. "Tyler." I glanced up. "I need you to stay calm, whatever happens. If you interfere, there's going to be trouble. And this goes without saying, once she wakes up, she's going to need her space. Freaked-out is what I'm expecting."

"I'm fine," he said. "Just do it already, she's barely breathing."

He still looked a little unstable. I needed to know he wasn't going to act. I nodded my head toward an area a bit away from us. "Go sit down." My voice held an order. We were wasting time. "Now."

For a moment it appeared like he would argue, but then he closed his mouth and sat with a thump, closer than I would've liked. "Fine. I'm sitting. Fix her."

I took a slow breath to center myself as I pushed more power into her tiny body. This time I wasn't seeking anything but trying to force it into her cells—like giving her magical mouth-to-mouth.

At the end of a draw, she gasped and her chest jumped. But she remained out cold. I threw another dose into her, making sure I kept it in check. I didn't want to give her too much. Her body reacted like it'd been charged, her chest heaving up twice before she finally blinked awake, terror on her face as she glanced up at me. "Don't move just yet," I said quietly. "Let me give you a little more so you can heal yourself."

She didn't listen. Instead, she clawed her fingers into the ground and twisted, stifling a scream as she tried to scramble away from me. "No, no, NO! It can't happen like this," she cried. Her voice was soft and breathy. "I have to complete my task! You have to die!"

Her eyes were incredibly striking. The irises were a full kaleidoscope of browns and yellows, colors that seemed to churn on their own. They dazzled, almost hypnotically. "That's not going to happen," I told her as I held her in place. "No one is dying here."

Marcy leaned over her, commanding, "Stay still, or I'll have to spell you. You only get one chance to cooperate with us. I suggest you take it."

"The hell I'm going to cooperate!" she shouted, surprising us all. Her foot shot out and connected with my jaw, effectively breaking it.

My head snapped back and there was an ugly sound. I rocked backward and held my aching face as she sprang up, lithe and agile, the well-defined muscles in her small arms tensing as she got down in a defensive position. She was obviously well versed in combat, and strong as hell. We'd underestimated her, thinking she'd act like she looked—fragile.

"*Ow*, that hurt." My jaw popped into place as it mended. She was so focused on me, she didn't hear Tyler come up behind her. He quietly took hold of her around the waist. She immediately kicked and squirmed, but he held her still, not saying anything. Marcy was ready next to me, chanting a spell under her breath. I stood before I addressed the necromancer once again, totally healed. "Nobody is dying," I reiterated. She met my gaze reluctantly as she continued to struggle in Tyler's grasp. "We're taking you with us, and if you don't cooperate, my friend here will spell you. It's that simple."

"Please," she moaned, changing her tune quickly when she realized she was out of options. "You have to let me go. I won't call on any more dead. I promise! But I have to leave right now."

"Why?" I asked, coming closer. Her voice had broken at the end, anguish seeping through. She had my attention.

She snapped her mouth shut and wriggled again, trying to get free.

I stopped in front of her. "We can't let you go. It's not an option." My tone indicated that we weren't giving in on that point. "You're a liability and you're coming with us. But you can tell us what's wrong, and if it's possible, we will try and help you."

She pointedly looked away from me, refusing to answer. I nodded to Tyler, who began to half drag her toward the van. Marcy followed close on his heels, her fingers still up and ready.

A few feet from the van, the necromancer finally found some purchase and dug her dirty bare feet into the ground, twisting in Tyler's grasp, angling her head back toward me. "No, please, you have to listen to me! If I leave with you, she will kill him. I can't let that happen. You don't understand! Please!"

At the mention of "him," Tyler stopped moving, tensing, his breath labored.

I moved around to face her. "You need to be more specific. Who's going to kill whom?"

Behind us, Rourke, James, and Nick came jogging down the hill, their jobs with the ghouls done.

The waif saw them, her face panicked as she shot her gaze from them back to me. "The woman who kidnapped me! She said if I failed to do what she ordered, she would kill my brother. Please! He's only fifteen and he's all alone. I have to get back to him before it's too late."

The guys pulled up behind her and fanned out. "I hear what you're saying," I told her, "but you have to come with us now. We can't linger here and you have no way to get home that I can see. It's going to take us a bit to figure this out. We'll do it in the van." Her face dropped. "But I'm giving you my word. If your story checks out, we will help you and your brother."

She didn't respond, only continued to look stricken. Rourke

walked up next to me and addressed her. "If you want our help, get in the vehicle." He gestured to the idling gator van. "If we don't buy your story, we don't help. We need to vacate this area. Now."

James walked around the driver's side and got in. Tyler guided the girl toward the side door, keeping a firm grip on her. I stepped in front of him and yanked it open. Tyler lifted her up and tugged her into the middle row. I hesitated before getting in. Jeb had told me to stay out of any vehicle. "I'm not sure if I should go with you. Enid might not be done yet."

A buzz sounded.

Marcy had her hand on the front passenger door and pulled her phone out of her back pocket. She cackled as she turned, showing it to me.

GET IN, CHICA.

I smiled. It was about time we heard from her. "Okay, I'll ride." Then I called into the air, "It would be nice to actually talk to you. When I get home, there are several things we need to discuss!"

Marcy glanced down at her phone. "No answer."

I chuckled as I got in, Rourke and Nick climbing in behind me. "I didn't think she would reply, but I feel like I at least have to try. Her tactics are frustrating as hell."

Tyler and the necromancer had taken the middle bench, Rourke joined me in the back, and Nick scooted in next to the girl to make sure she stayed put. She didn't look too happy, but she kept her mouth shut.

As we drove away, I glanced out the back window.

In the distance, Ray held a huge torch, and just as we careened out of view, he leaned over and lit the stack of bodies. It would be a raging inferno in seconds. We took off through the woods. I leaned forward and tapped the necromancer on the shoulder. "Can those bodies be of harm to anyone after we burn them?"

She shook her head but didn't turn around.

"Are you sure?" I prodded. "The humans in this city are in for the shock of a lifetime when they discover this. There will be no explanation for what happened, so rumors will run rampant, but if the humans who handle the charred bodies of the ghouls and wendigos are at risk, it's unacceptable."

"The wendigos are not contagious. You can kill a wendigo by fire if the brain has been destroyed—which I know you did, because I felt it." Her voice held a hard edge. "I have fully withdrawn from the ghouls. They will not harm anyone. They are only corpses now."

I sat back, nestling into Rourke's shoulder. "What's your name?" I asked as the van continued to bounce over the grassy hills before James was able to maneuver us onto a small country road.

After a long pause, she replied, "Kayla." It was clear that was all she was going to give willingly.

I glanced at Rourke. He nodded and I scooted aside so he could take over. We needed information from this girl whether she wanted to give it or not. I was not opposed to using whatever it took. "We understand you did all this against your will, Kayla," Rourke started, leaning up so he was over her shoulder. She straightened her back and tried to inch away, but there was nowhere for her to go. "But we also know you're a powerful necromancer, and we won't hurt you, if"—he let that settle for a moment—"you tell us what we need to know. So why don't you cooperate and start from the beginning? How did you come to be here?" He ended on a growl to force the seriousness of his request.

She shifted in her seat with obvious irritation. "I have no time to start at the beginning, because by the time I reach the end, my brother will already be *dead*."

26

James pushed the van faster than I'd thought it was capable of going. It zipped along the country back roads at breakneck speed, tossing us around in our seats continually. But James was a skilled driver and Marcy was keeping lookout.

We'd waited for her to spill, but after that confession, Kayla still hadn't divulged any information. Even though Rourke had stayed in her space. I tried again. "Kayla," I reasoned, "we can help you if you give us a chance. But in order to do that, you need to give us more information than 'she's going to kill him.' We can see you were kidnapped, and by the looks of it right out of your bedroom, but we need concrete details. And once we have them, we can figure out the next move. We are not your enemy. Enid is." Still nothing. So I used a different angle. "If we decide to take you home to rescue your brother, are we at least heading in the right direction?"

"No," she snapped, finally angling her body around to face me. "In fact, each mile we go is another mile away from him."

Her voice was full of anger and emotion, and in that moment I knew exactly how she felt. I'd just traveled to the Underworld to save my own brother. Sibling bonds were important, especially in the supernatural world—since the odds were against you having them from the start.

Before I could form a reply, Tyler said, "I say we go after him." His voice was firm and authoritative. It was the first time he'd spoken since we'd gotten into the van.

We all gaped at him, including Marcy, who turned in her seat, eyes wide. But she had the wherewithal to keep her mouth shut.

Kayla turned from me to glance at my brother.

She was frowning.

I cleared my throat. "What my brother means is we'll listen to what you have to say, and once we have the information—"

"No," Tyler said with an edge. "What I mean is we're turning this van around *now* and going wherever Kayla tells us to go." His power jumped to show his seriousness.

Kayla's frown turned into a tentative smile.

I could see only her profile now, but she really was lovely. It was hard to think of not helping her. She was obviously in a lot of distress. She was a perfect blend of both delicate and hard. Her features were soft and rounded, but her body was toned and angular, ready for battle. She had full lips and high cheekbones, with a slight blush to them. Her long, dark hair seemed to war with her coloring, which was pinker now that she was breathing again normally. She was a serious mix of backgrounds, but I had no idea which ones—possibly Greek or Italian with a mix of Scandinavian? It was hard to know exactly.

"Tyler, we're not turning around. We're heading home first," I said with finality. "Once we figure out the threat, we can decide what to do for Kayla—"

He turned in his seat to look at me, his face set. "Are you really telling me you're choosing not to save her brother while we still can?" Anger welled in his voice. "Since when do we not try and save an innocent? Kayla is as much of a victim in all this as we are. We help her and then figure out our next move."

Nick interjected before I could form my rebuttal. "Tyler, until we hear what Kayla has to say, we don't really know who's innocent and why we should risk our lives to help her. If she decides to trust us, and share her story with us, it might help sway us. And for the record, I agree with you—we should help—but not without more information first. She could be leading us into a trap or worse."

"It could take hours to get the full story from her, like she said," he retorted. "By then we'll be too far away." He glanced back at me, his eyes pleading. "Let's at least get this van in the right direction, and *then* Kayla can tell us her story." When I didn't respond immediately, he switched to internal communication. *Jess, I need you to do this. We have to help her.*

We will help her. I'm not saying we won't. But we have to hear what she has to say first. She's extremely powerful and dangerous, and we can't discount that. What if Enid had a backup plan and Kayla's new route leads us into a trap? Nick is right.

Tyler rubbed the back of his neck as a fine sheen of sweat dotted his upper brow. *It doesn't feel right that she'd lead us into something,* he countered, *but if that's her plan, wouldn't Juanita let us know? She told you to get in the van. Honestly, I don't even care anymore. If you're not going to help her, I will. Just pull over and we'll get out and figure it out on our own.*

I can't let you do that.

Jess, my wolf is about to jump out of my skin. I can't contain it anymore. Everything inside me is in turmoil. If you don't let us out, I could go full shift right here.

I could scent Tyler's change and his agitation. He was telling the truth. I took a deep breath and made a decision. "Okay, Kayla, where do we go?"

Relief swept through her features as she turned. "Baltimore."

"Baltimore?" Marcy said from the front seat. "Are you telling us Baltimore is a hotbed for necromancers? Who would've guessed?" She turned toward her mate and said, "You heard the lady, turn this van around. According to my awesome navigational skills, we need to head east."

James opened his mouth once to protest, but instead glanced into the rearview mirror at me. I met his gaze and nodded once. He slowed the van and did a U-turn.

As James nosed the van in the right direction, Kayla's entire demeanor changed drastically. I waited to see what she would do, and she finally decided to address Marcy's comment. "Baltimore is not a hotbed for anything. That's why we chose it. We move around often, and we've only been there for a year." She glanced down at her lap. "I left him there...alone in our apartment. I didn't have a choice—I know that. She threatened to kill him if I didn't go, so I went. But that doesn't make it any more bearable. He just turned fifteen."

"Why do you need to move often?" I asked, staying away from the heavier issues for the moment.

She turned in her seat, trapping me with an intense gaze, her irises radiating brilliantly, a soft yellow hue sparking deeply. "You will not get me to tell you my secrets whatever you do. I owe you no allegiance."

I sighed. "I'm not asking for your secrets. I agree with you. You don't owe us," I said, "but if you want our help we need more. I refuse to walk into this cold. I want to trust you, Kayla. I do. But you're making it extremely tough. You want us to free your brother, but you don't want to give anything in return. That's not how this game is played and I think you're well aware of that. So give us something to go on—*anything*."

She openly assessed me, her eyes seeming to dip into my soul. Then her head bobbed down once in acceptance. "Fine, I'll answer your questions, just as long as they stay on the surface, nothing more."

"Fair enough," I said. "How old are you?"

"I don't see why you need—"

"Just tell me," I said, a growl in my voice, my wolf agitated with my decision to help this girl.

"Twenty-three," she said.

"Why did Enid pick you? Out of all the necromancers she could've chosen in the area, why you?"

"I don't know." Her eyes stopped churning for a split second.

"You're lying, but we'll come back to that," I said, waving my hand. "Why Baltimore?"

"Just like I told the witch, because it's under the radar," she answered.

She's running from something, Rourke interjected smoothly in my mind. *But she's not going to tell us what it is and I can't really blame her. She doesn't know us.*

She's fiercely loyal to her brother, I answered. *It strums off of her. At least that's a trait we can embrace. I'm also not getting an evil vibe from her, but I can't be sure. Her magic signature is incredibly strange. It has its own pulse.*

I want to know what she is. She's a mix of something. "Where do your people hail from?" Rourke asked.

I guess that was one way to find out.

She turned her head slightly in Rourke's direction but didn't make eye contact. "I am half Greek and half Icelandic. My mother was from Iceland, my father from Greece."

"Your parents mated out of species." Rourke said it as a fact. That meant she was a supernatural mix, with more than one supernatural trait possible. Maybe that's why her signature was so strange. When she didn't acknowledge him, Rourke leaned forward, his mouth inches from her ear. "Iceland is known for only two things: elves and trolls. Your mother was an elf, wasn't she? Your father a necromancer?"

I hadn't noticed her ears. Elves usually had pointed ears. But she could've had those surgically altered. An elf would certainly explain her tiny stature and fierce strength. Elves were rare, from what I knew. They were ancestors of the fae, and they were rumored to be great archers and quick on their feet. I'd never met one.

Tyler shifted in his seat, clearly uncomfortable with our line of questioning.

Kayla didn't answer Rourke, but her refusal was enough.

I peered over her shoulder. Her hands were clasped tightly, her knuckles white. I decided to give her a break. I sat back, patting Rourke's leg to let him know the plan was to ease up. "Tell us about your brother instead," I said from my relaxed position, trying to calm her down. "You obviously love him and want to keep him safe. That's admirable. I can relate, because I love my brother too. He's the one you're sitting next to, who's championing you. I would do anything to save his life—and I have."

Tyler grunted, turning to give me a small smile, relief apparent in his shoulders and face. His wolf must have eased up now that we were headed in the right direction. "It's true," he said. "Jessica just pulled me out of the Underworld. But truth be told, I'm not the one who usually needs saving. If she'd stop getting into trouble every five minutes, my life would be so much easier." He tossed me a lopsided grin, one of his dimples showing for the first time. "Keeping my sibling safe is a full-time job, so we get it."

Kayla took in a small, quick breath.

My brother was incredibly handsome. His blond hair was longer than I'd seen in a while, curling in the back over his collar. That coupled with his sky-blue eyes and dimples gave him a sweet, rugged look. He looked like the kind of guy who could easily pick up a surfboard one day and scale a mountain the next.

He was also loyal, fierce, and competitive as hell. I'm certain Kayla had picked up on all of it already.

When Kayla didn't seem to want to answer my question about her brother, Nick prodded her gently. "Okay, so at least tell us your brother's name."

"He goes by Jax."

"Is he a necromancer like you?" I asked.

"No."

"Is it possible for him to hold his own against Enid until we get there?" Nick asked. That was a crafty way of asking how powerful he was. Nick was always thinking.

"No, he's in danger. He won't be able to…he can't…" She sighed. "We just need to find him."

I caught my brother's eye. *She's not going to give us anything more,* Tyler said. *Can we just give her a break now?*

We need to know a few more things, and then we'll stop. I glanced at the back of Kayla's head, assessing her. "Kayla, we need for you to answer a few more questions. Then we'll be done for a while. I need to know how and when Enid found you. Did she come ahead of time to set it up? Or did she surprise you recently? And had you ever come in contact with her before? She's a huge threat to us, and we have to understand how this happened. After that, we can all get some sleep."

"She came to me in my sleep two nights ago." Kayla's voice was low, barely above a whisper. "I could not resist her calls. She warned me that she would come if I didn't cooperate, but I didn't believe it—I refused to think she could force me when she only came to me in my sleep. Then in the early hours of the morning she woke me and led me to my brother. He was bound to his bed. I couldn't get the chains off. They were spelled by something powerful." She choked. "Then she somehow knocked me out. I have no recollection of how I arrived at the cemetery. My hands were tied. Once I was coherent, she was in my mind again, ordering me to raise the dead. At first I resisted, but she showed me horrible, awful pictures of what she would do to Jax—or had already done. I had no choice but to do as she asked." She quietly sobbed, her head down. After a moment she cleared her throat and finished with "I don't regret what I did to you. I would do it again in a heartbeat to save my brother. He is the only family I have left."

"I don't blame you, Kayla." My voice was sincere. "We'd all do the same thing. When she was in your mind, did you ever see her face? Or get a clear picture of her?" It would help if we knew what she looked like.

Kayla shook her head. "No. Only a great, foreboding presence."

"Damn, I was hoping—"

James slammed on the brakes and swerved, shouting a curse. "That vampire is a bloody nuisance!" As he regained control of the van, he slowed and eased it over to the shoulder.

Ray stood in the middle of the road ten paces ahead of us, his hands on his hips.

"Well," I chuckled, "he could've landed on the roof. That's a favorite of his. He must have spotted something urgent or he would've chosen another means to stop us." Or maybe not. You never knew with him.

Ray gestured for us to park the van on the side of the road as he strode toward us. James shut off the van.

Nick reached over to the passenger door and opened it as I called to the front, "Marcy, check your phone."

"Already on it," she commented over her shoulder. "All's still dead in Juanita-Land."

Before any of us could ask what was wrong, Ray stuck his head in the door and launched in. "There's a goddamn house up ahead, and it's glowing. I'm trying to ignore it, but it popped up about three minutes after you turned the van around and headed east. Now its blinking like a lighthouse beacon. What the hell is going on? Why did we change course?"

He hadn't been privy to our van chat.

"We've decided to help Kayla find her brother," I answered. "We're hoping to get to him before Enid does. We're heading to Baltimore."

Ray's eyebrows hit his hairline, but if he thought our new plan sucked, he kept his mouth shut, which was a Ray-sized miracle. "Well, what do you want to do about the blinking house?"

"How close did you get?" I asked, knowing he would've tried to investigate it.

"Not very," he said. "I didn't want to stray too far in case a passel of dead bodies started chasing after the van." He arched an eye at Kayla. "But the way it's acting now, there's no mistaking it. It's some kind of beacon. It's blinking at me like a disco ball, almost like it's trying to piss me off. I wouldn't be surprised if it's some kind of Morse code, but I don't know how to decipher it."

"Did you detect any magical signature?" I asked.

"Nope, it seems clean." He shrugged.

I turned to Rourke. "What do you think?"

"Sounds to me like someone wants us to visit," he said. "How many miles away is it?" he asked Ray.

"Looks to be about fifty or sixty by back roads," Ray answered. "It's due east, so it's right on the path we're taking to Baltimore.

The sucker started blinking right when you turned around. It can't be a coincidence."

"Likely not," I said. "But the question is do we trust it's not a trap? Jeb told us to stay out of vehicles, and here I am. Maybe this is his warning and he wants us to pull over and stop for the day?"

"Could be," Rourke said. "Or it's a message of some kind."

"Marcy, anything yet from Juanita?" I asked.

She waved the phone at me. "Nope, but you know, if you're looking for my two cents, I'm for getting out of this crusty van. We all need rest, and Jeb is powerful. If he wants us there, he could ward that house and make it safe. I say we go and check it out."

James turned from the driver's seat. "I second that. It sounds like something we should investigate. But we go in slow, each of us from different locations, and Ray from above. We don't take any chances."

I glanced at my mate.

Rourke nodded. "Let's go check it out. Better safe than sorry."

"Ray," I directed, "you go ahead and scope it out. But don't get too close. If you feel any danger, come back and let us know."

"Got it," Ray answered. Then he turned and gave James rough directions to where the mysterious house was located, as the bird flew—or in our case, how the vampire flew. He told us he'd check back in the last few miles and ended with "And don't wet your pants when I stop on the road again, Irish." He chortled, using Rourke's nickname for James. "You shoulda seen the look on your face. Priceless."

He nodded once and shot into the air.

27

It took us over an hour to get to the house. The back roads were small and twisty, not to mention we made several wrong turns. Ray had checked in twice, guiding us closer each time.

The sun was high above the trees when we finally pulled onto a dirt road off the main drive of what looked to be a secluded cabin next to a quaint lake in northeastern Georgia. It was fairly remote, heavily wooded. Any other cabins were acres away. Ray had already checked it out.

It was a perfect place to hide—or ambush—because there were no human witnesses for miles. The NO TRESPASSING signs we'd seen along the way made sure of that.

"This has to be someone's summer estate," Marcy said. "Judging by the gates and the driveway alone, it's huge. The entire area looks well manicured and taken care of."

Most supernaturals were wealthy, so we couldn't rule out this might be owned by one.

We all piled out of the van after Ray assured us he didn't detect any threat outside.

Rourke walked to the front of the gator van, its presence shouting, *We aren't from around here*, gesturing his arm up the drive. "We go up to the cabin in twos. Jessica and I will circle around to the north, Irish and Marcy west, Ray and Nick south." He glanced at me for my approval. I nodded. "And Tyler and Kayla east."

If Kayla ran, Tyler could catch her, no problem. She hadn't said anything more on our drive here, not even trying to dissuade us from stopping, so I was actually wondering what she would do with a little bit of freedom. Even if she managed to reanimate a dead body or two, if there were any around here, we'd be able to knock her out before it became an issue. Once she had collapsed back at the cemetery, all the ghouls had fallen.

I glanced at my brother. *Keep her in your sights at all times. We still don't know anything about her. If she runs, catch her quickly and let us know. We can circle around to meet you in less than a minute.*

I'll keep an eye on her, he said. *I hope she doesn't try to run. That would be tricky and another headache we don't need.*

Everyone nodded in agreement with Rourke's directives. "Go in slow," he cautioned. "I'll give a low whistle when it's all clear. Tyler and Kayla, meet us by the back door. Ray, you take the roof. Nick, you meet Irish and Marcy at the front. We enter at the same time."

We had to be careful. Anything could be a potential trap. I was feeling some trepidation that Juanita still hadn't made contact, but my wolf and I agreed that it felt right to stop. Juanita had made the trees glow in the swamp, so this could easily be her doing as well. But why she hadn't pinged Marcy's phone to tell us to stop was perplexing. That would've been the easiest route.

But when had any of this ever been easy?

"Marcy," I called as we took off. "If you feel any wards or spells, let us know."

"Oh, you'll hear me," she replied. "But so far I'm not picking up on anything. If a spell caster lived here, this entire gate would be warded. My best guess is a human owns this residence and it was chosen by whoever because it's remote and said human doesn't visit very often."

"I guess we'll know in a few minutes." We all went different directions. Rourke and I circled to the east first, ahead of Tyler and Kayla, who headed into the surrounding woods.

Once we were clear of the group, Rourke grabbed my hand and gave it a squeeze. I brushed my body against his as we walked, running my other hand along his forearm. It felt good to be close. I needed to feel him.

"Do you sense anything?" he asked, scanning the woods like the predator he was.

"Nothing but your pheromones," I joked, drawing in another luscious breath of his scent. I pushed my power out ahead of us to see if I could sense anything paranormal that could be amiss.

"I can't help it," he growled, leaning over to kiss the top of my head. "Getting a few seconds alone with you has become a feat of epic proportions on this journey. It's all I can do not to take you now while I have you." He rubbed his stubble into my hair, which gave me goose bumps. "When we are allowed two seconds of freedom, be prepared for me to tear your clothes off."

"That sounds like a perfect plan." Tingles raced through me at the thought of his hands on my bare skin. "Hey, look." I gestured toward the back of the cabin, which was just becoming visible as we circled through the trees. "There's a guesthouse and it has its own fireplace. Dibs."

We continued to make our way around, but before we fully stepped out from the cover of the trees, Rourke stilled. "Let's do some recon first," he said as he lifted his nose in the air. He shook his head. "I don't scent a damn thing. Whoever owns this house hasn't been here in a long time, and even though the lawn was mowed a few weeks ago, there doesn't seem to be a full-time caretaker living on the grounds. There's barely anything left in the air, and all of it is human."

I sniffed. "I can smell leftover gasoline and old grass, too, but you're right, no one has been here for a while." I glanced up at my mate, my hand caressing his forearm. "This is definitely why whoever wanted us here chose this place. It's perfect, really. Remote, yet civilized."

"Yes, but remote could equal a problem. It's quiet enough to kill us all without much interference."

"True, but I think that between the eight of us, we would be able to detect something evil, don't you think? And if a bomb does drop on our heads, we should be able to fight our way out."

"I do think," he said. "Which is why we're standing here and not in the van heading back down the road."

I hit his arm playfully. "If I thought for a second this was a trap, we never would've stopped in the first place."

He bent down and brushed my lips with his. "I know," he chuckled into my mouth, his tongue tracing my bottom lip, "but I like to pretend I make the rules when it comes to your safety. Now, let's head down to the back door."

We went stealthily, moving fast and staying low. The back door was actually a huge set of French doors. There was an abundance of windows in the home as well, but the shades were drawn, so we couldn't see in. As we neared, I didn't sense any movement inside. The lake was to our right, and left us a little exposed, but looking out over it, there wasn't any other cabin I could see. "I think whoever lives here might own this entire lake," I said. "I don't see any other homes and this lake looks like prime real estate."

Rourke grunted, telling me he couldn't give a rat's ass who owned it as we rushed up to the door. Once we arrived, he placed a single finger on the doorknob. Nothing happened. "All clear," he said. "I don't sense any magic or any movement inside."

A moment later Ray landed on the roof above our heads, and Tyler and Kayla turned around the corner from the east side. I was happy to see she'd followed the program, even though her mouth was set in a thin line. She wasn't happy about it, but she'd done it.

I nodded to her.

She ignored me.

To my brother I said, *Once we get inside, find her some clothes and get her cleaned up.* I eyed her tattered nightgown. *Looks like she could use some sleep too, though it's unlikely she will agree to it.*

Will do. She hasn't said one word to me, but she didn't try to run. I'm counting that as a win.

Rourke lifted his head and whistled low, signaling it was time to enter. He turned the handle. It was locked. He pushed his shoulder into the door, and it gave with a quick pop. On the other side of the house, James was doing the same thing. Ray broke a window on the second floor and we were all in.

The back door swung open into a huge vaulted kitchen–living room combo area. The eating space was nicely appointed with granite counters, expensive lighting, and stainless steel appliances. The living area had three couches, set in a U around a huge fireplace made up of dark stones that reached all the way to the ceiling. There wasn't much of a cabin feel going on here. It was obvious that the owner had lots of money. James, Marcy, and Nick strode in from a wide hallway on the other side of the kitchen, just as Ray emerged from a stairway nestled between the two spaces. "Nothing up there," Ray announced. "And it reeks of mothballs. This house has been locked up tight for a long time, maybe years."

Marcy ran her fingertips along the kitchen counter, which was gray veined granite, and then wiped them together. "Dusty," she said, "but nice. They spared no expense with this place."

I glanced around. "Okay, we're here, and there's no apparent threat. So now what?"

"I don't know about you guys"—Marcy walked over to the cabinets and began to open them—"but after I find some chow, I'm taking a breather." She arched a brow. "And by the sounds coming from your stomach, you could use something to eat too." She continued down the line, finding only dishes. "Let's get fed and then we can start to unravel the mystery of this abandoned mansion in the woods."

Ray walked over to the fireplace, picking up an old magazine, and sat down. "Hell, you don't have to twist my arm to take a break. I need a shower too—"

The entire house blinked.

There wasn't a better word for it.

It was like the house tripped its own circuit breaker for a split second and all the appliances and lamps jumped, flickering on for a second and then off.

All of us were instantly on high alert.

"Do you feel anything?" I asked Marcy. "Any magic in the air?"

"No, there's nothing." She had her fingers out and ready.

We all stood still for a few seconds, trying to sense the threat, then moved around the space slowly and quietly.

The silence was interrupted by a shrill ring.

It was the cabin phone.

It was mounted under the counter in the kitchen. We all stared at it until Ray broke the silence. "That's not for us, Hannon." He flicked his wrist toward the smooth black phone. "I'm thinking you might want to take that so we can find out what the fuck is going on."

Rourke nodded and I walked forward. After a few more rings, I picked it up. "Hello?"

"Chica! I am so relieved to hear your voice. So happy you came to the house. I did not know if you would get the message. We have very little time, so we must hurry."

It was a jolt to hear Juanita's voice. She sounded exactly the same, heavy Spanish accent and all. A picture of her with her cherry red nails and perfectly coiffed hairdo flooded my mind. "I'm here, Juanita. The glowing house was indeed effective," I answered. "But why not just hit Marcy's phone and tell us to come?"

"Because I am being monitored, and this es the only chance I have to meet before I must leave for a very long time. It was good fortune you turned around. If you had gone the other way, we would not have this chance."

"Meet? Are you here?" I went to the window above the sink and moved the curtain, glancing out. I saw nothing out of the ordinary, so I turned and mouthed to the group—who had heard everything Juanita had said—*Do you feel any magic?*

Everyone shook their heads no, but they all spread out to different corners of the room to pry back the curtains and blinds and take a look outside.

"I am in the guesthouse. You cannot see me," she said after a few beats, "but, Chica, you must come alone."

"I'm not sure I can do that—"

"I have just warded the grounds. That es what you felt when everything flickered. No supernatural can break in and none can track you, including my very dangerous sister." The word sounded like *see-ster*. "You are safe. But only for right now. We must take this time, as we will not have another chance."

I knew Rourke and my family had heard. I glanced around to see what they thought.

One by one they all nodded reluctantly, agreeing to let me go alone.

"Okay, I'll come out and meet you."

"Your *familia* may take up a perimeter around the guesthouse, which I can see will happen anyway, but they must not enter. Warn the witch to take heed. If they enter, it will throw everything off. And, Chica, I am taking a great risk by being here to see you. Do not forget."

"Got it. I'm on my way." I hung up the phone. "We have to choose to believe that was really her. I think it was. It sounded exactly like her."

Rourke crossed his arms. I could tell he was having the most trouble with this sudden turn of events. "It could be Enid posing as her sister. There's no real way to know. You could be walking into a trap that will leave you an easy target. They are both powerful and can cloak their signature. If she's here, she left no scent. There was nothing around the guesthouse."

I nodded. "I realize this is dicey, but we have no other choice. This is my chance to finally talk to Juanita and get some much-needed answers. If what she says is true, I won't get another shot. She alone can give us an insight into what the future will hold. It's a calculated risk, but I have to take it. You know I do." I started for the back door.

James opened it. "We will take up a perimeter around the guesthouse, like the Hag indicated," he said, "and we will refrain from going inside unless there's an emergency." He didn't have to add: The word "emergency" will consist of any whiff of blood or guts being spilled inside.

"Jessica," Rourke said, following me out. Once we were in the yard, he grabbed my arm gently and I turned to face him. "If I don't hear from you every five minutes internally, I'm going to break that door down. I don't care what she said. There's no other way I'm going to let you go in there alone."

I placed my hands on his chest. "Okay. I promise to check in," I said. "I wouldn't expect anything less. And if Juanita is all knowing, she's expecting that. I promise I'll keep you posted."

They all followed me toward the guesthouse. It sat fifty yards to the north of the cabin, right on the lake. It was picturesque.

Ray strode up next to me. "I'm going to settle myself on the roof. Just in case." His voice was calm, but he was on edge. We were all on edge. This was a Hag we were dealing with, someone with an insane amount of power.

It didn't matter how much I felt like I *knew* Juanita. It was clear I'd never really known her. But I was happy to get a chance to ask her the questions I needed answers to—which was basically everything.

The little house was shuttered. We couldn't see in. There was only one door, and it was situated on the side facing us. I walked up and tentatively touched the round handle. It was clear.

"Okay," I said, "this is it. It's either Juanita or Enid inside. We either gain an advantage or we fight." I glanced around. "Everyone ready?"

They all nodded. I knew they would defend me to the death and it was humbling.

"Spread out," Rourke ordered as I turned the knob. "I want every inch of this cabin surrounded."

I put my other hand on my mate's chest one last time. "This is going to be fine," I murmured. "I'm not getting any strange vibes or a warning of any kind. My wolf is on board and anxious to get this over with. Rourke, we need this information, as much as we can get. Tally is still missing and things are happening in Europe."

"I know," he growled, "but I don't like it. I'll never get used to you walking into an unknown risk."

"It's a calculated risk," I reminded him. "I have to believe that one of us would feel if something was off. There are eight of us here, all strong, powerful supernaturals. This is going to be fine."

He nodded, leaning down to kiss me. It was a fierce, protective kiss that seared my insides. "I'll be right outside," he whispered into my ear. "Call out to me if you need me. And like I said, I want an internal message signaling you're okay every five minutes. If I don't get one, I'm coming in. I don't care what she says."

"Fine by me." To my wolf I said, *Are you ready for this?* She barked once firmly, bringing her muzzle down in a *let's get this over with* gesture.

The door opened freely. I gave Rourke one last kiss and slipped inside, shutting it behind me.

"Oh, Chica, I'm so happy to see you!"

28

"Wait a minute." I stopped in my tracks. This was not the guest-house. "How did I get here?" I looked around me, bewildered. I'd just walked into Juanita's apartment. The one that sat across from my own back home. It was the same layout as mine, except her furnishings were bright and cheerful, yellow tables, red accents, and green throw pillows. It even smelled like her cooking. How could that be?

Juanita shot up from her seat at the kitchen table and came to greet me.

As she clacked toward me in her four-inch heels, she appeared exactly how I remembered her. She wasn't more than five feet four inches tall—*in* her heels. Her hair was perfectly done, as always, her nails painted the same bright red. She wore a pink sleeveless top and red skinny jeans. "I don't want you to worry, Chica," she said in her heavily accented Latina accent, "but I had no choice. Your family will break in soon, but they will find you peacefully sleeping on the sofa. Once they do, we will have limited time."

She embraced me in a big bear hug and then gestured to the kitchen. "Come, sit down."

"How are you doing this?" I asked as I followed her to the kitchen table. It felt completely real, right down to the garlic bread smell lingering in the air.

"We are meeting inside your mind right now, but I assure you, this es very real. I could not risk coming to you, but you are safe, as es your *familia*." She tugged me gently to a chair and I sat. "But we must hurry. There es not much time. I am taking a great risk by bringing you here, but we must speak."

I opened my mouth, but nothing came out. There was so much I wanted to ask, so many things I needed to know. I settled on the most important thing running through my mind at the moment. "Is Rourke going to think I'm dead? Please say no. I can't fool him like that again. He's already been through too much and we've only been mated a short time. I don't want him to panic."

She shook her head and reached out to grab my hand. Electricity shot up my arm as she held it, patting it on top with her other hand. "No, your vital signs are functioning normally. You are breathing peacefully. The witch should guess what es happening, but I cannot lie, your mate will have a problem with this. It cannot be helped. And just for you, I will make my spell tangible." She flicked her wrist. "You see, all es well. Now the witch will know exactly what has happened."

I didn't know where to start. "Juanita, how can . . . it be you? I never suspected anything. You don't have a power signature and you smell like a human. How is any of this possible?"

"Of course I smell like a human." She chortled, her sweet, high voice pinging the air. "I was reborn as a human fifty-four years ago for a specific reason. If I let my power signature show here, it would be like announcing to the world this es where I am." She tossed out her hands, letting go of me, to simulate an explosion.

"And that wouldn't do me much good protecting you, now, would it, Chica?"

"So you kept yourself cloaked the entire time you lived here?"

"*Sí*," she said. "I have been—how you say—undercover for a very long time. Since you were a bambina."

I shook my head in wonder. "I don't know where to start. There is so much I want to know."

"You may ask me, but I warn you, I cannot tell you very much." She shook her head gravely. "It would place you at too much risk. I have brought you here only to tell you a few precious things." She put together two of her fingers about an inch apart to indicate how little she could tell me. "But I also wanted to see you once again with my very own eyes." She brought a hand to my face and touched me, genuine happiness in her smile. "I have missed you, Chica. I had not known when I made the decision to advocate for you that I would find so much...affection for you. I have become attached. This, of course, has made it very hard for me to stay impartial. But what's done es done." She waved a hand dismissively and got up from the table. "I will bring us some tea and then we will chat."

She busied herself in the kitchen and I sent a silent plea to Rourke to let him know I was okay. *You're going to find me out cold, but I'm okay. I'll be back soon. I promise.*

"He will be all right," Juanita said, interrupting my thoughts. "He es a fierce protector for you. One of the finest warriors we have. You are one lucky woman." She turned, waggling her eyebrows in the old Juanita way. "I sent him to you early." She swished a hand over her head to indicate it was nothing as she continued to make tea. "It had to happen this way or I think you would not have survived. So many things to think about, all the time. They always occupy my mind."

My eyebrows shot up. "You sent Rourke to me—*early*?"

"*Sí*," she answered as she brought two steaming cups of tea to the table. "He was your fated mate, of course, but you were not supposed to find each other for quite some time. The future— it es always murky." She sat down, scooting her chair closer to mine. "So I made the choice to bring you both together, because without him, I fear, you would not have made it this far. So much trouble in your short life, Chica. Es hard to be your guardian. You have made it very tricky for me."

"You've been my guardian since birth? Like a guardian angel?"

She laughed, and again it was a lyrical, lovely sound, full of joy. I smiled along with her, realizing I'd missed her. I guess without knowing it, over the years I'd grown fond of her too. "You can look at it like that, I suppose, but really, it has been my pleasure to watch over you. You are the center of things in our world, for a reason. You are a *changer*. I chose to be reborn at the right time to make sure you survived and I take my job very seriously." She smiled wide, like I shouldn't be so surprised to find I had a guardian angel living next door to me for all these years.

"Jeb called me a catalyst," I said, "but he said my birth was late."

She nodded. "*Sí*, Jebediah Amel is correct, and you must learn to trust him, even though he can be a bit...*prickly* at times." She chortled at her own joke, which was referring to his spiky hair. Abruptly her face turned serious. "He will not lead you astray and you will learn much from him. Fate has been unstable for too long, Chica. When Lilith killed my sister and Ardat Lili took her seat on the Coalition, the damage they caused was grave. Only someone with a great magnitude of power could have derailed Fate's true path so effectively. Lilith was one of only a handful of supernaturals with the kind of power to do what she did, and she knew what she was doing—relished in it. Because of that, we are still reeling from it. My sister Enid and I miss our third sister,

Bianca, very much. But when Fate gave us the sight, right after she was killed, Enid and I interpreted the signs differently. It was the first time that had ever happened. We have disagreed about it for centuries. This es why we are sitting here at this table." She rapped her knuckles on the wood. "I believe *you* are the key to fixing everything that went wrong, and Enid believed that Lili was. And now that she es dead, without giving birth to our sister, Enid believes your death es the only option to give us a fresh start. But that es not the truth, and to prove it we must get down to the business of solving it before Enid can end your life."

My mind spun. "And how do we do that? How do we put things back on track?" I hoped she had an easy checklist that I could follow to the letter, and once completed, everything would miraculously go back to normal.

I somehow knew that wouldn't be the case.

"Before I go into that, I must be completely honest with you, Chica. Everything on the table." She rapped again on the painted wood to emphasize her point. "Enid's way es the only way that es *guaranteed* to work. My way es trickier, and all of the things must happen in the right order, but if they do, we have a chance." Her face was grave. "We will not take Enid's path if we can help it."

She was talking about my death. "If I die, you're certain Fate will set itself to rights?"

"*Sí,*" she answered. "If you die, it will trigger the birth of a new catalyst, and this time the rebirth would be my sister." She bowed her head. "Enid and I both saw it the night you ended Ardat Lili's life. That es why Enid has acted so quickly. She es desperate to have Bianca back, but I know there es another way. We saw it the night Lilith took Bianca's life."

"Jeb said it would be very bad if I died," I said.

"Oh, *sí,* it would be much worse in our world before it got better, which es why I don't agree with Enid. I am anxious to greet my sister Bianca once again, but we will get there another way." Juanita grinned as she picked up her mug and took a sip. "Enid thinks this es an acceptable loss in the short term, but I do not. My sister and I can both read the signs, but there es still quite a bit of mystery involved, you see? If we could *control* Fate, then we would *be* Fate. That es something my sister Enid cannot comprehend. Her grief es too great and she cannot think clearly any longer."

"What do I have to do to get Fate back on track?" I asked. I really didn't want to die if I could help it. "Tell me and I'll do it."

Juanita crossed her legs and grasped my hands again. "In the end, you will have to sacrifice something precious to you," she began, "but I cannot tell you what. I also cannot tell you anything specific about your journey, except that it will happen very soon. If I give away too much, it will influence your choices and that es a no-no." She wagged a single finger at me. "Moving forward, I must implore you to make all the decisions with your heart, even if they seem...hard to do. Just like turning the car around to help the necromancer. That was a choice you made with this." She gestured to my heart. "Without doing that, we would not have been able to be here right now, and you would not be on the right track."

Sacrificing didn't sound ideal, but it was better than dying. My brain instantly jumping to my mate. I couldn't give him up. I prayed it wasn't him. "I'm willing to do what is necessary." I didn't say any more. I'd cross that bridge when I came to it.

"Don't worry. This es something you can handle, Chica. I swear to it or I wouldn't be here. Inside of you, deep inside"—she motioned to my chest—"there es knowledge. Your wolf will help guide you. Now that she es whole for the first time, you are both complete. This es the place where you need to be. It was necessary for that to happen first, before we could move forward. In time, you will learn more. But you must always try to listen to your wolf on matters of the supernatural."

"Did you orchestrate my entire encounter with Marinette, then?"

"*Sí*, all of it was necessary, including taking the plane down where I did. But as much as I am able to lead you—to direct you toward something—we are forbidden to manipulate it once it es set in motion. The outcomes must be organic. But I did cheat a teensy bit with Marinette by giving information to the witch." She winked. "But it was necessary or you would've died. Meeting your creator was—how do you say—a tricky result? Many outcomes could have erupted from that. We were lucky it came out as it did in our favor. But that es a testament to you. You are tenacious, as I knew you would be. Marinette was a powerful goddess in her day, and she was indeed responsible for the creation of shifters, but her life ended for a reason—one that she was never able to fully grasp. Even if she had successfully inhabited you and taken over your body, she was no longer capable of being powerful. Her only reason for continuing to exist was to pass on to you and your wolf what was rightfully yours—the other half of her soul."

"You had to have set all this up a long time ago. The fracture pack coming down here months ago, my father following, the leader of the resistance pack meeting the priestess. All of it."

She shrugged. "Some, and some I did not have anything to do with. Your birth triggered a path, and up until Lili, everything had stayed mostly on track. You had some ups and downs, but I did not need to interfere overly much. I knew it would be a hard road for you, and I was very sad about that, Chica, but I didn't have to prod you much to stay on course."

"What about the cemetery? How did we survive that?" I asked. "I tried to change the game by jumping on top of the mausoleum, but I hadn't expected it to be that easy in the end." If chopping off wendigo heads was considered easy.

"Enid made some *grave* mistakes"—she chuckled—"but you were shrewd, as I knew you would be." Her face beamed with pride. "Your choice to stop running for nothing more than a brief second"—she snapped her fingers—"changed that outcome. You were right to stop. You listened to what your heart told you, even when your mind felt it was wrong. But Enid was greedy, and her true undoing was Kayla. She did not factor in the young girl's stamina—or lack thereof. She chose the best necromancer in the country, but not the most experienced. That, coupled with your move, and you became the victor."

Juanita flickered in front of me and the table began to fade.

She kept talking, but I couldn't hear her. "No, wait!" I cried, feeling frantic, grabbing at the table. "We can't be done yet! There's so much more I need to ask you. What about Tally? Is she safe? What about my father and Danny and Naomi?"

Juanita's visage cleared for a moment, but I knew we were out of time. "The great witch es safe but needs your help," Juanita murmured. "Your path will become clear to you soon. Remember, you must do what needs to be done, no matter how difficult."

"Are we going to meet again?" I asked quickly as the room around me dimmed and I heard a desperate roar.

Rourke was angry. *I'm coming soon,* I told him.

"No, Chica. Once you leave here, I must not interfere again. It's the way it must be." I could barely see her, but she reached for my hand again and stroked it. "You will be protected this night. Have no fear when you return. But when the dawn comes, you must make a critical decision and leave with all haste. Enid looks for you even now."

"No, please, tell me what to do. What is the decision? I don't want to screw this up!" I was bordering on manic, my hands scrabbling to hold on to her, but I couldn't feel her in the physical sense any longer. "Juanita, give me something more than that.

Help guide my next move. My mind feels divided. I want to go home and be with my Pack, close to my father. I want to help Tally. But my heart is telling me to do something else, to go help Kayla. To find her brother."

The entire room took on a hazy white glow and I began to float backward toward the door against my will.

Juanita stood, her ceramic mug in her hands. She waved and blew me a kiss. "I will miss you, Chica. And I will grant your last wish. Find her brother, the one called Ajax. Do that and you are on your way to fulfilling your destiny."

I blinked my eyes open.

29

"Hiya," Marcy said, glancing down on me. My head was cradled in her lap. "Was it fun? I've heard of astral spells, but I've never known a witch who could successfully perform one. Did it feel like you were really there? Or was it all blinky and weird?"

I lifted my head and glanced around the room. "Where's Rourke?" I needed to know that before I could answer her questions.

She paused, and then gave a dramatic sigh, looking resigned. "The boys had to escort him...outside. He was destroying too much stuff in here, so we all thought it might be better for him to take a tiny"—she inhaled—"time-out."

I glanced around. The cabin was a wreck. Cushions were shredded, lamps overturned, walls punched in. "How'd they get him out there?" I asked, sitting up. That must have been a feat.

Marcy slid over on the sofa to give me some space. "Well," she answered, setting a throw pillow into her lap, curling her legs under her, "it wasn't easy, I can tell you that much. I had to spell him and the boys had to manhandle him out of here. He's heavy, not to mention he's one tough son-of-a-biggen, and when he's pissed off he puts everyone in jeopardy. Once they got him out the door, Ray flew him someplace so he could...cool off. Like, literally cool *down*."

"Where exactly did Ray fly him?" I arched a look at her. She was evading me on purpose, but at least she had the decency not to smile.

"I believe he dropped him in the middle of the lake." She glanced away from my penetrating stare to gaze at her fingernails. "But, honestly, we had no other choice." She began to fidget with the corner of the pillow. "I begged him not to break down the door and come in here. James tried to hold him back. Once we were in, I told him what was going on with you, since Juanita left a huge imprint of her spell for me to find, like a big ol' witchy flare. I knew you were fine. But he kept pressuring me to wake you up. And if I'd tried to do that, it could've left your mind damaged, or worse, which is why Juanita had warned us away." She blew out a frustrated breath. "I wasn't willing to risk it, and everyone else agreed—except for him. So we did the only thing left to us. We dropped him in the lake."

I wasn't going to laugh or smile. What they did was harsh. "I heard him roar at one point during the astral trip," I said. "But, honestly, you can't blame him for being worried about me. The man loves me, and it's, what, the millionth time he's seen me near death?"

"The roaring part was tame, believe me," she said, meeting my gaze for the first time. "It was the claws that were the problem. I mean, look at this place. It's holding on by a thread!"

I glanced around. She was right. It was completely damaged. Not much was left that wasn't shredded to bits and pieces. "You can fix this, right?" I asked.

"Well, yes," she answered. "But that's not the point! He was endangering you."

I nodded to her while I called out to him in my mind. *Rourke, are you there?* I walked to the front window and opened the shade. I couldn't see him. *I'm back safe and sound. Where are you?*

Swimming, he said curtly. *And when I get back, I will annihilate anyone who gets in my way.* He was furious and I couldn't really blame him.

I'll be here waiting.

He growled his response.

Tyler, I said, switching channels. *I'm back, and if you know what's good for you, stay out of Rourke's way. Tell everyone to head back into the main house. We leave tomorrow to find Kayla's brother at dawn, not a minute later. Find out as much as you can about where we're going, what kind of a supe he is, and formulate a work- able plan with everyone else. We'll see you in the morning.* Rourke wasn't going to let me out of his sight, and once he got back, he wasn't going to be fit for company. We all needed some down- time and Juanita was warding this place until sun up.

Got it, Tyler said. *Jess, we had no choice but to intervene.* He paused in mid-thought. *I'm not sure dumping him in the lake was the best plan we've ever come up with, but it seemed like the only option at the time. Marcy was panicked about hurting you and he was forcing her to wake you up.*

I'll handle it from here, I replied. *Just make sure to give him some space once he's out. We've been on the road a long time, and it doesn't look like it's going to stop anytime soon. Let's use this break to our advantage.*

I hear you, sis. A break, even for a night, is a gift at this point.

Juanita has this entire place warded until dawn. Tell everyone. And make sure you tell Kayla we will help her. She won't be happy we're bunking here for the rest of the day and night. We'll meet you outside just before dawn. I clicked off and turned to Marcy, who was waiting patiently for me to finish. "How come you stayed with me? Did you draw the short straw for babysitting duty?" I joked, settling myself on the couch across from her.

"Nope, I picked it willingly," she answered smugly. "And babysitting, my aunt Betty's ass. Being with you is like trying to keep track of a whirling dervish hell-bent on injuring herself. It takes all my considerable skill and talent to keep you alive and functioning. And what if that astral spell had backfired and you went into convulsions? What then, huh? You should be grateful I was here."

"I am grateful," I said as I lay my head back, trying to enjoy these two minutes alone with my friend, especially since we weren't in any danger. "Your considerable talents *have* kept me alive. And I haven't had a chance to say thank you properly for what you did for me back in the swamp. Without you, I wouldn't have made it out alive. Juanita hinted that there were several outcomes that could've happened, but they didn't. I'm crediting you for your spells and quick thinking."

"*Phish.*" Marcy flipped her wrist at me like I was a silly person. "You had that entire thing covered from the moment we arrived. For the most part I was just in the way, bumbling along like your inefficient, but incredibly clever, sidekick."

"No way." I shook my head adamantly. "If it wasn't for the dark spells you brewed, we would've been overpowered in minutes. The potions gave us precious moments to get ahead. We wouldn't have made it otherwise. That's why Juanita sent you with me, like a barnacle clinging to a ship. Without you, I would've died." I raised a single eyebrow to dare her to contradict me. "I'm not invincible and never have been. This is a team effort, and I'm so thankful I have you—you and your cleverness—clinging to my boat like a moochy crustacean, so thank you."

Marcy picked up her throw pillow and tossed it at my head.

I ducked, laughing. "I'm hardly a mooch, and let's face it, you're the one who clings to *my* boat by the tips of your claws hoping I'll toss you a life preserver. Face it, without me you'd be bored out of your gourd, dragging yourself from one dangerous escapade to the next with no joy, only sadness."

"You're right, you do brighten my day, and honestly, I'm glad you're so humble about it. Always makes for such a self-effacing conversation—" Another throw pillow smacked me in the face. When I was done laughing, Marcy's demeanor had shifted. Her face had become serious. "Okay, now what?" I asked.

"There's one thing I have to know before your mate gets back. I have to ask, since you haven't had a chance to explain exactly what went down with Marinette after I was knocked out." Marcy leaned forward. "Is she part of you or what? I know she didn't come out. I saw you lying there, looking dead, and I'm sure she was inside. And then—presto—you woke up and she was gone. Nowhere to be found."

I closed my eyes, remembering. "I'm not sure I can put what happened into perfect words," I began, opening my eyes and leveling them on my friend, "but I'll give you my best interpretation of what happened."

"That's good enough for a barnacle."

"Marinette split her soul in two to create the first female werewolf on earth. My predecessor. She went against edict to do it, because she wanted her supernatural race—the race of shifters—to be the most powerful, and to have control over the supernatural race through her new toy. At least that's how she explained it to me. But when she possessed me, hoping to claim my body for herself, she presented my wolf with the other half of her soul. Once we stopped fighting the possession, thanks to Juanita, my wolf sort of...claimed the rest of the soul for herself. No power went with it. It's sort of creepy to say out loud, but I assure you,

Marinette is nowhere inside me. The only thing left is my happy, complete wolf." My wolf barked her agreement.

"That *is* strange and creepy," Marcy remarked, "but totally cool. You Ghostbustered her. I've never heard of someone swallowing up a soul like that, but I've also never heard of a supe splitting their soul in the first place. If Marinette was only made up of half a soul, I can see why she didn't have any power. She could be strong for a moment or two, when she used the bokor, but she would never have been a contender."

I chuckled. "You make the ordeal sound easy."

"Of course I do, I'm good like that. I like to take the fried and make it chicken fried," Marcy agreed. "Much more flavor that way. And now I can see by the bags under your eyes you need some time to recover. It looks like a truck with big, fat tires rolled over you and left you for dead. Get some sleep if you can. Your beast is getting out of the water as we speak." She stood. "If I'm here when he comes back, things will get ugly."

I stood along with her and gave her a hug. "Thank you, Marcy," I whispered in her ear. "For not only being my friend, but becoming a powerful ally."

She hugged me back fiercely. "I'm your Pack sister-in-law and don't you forget it. I'll always volunteer to babysit you, Wonder Wolf. We're in this together. All of us."

We stepped apart, both of us smiling and a little teary-eyed, even though neither of us would ever admit it. "Marcy, when you get back to the house, tell everyone we're leaving just before dawn. I already told Tyler, but our next step is to find Kayla's brother. Juanita told me the path I need to take right now, so we're taking it. She said once we find Ajax, my destiny will be clear—and I'm praying that will be true."

"Wait a minute, did you say Ajax?" she asked, her eyebrows furrowing.

"Yeah, why?"

"Because Kayla called her kid brother *Jax*, not Ajax."

"Jax must be short for Ajax." I shrugged. "That's not a huge stretch."

"No, but in mythology Ajax is a mighty warrior known for his strength, little missy." She shook her head. "He's not known for raising the dead, so that means her brother is not a necromancer."

"I guess we'll find out tomorrow, won't we?" I said. "I doubt she'll tell ahead of time, even if we beg."

"She's a little slippery, that one." Marcy walked to the door. "We'll have to keep a close eye on her. I don't intend to wake up with ghouls eating me as a midnight snack. I'm outta here. I hear splashing."

The door burst open minutes after Marcy left. My mate walked in looking fierce and sopping wet. He shook his hair out and ripped off his T-shirt while he paced toward me.

I met him halfway.

My mouth covered his before he could verbalize what seeing me out cold had done to him. I'd been incapacitated too many times, and instead of talking about it, I was going to show him I was okay the best way I knew how.

The electricity of our connection was immediate.

His hands clutched me from behind, pulling me roughly toward him so all our parts were touching. His lips were hot and firm, and a loud rumble issued out of his chest as his tongue lashed over mine again and again.

I angled my head to take him more fully and ran my hands up and down his torso, sliding over the wetness still clinging to him, then gripping his shoulders just as fiercely as he was holding on to me.

With a snarl he picked me up, our mouths still melded together, and stalked toward the only bedroom in the tiny guesthouse.

Once we were through, he kicked the door shut. It slammed so hard, it cracked.

In front of the bed, he broke our kiss, his mouth trailing down my neck and along the column of my throat. He nipped and licked me until I couldn't take it any longer. Moaning, I rubbed myself up against him. I was too filled with need to do much more. This coupling was going to be what it had to be.

Hard and thorough.

Only after we'd had each other would we calm down and talk rationally. My mate was wound past the point of snapping, and I was right there with him. I needed his touch. My body craved it like no other. It had been long enough.

I squirmed in his arms and he growled, laying me roughly on the bed, neither of us speaking. He stepped back, yanking off his jeans, almost ripping them in his haste, his gaze locked on my mine.

I stripped off my own clothes as he moved forward. He was glorious. His power jumped out ahead of him, stinging me with its delicious currents. Once I was naked, he covered me, entering me in one hot rush.

I arched up, taking him, welcoming it, my hands fisted in his hair as I dragged his body closer. As he began a frantic rhythm, I tossed my head back, luxuriating in his fullness and the sensations of our coupling. He roared as I gripped his backside, urging him faster. His hand slid under my neck, angling me up, his mouth slanting over mine, his tongue plunging deeply, ravaging my mouth. I returned his kisses, slash for slash, rocking my pelvis in tandem with his thrusts.

Breaking the kiss, his lips seared my neck as he inched down my chest. "Jessica"—his voice was full of anguish coupled with pleasure—"I can't . . . I need—"

"*Shhh*," I said, guiding him back to me, kissing his face, running my tongue along his beautiful stubble. "It's okay."

Slowing the pace, he rose on his forearms, gazing down on me. I reached up and stroked his face, murmuring loving words to him, wanting to soothe him and comfort him. My toes curled as the pleasure mounted with each thrust.

Without needing to be asked, he increased his rhythm, not breaking his gaze. "I cannot lose you." He rocked into me hard, hitting my core. "Ever."

"You won't . . . I promise." My voice broke on a moan.

"Come for me." He angled himself forward, his forearms bracketing my body, his thrusts coming fast. My hands fisted in the covers as I gave in to my pleasure, crying out his name.

Before I could recover, he roared his release, his thrusts triggering blissful aftershocks. "Rourke." I rolled my hips up, savoring the feelings. "You are . . . an amazing lover."

He collapsed on top of me, both of us breathing hard. After a moment he gathered me in his arms and rolled to the side. We lay locked together like that, legs intertwined, under the covers for a long time, neither of us saying a word. His hands continually ran over my body as I burrowed as close to him as I could get.

We would talk when we were ready, but for now, all we needed was physical contact and nothing else.

"Jessica," Rourke whispered.

"What is it?" I rose immediately on my elbow, blinking. "What's wrong? Was I asleep?" I glanced around the room. It was pitch black. "What time is it?"

"Relax, it's only ten."

"Oh," I said, my brain foggy from sleep. "That's a relief." I burrowed back into his warmth as I yawned. His arms braced around me, tugging me close. "I can't believe I fell asleep. I've been out at least eight hours. You should've woken me up sooner. We have a lot to talk about." I slung a lazy arm around his torso and snuggled deeper.

"You were too cute to wake up." He pulled the sheet up around us. "You kept making little growling noises and gnashing your teeth. It was like watching a puppy have a nightmare."

"Very funny," I mumbled, smiling into his neck. "You purr like a cat when you're out cold, so we're even." He laughed, whipping me effortlessly onto his chest. I leaned in to kiss him. "*Mmm*, I love the way you taste."

His irises sparked. "You don't taste half bad yourself."

I nipped his bottom lip.

He groaned, angling his head up to kiss me, but he broke away too soon for my liking, so I protested with a loud growl.

"Believe me," he said, "all I want to do is kiss you senseless, but you're right. We have to talk first. I need to know what happened when you were with Juanita. We can't put it off any longer."

I sighed, resting my cheek against his broad chest. "I know. But first I have to tell you I'm sorry I worried you again. Juanita said it couldn't be helped. I know seeing me unresponsive is hard for you."

"Jessica, I thought I lost you again when I kicked the door down and first saw you in that state." He cleared his throat. "I'm not sure how many times I can see you like that and keep it together. I thought Enid had taken you. I'm pissed they threw me in the lake, but they probably did the right thing. I pushed Marcy to wake you up even though she kept telling me she couldn't do it without hurting you. I wasn't in my right mind."

I caressed his cheek with a thumb. "I know this has been hard on you, but I can't promise that something like that won't happen again. If it helps matters at all, I like you vigilant. I love that you have my back. You're my rock. You were right to think it might have been Enid when everyone else was complacent to believe it was Juanita. In the future, we just have to make sure we work better as a team, and we have to know when to trust the people around us. Each of us has our own skill set. Marcy has to be the one with the last word when it comes to spells. We have to believe Ray when it comes to reaper things. Moving forward, that has to be our mind-set."

He shook his head. "I agree with you. But fear made me irrational. Marcy told me the signature was Juanita's. She's the professional. But I didn't listen. I just…couldn't. Not after everything we've been through recently."

"It's okay, I don't blame you for being fierce," I said, leaning down to kiss his bottom lip, lingering there for a moment. "It's not always going to be like this. It can't be. We won't survive long living in constant upheaval and danger. You and I are going to just have to keep moving forward. We have no other choice. But we *will* reach the finish line. Juanita told me something while I was with her, and the way she said it felt like there would be an ending. She said I'd find peace at some point, but in order to get things back on the right track, I did have to sacrifice something, but whatever it was I could handle it."

"Tell me everything she said."

I recapped the meeting as best I could, leaving nothing out, including the realness of the smells and how everything affected my senses. "The last thing she told me was we needed to find Kayla's brother, and once I did, I would find my destiny. When she said the words, they filled me with hope. I had the feeling that if I succeeded in this next mission everything would finally come together. At least that's how I interpreted it. I truly believe she thinks I can succeed and my death isn't necessary. I have to as well. Being hopeless is not an option."

"Damn right, we believe. Your death is *not* an option. I don't care what Fate or Enid think. Juanita has been your champion since the beginning, by her own admission. She knows there's a way around this and we are going to move in that direction. And once this is all over, the first chance I get I'm squirreling you back to the Ozarks and keeping you under lock and key for a while."

I sighed, laying my cheek against his chest again. "That sounds like heaven." I ran an open palm along his contours. "I fell in love with that place the first time I ever saw it."

"I did too," he grunted. "Kind of like the first time I set eyes on you."

"Liar!" My head whipped off his chest. "You disliked me the first time you saw me! Don't you dare lie. When you carried me out of that bar against my will, I was your burden—not your conquest. Admit it!"

Before I could blink, he flipped me over on my back and pinned me, wrists over my head. He was grinning, his eyes a kaleidoscope of emotion. "The very moment I saw you, I fell in love. It was instantaneous. Like nothing I'd ever experienced before." He leaned over and nuzzled my neck. I shrieked as he deliberately grazed his stubble over my chest. He met my gaze with a wicked look. "Now, there's a possibility I fought some of those feelings for a brief second or two but—"

"Brief!" I hooted. "You were *so* not into me. We traveled for two days before—"

"Wrong," he interrupted, silencing me with a kiss. His lips lifted off mine as slowly and seductively as he could manage. "From the very moment I took you out of that bar, I was trying to seduce you."

"You were not!"

"I was too. Remember our time in the swimming hole?"

"Of course I remember, how could I forget? We had to douse ourselves in sulfur water to mask our smell before we could climb up to your cabin."

"Wrong." His face broke out into a huge grin. "That sulfur was just a tactic because I wanted to see you dripping wet in that little white cami. And it was well worth it." I kicked my legs out, laughing. "It clung to your delicious curves like a glove. I've never been so turned on in my life."

Before I could protest, he kissed me soundly.

I lost myself in his lips, and I couldn't really argue, because I'd wanted to see him without his clothes on just as badly. I finally broke the kiss, giggling. "You're such a bad boy," I scolded.

"Yes, yes, I am. And I'm planning on proving that to you again right now." He ran his chin down the middle of my chest, abrading me all the way to my belly button.

I laughed, my hands twining in his hair. "You have until four-thirty a.m., tiger."

"And I plan to use every single minute of it." He winked.

I licked my lips. "I can't wait."

Acknowledgments

As always, I want to thank my readers, supporters, and fans. Without you, this entire ride wouldn't be nearly as sweet. Bill, I love you. There isn't a more supportive spouse on the planet. You roll up your shirtsleeves and do whatever needs doing. I appreciate that more than you can ever know. To Paige, my college-bound daughter, I'm so proud of the woman you've become. May the road ahead be paved with opportunity and unforgettable experiences. To my son, Nat, you are amazing and insightful. I enjoy watching you grow every day. To my daughter Jane, you make us all laugh, and I thank the stars above for it. Sweat is not the only thing you got from me. To my parents, Daryl and Koppy, I love you so much. Thanks for continuing to support me in everything I do. Kristen Painter, you are a rock star, and I'm so happy to call you a friend. Amanda Bonilla, you are my shot of caffeine. Without you, my day wouldn't be complete.

And to Orbit and all the great people at Hachette who make this book a reality, I thank you.

extras

www.orbitbooks.net

about the author

A Minnesota girl born and bred, **Amanda Carlson** began writing in earnest after her second child was born. She's addicted to Scrabble, tropical beaches, and IKEA. She lives in Minneapolis with her husband and three kids.

Find out more about Amanda
at www.amandacarlson.com
or on Twitter @AmandaCCarlson.

Find out more about Amanda Carlson by registering for the free monthly newsletter at www.orbitbooks.net.

if you enjoyed
PURE BLOODED

look out for

JINN AND JUICE

by

Nicole Peeler

Chapter One

The chubby little human was doing his damndest to hump my leg, but the palm I'd placed on his forehead kept him at arm's length.

"You're so beautiful," he said, panting up at me as he air-humped, his eyes glazed.

I sighed, feeling bad for the guy. He was wearing full nerd garb, including a pocket protector and an extremely unfortunate, thin, brunet comb-over. One leg of his corduroys was pegged for biking, and I thought I could see a fanny pack peeking at me from over his rounded hips.

He was hardly Purgatory's average customer, since our clientele was more apt to sport fangs, gills, or claws than this guy's sad clip-on tie. This dude was all human and also, considering his dilated pupils and complete lack of reserve, very obviously glamoured out of his mind. He wasn't here by choice.

"Mister, you've got so much mojo in your system you'd hit on a grizzly. Who brought you here?"

The man jerked his head toward the bar, where a blonde wearing a pornographically tight silver dress flirted with Trey, tonight's werewolf bartender. I'd seen her around a few times—the daughter of a succubus and a human, she'd sought refuge in steel-stained Pittsburgh after being rejected by her mother's Tribe.

But a sad childhood was no excuse for a messy feed.

"Let's get you home safe," I said, putting an arm around the human to lead him to the door. He acquiesced willingly, his arm fumbling around my waist, one hand moving to my ass. I gave a warning shimmy, the coins on my scarf-belt jingling like a rattler. He jerked his hand back, only to sweep it up my bare back.

"Lyla, what the fuck?" The voice came from behind me, pitched to a petulant whine. I turned to find the silver-clad hoochie eyeing me reproachfully.

"He's my catch," she said. "You don't even eat people."

My lips pursed as I sought her name. I never forgot a face, but after a thousand-something years on this earth, names weren't my strong suit.

"Crystal?" I hazarded. I knew it was something strippery.

"Diamond," she said, hissing like a cat and taking a step toward her prey.

"Right. Sorry, Diamond. I wasn't poaching, just helping this gentleman outside. You know the rules."

Diamond's wide red mouth bowed in a frown. "This place has rules?" A long, graceful arm swept open, indicating the pool table, where a pooka was currently snorting a line of faux-brosia off the bared tits of a weredeer.

"Granted, not many," I acknowledged. "But there are a few. One of which is no luring humans on premises. If they wander in on their own steam, they're fair game. But something tells me that's not the case here, is it?"

As if to prove my point, the human stared fixedly at my

cleavage, one glassy pupil dilated, the other a pinpoint. He looked like the CPA version of Marilyn Manson.

Narrowing her eyes, Diamond took a step forward. "I'm sure we can work something out. I just want a little of his vitality. You can have his wallet."

I moved between her and the little man. Annoyingly, he took his opportunity to grind up on my behind like a corpulent schnauzer.

"That's generous," I said, swatting him away. "But no. What we *are* going to do is put this guy in a taxi and send him home to his wife." I grabbed for the pudgy hand groping for a boob, raising it so Diamond could see the gold wedding ring glinting on the human's finger. "As for you, feel free to stay for the show. I'll buy you a drink. But you'll have to find your next meal elsewhere."

"Fuck you, Lyla," Diamond said, her red lips receding alarmingly, succubus-style, to reveal her hitherto-hidden fangs. "You're not the boss of this place."

"No," I said quietly. "I'm not."

And with that I let my Fire flare as much as my unBound state would allow. Unnatural black flames licked along my pale skin, blending upward to ignite my long tresses till they lifted like raven wings framing my face.

Behind me I heard the human groan. I hoped he hadn't soiled his pegged corduroys.

"But I can easily be the boss of you, dear Diamond."

She crouched, hissing at me again, but my flames were already licking at her skin like thirsty tongues. Not burning, though. Not yet.

Her head drooped and she dropped to one knee, submissive.

"Bertha, call this gentleman a cab," I said to the bouncer lurking at the corner of my vision. Big Bertha nodded, her massive frame lumbering over to where the human stood, quivering in genuine fear and glamoured lust. Bertha's fuzzy monobrow twitched at me, waiting for my next move. This was why we all loved her: despite her size, she let us fight our own battles, unless we needed her.

"Diamond, release him," I said, keeping my voice pleasant.

Resting on the carpet, Diamond's hands clenched into fists, but I felt a small *pop* as her magic fizzled.

"Wha'?" said the human, Bertha already leading him up Purgatory's stairs, toward the entrance guarding the outside world from the freaks that found shelter behind our doors.

I approached the figure hunched on the carpet. "Thank you, Diamond. Like I said, your next drink is on me. But please remember not to bring your own dinner into the bar next time."

She didn't look at me. I felt the resentful shift of her power, but she didn't attempt another challenge. An Immunda, Diamond was no real opponent. She could glamour using the magic she took feeding from humans, but other than that she may as well have been one.

Her vulnerability made me sad. I'd been powerless once, after all.

Pushing thoughts of my curse aside, I stepped over Diamond and headed backstage to our dressing room.

The show must go on.

I could hear Rachel's bass voice crooning even before I opened the door.

> The not-so-eensy willy
> Went up between my legs
> Up go my berries,
> So pretty like Old Gregg's…

"It's tucking song time!" I called as I entered the dressing room I shared with my best friend, Yulia, our resident will-o'-the-wisp, and Rachel Divide. Rachel was a human, but a powerful psychic. She was also a drag queen and the lover of my oldest friend and current boss.

"You bet yo' white ass it's tucking time." Rachel's syrupy Southern accent wrapped around me almost as tight as the gaff she was hauling up between her legs. She reached for her Spanx as I sat down at my dressing station.

"Are you doing 'Old Man River'?" I asked, noting the sequined gown hanging off the corner of Rachel's trifold mirror. It was extra glamorous, which usually meant we were in store for some *Showboat*.

" 'Old Man River' is my favorite," Yulia said, peering down her nose at herself as she layered on her signature silver eye shadow. Her Slavic accent was thick, proof she was concentrating.

"Mine, too," I said, reaching for my liquid eyeliner.

Rachel was shoehorning herself into her Spanx, sweating with the effort. Not for the first time I was grateful that belly dancing precluded support garments.

"Jesus H. Christ, I swear to God that one day Imma burn these damned drawers." Rachel hauled the Spanx the last of the way up, then did a few deep squats to get them situated. Her tucked-away junk didn't move an inch, and I wondered how the hell that could be comfortable.

When she was done, Rachel smoothed her hands over her round belly, then pivoted on her heel to check herself out from the back. Obviously satisfied, she reached for her sparkly tights.

"You doing the snake dance again?" Yulia asked me.

"Yep. That head took forever to make. I'm getting my time's worth."

"Whatever, girl. You just like getting your hands on my man," said Rachel, leering at me mischievously in the mirror.

I grinned back, finishing the thick lines of eyeliner with expert precision. "He's certainly not bad eye candy, for an antique."

Rachel grunted obscenely, fanning herself. "He's not old, he's wise. Lawd have mercy, the things he can teach a girl!"

"Age does have its benefits," I acknowledged, reaching for the glittery bronzer I used all over my body.

"And you should know, old lady." Yulia was belting herself into her own costume—a sort of dominatrix-meets-ice-queen-meets-showgirl hybrid.

At over a millennium old, I didn't take offense at that comment. However... "You're hardly a spring chicken," I said, dryly. Yulia had been leading unwary strangers off the path for a few centuries herself.

"I was never a chicken anything," she said, letting her wisps glow faintly, individual strands of light floating around her like celestial tentacles.

"She's more of a peacock," Rachel clarified, hitching up her tights and reaching for her gown.

Yulia's graceful white arm extended along with one of her wisps to pluck the gown off of Rachel's mirror and hand it to her. Rachel nodded her thanks, the heavily eye-shadowed skin around her rich mahogany eyes crinkling in amusement.

"Hey, you heard from Aki?" Rachel asked.

"The kitsune?" asked Yulia.

"Yeah, he didn't show up for work yesterday, or today. That ain't like him."

I frowned, thinking. "No," I said. "I haven't. And come to mention it, he was supposed to borrow that costume for me, from the Heinz Museum."

Aki was technically Purgatory's dishwasher, but like any kitsune worth his fox fur, he was also a fabulous thief, spy, sneak, and general ne'er-do-well. Needless to say, he was a great friend to have in your corner. Able to get virtually anything, he also knew everyone and everything that was happening in our fair city of Pittsburgh.

"I'll text him," said Yulia, reaching for her phone.

"Please do," said Rachel. "But I already did, like nine times."

"He's probably on a job. Or lying low," I said, since lying low was the natural consequence of the majority of Aki's jobs outside of Purgatory.

Yulia tapped away at her phone, while her wisps delicately placed feathers in her hair, much to my jealousy. My own Fire was nowhere near as compliant as her wisps, even if it was worth a hell of a lot more in a fight.

"Maybe he finally quit after being spurned by Lyla too many times," Yulia said, arcing a brow at me in her mirror as she tapped one last time and put down her phone.

I rolled my eyes. "Ohmigod. You're not bringing that up again. Aki is like a zygote compared to me."

"Girl, everybody is a zygote compared to you," Rachel said, tutting at me in her own mirror. "You are like a gabillion years old. If you use age as an excuse not to get any, you will have to go down on Methuselah."

"I am not going down on Methuselah. That shit's gotta be bitter by now."

"Well, then, you will never get some." Rachel slipped her ball gown up her generous frame, a frame that needed very little extra in the way of padding to look utterly feminine. "'Cuz Methuselah," she added helpfully, "is the only motherfucker on this planet older than you."

"Mmmhmm," purred Yulia.

I glared at both of them. "Ladies, I have bigger fish to fry than dudes."

"Like what?" Yulia asked, turning around to face me.

"Like my curse, for one," I said.

"Whatever, Lyla," she said, rolling her eyes dramatically. "The point of your curse is you don't have to do anything. Just not get Bound again. And there haven't been any Magi in Pittsburgh since... well, probably since forever."

"I know, but still," I said, sounding prim even to my own ears.

"But still what?" asked Rachel, motioning toward Yulia, who sent a wisp snaking out to pull up Rachel's zipper. "The fact is you've been alone for longer than I've been alive. And that's fucked up, girl."

"I haven't been alone! What about that siren? And that werewolf. And those two trolls... they were brothers!"

"And yeah, you fucked the hell out of them," said Yulia. "I had to leave the apartment you were so loud. But those were all one-night stands, Lyla."

"Hey," I started, but Yulia cut me off.

"Fine, one-week stands. But they were stands, *angel moy*."

"So what?"

"So, there's more to life than your curse," Rachel said, gently.

It was my turn to roll my eyes. "How can I do anything when I'm not even free?"

"But you *are* free," said Yulia. "You haven't been Bound in centuries."

"As long as I'm living as a jinni, I'm not really free," I said, my jaw clenching involuntarily.

"I know you think your situation is different, sugar," Rachel said, her voice gentle. "And it is certainly unique. But when it comes down to it, we're all bound to different things. And one of the only bindings worth anything is what you make with other people."

"And I do have those ties," I said, my exasperation coming out in my voice. "Look at you assholes, grilling me an hour before I have to go on stage. If I'm not bound to *you* bitches, whom am I bound to?"

Rachel laughed her big, booming laugh and Yulia smiled, but it was sad. "And we'd do anything for you, *zaychick*. But just as there is more to your life than your curse, there is more to any life than freedom. I worry about you."

I stood up, opening my arms to my friend. "Don't worry, you two. Seriously. I'm so close to being human again. When I am, I can start over. I'll be different. I promise."

Yulia came and gave me a hug, her always-cool skin making my own flesh goose-pimple reflexively.

"Not too different, please," she whispered, and I hugged her hard.

"If you two hookers make me cry off my makeup, I'll shave your eyebrows," said Rachel, her voice quivering slightly. We broke off our hug immediately, knowing she was completely serious.

Nothing, not even friendship, could get between a drag queen and her makeup. Not without feeling the wrath of fabulous scorned.

Chapter Two

The air whispered cool over my arms as I stood on stage, ready to be announced. The room was dark, the wisp-lights glowing on our small café tables the room's only illumination.

Suddenly Charlie's smoky voice oozed over the audience like KY at a porn shoot, getting all up in the audience's aural cavities.

"Ladies and gentlemen, I know you've been waiting for this. Straight from the sultan's bedchamber, a woman of fire too hot for the harem—put your hands together for our very own... Lyla La More!"

Applause, wolf whistles, and a few ululations echoed from the crowd, but the lights stayed off and I remained still. The crowd quieted, growing totally silent as it heard the first low strike of the bass drum. A deep, dark sound, it echoed through my bones as it thumped again, and again, speeding up by infinitesimal degrees. Stock-still, I moved only when the low sweet strain of a cello cut across the drum, and my left hip lifted and dropped. The cello sounded again as my right hip lifted and dropped. And then my hips erupted in a chaos of shimmies with the entrance of more drums and a violin. Beats Antique rocketed out of the speakers, taking the audience out of its seats and my limbs into hyperdrive.

The dance was a serpentine one, my costume signaling the theme with tight, sheer green fabric sheathing my legs from where it hung off the heavy, crazily Bedazzled belt slung low on my hips. The smooth, soft skin of my belly was bare, of course, and above my ribs metallic serpents cupped my breasts, holding more green fabric to protect my modesty.

It was the headdress that stole the show: a great papier-mâché serpent reared above me, its fangs glittering with rubies and its eyes with emeralds. Or the craft store versions of precious gems. It was heavy and awkward, but it looked marvelous in the low light, winking malevolently at the crowd as I danced for their entertainment.

My hips slowed as my chest took up the dance, lifting and shifting, my spine arching as I raised my hands in snake arms. I did a slow circle, alternating movements between hips and chest. As the music swelled into a crescendo I faced the audience again, letting my hands fall to frame my hips. My belly bowed and swooped, muscles pulling in and then relaxing. The beat increasing, I moved as much as my tight costume would allow, darting my hands at the audience like another pair of striking snakes doing the bidding of the great snake that loomed above. The audience went wild, thumping the tables and calling for more. But the music slowed, and I let my shifting carry me downward, my hands above my head. I knelt before them, my snake's head weaving and my arms undulating as the violin cut out, then the cello, leaving only that slow thrum of the bass drum once again. The lights lowered, and for a split second I could hear only the thudding of my heart and the rough pant of my breath through my toothy smile, until the first clap sounded in the room, sending everyone into another round of applause. The lights went up again and I stood, Charlie coming to take my hand.

Charlie was wearing all of his clothes, since it was relatively early in the evening. Soon enough he'd be stripped of his red velvet ringmaster's coat, underneath which he wore only lovely white skin and black suspenders holding up tight black jodhpurs. His mustache was twirled into two rakish whiskers flaring over thin lips, black guyliner smudged around his eerily colorless eyes.

He gave me his sexy ringmaster's leer as he approached, those pale eyes sweeping over my body. His interest was all part of the show, though—Charlie was both gay and taken.

The clapping slowed as Charlie grabbed my arm, jerking me around and toward him. For a split second we were nose-to-nose, me on my tiptoes and him bending over me. Then his arm wrapped around my waist, pulling my hips against his and arching my back. I melted against him, my hands slipping inside the lapels of his coat to lie against his chilly skin. We stayed in that classic pose for a second, Charlie's lean frame looming above me—the alpha male subduing his exotic female. I let my Fire flare just enough to swirl my hair, its sinuous weight mimicking the natural movements of the snake I still wore on my head.

On cue, Charlie whipped me around so I faced the audience. He stepped behind me, his hands moving to my headdress. He undid the strap beneath my chin, lifting the heavy snake's head off me. He set it by my feet, reaching for the belt at my waist.

The audience, having fallen silent when Charlie first grabbed me, began to clap with Trey, who'd initiated a slow beat from behind the bar.

The clapping sped up as Charlie's hand reached for the knot of the belt, undoing it with theatrical slowness. On cue, my next song began. "Hey, Miss Kiss, let us dance," echoed out of the speakers as Charlie whipped my skirt off, leaving me clad in a coin-covered G-string. The audience was on its feet, clapping as Purgatory's ringmaster grabbed my serpent head and, wielding my skirt like a bullfighter's cape, plunged offstage.

It stayed on its feet for the second half of my act, a traditional burlesque number to which I gave only the slightest belly dance flair. I was already pretty nude, but that didn't mean I couldn't tease. And tease I did.

In fact, I got so deep into the dance I went ahead and let my Fire flare again, its dark shadow swooping around me like a doppelgänger, its preternatural heat caressing my skin like a familiar lover.

I would miss my Fire when my curse was lifted.

As the song ended I let the black flames fall around me like a cloak. My hands went behind my back, finding the knot that held on my bra. Then I let the dark swath of my Fire peel away, letting the coin bra fall with it and leaving me clad only in my coin G-string and a pair of pasties in the shape of genie lamps. The audience hooted as my Fire dissipated and my arms fell to my sides, leaving my mostly bare flesh sweating in the hot lights of the stage. Charlie came out again, leading me stage left, where I made a deep curtsy, peeping up at the audience provocatively through my lashes. I repeated the movement stage right, and then finally center.

Straightening from my final bow, I caught a glimpse of a man sitting toward the back, his silver eyes opened wide.

And glowing like fucking headlamps in the dark.

Magi, chimed my brain, unhelpfully.

I pulled sharply away, startling Charlie, who dropped my hand. A smart move on his part, because I was already running.

Panties a-jangling.

Trip hissed at me as I leaped over her and Trap. The twin spider wraiths were currently conjoined at the waist, their legs splaying around them as they prepared for their act.

I didn't respond, since I was in fully panicked fleeing mode. Trip and Trap, after all, couldn't help me. Neither could Trey, or Big Bertha, or Charlie, or any of my other friends. Not unless they ripped that fucking Magi's tongue out before he could speak. For Magi he certainly was, his eyes Flaring to my Fire.

I heard crashing behind me as Trap cried out, "No humans backstage!"

The Magi ignored the spider wraiths, his footsteps closing in behind me. But he hadn't Called yet, and I used my Fire to propel me forward, pushing me toward Purgatory's stage entrance and the street. There I could hopefully put enough distance between me and the Magi for Pittsburgh's steel-stained environment to help me hide.

The cool spring air hit all my bare skin like a slap as I plunged into the night, cutting right down the alley. It was a wide, empty East Liberty alley, giving me plenty of room to run. But the guy chasing me was fast, and his hand managed to catch my elbow, twirling me around to face his glowing eyes. He stared at me in wonder for a split second and I thought I might just have time to kick him in the balls before he could speak.

But it was too late.

"Hatenach farat a si." I See you, he said, in a language older than humanity. Older than time. A language of smoke and fire; a language of magic. The language of the being that made me what I am today, which had the power to make me a slave.

Fuck if I was ever going to be a slave again.

With a harsh cry I launched myself at the man, skimming off the surface of the magical Node beneath the city to shift my nails into long, wicked talons. A look of surprise twisted his features, but he had good reflexes. He threw himself out of my way with a neat somersault that had him back on his feet, his fists raised as he balanced on the balls of his feet—the stance of an experienced boxer.

I lunged at him again, calling my Fire to flame around me. I hoped to intimidate him even if a jinni's black flames wouldn't burn a Magi. His eyes grew even wider at the sight, but he didn't budge. So I slashed at him again with my talons, but he got under my guard and I overextended badly, cursing my inability to use my strongest weapon even as I fell.

I landed hard on the ground, my breath knocked out of my lungs. He kicked away my hands and jumped on top of me. Concentrating on the words, he opened his mouth to speak. Before he could get out the rest of the spell, I struck upward with both my hands bent, the heels of my palms striking him in the chin.

His eyes, already glowing in reaction to my presence, Flared brighter in the darkness, causing my anger to blaze with them.

"Magi," I hissed, and I hit him again. This time he caught my wrists, his hands like vises. Now that he had me on the ground, his bigger size gave him the advantage.

At least for those few seconds.

It was his turn to hiss as suddenly, instead of being a tiny Jasmine-stripper look-alike, I blossomed into obesity. My fat hips knocked his thighs open, pushing him off balance. I heaved myself over, morphing into a taller, more muscular version of me as I did so. Unable to tap the Deep Magic unless Bound, I couldn't get that much bigger, but it made the fight a little more fair.

"Why don't you take on someone your own size?" I growled as I dove for him.

In retrospect, I should have taken the fight slower. I was just so pissed and so panicked. I hadn't heard anyone with those eyes speak that language in a century—not since I'd escaped Europe for the New World, and found refuge in steel-soaked Pittsburgh, where only Immunda could survive. Recognizing a true, Initiated Magi, my crazy inner she-bear emerged, gibbering about never being taken alive. If I had any thought at all it was that my sense of self-preservation would give me an edge. I was fighting for my life, after all, while this guy was just a jerk trying to Bind a jinni.

Unfortunately he didn't fight like a jerk; he fought like a cornered wolverine. He fought as if he were the one who'd be enslaved if he lost this match. He fought like his life depended on it. Which, considering I was intent on killing him, I guess it did.

He fought better than me.

I was hitting him, hard, but I'd lost my talons shifting to a bigger size. Being unBound meant I was far less powerful, even with my unusual access to all of Pittsburgh's corrupted magic swirling at my feet. And now that I was unarmed, he wasn't hitting back, just using his big body to deflect the majority of my blows. Until I overextended a kick.

His own booted foot lashed out, knocking my leg out from under me. I was on the ground again and this time he didn't underestimate my abilities.

He pinned me down with all his weight, his knees pressing painfully into my thighs and his chest blanketing mine, his hands holding down my wrists. His face was inches from mine, but his features were entirely obscured by the bright glow of his Flaring eyes.

Not me, my brain howled. *Not when I'm so close to being free.* I started to shift again in a last, desperate attempt. But before I could change, he'd spoken.

It was the second part of the spell that was the real bitch. And I was too late to stop him.

"Te vash anuk a si," he chanted over and over. *I Call you.* His pronunciation grew more confident with every repetition. The harsh sibilance of the language of the jinn reached toward me, wrapping around my soul. I cried out, but the spell blanketed me, muting my powers. I stopped mid-shift, my power whoomping out, leaving me beneath him in my own small form.

My wide brown eyes stared up at him, begging him silently to stop, not to say the last bit. The bit that made me his; that made me do his bidding; that made me a slave until he either let me go or died.

He spoke the words.

"Hatenoi faroush a mi." I Bind you.

And just like that, I was caught. Bound to a human. Again.

There were no lights or sounds or other magical occurrences, but we both felt it. I was his. He stared at me with eyes gone wide with shock, his Flare fading as his magic accepted my acquiescence.

He was my Master.

"Göt," I muttered. Then I switched to English, so he'd understand.

"Asshole."

Chapter Three

Charlie's dagger ground to a halt inches from the Magi's face, caught in a black tendril of my Fire.

"It's too late," I told my friend, but he didn't listen. He pulled another knife from inside his ringmaster's jacket and let it fly.

I caught it, too, letting it drop to the ground with a clatter. But he just reached into his pocket of Sideways and grabbed another. I caught that one before it found my new Master's throat.

We could play this game forever, as Charlie had an infinite number of knives stashed Sideways.

The rest of my friends piled out onto the brick alleyway and, loyally, they all attacked. A deadly wisp shot at the Magi, courtesy of Yulia, which my Fire snared.

It also caught the twin nets that Trip and Trap shot out of the spinnerets located near the bases of their spines. The spider wraiths had turned as one, their midsections still joined by a thin veil of skin that was separating to let them run free. Trip kept spinning, leaping up onto the neighboring building and shimmying toward the sky. Trap did the same on Purgatory's rough brick. When they had enough height, they turned as if on cue to drop out of the sky like creepy missiles trained on their target.

Both bounced off the dome of black Fire with which I automatically shielded the Magi.

It was Big Bertha who intervened, although she didn't look happy about it. Half human and half troll, she towered above all of us, her enormously muscled frame clad in her usual dark suit, huge breasts straining at the buttons of her blouse. Like all troll women, she wore her beard long, framing her surprisingly delicate features.

"Stop it!" she roared.

Everyone stopped. Bertha rarely had to roar, given her size. So when she did, people listened.

"You're too late. She's Bound," the troll explained, using her Patient Bouncer voice.

Yulia, being Yulia, acted like she hadn't heard and shot a series of wisps at the Magi that my jinni caught. Charlie reached for another knife.

With a sigh Bertha snagged her boss around the midsection, pinning his arms to his sides. "She has to protect him, sir. You're just wearing her out."

Trip and Trap looked at each other and skittered into the shadows, undoubtedly planning a new form of attack.

Bertha looked at me. "Get him out of here," she said. "They're not going to listen."

I nodded gratefully to her, turning to collect my new Master. The Magi who'd Bound me was standing there, staring ahead of him, eyes round as a tarsier's. In the dim light of the streetlamp, I could see he was a large man—tall and well muscled, dressed in raw denim jeans, wide cuffs light against his solid black boots. He wore a T-shirt under a thick flannel shirt cut in that slim-fitting hipster interpretation of Western gear. In the hollow of his throat I could see a tattoo—an anchor.

"Nice ink," I told him. "Now run."

When he only blinked at me, I grabbed his arm and dragged him toward my scruffy black El Camino, throwing up a huge wall of my Fire to protect our progress.

As I threw my new Master into the passenger seat I used a spark of magic to start the car, since the keys were still in my purse in the dressing room, and another spout of black Fire carried me up and over the car to my own side. As I dove in to drive away I heard my friends shouting and Bertha, above the din, using her outside voice to remind them, over and over, that it was too late. They couldn't do anything.

I was Bound.